Strains of Silence

Bethany Kaczmarek

This is a work of fiction. Names, characters, places, and incidents either are the product of the author's imagination or are used fictitiously, and any resemblance to actual persons living or dead, business establishments, events, or locales, is entirely coincidental.

Strains of Silence

Cover Art by *Nicola Martinez*
Harbourlight Books, a division of Pelican Ventures, LLC. Harbourlight Books sail and mast logo is a trademark of Pelican Ventures, LLC.

Publishing History
First Harbourlight Edition, 2017
Paperback Edition ISBN 978-1-61116-966-9
Electronic Edition ISBN 978-1-61116-967-6
Published in the United States of America

Dedication

Fly the W.
To my very own baseball player, who gave me the courage to dance. Thank you for leading.

Acknowledgements

I remember my little sister's face blinking back at me as I realized I had a story to tell. And from those earliest moments, Erynn, you've encouraged me, learned at my side, gotten me to laugh at my n00b mistakes. I don't think I'd have ever had the courage to write if it hadn't been for you. Thanks for the nudge and the company.

And Sue Quinn, who read and critiqued those two early years-ago versions chapter by chapter, you sharpened me, challenged me to take what I'd written for myself and to make it about my readers. Your belief that I could do this meant so much—still does.

Susie May Warren, Karen Ball, Rachel Noto, and Sandra Lovelace, each of you has said something to me that lifted my chin and spurred me on in this endurance run. I treasure those words, and I keep on.

Jeff Bourque, honestly? This book wouldn't have become what it is without "Nothing." Weaving those lyrics into the story moved my writing in a direction I couldn't have predicted. It was God's gift to me. I wish everyone in the world knew your song, and I'm thankful that we met you on the Polish mission field so long ago.

But God had a different song to break Kasia's silence. Sarah Sharrow, time spent worshiping and seeking God's heartsong for her story, time spent praying and writing new lyrics with you—I wouldn't trade those moments for a New York Times bestseller. They were sweet, and they knitted our souls together. You were one of my first fans, and you'll always be one of my favorites.

Light Brigade, soul-sisters, you have prayed me

through every high and every low of this ride. Ronie, your friendship is a mocha latte for my afternoon slump. Marney, you know what's up. You pull no punches, you push me to excel. Judi, my kindred spirit, bosom-friend. I want to write books and characters you'll like having around as much as me (and bonus: they'll be able to be around on demand). I miss you every single day.

Mom and Dad, you loved us with grace, Truth, and fierce determination. I love you cowmootillion.

Boyfriend-Husband, some of my berry favorite things about you made it into this story, because I wrote what I knew. Your patience and grace, your ability to make me laugh no matter what's going on around me. You befriended me at a time when I didn't believe in love, and you showed me what it looked like. But you never claimed to be my hero. You just pointed me to Him. And that's what I love the MOST about you. Keep it up until we die, love.

To the Kacz clan, those dinner-table conversations and couch-snuggles and loud laughter and heartspills—they're more precious to me than jewels. I love watching you each discover your own stories. Giant, you are the Man. Bean, aš myliu tave. Short Son, I'd love you if you wore a ten-gallon hat. Smalls, you're magical with love. And Pound o' Puddin', I love your little heart. You all rawk.

Julie Gwinn, agent-friend, you are The. Best. Thank you for championing me and pushing me to write and write and write. Even if I don't have pink hair, you still tell me I'm cool. And even when I stole your pillow, you didn't leave me behind. I shall keep you. Here's to many more books to bless us both.

And to my readers, you are the reason I tell stories.

May you find the powerful, unshakeable Love that calls your heart. He’s waiting for you.

What People Are Saying

[Strains of Silence is] an intimate portrait of the impact abuse has on not only the victim but on the circle of loved ones surrounding her. This tenderly told story resonates as a true and important testimony to the beautiful redemption of a broken silence.

~ Serena Chase, author of The Eyes of E'veria series

"Honest, raw, and relatable, Strains of Silence shatters the stigma of shame, abuse and regret in one beautifully written novel. You can't help but find a little bit of healing for yourself in every page."

~ Betsy St. Amant, author of All's Fair in Love and Cupcakes, and Love Arrives in Pieces

"Strains of Silence gives poignant words to an unprecedented epidemic young adults face—partner abuse. Set here and abroad, readers will grow to love Kaczmarek's well-drawn characters and appreciate unique storytelling."

~ Mary DeMuth, author of The Muir House

"Bethany Kaczmarek engages readers with accessible, yet astute, writing. As a result, Strains of Silence achieves much more than a well-constructed plot; it gifts readers with life-changing principles."

~ Andrew Greer, Dove Award-nominated singer/songwriter

"Strains of Silence is a powerful journey from fear to freedom. This gripping, timeless story recounts one young woman's courageous stance against abuse, and the strength she discovered lived within her when she began to believe again. "'If it meant brighter stars, she would follow God into the darkness.'"

~ Jackie Marushka, CEO, Marushka Media, Nashville

"Bethany Kaczmarek has a knockout debut novel. Strains of Silence produces intense emotion, deep characters, and forces the reader into a voracious desire to continue turning the pages. I look forward for more from this breakout novelist. A must-read, a glad-you-did novel."

~ Cindy K. Sproles
Best-selling author of award-winning Mercy's Rain

Bethany Kaczmarek's passion for millennials shines in Strains of Silence. Beautifully balancing the raw and the lighthearted, she brings to life a powerful story that will strike a chord with old and young alike. Kaczmarek is a talented author and not one to shy away from tough conversations—definitely a book to read and an author to watch!"

~Ronie Kendig, author

"Bethany Kaczmarek's clean prose and deep understanding of her characters work together to create Strains of Silence, a novel at once charming and terrifying. Her portrayal of abuse is both believable and chilling, and yet she handles the subject with confidence and unflinching courage. Her protagonists are far from perfect, but they each find hope in their respective darkness. Strains of Silence is a gripping novel that arrests the reader from the beginning and holds them through to the end."

~ Aaron D. Gansky, Author of The Hand of Adonai Series, Write to Be Heard, Firsts in Fiction: First Lines, and The Bargain

"Author Bethany Kaczmarek weaves music with her words. The Strains of Silence immediately captures the reader with a compelling story and characters who step off the page. She approaches real-life situations with believability and grace. She offers hope and honesty in such a way that makes us all remember we are loved. Definitely an author who has moved to the top of my favorites list.

~ Edie Melson, Author of While My Child is Away & Director of the Blue Ridge Mountains Christian Writers Conference

1

Kasia Bernolak's fiancé waited for her back on campus.

She could allow that thought, thick and smothering, to choke her. Or she could fight it. When she'd taken off that morning, left Huntington to free-climb Beekur's Bald, she'd ached for spring's vitality. Over the past year, her heart had become almost as unfeeling as the granite beneath her—tough enough to withstand the storms, hard enough to cope.

Her father always said she'd been born with sun in her hair and its heat in her veins—all hope, all conviction, all passion. But if her daddy, her *tatuś*, were here now, his disappointment would fall on her like the rain had. Sudden and cold.

Her lungs burned from exertion, but she relished it. If only navigating relationships were as easy as climbing. The mountain under her feet could be conquered one foothold at a time. Even when she got jarred and bruised along the way, she could best it. The rock may be unforgiving, but it was solid, constant.

Unlike Blake. He was as changeable as the weather.

The rainclouds had finally—mercifully—moved on. They now hung above Huntington proper. She pressed her palms flat against the wet, gritty stone at her back and let her gaze trace the winding road up the far side of the valley. Any GPS would say home was a thirty-minute drive away. But true home—with its piping hot, herbal tea, whispered Polish conversations, and strong-armed hugs—was out of reach.

Mama and Tatuś would argue that homecomings were always a good idea, but some things couldn't be undone. Apologies couldn't fix everything.

She'd probably stayed too long up here already, but the rain had slowed her climb. Rather than waste time on the switchbacks, Kasia cut through the trees wherever she could, her footfalls muted by the moss and damp earth. Near the bottom of the trail, she paused to catch her breath and listen to the chittering songbirds. She gripped the slick bark of a birch and inhaled the peace, steeped in it. The scents of damp earth and mountain laurel conjured images of better times, times when she had the freedom to lose herself in the mountains for hours.

She hiked the trail carefully as it sliced down toward the valley. A twig snapped, and a rabbit darted beneath a fallen log a few yards to her left.

Bless it. She recognized desperate fear when she saw it. She slowed, tugged her wet T-shirt from against her rain-slicked skin, put the previous night on replay.

It hadn't been so out of the ordinary.

At Blake's too late, curled up with him on his couch, she'd been half watching a gory zombie flick and half enjoying the familiarity of his arms around her.

Just half.

And when he'd shifted at her back—it was bizarre, really—she felt...hunted. She'd jumped up, coughed out a flimsy excuse, and left.

Would he mention that today? Or just let it hang over them like a storm cloud?

~*~

Kasia shoved open the cafeteria door and stepped inside. She took a moment to collect herself beside a small palmetto that'd been transplanted into these South Carolina mountains just like her Polish family. Her shirt had dried quite a bit on the way back to school. She tugged on it, tried to convey confidence. Strength. All the qualities she used to have.

If Blake *hadn't* waited, she could get in, eat, and get out. She needed to shower before she spent the afternoon at the homework club. Her sneakers squeaked across the floor and past the serving lines. The smell of garlic and oven-fresh bread made her stomach grumble as she scanned the room.

Blake eased back in his chair, laughing with guys from the business school. The picture of charisma.

Kasia willed her heart to match the steady cadence of her footsteps, prayed a calm façade would hide her discomfort. Under the surface, her mind composed a discordant tune, all sharp words and flat explanations.

He pointed at his classmates. "I'll catch you gentlemen later. Kasia *finally* decided to join me."

"Oh, don't leave on my account, guys," she said. A crowd could take some pressure off.

Blake shook his head. "They know I've been waiting for you. It's all good." Blake's friends meandered elsewhere. And his gaze landed squarely on her. "Drowned rat isn't your best look. Probably a good thing you missed the rush."

She balled her toes in her soggy shoes and pulled her long ponytail over her shoulder. The sudden rain shower on the bald had dulled her fiery hair to mud-brown. She looked up and noticed an empty plate smeared with tomato sauce near his elbow. "You already ate?"

He tapped his thumb against the tabletop. "Really? You ditch me last night with no warning, you're late today, and now you're going there?"

"Sorry." She touched the hard, angular stone on her finger, held the engagement ring firmly in place.

"Sit down. I'll go get you some lunch."

She blinked in surprise, and he was gone. The air conditioning kicked on a second before ice-cold air whooshed over her damp skin.

Blake's sweater peeked out of his backpack, taunted her. A minute later, a plate clinked against the tabletop, and he slid her a fork as he sat. "Here you go."

Yum. Yesterday's chicken cordon bleu masquerading as something Italian. Her stomach wobbled. "Did they not have soup?" She longed for one of her mom's signature winter dishes—a deep purple *barszcz* or chicken *rosół* with potatoes and fresh dill.

"Sure. But I just sat down."

As she reached for the fork, her diamond caught the light and sparkled.

As if the promise of marriage were a beautiful thing.

Fear swallowed her like the pitch-black of a cave. In three months, she'd be Blake's wife. His *wife*. Every other option would cease to exist.

But to be realistic, she'd blown her chance at anything else when she gave herself to Blake. She had to make this work—to redeem their relationship.

She missed the old Blake. In the beginning, he'd have jumped at the chance to get her soup, hot tea—

anything she wanted. He'd have offered the sweater the second he saw her wet and chilled.

She could make him smile just by being herself.

He reached out and fingered the hem of her soggy shirt. "So, you were climbing again. What is it about that place? Every time you're up on that ridge, you come back with your head full."

I have to climb to get out from under you. "Just struggling with some stuff." She forced down a bite.

He crossed his arms and rocked back in the chair.

She didn't have time to play his game. "I might switch from Elementary to Secondary Ed. I…I feel weird about where I'm headed." It wasn't a total lie.

He squinted.

Had she played the role of blissful fiancée that well?

"We've already discussed this, Kosh. We'll travel, see the world. Dad's got big plans for me as the international liaison—Paris, Bangkok, Dubai. Your sole responsibility will be keeping me entertained."

She let the dull murmur of others' conversations fill her head, wished she could rewind, delete the innuendo. But it played back.

He wasn't talking about her music.

Did he not remember all the things he'd said made him fall for her?

Or did he simply not care anymore?

She'd been somebody—the musical daughter of that gracious Polish-American pastor from the church on the ridge. Her family had always won everyone's affection and respect without even trying.

For Kasia's whole life, music had been her driving passion—the truest expression of her faith. Her music had blessed people. Then she'd quit it all. Blake didn't like her in the limelight.

If she still wrote songs or sang, that might bother her more. But since her well of music had dried up, it hadn't been worth the battle.

When *was* the last time she'd enjoyed the weight of the guitar, the taut strings against her fingertips? What had changed?

She should've asked those questions long before now. Doubt breathed down the back of her neck.

Blake stroked the back of her hand. "Your chicken as bad as it smells?"

"It's fine." She poked at a piece of melted mozzarella with her fork. "Do you remember that song I wrote for you the summer we met?" she asked.

"All I remember is your crazy possessive parents."

They were never possessive. Tatuś protected his girls was all. "Overnight stays weren't the kind of thing his girls did—even at your parents'."

Past tense. She hadn't been back at school long before she spent most nights at Blake's apartment.

Tatuś probably still thought she was worth protecting.

As Blake sat there people-watching, she searched for a trace of his former sweetness—the letters he used to write her! No luck. "I'll be at Heritage Acres today—running the homework club."

He sat straight. "We've been over this."

"Jen has a doctor's appointment—just today." She hadn't realized how much she missed it.

"It's pointless, Kosh. You change nothing for those ghetto kids."

Maybe she wouldn't change anything long-term, but she could certainly make them smile and laugh before they went home. Somebody needed to tell them they could amount to something. She wished someone would offer her the same hope.

She wadded her napkin and set it next to her plate.

"Pointless." He shook his head like a disappointed teacher. "What you need to do is—"

Enough. She stood. "What I need to do is go. I've got to shower before I leave." She left her tray and stalked off.

"Do not walk away from me." Blake's voice kept on, but she tuned him out. He wouldn't cause a scene in front of all these people. "Presentation is key," he always said. Stupid catch phrase.

Let him feel the embarrassment this time.

She passed a guy she'd seen in the music building a few times. Kasia smiled, chin high.

For the first time in months.

Twice now, in twenty-four hours, she'd left Blake in the dust. And she sort of liked how it felt.

~*~

An hour later, wearing a dressy T-shirt and capris, her curls barely tamed into submission, Kasia grabbed her keys off the desk and headed to the parking lot. Thankfully, the rainclouds had vanished.

Heat poured out the door of the old sedan Tatuś had given her before she left for Oconee State. Inside, she soaked in the warmth of the sunbaked vinyl. As the engine turned over, she focused on the slight vibration and the hum of the engine, rested a hand on the wheel. The car always felt safe—like a place where her dad watched over her.

She pulled out and left campus, wound along side streets through east Huntington. She decided to take the bypass around town, merged seamlessly, hit the gas.

All she needed now was her music. A little Eric Peters would suit her nicely today.

Thunk.

The car shimmied and lurched to the left. She yanked the wheel right, fought against its pull toward oncoming traffic. One glance at her rearview mirror and her heart turned percussionist.

A horn blasted.

A semi swerved.

In the right lane, car after car snaked past, kept her from the safety of the shoulder.

She punched the hazard lights button, slowed to a stop, waited for an opening.

Show some mercy, people.

Eons later, she saluted the final vehicle, edged her car onto the shoulder, and parked.

She got out and checked all four tires. A flat. The absolute last thing she needed. At least it was on the passenger side.

She ducked in to grab her cell and touched the screen to bring it to life. Nothing but black. *Ugh.* Now she couldn't call for help or let Mrs. Peat know she might be late. Could today get worse? At least Tatuś had taught her how to change a tire.

It was different now though. Last time, she'd done it with him. When he was close by, smelling of aftershave and wood chips, she could do anything.

She popped the trunk and hoisted the jack. The spare took a little finagling. She gripped the rubber and lowered it to the gravel.

With the jack crank, she pulled off the hubcap and set it behind the wheel. The stubborn lug nuts held on, though, and the edges cut against her skin. They hadn't been this difficult to unscrew when Tatuś was here.

Kasia imagined him coaxing her with his familiar accent. *Get some leverage, Kasiu. Use your body weight when you must.* She maneuvered the tire iron, shoved down on the left, pulled up on the right. Her arms shook, palms burned. Kasia stood, brushed tiny stones from her knees and considered grabbing one of the hair bands she kept on the gearshift. Hair clung to her neck, prickly, annoying. She placed her right foot on the iron and stepped up, bounced her full 120 pounds.

The lug nuts moved about as easily as the guilt she kept wishing away.

What now? If she flagged somebody down, she might get a psycho. If she stood there like an idiot, a psycho could volunteer.

Tires crunched on the gravel as a black military-style vehicle rolled to a stop behind her. Kasia prayed for someone sane, helpful, gracious. A tall guy about her age jumped down from the driver's seat and strolled over. His hair was a mess—a haystack all gold and shadow. Laugh lines creased his eyes, and deep dimples punctuated his cheeks as he smiled.

Careful to keep her distance, she moved to the front of the car.

"Got a flat?" The barest hint of a southern drawl played in his words—more gentleman than country.

She eyed the deflated tire. "The lug nuts are too tight."

"Mind if I give it a try?" He didn't wait for an answer. He stepped onto the tire iron and used his body weight to kick-start it. For him, it worked. Of course.

"I did try that."

He peeked from underneath a few strands of gold. "Were you standin' on the right side?"

"What?"

A black sports car blew past and laid on the horn.

"The correct side? Righty-tighty, lefty-loosey?" He made a letter *L* with his fingers.

Her mouth hung open, and she parked her fists on her hips. "Not all women are inept." In fact, she could change her own oil without any help, thank you very much—if she could get the filter unscrewed.

Both his hands popped up in surrender. "Whoa, not even going there. Just checking." He smiled and muttered "inept" as he knelt to work the iron with his hand. He glanced up at her. "And not all redheads are feisty." The smile in his voice disarmed her.

"It's auburn."

He wiped his jaw with his shoulder. "Auburn, then."

"For the record, I stood on the correct side. And jumped on it."

He chuckled. "Sorry I missed that."

She watched him work, watched his shirt dampen between his shoulder blades, watched ropey muscles move beneath his tan skin as he turned the iron. Even with the hours Tatuś spent in his wood shop, he didn't have that much definition in his arms. How did a guy get forearms like those?

The lug nuts were off in minutes, the last one clinking against the others as he pocketed it. He reached around both sides of the tire to haul it off. "Maybe we could grab somethin' cold after this."

"I don't think that's a good idea." She spun her engagement ring around her finger and swung her hand behind her, out of sight.

Mr. Forearms shoved her spare into place and met her gaze as he hand-screwed the nuts back on. "Come on. I'm doin' you a solid. Cold glass of sweet tea sure sounds nice."

She leaned against the hood. "Does that line usually work?"

"Ouch. Go easy on me, Auburn." He winked and reached for the tire iron.

"Kasia."

He swiped a hand across his sweaty brow and glanced up at her. "Sorry? Kosh-what?"

"I'm introducing myself. My name is Kasia, not Auburn."

"Zan Maddox. How about a truce?"

She offered a single nod and half a smile.

He worked in silence until he finished the job and then moved the flat to her open trunk. She caught a scowl as he set it in and wiped his hands on his jeans.

"Is something wrong?" she asked. "You, um, looked concerned."

"I am. You've got a nail in your tire."

"Oh." She waved him off. "I've run over those before. It's no big deal."

"You didn't run over this nail." He pointed midway up the sidewall. "Somebody had to hammer it in there."

Kasia swallowed. Blake would never intentionally hurt her. "I have no idea who would…" The words stuck, thick and false on her tongue. She fell silent as a semi blew past, rattling the car windows. Why bother with a convincing story?

His arched eyebrow told her he knew it was a lie.

2

Back in his classic Jeep CJ, Zan cranked up his Amos Lee playlist and followed Auburn awhile. He'd been driving into Huntington to check on Bailey, but his mama had brought him up well enough that he'd still make sure Auburn got where she was headed. He shouldn't let himself get derailed by a gorgeous face.

She drove about like he did—five over the limit, window down. He hadn't been able to get her to go for a drink with him, much less give up her phone number, but he had to admit he'd enjoyed watching her braid that fiery hair and flip it over her shoulder before she took off.

What kind of loser would put a nail in a girl's tire? Zan knew the answer as sure as hurricanes in September. Somebody like Mike.

His brother-in-law was exactly the sort of jackleg who would sabotage a tire. Hopefully, Kasia would be smarter than his sister. Keep herself out of danger.

His sister usually called every few nights, but a solid week had passed, and that didn't sit well. "Call Bailey." His Bluetooth dialed. *Again.*

He rolled his neck as it rang.

And rang. How many times had he called already? At least ten. Possible scenarios filled his stomach with lead. Bailey'd dropped out of contact twice before, and both times, he'd found her messed up—broken nose, busted lip, too hurting to stand.

"C'mon, Auburn. Let's move." Instinct suddenly shouted that it might be a good thing she'd turned down the sweet tea.

Auburn's right blinker flashed. Wait. What? She was turning into the projects. Did Nail-in-the-Tire live there? Surely Kasia knew what kind of neighborhood Heritage Arms was.

He shoved his fingers into his hair, grabbed a fistful. Should he follow her?

Family trumps everything. His father's voice blew into his head. And right now? He was afraid Bailey needed him more than an auburn-haired stranger. Zan wished Kasia well and hit the gas.

A few miles farther into town, at the stoplight across from Bailey's upscale digs, his neck bristled with unease. Why hadn't she picked up the phone? Was she hiding somewhere? Beaten senseless?

Or worse this time?

He hit the gas as soon as the light turned green. He cranked the wheel, careened into her neighborhood, gunned it toward her house. Everything looked dark. Her coupe sat in the driveway, but—wait. Was the front door ajar?

He parked at the curb and catapulted out. "Bay! Bailey!"

At the door, he hesitated, listened. Knocked as he entered.

Pieces of her splintered rocker littered the living room. Shattered glass glinted in the sunlight. The mirror. He froze. Glass snapped under his shoe. His pulse hammered. Nothing else.

He charged from room to room, desperate to find his sister. All he found was a mess—a desk flipped, papers strewn all over. The shower curtain torn down.

The house was empty.

He whipped out his phone and dialed his mom. Checked the pantry. Checked the closet in the guest room. *Answer already.*

"Hey, hon. What—"

"Have y'all heard from Bailey?"

"No, not since Tuesday. What's wrong?"

"I'm at her place. It's a wreck, and there's no sign of her."

"Check her closet." Panic laced her voice.

He should not have called his mom—she'd fall apart with worry. Better dial it back.

Inhale. Count to three. Ease her mind now that you got her agitated. "You know? I bet she's just out of town."

No response. He'd better keep talking. "You think? Maybe she was just in an all-fired hurry or something."

Still quiet.

Don't miss anything, man. Zan's fingertips traced the walls of the dark hallway once more as he inched toward her bedroom.

He paused in the doorway, gripped the frame. *Catch it all. Every detail.* The bedspread lay crumpled on the floor, and two dime-sized drops of blood stained one of the pillowcases. He squeezed his eyes shut and turned away. It didn't have to be Bailey's blood. Might be Mike's. The closet had been ransacked. Hangers and boxes cluttered the floor, and not a stitch of clothing remained.

"Zan? What is it?" His mother sounded squeaky and scared. He should've called his father.

Deep breath. *Be convincing.* "Huh. Looks like she's gone, Mama. Finally packed up her things and left."

A shaky sigh was her only response.

He tried to slip a smile into his lie. "I bet she found a safe place to stay."

"She's safe, you think?" Her voice sounded a little steadier.

"You know? Now that I think about it, I'm pretty sure she mentioned visiting some friends awhile. I'll track her down and call y'all later to say how she's doing, all right? Sorry I got you all worked up over nothin'."

She tried to laugh. "It's fine. Good to hear she's out of there for a while, hm?"

He wanted to hug her—promise her everything would be all right. "Yeah. I'll call you soon."

"Bye, sugar."

His father needed to know about this, but first things first. Zan dialed the police as he stared out the window at his sister's car. "I need to report a missing person."

~*~

Whew! She'd rushed, but Kasia had the tables set up in five minutes flat. If Zan hadn't come by when he did, she'd never have made it. The kids swarmed into the Heritage Acres Community Center and sucked the cool out of the room in a single beat. Kasia opened the last window and wiped her hands on her khakis.

"You all remember Miss Kasia?" Mrs. Peat called from the doorway of her office.

Heads nodded, some still half involved in conversations.

"We're going to have a great time, Mrs. Peat. They'll behave." Eyeing them like Tatuś always did when he needed to be stern, Kasia scanned the room. A tiny freckled girl sneaked in the back and pulled out a folding chair. Her eyes shone with tears. She knocked Kasia's authoritative façade right off. That girl needed a hug.

"If you ladies and gentlemen will get started on your homework, I'll walk around and help wherever you need it." She'd start with Freckles. "And remember, it's fine with me if some of you older and wiser guys assist the little ones if I'm busy with someone else."

Kasia made her way across the room, pausing only a few times to answer questions. She rested a hand on the chair beside Freckles. "Mind if I join you?"

Freckles bit her bottom lip, balled her hands so tightly they shook.

Instead of taking a seat, Kasia knelt beside the girl and reached for a small fist. It stilled instantly, tiny and clammy against her palm. Kasia risked the dam break, traced a tiny knuckle, and whispered. "Need a hug?"

The girl slid out of the chair and into her arms. The willingness to crumple into a stranger's embrace saddened Kasia more than it surprised her. She searched for words—anything—to wrap up this frail little girl and warm her spirit.

"He's gone."

"Who's gone?" *Please say the dog. Let this be as easy as making flyers.*

Freckles settled her head against Kasia's shoulder. "Daddy. Loves somebody else now, Mama said." A shiver ran through the slight frame nestled against her, and Freckles whispered into Kasia's hair. "It's my fault."

A fire roared to life inside Kasia. "No, ma'am. Not possible."

Silver-blue eyes, rimmed with unshed tears, lifted

to meet her gaze.

"Nothing you did made him go away. Wherever he is, he misses you. I'm positive."

Freckles blinked. She dashed away a tear with the heel of her hand. "If Daddy doesn't love Mommy anymore, he'll stop loving me next."

Lord, forgive me if this is a lie. "Daddies never stop loving their little girls. No matter what."

A mournful tune wound its way into Kasia's head, and she hummed softly, sifted through mountains of sweet childhood memories and identified it. A song like that hardly belonged. *Oh.* It was the one Busia, her sweet grandmother, had sung all those summers ago.

Busia. Kasia ached to see her. Had it been too long since she'd visited?

It didn't matter. She'd go tonight. Busia would know exactly what to say to a little girl who needed to believe she hadn't wrecked everything.

3

It was a waiting game now. Platitudes were useless. "Every possible lead" had produced squat. Even by Thursday, Zan couldn't shake the effects of Tuesday afternoon—Kasia on the roadside, Bailey's place deserted. He constantly wondered where they both were. Whether they were safe.

And he needed to get his head in the game.

Lungs on fire and calves aching, Zan tagged the fence and spun, sprinted back toward the dugout. His team was a force to be reckoned with, but the playoffs required skill, 110 percent effort, and a decent bit of luck. Postseason, more than ever, every hit counted, every run stoked the team, and every error put a target on somebody's back.

Tonight a slow jog back to his apartment suited Zan better than a locker-room shower. He could do without the ruckus…and the praise everybody kept tossing Firelli. First-year student or no, the kid was unbelievable—should've been drafted out of high school. So Zan was a glorified benchwarmer now. What could he say? It stung.

He followed the guys in and grabbed his duffel from his locker. He dried off, draped the towel against his neck. "Later, Adams."

"You out already?" Adams untied his cleats and chucked them under the bench.

"Mind's on other things." Zan readjusted the

towel, hung it below his neck. The sweltering locker room made everything sticky.

"Kent and I are cramming for exams at Rose's tonight. You in?"

"Why Rose's?" The coffee at that place could fuel his Jeep.

"Cheap coffee. Cheap food." Adams shoved his practice shirt into his duffel and grabbed his soap.

"Y'all up for a drive? Huntington's a half-hour away, but I know a place with some serious coffee." *And Bailey goes there once in a while. Maybe she'll show up.*

Adams nodded. "I'm in. I'll tell Kent. See you back at the apartment?"

"Yeah." Zan headed toward the exit without a word to anybody else. Maybe luck would smile on him tonight and he'd run into Auburn too.

Outside, he relished the unseasonably warm sun on his neck. He shoved a hand into his mop and scratched his head till his hair just about stood on end. Man, things had been simpler in high school.

Coach had offered him a scholarship to play right field—nothing to shout about. He could've gotten a full ride elsewhere.

But his school was close to Bailey.

Then the scouts found Firelli. Zan flipped up a corner of his towel and roughed his face.

Firelli.

Rumor was the kid could have had his pick of Division I schools, but his family'd pushed this school since he wore diapers. Firelli was a right fielder too, and Coach'd made him starter from day one. Zan never stood a chance, and it ate at him. Coach would always choose Firelli over Zan.

Any good coach would. Even Markman. Best

coach ever.

He swung over to the activity center to check his mail. He dropped his backpack on the floor, stabbed his key into the lock. He pulled out a bill and something else—a letter? Bailey. A letter after nothing for a week and a half?

Falling back against the metal mailbox doors, he tore into the envelope and tugged out the paper. Nice stationery. Normal handwriting.

A phone number.

Zan dropped to a squat and pulled his cell out of the side pocket of his pack. He punched in the number at the bottom of her note, skimmed the text for more clues. The reverberating shouts and laughter around him fell silent. All that mattered was hearing Bailey say she was all right.

Why couldn't people answer the freaking phone?

Some other woman picked up. What was the deal?

"I'm looking for Bailey Weston."

"I need to ask who's calling."

All right, good response. "Her brother. Alexander Maddox."

"Just a minute." Muffled conversation.

"Hello?" Her voice was a grand slam.

"Bay, where are you? Are you all right?"

"I'm good, actually. Sorry I scared you. I know I must've."

You think? He pinched his eyebrows together and willed himself to keep it cool. "Tell me you're somewhere safe."

"I am. Some friends got me out—to stay this time. I'm getting help."

"So, you're in a clinic or something?"

"With people from this new church I've been

going to."

No. Way. What could they do besides fill her head with fairytales? "Can I see you?"

"Yes! I…I know I should've called sooner, but I was sleeping a lot."

"You couldn't call because—what would it have taken, two minutes?" He needed to curb the irritation. Focus on the relief that he knew where she was—that she was all right.

"Honestly, I thought it would be easier to write. I know how you are about anything churchy, and I didn't want to hear it when you disapproved."

Touché. It was all he could do not to give her an earful. He tugged at his hair. What kind of help did these people offer exactly?

"When do you want to come by?"

"Saturday's the big game. Any chance you can come watch?" It wasn't like he'd get any playing time, but family in the stands would be nice.

"Michael might look for me there."

Right. Of course. "Sunday afternoon, then. As long as you're safe, I can wait."

~*~

The conversation with Freckles at the homework club kept flitting through Kasia's mind. She needed to hear that daddies don't quit loving their little girls.

But Kasia shouldn't be at Loch Haven this late. Her grandmother didn't know she was coming, the center's visiting hours would be over soon, and every time she rounded a corner, her stomach knotted.

What would she say if she ran into Mama or Lenka or somebody?

Kasia wrinkled her nose and tried to smile at the nurses as she walked down the unfamiliar, fluorescent-lighted hallway. This retirement community had been Busia's home for a full year, and this was her first visit. Could she be a worse granddaughter?

The buzz of overhead fixtures and an occasional blaring television were the only soundtrack as she made her way into the labyrinth of hospital-like rooms. The blend of antiseptic cleansers and lavender unsettled her. She missed opening the kitchen door at Busia's house and inhaling the mouth-watering scents of *kuchnia Polska—kiełbasa*, cabbage, and onions.

Mama had given her Busia's room number at Christmas, and the note was exactly where she'd stuck it all those months ago, tucked securely in the back of her Bible. She pulled out the pocket-crumpled piece of violet paper. Room 407.

A blue sign with three-inch numbers declared she'd reached the four-hundred hall. Busia's room would be all the way at the end. Kasia padded quietly past the open doors and peeked into room 407. Next to the window, her grandmother rested, eyes closed, in the walnut rocker Tatuś had handcrafted. A blanket lay across her knees and an open Bible in her lap.

What peace she exuded.

Stepping quietly into the room, Kasia set her keys on the dresser by the door. The slight noise caused Busia to stir.

Her eyes evidently took a moment to focus. When they locked on Kasia, they widened. "Kasiu," she said. "I prayed I'd see you soon."

Kasia missed so many of these sweet details—like Busia adding a *u* to her name. The Polish flavor in even her most casual greetings made Kasia's throat tighten.

When her grandmother pulled at the afghan across her legs, Kasia hustled over to her. "Oh, you don't have to get up! Let me come hug you, Busiu."

"*Oj tam.* Hush with that. I'm standing to hug you right. No half measures today." Kasia took the blanket, set it on Busia's bed, and helped her up.

The moment Busia stood, her soft, weathered hands found Kasia's cheeks, and tears filled her eyes. "Look at you, my lovely, lovely girl. You're the picture of my Marta. So dear." She patted Kasia's face and embraced her with surprising strength. Kasia's arms circled her grandmother's sweet shoulders, hunched with age and a lifetime of hard work.

They rocked side to side for a moment before Busia pulled back and kissed her right cheek, then left, and right again. "*Usiądź. Usiądź.* Sit down, *proszę*."

Kasia laid the blanket back across Busia's legs and perched on the bed.

"Now, tell me how you are. Not quite home for the summer, are you? Your mother tells me she's got a few weeks to wait."

"No, ma'am. I, um, I just missed you. How have you been?"

"The Lord must have a purpose for me yet, because I woke up again this morning." Her eyes twinkled. "I imagine it's to keep my friend Ida in line. She's a handful, that one, but does she ever keep me entertained."

Kasia's heart filled with affection. Busia's sweet face was wrinkled by decades of pouring herself out for her family. Nearly overcome by regret, Kasia shoved those thoughts aside and determined to make this moment count. "I brought you some Leibniz biscuits. I found them at a little deli in Huntington."

"Z mleczną -czekoladą?"

"Dark chocolate, not milk. I know what you love best."

"Ha! Better and better. How about we taste one now?" She reached out an arthritic hand.

"Don't worry about me." Kasia pulled out a cookie for her grandmother and set the package on the table. "These are all for you—and one or two for Miss Ida if you want. I bought a pack for myself too."

"Oh, but have one now, with me." Busia reached for the package and offered it to her. Once Kasia had a biscuit in hand, Busia nodded. *"Smacznego."*

"Dziękuję, Busiu."

Busia's eyes closed as she savored each bite. *"Pyszny*, Kasiu." Delicious.

Kasia pointed to a cut-glass vase on the table. "Those flowers are lovely."

"Dziękuję. Lenka brought them over yesterday. She found them up in the meadow. Tell me, are you ready for your wedding?"

Kasia's shoulders tensed. Had she come for honest conversation or not? "Busia, how did you feel when you got married?"

Her grandmother's face beamed with unfathomable love and joy. "I felt I had been made for that very moment, that very man. Your *dziadek*, Kasiu, was my dearest friend." She settled back into her rocker. "My greatest champion."

The answer rendered Kasia empty and brittle, as if a single blow would shatter her. For a moment, she wished someone would just do it.

End her.

Her throat squeezed shut. Her eyes burned.

The tears would let loose any second.

She waited.

Nothing.

How could she feel such utter pain and not cry?

"Kasiu?"

Her eyes focused on the speckled tiles.

"Kasiu." Smooth fingertips grasped her hand. Busia's touch offered none of its usual comfort. Only strength and determination.

"Czy kochasz tego chłopaka?"

Did she love this boy? "I…I don't know." She pressed the heel of her hand into her knee. "I know I *did*. But the wedding—I feel like I'm in the last car of a bullet train, racing forward. And nobody knows the bridge is out but me. I can't stop. Nobody will listen, but—I want to get off."

"So jump."

Kasia snapped her head up. "But what if—"

"I may be old, but I am sitting here, looking at you. The first time I've been able to do so in a year." She sat back. "I think maybe some things are worth the risk, no?"

A knock sounded at the door. "I hate to interrupt, but visitor hours are over, Ms. Kowalski. This your other granddaughter?"

"This is my Katarzyna, but we call her Kasia—the Polish nickname."

"Nice to meet you, Kasia."

"Celeste, you have already spoken to everyone else?"

The woman smiled and looked at her watch. "I can give you about five more minutes. How 'bout I go and get you a glass of warm water?"

"That would be kind, dear."

As soon as she left, Kasia busied herself by picking

at the side seam of her pants.

Her grandmother's gaze settled heavily on her. "It's been a year, *kochanie.*" Beloved. Even Busia's reprimand was gracious.

"*Przykro mi,* Busiu. *Bardzo.*"

"I know you're sorry, dear. I simply want to know why. What kept you from us?"

As much as she wanted to, she couldn't place the blame solely on Blake. "I'm not the Kasia you knew."

"Where did that Kasia go?"

A thread began to pull loose. "I'm afraid I've lost her."

"Do you know what has always made you stand out to me?"

Kasia leaned out to straighten Busia's blanket.

"Your selfless love for others. You found joy in making others smile. *Zawsze byłaś piękna.*"

"Beautiful?"

Busia's eyes wrinkled. "Inner beauty. Perhaps that might be the best way to find yourself again, hm? A little mission project."

Hope sparked. "You think it would work?"

Busia took her hand again. "Only God can change you. But I know He hasn't given up on you. Nor have any of the rest of us. You jump, and your family will meet you where you land."

All nice to hear. With another bite of her cookie, Kasia prayed Busia's words were true.

And that she'd find enough courage to jump.

4

Once a decision was made, a girl could stand a little taller.

An early-morning thunderstorm cooled the mountain air, so Kasia spent Saturday morning jogging the cross-country trails beyond campus. Her feet pounded the packed dirt as she tried to hammer out every one of her doubts.

And failed.

But each time she wavered, Busia's challenge pushed her onward. Kasia skirted the commuter lot, equally exhausted and invigorated.

Her plan was straightforward. She'd shower, eat a late lunch, and then call Blake to break up with him.

Between now and then, all she had to do was come up with the words.

"Kosh!" His voice stopped her like a brick wall.

Didn't Blake have plans with Travis all morning? She pasted on a smile and turned to face him. "Hey. I didn't think I'd get to see you before dinner today."

"You never know where I'll turn up."

What was that supposed to mean? "Where's Travis?"

"Busy." He shrugged. "Everybody's busy."

Blake hadn't smiled yet. That needed to happen fast, or this could get dicey. "There's always so much going on at the end of the semester, you know?" She stepped close and playfully grazed his arm.

He took the gesture as an invitation. His mouth

was hot on hers, his hands strong on her neck and shoulders—a stranger's mouth and hands. She didn't know him, didn't want him. Any of this.

But she knew what to do. When passing voices made her want to disappear, she smiled against his lips. Switched off her mind so she wouldn't feel any of it.

Blake broke the kiss and touched his forehead to hers. His gaze was all heady expectation. Breathless need. His eyes seemed to darken. "It's been a while since I had your undivided attention. We should go back to my apartment."

New, not-so-improved Kasia was entirely too good at distracting Blake.

She had to avoid his place. Not the ideal breakup scenario. "Why don't you walk me to my room? I've got to get cleaned up, but we could talk about the wedding."

He took her hand and went along with her suggestion. For once.

Her stomach felt like a solid ball of lead.

Oblivious, Blake yammered the entire way about how he and Travis had embarrassed some poor freshman in the library. She let him. She rehearsed her spiel, wished it was over. Near her dorm, a rush of determination bolstered her strength.

She pointed to a bench. "Can we sit a minute?"

"Sure."

Her mind was a jumble. If she didn't speak soon, the awkward silence would betray her. She flashed a smile, prayed for mercy, and sat.

Blake joined her. His fingers traced a slow circle on her back. "Kosh?"

All she wanted was to arch away, shake off his

touch. Throw the words at him and run. She twisted the ring he'd offered her five months before. "So, I think I've got to make some changes, to more than my major." She forced out the rest. "I can't marry you this summer."

His hand paused beside her shoulder blade. "What?"

She peeked at him. His jaw muscle was a solid knot, his gaze riveted on her hands as she worked the engagement ring around. He pulled his hand away.

If God would let her lay this on Him, she could make a clean break. "I feel like the Lord wants me to wait. I mean, I should've waited before. I'd always hoped…" Words failed her again—allies turned enemies.

Her fingers stilled. "Blake, I don't think I've been very clearheaded. I guess I regret…well, we've done…" He tensed, and her stomach dropped to her heels. She scrambled for a different approach. "Look, my reasons won't make sense to you, but—"

Commit to it. "I need to walk away for now and focus on my faith again."

"What do you mean 'for now'? Are you trying to break up with me?"

Her voice went AWOL. She dug the toes of her shoes into the gravel and mud under the bench, half searching for the right answer in the dirt, half tunneling out a place to hide. Terrified of what she'd see in his face, she tipped her head forward and used her hair as a shield.

His knuckle forced her chin up and gave her no choice. She stared into his eyes, almost crumpled at the confusion in them.

"And you're blaming this on God."

She clamped her eyes shut tight. He'd nailed it. She had no right to expect God's help. Maybe she could've asked Him two years ago, when innocence and possibility were the norm, but not now. Now this wild pastor's kid deserved any trial she brought on.

"Blake, believe me." She pulled her face away, studied the grass, straight and proud. So unlike her. "I wish I had answers you liked better."

He white-knuckled the bench. The yelling would start any second now.

A few people approached, and Kasia's head swam with relief. "Maybe one day it'll be different." She held the ring out to him, and he glared at it, unblinking.

Strength came from somewhere—filled her—and she didn't question it. She opened one of his hands, pressed the ring into it, and closed his fingers. "I'm walking away. To figure out what God wants for me, so…this is the end."

Blake sat, tense and too silent.

People were still around. "I'm sorry, Blake, but I need to go." She stood.

"Wait. Please." He shot off the bench. "Can we pray about this together? I can do that. Just…don't leave."

He'd never offered to pray with her, not once in all the Sundays they'd attended church together. Had he simply needed an ultimatum? A tear slid down his cheek, sliced her heart.

"Blake—"

He pressed his lips to hers. This time, the kiss hummed with familiarity and warmth. Her resolve faltered. What if they could make changes? Follow God together? She reached for his fingers, longed for the simple and sweet moments they'd shared in the beginning. A shuddering breath escaped her.

She immediately wished it back. But too late.

He pulled away, and his mouth tipped up in a rueful smile. "You still love me."

She blinked. No. Somewhere along the way, love dried up. Along with her music.

His smirk taunted her. "You won't stick to this, Kosh. That kiss told me everything I need to know."

She wiped her mouth with shaking fingertips. "One kiss changes nothing." She spun away and strode toward the dorm, furious at herself. She'd acted like a sickening fool.

Again.

She stomped to her room and locked the door behind her.

Then she locked the window.

Closed the blind.

Stood there, expecting tears to come.

And then flung her keys at the wall when they didn't.

Kasia stepped into the bathroom and turned on the water, washed her face to cool it down. But the humiliation kept her cheeks blood-hot. It was over.

Finished. *Koniec.*

She wanted to slam her fist into her reflection and smash the glass. Why did he never listen to her? Was she that weak?

Probably.

If she could only be home, near Tatuś for his evening reading. Maybe she could soak in his strength. She dried her face and hung the hand towel on the rack, studied herself in the mirror. What if she got home and couldn't even look her dad in the eye?

Her heart sank into her feet as a worse possibility

hit her. What if those eyes—open and welcoming as home itself—shut her out? Saw who she'd become and turned away? If a pastor couldn't keep his own household in order…

She flicked off the bathroom light and shut the door.

But what about Lenka? She and her little sister had always been so in tune, the two-year gap practically nonexistent. That didn't have to change, right? When she got home, they could hike up to their rock as always, just sit and soak in the sunshine and fresh air.

Suddenly, the need for her sister's voice overwhelmed her. Kasia grabbed the phone.

Lenka picked up right away. "Kosh! When are you coming home?"

Her heart warmed. "Three weeks. You almost done with school?"

"Yeah, summer's not getting here fast enough. What's up?"

The reason for the call slammed into her, and she buckled behind the weight of it. "I just broke up with Blake."

"*O jejku.* Are you all right? Did he do something?"

"No, nothing different. I felt…*niespokojnie.*" The Polish word fit better than any English one she could drum up. She'd lacked peace, as much as she'd longed for it. That theme was the soundtrack to her life these days.

"How did he take it?"

Kasia went cold then hot again as she remembered the humiliation of their last kiss. "Not well." She slumped. "But I probably should've handled it better." Honestly? She deserved to be reamed out for the way she'd made a mess of the breakup.

"I noticed you didn't say much this Christmas. Is this what it was?" Compassion sang out in Lenka's voice.

"I guess." Kasia chose a granola bar from her basket.

"What'd you tell him?"

"'This is what the Lord wants.' Sounds like a total copout, I know," Kasia said. "I just had to get out." *Copout* had been an accurate description at the time. But now—only fifteen minutes later—she meant it. If God wanted her away from Blake, wanted her attention for Himself, she would follow through.

"Think it'll be weird at school with him, still?"

"Not if I don't run into him. I plan to stay in lots."

"But you'll make a point of escaping sometimes, right?"

Kasia rearranged her desk. "I mean, I'll probably go hang out off campus. I might go catch some live music at Common Grounds tonight."

"The coffee shop where you used to play? On Fifth?"

Kasia blinked. "Yeah."

"So I'll come down and be your date. What time?"

"Lenka, you don't have to—"

"Actually, why don't you come home with me for church tomorrow?"

Uh, no thanks. Their church family meant well, but…Kasia wasn't ready to go under the pastor's-kid microscope just yet. "I've got too much to do. For school."

"So what time do you head out?"

"Music starts at eight. Are you sure?" She could do this on her own.

Lenka was quiet a beat too long. "Sorry. Mom

called me to help cook."

"What's for dinner?" Kasia picked a chocolate chip out of her bar and bit it in half.

"*Pierogi*, I think."

Mama's Polish dumplings were ultimate comfort food—Kasia's favorite. "Lenka? If I ever ask you that again from my dorm room, feel free to tell me you're having cereal or something."

Lenka's laughter got Kasia to smile again. "Right, when I said *pierogi*, I totally meant Choco Puffs. And I'm pretty sure they're stale. I love you, nerd. I'll call if I can't come for some reason. Otherwise, see you in an hour or so."

Kasia tore off a bite of her granola bar. It was all she'd get for lunch, because she wasn't about to venture out to the food court and risk facing Blake. She brushed the crumbs into her hand and threw them away.

The neck of her twelve-string guitar peeked out at her from her the closet. She stood, rolled her neck, stretched her fingers.

The guitar felt cool and solid in her hands. She sat on her stool and fingered a G chord. Strummed. *Whoa, that's flat.*

Kasia tuned it, thought of her songs. "Shelter." "Empty Me."

Nothing felt right. No melody or familiar chord progression surfaced. Instead, a nameless dread buzzed at the edges of her consciousness, and she couldn't mute it. Why was she so rattled?

Kasia reached for her mp3 player, selected her indie playlist, and cranked it up. She'd just drown out the fear.

5

Adrenaline pumping through his system, Zan jumped to his feet and gripped the cool chain-link fence in front of him. A cold front had blown through early Saturday morning and perfected the weather in time for the final game in the conference tournament.

Bottom of the ninth, the title was within their grasp—but barely. Of course Firelli would be the batter. There was a full count on the freshman—three balls, two strikes, and two outs. If anyone could produce under pressure…

Zan clapped a few times as he shouted from the dugout. "C'mon, Firelli. You got this. Make it happen." There was a significant part of him—the part that loved college ball, loved victory—that wanted Firelli to come through no matter what it cost him personally. The other part knew Firelli could seal his fate with this at bat, and he almost couldn't watch it happen. But he buried the naysayer deep inside and concentrated on the game.

Fans shouted from the bleachers. "Keep it alive, Firelli."

Firelli dug in, and the crowd stilled. Zan's heartbeat thundered in his head.

The pitcher threw a low-breaking ball, and Firelli went with it. A metallic ping sounded as the bat made contact. The crowd sucked in a collective breath.

And there it was. Firelli nailed it. The ball smoked

through the right-center gap. Kent scored from third, Adams from second. The crowd roared as Adams slid into home. Firelli was their new hero.

Zan swallowed the bitter taste in his mouth and rushed out to the plate with his teammates, allowed himself to get caught up in the rush of victory. Shouts, backslapping, cheers, and laughter culminated in a sweaty dog pile on top of Adams. East Coast Conference champions, again, and Zan was part of the team.

Sort of.

Adams knocked the bill of Zan's cap down over his eyes and punched him in the shoulder. "Conference champions, Zan! You headin' to the house for the party tonight?" He leaned over and spoke out the side of his mouth. "Heard there's gonna be some good stuff."

"What are you? Popeye? After a game like today, yeah. I'm thirsty." He smirked. The sooner he could catch a buzz and forget about his life, the better. He'd figure out what to do later.

If there was anything he could do.

Ever the good sport, Zan shook hands with the losing team and felt numb.

For about two seconds.

Then he spotted the perfectly coiffed blond hair of his brother-in-law. Suddenly, he was on fire. Michael Weston stood over the dugout, scanning the stands with a pair of binoculars. Hunting Bailey, no doubt. How good would it feel if his fist could connect with that wifebeater?

With one eye on Mike, Zan shook somebody's hand. "Good game." On to the next. "Seriously. Good game." As he passed the last player, Zan stayed on the path only he could see. Straight as a baseline. Right over the wall and into the stands.

He was in front of Mike before the fool knew it. Zan itched to knock the spit out of him, balled up his fists. "You see her, man? I thought she'd be here for sure."

Mike lowered the binoculars and pivoted toward Zan. They were dead level.

Zan clenched his teeth. "What are you doing here?"

"I came to watch you sit the bench, little brother. Hey, have you seen my wife?"

Zan's hate could've been clocked at ninety miles per hour. He shoved Mike so hard the loser landed on a bunch of bystanders.

Mike shook it off and lunged back.

"Hey! Break it up!" Hands pulled at Zan from different directions. Well-intentioned but totally ignorant people yanked the two of them apart. They didn't know—couldn't know—what Mike was, or they would've all turned vigilante and helped Zan take him down.

"Zan! Buddy!" Adams picked his way through the mob. "Come on, man. Get outta here." He pulled Zan away, back past the dugout, away from the face he wanted to shatter.

Away from Mike's eyes. Eyes that mocked him and sneered at his sister.

Away from justice.

After the debacle, Zan needed to get lost. Needed his head to be anywhere but on Bailey and Mike.

Or the ball field.

He burned rubber out of there.

~*~

A night out for live music was an act of rebellion. Kasia had a bounce in her step.

Tonight was about her future—without Blake. Flanked by Lenka, stuffed with Mom's homemade *pierogi* and cream, Kasia headed toward Common Grounds. "Dinner was awesome."

"Glad I could deliver it, then." Lenka's smile shone brighter than the fading sun, and Kasia soaked in the warmth of it.

"Best *pierogi* ever."

Lenka waved off the opinion. "You've been away from home too long."

Kasia winced. She could forego the reminders of her truancy.

Downtown Huntington smelled like coffee, mesquite smoke, and a touch of diesel, courtesy of the city public transportation system.

They crossed the street and took the steps down into the alley entrance of Common Grounds. Muted lights and the warmth of the deep red stucco-and-brick walls welcomed them. A local guitarist provided the soundtrack as quiet conversations hummed in the air around them. The lyrics of his song were spiritual—not overtly Christian.

But Kasia wondered. Maybe God was reminding her He was with her. She inhaled the scent of fresh-brewed coffee and managed a half-hearted smile for Lenka.

Lenka pointed to the only open booth. They sidled over, squeezed between the other patrons.

As Kasia sat, her gaze settled on a thick and tattooed arm propped on a corner table.That guy from the music building. What was his name? He ran a hand through his shock of black hair and whispered something to the artsy raven-haired girl at his side.

She punched his arm and laughed.

He pointed at Kasia. "Hey. We had a class or two together, yeah?"

She nodded. "I think so. Music?"

"Right, right. I'm Jayce, short for Jayson. A.J.'s an art student, so ya might've missed her around campus." Jayce had to be from Massachusetts. Absolutely no *r* in *art*.

"Kasia and Lenka." She pointed a thumb at her sister.

Lenka rolled her eyes. "Lena, actually. Only family calls me Lenka—short for Little Lena. It's Polish."

"That's cool," A.J. said. "So, do you guys know Kyle or are you just out for coffee?"

Lenka mumbled something about wanting to know Kyle.

A.J. chuckled, her perceptive blue eyes amused.

"Sister date," Kasia said. "But…we forgot our coffee."

Serious fingerpicking drew her attention Kyle's way.

Kasia studied her own fingertips—no longer callused. She shoved her hands in her pockets. Two years away from the stage felt like ages. She missed it all—the sound checks, the travel. The fade to black as the spotlight came up. She used to pretend the auditorium was empty, sing for her audience of One.

"So, Kasia. Music. Just one or two classes, or is that your thing?"

A.J. turned her chair to chat with Lenka about the music. Kyle's gritty voice really did deserve the stage.

Freshman year, it'd been her major. "I don't know

what I'll do with it now." Kasia's gaze jumped over the wide leather band on Jayce's wrist and traced the curling lines of ink on his pale skin. She gave his thick northeastern accent a try. "You from Massachusetts?"

A half-smile crept up his cheek. "Yeah. Boston. The Southside."

"Southie, huh?" That explained his accent, but not the Greek script in his tattoo.

"What do you know about Southie?"

"I saw *Good Will Hunting* and *The Fighter*."

"A.J., you hear this?" His smile stretched the rest of the way.

"Thought it was perfect," she said.

Lenka laughed and smacked her leg. "We should order something and not just sit here. Can you get me a mocha while I run to the back?" She nodded toward the restroom.

"Yep." But as she neared the counter, the murmur of Common Grounds turned to white noise in her ears.

Blake.

She should've smiled, should've disarmed him somehow, but she froze.

"Starting over?" he asked.

"I…just…" Why couldn't she ever think of what to say around him?

"Nah, it's good. Making new friends and all." The words apparently tasted like dirt.

Kasia dropped her gaze, away from all his intensity.

"Come outside." She felt his fingertips on her face, but his touch made her shudder.

Her feet moved backward.

"Kasia." His voice had softened. "Don't do that. Don't pull away."

Her mouth opened, but she was mute. She cast a quick glance toward the table but couldn't see Lenka. Jayce and A.J. were focused each other.

"Outside." Blake's vise grip on her elbow maneuvered her out the door and up the alley steps.

Her breath left, along with her confidence.

Outside, the night swallowed the music. They moved down the street toward his Daddy-only-buys-me-the-best custom sports car. The one mercy was that he'd parked right under a streetlamp.

"Sit with me a minute." He gestured toward the passenger door.

Absolutely not. Light-craving insects whizzed around her head, but she remained under the lamp.

Blake ground the heel of his hand against his eye. "Please?"

Guilt hit her like a gust of wind. He looked like he hadn't slept in days. Like he was broken.

He cleared his throat. "I need to apologize."

"For?"

"For whatever I did to make you so mad. There's got to be some real reason you broke up with me. I mean, we went from perfect to nothing. No warning."

No warning? Did he really believe what they shared was perfect?

He tugged on his collar. "You yanked the rug out from under me, and I…well, I think you owe me a chance to say something."

The weight of his accusation settled on her shoulders. "Fine." She met his eyes. "Say something."

Blake opened the car door, and she tensed. But he pulled out a bouquet of yellow roses.

Her favorite. She bent to smell them before she realized how weak it would appear. She straightened, lifted her chin.

Blake tossed the flowers on the hood and leaned against it, shoulders slumped, as people meandered past. How could one person appear so miserable? She pulled both lips between her teeth, waited.

"Kasia, do you remember how happy we used to be?"

She dipped her head.

"Don't you miss this? I wanted us to have forever, you know?"

"I don't think I did." She rubbed a hand over her elbow.

"No?" He pulled a picture from his pocket, thrust it at her. "Look at us." The photo, worn around the edges, bore a slight imprint from a frame.

She knew that picture, the night they'd walked the Kearnsey Creek Trail to get pictures of the autumn foliage. They'd been together six months. Blake called a hiker over to get a picture of the two of them. He'd wrapped his arms around Kasia and pressed his cheek to hers, whispered, "You're everything."

Her heart had been so full it ached. *In love.* There were no other words for it. It ached again. For all that could've been, if he'd just—if she'd—

"C'mon, Kasia. What happened to us?" Irritation laced his voice. He stood.

Dissonance replaced the harmony in her mind. She handed the picture back. "I don't know, but I settled things, and I'm not going back on it. I promised God a lot once—myself, my music, my whole life. I owe Him all of me."

He laughed. "Your music. When was the last time you sang or played anything?"

She snapped her head his direction. "Maybe that's

my point."

"You made promises to me too, as I recall." He leaned in and whispered against her ear.

Shame sapped her indignation. Jesus couldn't really forgive all that. She stepped closer to the streetlamp—wished she felt more light than shadow.

He grabbed her arm. "I didn't follow you here so I could be left standing like an idiot again, Kosh. I asked you to come outside and talk." So much pressure on her wrist bone.

"But you did follow me here." His grip felt like a nail piercing her joint. "Blake, I am trying to start over. Just let me."

"Starting over without you is—worthless to me. I want you." Blake's grip was relentless.

She snatched her hand away. The sudden rush of blood warmed her fingers. "For the record—you also didn't ask me to come out here." She massaged her elbow to make her point.

"So I'm the bad guy now?" The tenor of his voice rose with every syllable.

Jayce strolled down the sidewalk into the light. "Kasia, this fella botherin' you?" His words were clipped with tension.

Embarrassment flushed her cheeks.

Blake's hard, penetrating eyes leveled a silent warning. And it almost worked.

She wasn't fool enough to say yes out loud, but Kasia met Jayce's eyes.

"Kyle's about to take a break. I want to introduce you two."

Her steps were tentative at first, but she walked toward the coffee shop. She didn't hear Jayce's footsteps behind her, so she glanced back.

He stood a few feet from Blake, simply staring.

After a minute, Blake threw his hands up in the air. "What?"

Jayce shrugged as his gaze lingered on Blake a few moments more. Then he shook his head and left Blake sitting in a lump.

He jogged up, wallet chain jingling, and walked her down the steps. "Ya good?"

She stepped into the shop full of music. He'd seen more than she'd wanted, and she needed a minute to get her wall in place.

"Thanks for coming outside, Jayce."

Jayce scraped the corner of his mouth with his thumbnail. "No problem. I'm gonna get something to eat. You?"

She shook her head and looked back toward the table. "Just our coffees."

With any luck, he would pretend none of this ever happened.

Lenka slid up and nudged her. "What happened while I was in the bathroom?"

Kasia shrugged. "Nothing big. Blake showed up, but I told him we're over." *Or something like that.*

6

Zan's blood was liquid apathy, the world adequately squidgy around the edges. This kind of night—the kind when he wondered why he bothered with college ball—demanded a buzz.

Walking down Frat Row, he felt the bass before he was within fifty yards of the party. A few more steps and he could lose himself in the mayhem.

In no time, he made it to the center of the throng, moved to the beat that vibrated the house and thrummed in his veins. He stayed where the music throbbed so loud in his ears he didn't have to talk to the girls who danced and pressed around him, couldn't have carried on a conversation if he'd wanted to.

Yeah, this was where he wanted to live until the night wore out.

He closed his eyes. Bodies writhed and swayed on every side. He felt soft, thin fabric against his palms, a touch of warm skin, hair ghosting over his fingertips. Delicious perfumes, fruity and exotic, suffused the air, and the slight tinge of sweat and the fermented odor of beer mingled with every scent. When he opened his eyes in the dim light, a gamut of tantalizing images played out before him. A sensory feast.

So why didn't he feel sated? Restless, he wandered back to the kitchen for a refill. Several of his teammates sat around the table, playing beer pong and getting wasted. But nobody was too far gone to miss it when Adams cranked up the TV to hear the ECC championship announcement. Zan's back hit the kitchen doorframe, his gaze riveted to the screen as Firelli's game-winning hit looped again. The room became a riot of whoops and hollers.

He only stood there. What had he done all year? Shagged foul balls and warmed up the left fielders? He'd personally contributed absolutely nothing to this victory. It wasn't his.

Nothing had ever been *his*.

"It's been a long time." A too-familiar voice purred in his ear, warm lips against his skin.

Tasha.

It definitely had been a while. Forgetting her—that face, that voice, that body—after their hot summer together back in Charleston had been less than easy, but he'd made a valiant effort. Popularity, prestige, and wild sorority parties mattered more than he did, so she'd cut him loose. During rush week, and the following year, throngs of guys clamored for her attention.

Well, they could have her.

Tonight, though, as her fingers dug into his hair and her body moved closer to his, he didn't have to ask what she wanted. It might mean nothing to her, might just be for old time's sake, but if he could have something, someone of his own—even for an hour…

He let her lead him away from the crowd and toward the stairs.

One step up, she locked eyes with Zan. Her fingernails scraped lightly against his stomach as she whispered the words he wanted to hear, full of invitation and promise. Zan smirked and answered with a scorching kiss.

A massive arm slammed into his upper body, and Zan swung his head around, disoriented.

The arm was attached to a tree trunk of a man. "Wanna tell me what's goin' on?"

Tasha batted her eyelashes at the hulk. "There you are, baby. He was helping me look for you." As if she hadn't just offered herself to Zan.

The giant's face crumpled as his eyes darted back and forth between them. Whatever was in his bloodstream—mercifully—slowed his reactions to a crawl. That moment of hesitation was the only reason Zan made it out the door.

~*~

As Kyle's set slowed, the song choices were familiar enough to calm Kasia, and convicting enough that she wished she could sink into the floor. Blake's reminders, still hot against her ear, didn't help.

How in the world had she had the audacity to think God would still use someone like her? She'd broken every promise she'd ever made Him, stepped on the shards of her commitments and ground them to dust. Kasia gripped her coffee like a lifeline and squeezed her eyes shut. Gravity compressed her will to nothing. *How do I get up from here, God? Unless You lift me, I have no chance.*

Soft guitar broke into her hopelessness, a plaintive melody drawing her attention. Suddenly, Kyle seemed only a small part of the music. His mellow voice sang a song new to Kasia, and the lyrics hollowed out a piece of her heart.

"...wrapped in shadows of good intentions..."

Exactly. She'd be better off fleeing God than trying to sing again.

His voice filled the room, filled her head. "Stronger, better, but not myself. Change me into—"

Something else, something new.

"Something that could bring You glory…"

In a breath, Kasia was ten again—and Tatuś her universe. On one of those countless nights her family had cozied up on the hearth rug to enjoy the warmth of the fire, Kasia's adoring eyes locked on her daddy's. Tatuś read to them from his favorite books—some in Polish, some English. But he always began with the questions.

"What is man's greatest end?" he asked. With a light touch to the tip of eight-year-old Lenka's nose, he'd leaned toward her and whispered, "I'm asking why we are here, *misiu*. Why did God make us?"

Kasia, nestled snugly under his strong arm, leaned with him in Lenka's direction, scooching even closer to his side as he straightened. He smiled down at her, the skin around his eyes creased with love, and he tugged one of Kasia's long curls. "Do you know, Kasiu? What is our greatest end?"

Suddenly shy, Kasia had whispered the words they were all committing to memory. "The greatest end of man is to glorify God and enjoy Him forever."

"*Och ty! Slicznie,* Kasiu." Wonderful. He squeezed her knee, and she proudly rested her small hand atop his oversized one as he tapped the rhythm of the answer, repeated it once more. "…glorify God and enjoy Him forever…"

Tonight, in Common Grounds, the warmth of her daddy miles away, Kasia wrestled with the second half. Would she ever be able to find joy again?

"So...Kyle's pretty great." Lenka's voice yanked Kasia out of her introspection. "A.J. said he wrote this one. You ought to get that chord chart from him. Maybe you could play with him sometime."

"If you want the chart, you can ask him." Lenka could sing it.

With a crescendo, the music commanded Kasia's attention once more. Kyle's eyes were closed, his face lifted in prayer as his voice resounded. "Make me whole, then make me wholly Yours..." He hummed as he played the final chords, hung his head and let the music fade.

"You've totally got to get the chord sheet."

"*Dobrze*. Fine. I'll get it." *Sheesh.* She would. Even if she couldn't make herself sing. Those words would be her prayer in the weeks ahead.

~*~

Kasia studied Kyle's guitar as he set it down. Great sound quality, beautiful coloring. She sort of hated it when people put stickers on the body though.

He strolled over to fist-bump Jayce. "Who are these lovely ladies?"

"I'm Lena, and this is my sister, Kasia."

A.J. chuckled. "There you go. They even answer questions."

"You two go to school at Oconee State?"

"I do," Kasia said. "Lena still lives at home." She wouldn't say "high school" in order to save her toes from her sister's vengeance, but she wouldn't lie either.

"Where do you go?" Lenka asked.

"Tri-County Tech. I study Broadcasting Media?" It was a question.

Lenka chuckled. "You're not sure?"

"I'm sure it's my major. Wasn't sure you'd know what it was." He shook his head.

"Radio and TV, right?" Kasia asked.

"Yeah. There are loads of technical details and small projects, but we each get a shift at the station too. I handle a weekday-morning broadcast, but my baby is the indie-music show I do on Saturday nights. It's a pretty cool course."

"Sounds like it." Kasia smiled. "I'll have to tune in this weekend and check it out. I'm always looking for new music."

"Did you write any of that music tonight? A few songs were new to me." Lenka brushed her long, straight hair back over her shoulder. "Kasia writes music."

What! "Thanks, Lenka. Even though I purposely kept it on the down-low that you were still in high school."

"Ohho. Bring it, sister. He probably doesn't care that you're mediocre."

"You guys are so sweet." Kyle laughed quietly. "But seriously, Kasia, do you write a lot?"

Kasia tipped her head to the side. "Been known to try."

"That's cool," Kyle said. "I'd love to hear something of yours. Why not bring your guitar next week. We can jam after the study?"

Kasia's emotions swirled in the pit of her stomach at the hope she saw in his face. She hated disappointing people. She looked away. "I, um…haven't really written anything new—or played—for a while."

"Oh, I guess…" Kyle quit talking.

"Who else is hungry?" Jayce said suddenly. "I feel like a meatball sandwich or two. Anybody in?"

"I'll get a dessert," Kasia said. Kyle and Lena picked up the conversation from there, but Kasia didn't listen. Her mind stayed engulfed in unanswered questions.

~*~

Back in Kasia's dorm room, her sister spouted opinion like an annoying fountain—on the music, on Kyle, on how hard it was to get Kasia's attention all evening.

Kasia hoped the well would run dry soon. She'd thought about inviting Lenka to spend the night, but no way. Kasia's nerves were as taut as guitar strings and humming already.

"So. Church tomorrow. It's cool A.J. invited you, since we need new people for you to hang with. And Kyle definitely seemed interested in talking music more."

Lenka clearly had no hesitations about it. Apparently, "we" were signing up for anything that presented itself. Kasia studied the floor, tried to expel her irritation somewhere other than all over Lenka. Her sister meant well, but—*just ask first*. People always assumed they knew what she wanted.

"Kyle had a whole lot of questions about you, actually." Lenka waggled her eyebrows.

"Slow down, Lenka. I'm not exactly ready to meet the world yet."

"You don't *miss* Blake, do you?" Lenka obviously wanted a no. "You know, I don't even know him. Anyone who's more important than family is—"

"He was never more important. It was just…I didn't want…"

Lenka's face softened.

Maybe Lenka could truly listen and withhold judgment. "I…did you have any idea Blake and I were sleeping together?"

Lenka rocked back on her heels. "No! I mean, I knew you were—" Her words fell into silence. She cleared her throat. "Kosh, what were you thinking?"

Kasia's ears heated up. From shame or the sting of Lenka's tone, she didn't know. "I didn't plan it, Lena. We just went a little further every time. And you knew we were what?"

Her sister's mouth formed a tight line. "I walked up on the two of you one time out behind Dad's wood shop—you had no idea I was there."

What had she seen? "Were we—?"

"Kissing, but handsy enough to scald my eyes."

"Sorry you saw that." Kasia aligned her Bible with the desk corner. Exactly.

"You're not sorry you did it?"

"*Jejku,* Lenka. Thanks for the judgment."

"I didn't mean that." Lenka rubbed her palms on her shorts—her signature I'm-uncomfortable move. "It was just a shock to see, you know? And to hear this now. You've always been my standard."

Kasia's gaze flew to meet Lenka's. "Not fair. Nobody can live up to that kind of pressure."

Lenka nodded. "You at least realize it was a mistake, right?"

How about some encouragement? "You think if I planned to sleep around, I'd announce it?"

"Sorry." Lenka blew out a breath. "I'm not doing a good job here."

True. Still, Kasia couldn't fault her sister for the reaction. She deserved worse. And she needed a friend. She steadied herself on the edge of her bed. "I understand why you'd think less of me. But there were a slew of good reasons I couldn't stop."

"Like what?"

"Forget it. Just…believe me when I say I'm done with all of it. Dating and everything."

"Sorry you have to deal with all that."

Kasia picked at the rubber on her flip-flop and felt a hand on her wrist. She glanced up.

"Really. *Przykro mi*. I'll pray for you."

The Polish apology warmed her. "Thanks. You, um, should probably head home. Don't want Mama and Tatuś to worry."

Her sister's strawberry-blonde hair fell in her face as she stood. "All right. Do you want me to drive down sometime this week?"

"I'll let you know, *dobrze*?" Lenka was right. She needed friends right now.

But she also needed to make some decisions for herself.

7

Zan woke the morning after the hellacious frat party and felt like he'd slept chained to a jackhammer. His body ached, his stomach churned, and his tongue wore a sweater. He poured a cup of yesterday's coffee, swallowed some aspirin, and tried to remember the last twenty-four hours. Based on the pieces he could recall, he might as well give up and move home.

His cell vibrated on the coffee table. Dad. Well, that ought to ease the headache. "Hello?" His phone said one o'clock already.

"Congrats on the championship, son. Wish you'd have gotten a little game time."

He did not want to talk baseball with Dad while his head was under this anvil. "I'm going to see Bailey today."

"Is she all right?" Protective-father mode. Immediately.

"Decent, I guess. Staying with some church people."

Dad harrumphed. "For how long?"

"I don't know. I'll ask though."

"We don't tell you enough, son. Taking that partial scholarship—that was a mighty selfless decision. It's good you're close to Bailey."

Zan's chest swelled a little, even though when he'd turned down two other offers—both starting positions—he hadn't been reaching for a compliment.

"As far as these church folks—you help Bailey make some wise decisions, hear? Maybe get her to come home."

No pressure. "Yes, sir." Zan knew he'd be hearing from the coach soon. May as well bite the bullet. "Hey, Dad?"

"What is it?"

"Mike was there yesterday, at the game. Looking for Bailey."

He'd never heard his dad swear so eloquently. "Did you say anything to him?"

"Yeah…more than that. I'm pretty sure I'm in serious trouble."

~*~

Kasia sat in the back of West Ridge Community Church next to A.J. and Jayce. Kyle, part of the worship team, winked at her from the front. Their pastor wouldn't preach that morning. Missionaries Mark and Patty Cleaven would only be stateside for two weeks more, so Pastor Sean asked Mark to share about his work in Peru.

From word one, Mark's obvious love for the people of Cajamarca held Kasia's attention. In the photos, she saw their highland village—snapshots of their work, side by side with the people, drilling wells, building irrigation systems.

As Mark spoke, Kasia's mind whisked her to the Andean highlands. She saw herself working with the bronze-skinned women, laughing at the antics of nearby black-headed children. The idea smoldered within her.

She tore herself from her reverie and listened as

Mark shared the immense challenge facing the team as they returned to the field. "We're torn," he said. "We spend most of our time in the highland villages. Up until now, we've only spent one day a week in the city, for shopping and daily business. But we've built relationships with the open-air merchants and shop owners. Any of you folks ever thought about teaching English as a second language?"

Kasia had. She'd helped her mom for years. Even before Mama let her help with her ESL classes, Kasia couldn't stay behind. She'd learned to greet everybody in their heart language, make them feel welcome. She sat and drew pictures for them while she listened. When she turned twelve, Mama let her help with the kids. But in that—*that*—she'd found joy.

Mark's eyes—full of contagious intensity—scanned the auditorium. "Before we came back to the States, they asked me to offer a conversational English class for their older kids—home from university for the summer. We'd be crazy to blow this opportunity. The highland families are responsive, but there are a hundred thousand more people in the city than the villages. There isn't enough time for my wife and me to do it all. Pray that God will give us wisdom as we choose how to invest our time."

Kasia nodded. That was the same thing she prayed for herself.

And then Mark Cleaven said the words that changed everything.

"And if there's someone here who'd be willing to go and work with us? Let me know." His words reverberated in the air, rippling waves in concentric circles. They crashed against her heart.

That's me.

It's not music, but it's something. And what held her back?

After the service—without a word to her new friends—Kasia hustled up front. She didn't want him to leave before she got to him.

Kasia stuck out her hand before doubt could kill her nerve. "Hi, I'm Kasia. I can do it."

Mark laughed. "Do what?"

"I think I'm your new ESL teacher."

~*~

Zan parked in front of a yellow Cape Cod. *Manicured* wasn't the right word, but the freshly mulched flowerbeds must be a favorite hobby. He hadn't meant to be impressed with these people who'd taken his sister.

Bailey hurried out to meet him, and he wrapped his tiny big sister in a hug. Nothing frail about her this time. She offered him an Adirondack chair by the front window, and an older lady waddled out with a tray of iced lemonade, set it on the weathered wicker table.

He extended his hand. "Alexander Maddox, ma'am."

She grasped it before swiping a silver strand of hair from her forehead. "I'm Mrs. Beistline. We certainly adore your sister."

Zan watched Bailey settle into one of the low chairs. She glowed, eyes vibrant. If he hadn't spent last week afraid for her, he might have warmed at the peace in her eyes. But it irked him.

He waited until Mrs. Beistline went inside. "I called off the search when I got your note." He needed to swallow the anger, but Bailey had to catch what he was pitching. "I went to your house, you know? Filed a missing-person report and everything." Her blindness to his frustration and concern drove him nuts.

Bailey frowned. "Sorry. My only focus was getting away. We thought it would be best for me to completely disappear. And I figured you were tied up with baseball."

"Really, Bay? In what world would baseball be more important than you? You disappeared! Not a word to anybody. We were all—"

"I know." She sipped at her lemonade. "I should've thought of everyone else."

The words punched him in the gut. "No. You did what you had to. It was just…scary. Listen, forget about it. Tell me about these folks."

"They're great. I met them at a support-group meeting at West Ridge Community Church. As soon as they learned about everything, they opened their home to me."

"If you want to get out for good, you could always move home. Mom and Dad would—"

"I don't want to leave Huntington, Zan. If Michael doesn't find me, I'll be fine. I love the church—the people."

"Bailey, when you're in a situation like this, you go to family. That's the way it's supposed to be. You don't need to depend on strangers, especially if they're filling your head with—"

"Hold it right there."

Zan blinked. Never. She'd never stood up to him before. To anyone.

"I'm content. I feel safe. I know I haven't made great decisions in the past, but I want you to trust me this time."

"Was Mike…" He rubbed his knee, couldn't figure out how to ask. He got up and leaned on one of the supports.

"You can ask me anything."

Zan reached across his chest and massaged his shoulder, grasped for words. "Was it just when he was drunk? I mean, did he ever…"

The words hung there, and Zan gave up trying to phrase his thoughts. When he turned to gaze out at the mountains in the distance, she spoke.

"He was abusive in just about every way you can imagine—he messed with my mind, screamed at me, threatened me, beat me, accused me of…all kinds of things. And I didn't even see it. I got really good at making excuses for him."

"What happened that night at the house? You had to be terrified."

"He did all the smashing and breaking after I left."

"Thank God."

Bailey snapped her head in his direction and one eyebrow slid up underneath her bangs. "I do, Zan. I might not have lived through that one. Of course, my decision to leave caused the reaction."

"What changed? That made you leave."

"One night, our neighbors called the police, and I—*whew.* This one's embarrassing." She kicked at the welcome mat.

"You don't have to—"

"I do, actually. It's good for me. I covered up the bruises while Michael met the officers at the door, and then when I came out, I basically fell all over myself declaring his innocence. 'He didn't do anything. I fell.' No one pressed charges."

Zan felt sick. He'd always wanted to believe Mike

was just gifted at smooth-talking his way out of trouble—without Bailey's help.

"The next day, while Michael was at work, my neighbor Sally came over. She brought her pastor's wife with her, and they invited me to come to a group that meets at their church. It took me forever to actually go, but Sally never pushed. She just showed kindness like no one I'd known in a while. And the group? After about four sessions, the Lord began to let me see what sort of shape I was in—and what was happening."

"Did you tell Michael you were leaving?"

"No. The Beistlines rented a trailer while he was at work." She reached for his hand. "Alexander. Let me figure things out. I need this."

Zan's chest hurt from the pride he felt for her. That took some strength.

He scratched his head. No more dark circles under her eyes. They were clear instead of dull and glassy. She'd been so frazzled and broken. Now? Stronger somehow. Clearly, she bought whatever these people were peddling. For today, he could get behind anything that made her feel valuable. "All right, Bay. You figure it out, but keep us in the loop. We love you."

"I know. I feel it."

"Stay in touch with Mom, if nobody else. Charleston feels a world away when she doesn't know where you are."

"I promise."

He reached across the table and squeezed her hand, willed her to pick up on his mental signal. *Hang on to the worthwhile stuff, but don't fall for the Jesus con.*

~*~

Jayce stood near where they sat for the service, a helmet tucked under his arm. "A.J. had a quick creative-arts-ministry meeting, but she wants us all to head over to her Uncle Frankie's for a cookout. You in?"

"Who's going?" Kasia asked.

Jayce gave Kasia that Southie nod. "Does it matter? There's gonna be a grill."

"I can make a salad if you want," Kasia said.

"I bet you make a wicked salad, but, ah, lettuce ain't really my thing."

"Can I ride with you, Kasia?" Kyle asked.

Jayce dropped his Bible into a worn backpack. "Let's just park at your place, Kyle. I'll drop the bike and we can all take Bond-O."

"What kind of motorcycle, a chopper?" Kasia asked.

Jayce's eyes crinkled with laughter. "Ah, no. No, I'm not the chopper type. I drive an old British cycle. My old man and me restored it together. Took us four years."

Kasia's eyebrows arched. "Four years? Are you serious?"

"Yeah." He had a pleasant, far-off look in his eyes for a moment. "Parts were a little pricey, so we just did a little at a time."

Kyle's face was full of admiration. "That is one sweet bike."

"If the bike is so special—why did your dad let his college-bound son take off with it? It's like a what? Fifteen-hour drive?" Kasia asked.

Jayce nodded with that wry smile again. "Yeah,

almost sixteen. My bike's better for an afternoon drive. Fine around town, but he wanted me to get down here all right."

A.J. jogged over. "Jayce, I've got to run over and pick up those canvases for the coffeehouse. That all right?"

"Yup. Pick us all up at Kyle's when you're done."

As they neared Blake's neighborhood, Kasia's shoulders turned into two solid knots of tension. She couldn't wait to drive past it.

"Oh, take the next right onto Finley Road." Kyle pointed out the window.

Her stomach hit the floorboard. Finley Road. She swallowed hard as she hit her blinker.

"Just pull in here—this first left."

Why here? Kasia stayed as far away from Blake's building as she could, pulled in next to the mailboxes.

As soon as she parked, Kyle jumped out of her car. "Be right back."

Kasia grabbed her phone and called Lenka. She leaned her head back on the seat and closed her eyes, imagined she was somewhere else.

"Hey," her sister answered. "So…what'd you think of everything?"

A smile commandeered Kasia's face. "I figured out what I want to do this summer."

"Good. Maybe we can carpool or something."

"Not unless you want a ride to Peru."

Silence.

"Are you still there?"

"You're serious."

"Dead."

"The whole summer."

"I've got no reason to stay. I can be back at school

in the fall, and I'm exactly the kind of person he's looking for. No job, no husband, no kids, no ties—other than a supportive family who I'm *hoping* will send me off with their blessings." Just saying it out loud was making Kasia's heart hammer.

"Huh." Kasia could practically hear the gears turning in Lenka's head.

"What? I felt alive again today, and…it's been a while." Kasia needed this as much as the Cleavens needed her. Nothing Lenka could say would change it.

"I think you'd be awesome at that type of ministry—and time away would be good for you."

"Really?"

"Really. I'm sure Mom and Dad will see it too."

"Lenka, you make me all sappy."

"Aw, I'm just trying to get you out of the country so I can have your room. You've got the view of the mountains back there. My window looks out on the road."

"Girl, if you help me persuade Mom and Dad, I'll give you my room willingly."

"Don't think I won't hold you to that, Kosh. You go and that room is mine."

Kasia laughed. "Done."

Someone tapped on the glass beside her head. She glanced back and her stomach hit the floorboard. "Blake is outside my car."

"What is he doing there? Did he follow you again?"

Kasia knew better than to answer that. He knocked again.

"Don't even think about rolling the window down."

"He's not going to go away if I don't."

"He's not—"

Kasia rolled it down halfway. She said nothing.

"Will you please get out and talk to me?"

"No. I'm on the phone with my sister, Lena. Remember her?" Kasia sounded all politeness, but a strength infused her that she'd lacked before.

"Put it on speaker," Lenka demanded.

"Kasia, listen," Blake began. "I'm sorry about the way things happened last night. I just…we didn't get to finish. Your friend interrupted." He wasn't quite able to hide the venom in those last two words.

"No, we were finished. I didn't really want to hear any more."

His fist shook. With obvious effort, he stilled it, stretched his fingers out. "There are still things I want to tell you though."

Kasia shook her head. And then she heard the tiger purr of a motorcycle.

As Blake looked behind her car, Kasia peeked in the rearview. The slick black cycle idled directly behind her. Jayce lifted the visor of his helmet and stared. Revved the engine.

Kyle appeared and leaned back beside Kasia's door, arms folded across his chest.

"What's happening? I need details," Lenka said.

Kasia's nerves hummed, but—with the guys looking out for her—it was far more entertaining than she thought it'd be. She gave Lenka the details and put her on speaker.

Kyle extended his hand. "I don't believe we've met. Kyle Compton. You are?"

Blake stared at Kyle's hand for a beat, then leaned down and hissed at Kasia, "This is getting old, Kasia. I'll catch you at school." He spun and stalked off.

Jayce pulled into a nearby spot and parked. Kyle climbed in the passenger seat.

"Is he gone?" Lenka huffed. "Yet another reason why a few months in Peru might be a good thing."

"Yeah, Lenka." Blake was right. This was getting old.

"She say Peru?" Kyle asked.

Jayce slid into Kasia's back seat. "All right. Ya gotta tell me: Is this guy a real threat, or is he just unbelievably irritating?"

Both girls answered at once. Lenka shouted on speakerphone, "A threat."

Kasia muttered, "Just irritating—" Then she added, "I…think." Her caveat was met with awkward quiet.

"On that note," Lenka said, "I'm going to hang up. But…you need to tell these guys the situation, since they're around more than I am. See you soon."

Kasia mumbled, "Blake and I used to…" Minimizing it would get her nowhere. "He's my ex-fiancé. He can't quite let go."

Jayce spoke again. "But ya made it clear that you were done, yeah? I mean, if ya need me to mess with him a little—"

"No," she said. "I think…I *don't* think it would help if you got involved. You know what I mean?"

Jayce dipped his head. "You lemme know if things change, all right?"

Kasia smiled. "Thanks," she said. "Both of you—for just being around a minute ago."

Kyle offered a sympathetic smile.

A deep rumble sounded behind them. "There we go," Jayce said. He chuckled as he turned in his seat to watch as A.J. roared into a nearby parking spot. "That girl makes me smile every time I see her." He hopped out of the car and spun back to duck his head inside. "You two wanna follow us over, then?"

Kasia nodded and found a smile for him. "Sure."

Jayce drummed twice on the roof, then closed the door and jogged over to meet A.J.

She felt Blake's infuriated gaze on her as they pulled out.

~*~

Kyle rolled down his window. "So…Peru?"

Kasia beamed. "I've decided to go work with the Cleavens—for the summer. I mean, I've got to talk to my parents about it and all, but it's perfect. It's exactly what I need."

"To teach? With the guy from church?" Kyle asked.

"Yeah."

"You'll be awesome at it," Kyle said. "Want some company down there?"

Kasia cast him a sideways glance. "Nope."

Kyle patted the top of her seat. "Kidding. I've got a bunch of concerts booked for the summer. Just sorry you'll miss 'em."

She relaxed in her seat, the smile back in her voice when she spoke. "Save some sample CDs and we'll catch up when I get back."

"You're on," he said. "It's a date. Oh! Did A.J. tell you about our small group?"

8

Kasia's alarm shattered her semi-peace, and she snapped her head up. Why was she on the floor?

A pain knifed her neck and shoulder as she turned and eyed the time. *Ugh.* Seven already? She pressed the knot with her first two fingers, bled the tension from her shoulders.

Only an hour to meet A.J.

She pushed herself off the rug, crawled over, and turned off the blaring clock. Floor naps were becoming too-familiar friends. No matter how she tried, Kasia couldn't outrun insomnia.

But Saturday night, she'd dozed fitfully. And her anxiety crescendoed.

She kept dreaming her legs were anchored to the center of a murky lake. Shadows slithered under the surface, slipped past her skin. She exhausted herself to keep her head above water. But she couldn't escape.

Even now, wide awake, dread dogged her. She needed an outlet, needed to do something strong. Kasia snatched her phone from the top of the dresser and paused with her thumb on the call button. Depending on who answered, her tactics would need adjustment.

"Hello?" Mama's voice.

A gentle approach, then. "Mamusiu? It's Kasia."

"Czy wszystko w porządku?"

"Yes. I'm fine. I just have a question." Did she only

ever call when she was in trouble?

"*Dobrze.* What is it?"

"Well, you know I visited Busia this week, right?"

"She's talked of little else. It was wonderful of you to stop by."

Kasia rubbed the back of her desk chair with the heel of her hand. "She, um…suggested I do some mission work this summer."

"You don't want to talk about this when you come home?"

"My idea has a deadline."

"Oh?"

All right, Lord. This is all You. "I met a missionary—the work sounded incredible. Similar to your English classes for other immigrants all those years. I know I can do it."

"It sounds perfect—'working with immigrants,' you said?"

She picked up a piece of scrap paper and threw it away. "Um, no…I said 'similar.' It's in Peru."

"Kasiu, you mean the entire summer? In South America? We don't know anything about this—"

"It wouldn't be the first time I've travelled internationally. I know right where my passport is. And—this is why there's a deadline—Mr. Cleaven will only be in town for a few more days. I thought maybe you and Tatuś could meet with him personally and iron out some details, where I would stay, all that. So you feel good about it when I go." *When. Not if.*

Silence. Then, "That's…that's huge."

"I won't leave town with them. I'll come home after exams, spend a couple weeks, prepare several English lessons with you, pack carefully…"

"You haven't been home in a long time. I'd like to

have time to enjoy your presence."

"I wouldn't have been home all summer anyway, if I'd gotten married in June." It wasn't a jab. Just a dose of reality.

"Hm. Another thing I'd like to talk about with you."

Not now, not now. "What if it's what I need, though, Mom? Like Busia said. I need to figure things out—figure myself out."

Shoes squeaked in the hallway outside her room. A dark blur marred the strip of yellow light under her door. Was someone standing there?

"And you think Peru is the best place for that. Thousands of miles from your family."

Kasia pressed her fingertips into the wall until they turned white, tried to sound sensible. "Mama, you wanted to be a missionary for years. Why are you against this?"

"I'm not against it, *kochanie*. I am for you. We haven't spoken often recently, so I can't pretend to know what you need, but I'd rather deal with all of this face to face."

"I've already verbally committed. Can you at least *consider* giving me your blessing?" Her heart sounded like a wild drum solo. She might be pushing it here.

"Your dad's been counting the days until his Curly-Q gets home, but I'll ask him to hear you out. In person. Best I can do."

She'd have to settle for that. "Thanks, Mamusiu."

"I miss your voice, Kasiu. I can't wait to share a pot of tea and hear how you're truly doing. I imagine it's tough, since Blake is around and you share the same friends. Has there—"

"Oh! I've got to go. I'm meeting someone to study,

and they're here." A scuffle in the hall concerned her. There was definitely someone out there—but the shadow had disappeared.

"All right, then." She heard the smile in Mama's voice. "Have a good study session. *Kocham cię.*"

"Love you too. Bye." Kasia ended the call and dropped the phone on the bed. The prospect of candor with her mom made her clammy. She didn't know how she was "truly doing," and her "trite answers and lies" tank was running on empty.

She opened her door and peered into the hallway. Deserted. As the door shut, an envelope caught her eye.

She bent and picked it up. The graceful, slanted address said it was meant for her, but the unfamiliar script made her stomach tighten. Who'd been out there?

Kasia opened the letter and pulled out simple white stationery. Something slipped out onto the floor. An old admission bracelet from…the Haven? She picked it up and stared, emotions warring in her head.

Blake. Her bracelet was still in her guitar case. Had he been the one in the hall? Did he hear her say she was starting over?

The smooth plastic between her fingers reminded her how easy everything had been that first summer. He'd surprised her with an invitation to his parents' home near Stone Mountain for a three-day concert event. Some of her favorite indie artists were on the program—people she'd hoped would become colleagues and friends.

Because of the chance to network, Tatuś relented. She'd seen the discomfort in his gentle eyes when he'd nodded yes. But it had been so worth the compromise.

Parts of the weekend she didn't remember well. She had her first drink that last night, at his parents' big dinner party. At least the buzz helped her not feel so…foreign…so out of place. But the concerts had been super. That's what she wanted to remember. Regret clogged her throat as she opened the letter, swallowed.

I'm sorry I made you hate me somehow. I don't want to make you run. I only want to talk. Please call me. It's the last time I'll ask.

Blake

She didn't hate him. Still, she wouldn't call. Odds were she'd say something stupid again. Or confuse the issue. She needed to avoid him for sure.

Decision gave her the necessary momentum. She dropped the envelope on the bed and grabbed her clothes. Blake always seemed to intrude when she most needed freedom. She couldn't let him make her feel caged anymore. Within ten minutes, she was dressed and ready.

Kasia locked her window and bathroom before she left to meet A.J.

She turned back to deadbolt her door. Every little bit helped. She wasn't sure exactly what she was locking out of her life, but she knew one thing.

She needed to feel safe.

~*~

Zan threw his sketchpad and charcoals onto his passenger seat, cranked up, spun his tires, and peeled out, away from school. He needed to touch base with his father after his chat with Coach, but that was dead last on his to-do list.

All the list said was *Get Out*.

Westminster, Seneca, Walhalla—the whole Golden Corner hemmed him in. He headed north, craving mountains. Half an hour later, he ended up in Downtown Huntington, pulled to a stop in front of the Warehouse—one of Bailey's favorite coffee spots. He strode in and ordered the tallest, sweetest drink they offered.

"I'm not looking at Alexander Maddox all the way up here in Huntington, am I?"

Zan spun in the direction of the voice, and a wide grin commandeered his face. "Yes, sir!" Coach Markman was exactly the medicine for his particular ill tonight. Zan gripped the extended hand.

"Sit down and catch me up."

Zan took a seat next to the window, pulled off his cap. His hair probably stood stick straight, but who the heck cared? "Seems like more than a couple years, doesn't it?"

"Sure does." Markman took a swig of his iced tea. "I saw you on TV yesterday."

"That's a pretty mess, isn't it?"

Markman laughed. "I meant the game, but I saw that too. Report only showed y'all being pulled off each other. Did you clock him?"

Zan allowed himself a wry smile. "No such luck."

"How *is* your sister?"

See, this was why he loved Coach Markman. He hadn't just coached the high-school team. He knew his boys, cared about what they were into. What went on at home. "She's out of there—permanently, I think. Staying with some church people."

Markman's brow lifted.

Exactly. "So, what are you doing these days?" Zan asked.

"Got a few offers from minor-league teams, but I decided to stick with coaching."

"Looking anywhere in particular?"

"Just signed a contract with Oconee State University, actually." Markman glanced over at the door as a group of laughing women walked in.

Zan thought he caught a flash of auburn and turned in his chair. He didn't recognize any of them. Disappointment punched him. But as he swung back around, his gaze did land on Kasia—climbing out of her car on the far side of the street. What were the odds? Would she come into the Warehouse?

"Know her?" Markman's voice startled him. Had he been staring that hard?

Zan lifted a shoulder. "Changed a flat for her once, but she played it cool."

Markman smiled. "Gimme a minute?" He pointed toward the restrooms.

Zan nodded.

Kasia stood on the opposite curb, waiting for a chance to cross. Her thick, penny-colored braid hung over her shoulder as her eyes scanned the street. He remembered that braid—and all the spunk that went with it.

"Bernolak!"

Was this joker yelling at Kasia? Right in front of the window, some lanky guy had stopped. Waved to her. So her last name was Bernolak.

If this was Nail-in-the-Tire, Zan would love to reach out and set him straight about a few things.

She jogged across the street and stepped up onto the sidewalk. Kept her distance though. Zan smiled.

He turned his body away from the open window and pulled out his sketchpad. He should at least *appear* to be otherwise occupied. No sense in looking like a creeper, even if he was listening in.

"I'm just on my way out," the guy said, "but I could come in and hang for a while…if you don't—"

"I'm meeting somebody." Kasia cut him off. "Probably in there already."

Poor guy.

Zan reached into his pack and picked up a soft lead pencil. It felt sturdy in his hand. He drew a careful line, the shape of her face as he remembered it.

"Cool," the guy said. "I just wanted to say we miss having you around. Not like we did a lot when you and Blake were together anyway…whenever we saw you."

The dude was tripping all over his words. But Zan caught the past tense. She wasn't with Blake, whoever he was. *Nail-in-the-Tire maybe? Good for her.*

"No, I didn't see you a whole lot, did I? Once you introduced me to Blake, you pretty much ditched me." *Ouch.*

"Is that what you think? That we all just took off?"

"Didn't you?" A question in the tone of her voice made Zan turn. Yeah, her expression seemed genuinely confused. He turned back around, antsy. Last thing he needed was for her to catch him staring.

"Blake said—" It got quiet outside the window.

Zan sketched her eyes. Shaded with the flat of the pencil. Erased. Couldn't do her justice.

"Never mind what Blake said," the guy went on. "I just wanted to tell you I miss you. And I'm sorry everything changed. Sorry Blake ever showed up."

Zan waited for Kasia to say something.

"Forget it." Dude was done trying.

"No, wait," she said. "I'm sorry. I miss…a lot.

Everything used to be better."

The guy had apparently decided to keep quiet. And Coach Markman was headed back. Zan shut his sketchpad and slouched a little, tried to appear relaxed. The metal chair bit into his back.

Markman stopped at the counter and pulled out his wallet.

"—best if we don't hang out," Kasia said. "I won't ask you to choose between friends. And—I really need a blank slate. New everything."

"I get it," the guy said. "I'll try to run interference."

She coughed—probably fake. "I'm going in, Trav. Tell everybody I'm sorry, will you?"

"You want some dessert, Zan?" Markman slid into his chair with one of those strawberry shortcakes. "Or are you filling up on the conversation outside?"

Zan's cheeks caught fire. *Both?* "I'm good. Thanks."

"So tell me. How much trouble are you in because of the throwdown with Bailey's husband?"

"There's a hearing on Tuesday." Zan needed to see if Kasia Bernolak had come inside, and if the guy she was meeting was here yet. Maybe he could snag a minute to say hi.

"Don't let this throw you, Zan. Explain the history—you'll probably need to get some documentation, maybe incident reports from the police. I know your parents must have a pile of stuff from early on. Be the respectful, standup guy you've always been. Give it your best."

He nodded.

"I'm not going to lie though. It'd be nice to build a team around some of my old boys." He winked.

"Wouldn't be legal for me to lure you away from your athletic program."

"Sometimes I wish I were anywhere else. It's not just this probation thing. There's—"

"Firelli."

Man, he missed Markman.

"If you get kicked out or something, I'll see what I can swing."

~*~

As Kasia turned toward the door of the Warehouse, her gaze ran across a black Jeep and her breath caught. It had to be the same one—older, bigger, more off-road-worthy than the average. Forearms was nearby. In the Warehouse?

Her heart somersaulted. He might ask her to join him, and if he smiled at her with those dimples, she didn't know if she could refuse.

A pair of sandals slapped hurriedly down the sidewalk. A.J. dropped her keys into a handmade bag. "I thought you'd wait inside! Get us a table."

"I ran into an old friend. But let's go. I haven't had good food all day."

Inside, they placed their orders and Kasia peeked around to find Forearms. Didn't see him. She exhaled equal parts relief and disappointment and picked up her sweet tea and chef salad.

"I love that skirt, A.J. Where did you find it?"

A.J. led the way to the only sunny spot in the restaurant. "I cut up some of my old clothes and made it. New life, new look."

Kasia took the seat against the wall and slung her messenger bag over the chair.

And spotted Forearms grinning at her from the table behind the door.

If it wouldn't have been the most obvious ploy ever, she'd have switched sides with A.J. Instead, she smiled at him and looked away, determined to ignore how his ball cap rested on his knee and that one piece of gold hair fell into his eyes.

"So you ran into somebody?"

Kasia sat. "One of my—one of Blake's friends. They grew up together."

Her stomach tightened at an unbidden memory. The one time she'd met Travis to study for an exam over coffee, Blake had knocked Trav's cup off the table and splattered the contents all over the wall. And they'd left him there to clean it up.

She'd never apologized to Travis.

"What's up?" A.J. tugged on her long, straight ponytail.

Kasia sipped her drink to wash down the knot in her throat. "It's easier to start over."

"I hear that. It can be daunting, but you look tough enough." A.J. bit into her meatball sandwich.

"Nice to know someone understands. Why did—"

"Hey, I meant to ask." A.J. swallowed quickly and cut her off. "Did you find something for this summer?" Her bright blue eyes were expectant. "What will you do?"

"Um, Peru. I'm going to teach English in Peru." Maybe she'd get to hear A.J.'s story later. "Tell me more about small group."

Forearms had his back to her now, so she could watch him as he set his hat on the table and ambled up to the counter. His T-shirt fit tight across his shoulder blades, and he wore cargo shorts and leather flops.

Looked like he preferred the beach to the mountains. Maybe it was his surfer hair. Even relaxed, though, everything about him shouted strength.

"…think you'll like everybody. We all take turns leading the study."

Kasia turned back to A.J. "Can I bring something for everyone to snack on?"

"Definitely. You'll be Jayce's new favorite."

"It's the Polish in me." She shrugged. "We never show up at someone's house without a gift. I like to bring food."

Forearms, a plate piled high with whipped cream and strawberries in his hand, slid back into his seat. He raised his glass of sweet tea to her and winked.

She stabbed a piece of chicken, but the corner of her mouth lifted. "How long have you and Jayce been together?" Something in her needed to know good relationships still existed—for more than just her parents and grandparents. For people her age.

Of course, that could make her feel more like a failure.

"Since the middle of our freshman year." She blew her bangs out of her eyes. "He came into my Uncle Frankie's body shop to get some detailing done. That's my gig." She popped a kettle chip into her mouth and shrugged, but the glow gave her away.

Before Kasia finished her salad, Forearms and the man with him stood and left their tips on the table. He nodded in her direction and walked out the door.

And Kasia didn't know how to feel about it.

9

Kasia was desperate for a new beginning…or seven.

On the way to Kyle's for Monday night small group, Lenka kept firing questions. Kasia turned up the music.

"What do you think about—"

Kasia reached for the knob again.

"*Jejku*. I get it. Conversation's not your thing." Silence reigned for a few beats.

As she pulled into the neighborhood, Kasia glanced over at Blake's building. She parked near the mailboxes again.

She hip-checked the car door and headed down the sidewalk, armed with a tray full of appetizers. Around the corner but still in sight, a hundred yards away, Blake's black sports car gleamed in the corner spot as always, where he could guard it from his bedroom window.

She and Lenka climbed the steps to Kyle's second-floor apartment. At the top, Kasia rested the tray on the railing and scanned the lot.

"Are you all right, Kosh?" Lenka asked.

"*Dobrze.* I'm fine. This is the right address?"

Lenka checked her scrap of paper. "1207 Finley. This is right. What's up?"

"Nothing." What if Blake spotted her?

Lenka pursed her lips. "Whatever. Let's just knock

on the door."

So stubbornness wasn't her premier quality.

A.J. greeted them, and Kasia hustled in. With the door closed behind them, Blake and everything to do with him sealed outside, Kasia breathed easier.

A.J. took the tray. "Smells delish."

"Southwestern chicken melts." Lenka cast a suspicious glance at her sister.

Kasia wiped her forehead, tried on a smile. "Thanks again for inviting us."

"Of course." A.J. sauntered into the kitchen and set down the tray. "You can get a drink if you want, or just follow me and I'll introduce you to everybody."

"Go ahead." Kasia pointed to the big pitcher of tea. She'd opt to avoid the center-of-attention scenario. "You thirsty, Lenka?"

"No thanks." Lenka followed A.J. into the other room, and the introductions started up.

She'd just filled her cup when an empty one appeared next to it. Jayce's tattoo gave him away. "Ya mind fillin' me up?"

"Not a bit. Hey, what's your tat about?"

"Justice."

She squinted. "It's Greek?"

His head jerked up in a Southie yes. "My ma's Greek."

"I thought Southie was mostly Irish…Catholic at least."

"It's a mix-up these days. But they didn't exactly roll out the welcome wagon for her. There's still a thing with anybody who's not good and Catholic."

Lenka nudged her. "Come meet some of the girls."

Kasia spotted Kyle by the hallway. Hands in pockets, he smiled in her direction. "Hey, Jayce," he called. "I'm gonna get ready to start playing, all right?"

Jayce nodded. "Yeah, just a sec. I'm all over these melt things."

"Kasia, you sure you don't want to play with us tonight?"

A fist squeezed her heart. "Maybe next time? Let me just get a feel for the group dynamics and see how everything works."

Jayce bumped her arm and leaned in. "No rush. It'd be kickin', but we got it. Whenever, yeah?"

She smiled her thanks, and he popped another melt into his mouth.

A.J. appeared, wrapping her hair into a bun and securing it with a pencil. She leaned back into the other room. "Jayce is in the kitchen!" Her almond-shaped eyes, back on them, lit with mischief. "All the best stuff is gone by the time the guys are done with the music, so Jayce stashes a plate in the fridge. A big plate." She nodded toward the living room. "Let's find a seat."

They settled with their backs against the couch and kicked off their shoes.

Kyle stepped around the coffee table, guitar high over his head, and plunked down beside Kasia. He set the chord sheet on the floor in front of them. Shaggy brown hair framed his face.

Kasia caught his eye. "Want anything from the kitchen before you're trapped there all night?"

"I'm good." His boyish gray eyes were all thanks and interest.

Kasia scanned the room of twenty-somethings. Some were in the local universities, some worked, a couple were married. Good mix. She could get used to this. *Help me to get Blake behind me. And please, fill my heart with love again—only for You though. Always, only for You.*

It was the only kind of love she could feel anyway.

At the opening chords of "How Deep the Father's Love for Us," Kasia perked up. Kyle glanced her way, and she offered him a smile.

Kasia closed her eyes and shut out the distractions. She sang along for the only audience that mattered, imagined herself at Jesus's feet, her voice an offering.

"Turn to Philippians three." The words called her to attention. An international student leaned forward and straightened his glasses before he read.

Kasia followed along in her own Bible, enjoying his unusual accent.

"Pastor Sean preached this on Sunday. Paul counted ev'rything loss compared to knowing Christ as Lord. He calls it 'rubbish.' What does he mean? What does he say 'bout how we spend our time?"

The question hung in the air. Then, one by one, others answered. "Nothing."

"Loss."

"Trash."

Trash *might be a bit harsh.*

After a minute, he went on. "Tell me: What kind of things do you pursue?"

"Success," someone answered.

"God-honoring relationships."

"A degree."

"Marriage." A few people laughed. Some nodded.

"A record label." Kyle winked at no one in particular.

Kasia traced the edges of the onion-leaf pages. A recording contract used to be her answer too.

"These things—they're not bad. But compared to all we can find in Christ, Paul says they're worthless.

Why?"

"'Cause whatever they are, they're not gonna last forever," Jayce said. "We gotta chase things worthy of Christ. Spend our time on what matters. Nothin' else."

Kasia's hand stilled. She didn't hear much after Jayce's answer. His words played on repeat awhile.

Around nine, the study wrapped up with a time of prayer, and people started moving again. Kasia slipped her Bible into her canvas messenger bag and said goodbye.

She and Lenka climbed into her car and rolled down the windows.

Blake's car hadn't moved.

He hadn't seen her.

A warm breeze caressed her cheek as she maneuvered out of the lot. As she pulled out onto the road, she let the wind whisk every distraction from her mind. The world faded and Jayce's voice echoed again. *Spend our time on what matters. Nothin' else.*

The words inked her heart, stained deeper than her new friend's tattoo.

She inhaled April-warmed air, fresh and full of life, as determination saturated every inch of her.

Lenka turned on some background music and stuck her hand out the window. She sliced through the wind. "What'd you think?"

Kasia gripped the wheel and smiled.

"You were right. I needed this."

~*~

Tuesday's disciplinary hearing bore down on Zan like an angry third baseman.

He swung by his apartment to dress up and get his

papers together. As he whipped into the lot, he spotted his father's sleek gray Italian car in his parking space. Zan swore under his breath and switched off his radio.

He drove around to the side of the apartment building and found a guest spot, let the engine idle awhile. He wanted to appreciate the parental involvement, but he didn't need the situation "handled" for him. What about that respect Dad mentioned on the phone?

Pressed and dressed, his father stood on the sidewalk in front of his door—on his cell. He never could set business aside easily. But he was here. There was that.

Zan jangled his keys and stepped past his father to let himself in. He grabbed a bottled water and leaned against the bar, waiting for the big entrance, but time was a-wasting. Should he make himself a quick lunch? *Nah.* He'd be willing to lay a hundred down his father would require better than sandwiches.

So he jogged to his room and threw his clothes on the bed, then pulled on the pair of khakis he'd ironed before he left. He buttoned his dark blue oxford as he walked to the living room. Still empty. When he'd finally perfected his tie and gotten his hair to lie down, the front door clicked shut.

"Felt like a four-hour drive this morning?" Zan gave his reflection a final once-over.

"I've been in town since yesterday afternoon, Alexander."

Oh? Glad they could get together. "Where are you staying?"

"The Fieldstone, of course. Your mother made the reservations."

Zan leaned against the doorframe of his bedroom,

took a long pull on his water, wet his lips. "What does she think of all this trouble I got into?"

"I don't suppose she likes it, son, but she certainly understands. We've all got skin in this game."

Zan screwed the bottle cap on and off. "I'm sorry it was so public."

"Michael chose the venue. And I can't say I'd have behaved any better than you." He pulled out his tablet and messed with the screen. "I've made an appointment to speak to the coach about all this."

"No!"

His father's head turned slowly and the warning eyebrow arched an inch.

Zan re-straightened his tie. "Let me do this, Dad. Please. I know you're only helping, but I don't want special treatment. I apologized for my conduct, but I have no regrets—and I'm prepared to accept whatever decision the board makes. It's not like I play ball anyway. Just because I was issued a jersey—"

"That's the point, son. We're not going to throw all this away."

All what? "I'm no Firelli. If he'd shoved someone in the stands, this might be a different conversation. It's—I'd…" He'd like them to take his name off the roster, so he wouldn't feel like such a quitter when he…if he had to walk away.

"You're better than Firelli."

"Not at baseball. And…he's a good guy. If I've got to play second to somebody…"

His father stood there, a great stone face.

Zan checked the oven clock. "Have you eaten?"

"No. Let me take you out, and then I'll drive you to the hearing." His sigh practically made the earth rumble. "And I'll wait outside. But you'll show them the documents I brought up from Lydia Johansen."

"Yes, sir. A courier delivered me some reports and files from the precinct up here too, thanks to Lydia."

"This is why we keep her on retainer."

Zan grabbed his backpack and swapped his textbook for the manila folder. He followed his father out the door, his mind too full to speak.

~*~

Zan gently closed the conference-room door behind him, paused in the hallway to collect himself before facing his father. Who knew what the board continued to talk about in there? He had been officially dismissed. Dealt with.

Suspended. Was he supposed to feel relieved?

He walked toward the lobby, loosened his tie. He needed to put the best possible spin on this decision. All they'd done was come up with enough sentence to satisfy the bloodthirsty and leave him as useless as he'd always been.

His father stood when Zan entered the lobby. "Well?"

"Suspended. I can't play or even travel for the super-regional. I can be in the stands, but on my own dime." If Firelli took the team that far.

"But not expelled or off the team. The documents were useful then?"

"Yes, sir. They understood the history between us, and it helped that I didn't 'hit' him."

"I'm sure it did." He strode toward the glass door and held it open. When they were outside, he added quietly, "Maybe one day, you'll still get the chance."

Zan turned, pleasantly surprised to see a wry

smile on his dad's face.

"It would be ideal if he just disappeared," Zan said.

"True. But if he doesn't, and you're not in uniform…" Both eyebrows lifted.

"I read you."

"So."

"So." Zan smiled. Good to know the encouragement and support were still there—at least where Bailey and Mike were concerned. As for baseball, only time would tell.

"I'll drop you off at your place, and we'll see you in a week, yes?"

"Yes, sir." They climbed into his father's car, and Zan rested his head against the sun-warmed leather. So different from the hearing, with its cold air conditioning and the chill of tough conversation. "You canceled your meeting with Coach?"

"I did. But I—"

"I'm going to talk with him this afternoon."

"About?" The question filled the car.

Zan cracked a window. "Where I go from here." If he would never get to play, what was the point of staying on the team?

Even as he asked it though, it stung. Baseball had always consumed his future plans. Starting over felt impossible.

Kasia was starting over too, wherever she was in the world.

He sure would like to see her again.

10

The Cleavens would depart for Peru tomorrow.

Kasia's nerves buzzed. Had Tatuś made time to meet them? If not, would he put his foot down and forbid her?

She hunkered at her desk, comparing ticket prices and making a packing list. If nothing else, she could plan. Preparation could only prove her determination.

A knock sounded, and Kasia's heart rocketed into her throat. "Who is it?"

"Lena."

She unbolted the door and let her sister in. "What are you doing here?"

"Thanks for the hug, nerd. I thought you might not mind me staying the night since we're going to Kyle's party together tomorrow. Aren't you the girl who needs friends?"

She slid the lock into place.

"Dad met with Mr. Cleaven this morning. Figured you might like to know that."

Kasia's eyes burned, and she squeezed her sister tightly. Lenka was still her best ally. "Did he say anything about it?"

"Nope. No idea what the verdict is. Just saying. What are you working on?"

"Planning anyway. Packing list and stuff." She pointed to her bed. "Have a seat."

"I think it's cool that you're so serious about this.

You remind me of a sister I used to know." Lenka threw her duffel on Kasia's futon and set a box on the desk.

"What's that?"

"Mom sent oatmeal chocolate-chip cookies of deliciousness for Kyle." She plopped down on the bed beside her bag. "Get back to work. I brought stuff to do. I knew you had exams and all."

Lenka rocked.

Kasia's ringtone pulled her attention. She grabbed her cell and frowned at the unknown number. *God, please don't let it be Blake.* She waffled a moment too long, and the call ended. Unsure what to do, she sat next to Lenka.

"Yeah?" Her sister pulled an old-school photo album out of her bag and flipped through some of her favorite shots from the last few weeks. For Lenka's birthday, their parents had given her an old manual 35-mm camera. She'd already been experimenting—on everything and everyone.

"Somebody called my cell a second ago, and I didn't recognize the number. Should I call back?" She hated having to ask Lenka. Blake used to call Kasia an oak, but she behaved more like a clinging vine these days.

Lenka shut the book. "Think it's the cretin?"

"I don't know. Might only be A.J. at home…but I can't make myself call."

"Hand it to me." Lenka took the phone and pulled up the number. She held it to her ear and pursed her lips. "Hey," she said. "You just called me?"

Then everything about Lenka's tense facial expression shifted, and she grinned. "She's right here, Kyle. Let me get her."

Lenka waggled her eyebrows and handed Kasia the phone.

"Hey, Kyle, what's up?" Relief colored her every word.

"I thought maybe—if you want—I could give you a tour of the radio station tomorrow. Before the party."

"Sure. What time? I planned to buy some things for my trip."

Kyle even agreed to swing back by school and let her pick up her car before the party. If he drove her back afterward—too much like a date.

After he hung up, she punched through the menu, added Kyle to her contacts. No more mystery numbers. Lenka's watchful gaze was on her again. "What?"

"Hanging out with Kyle tomorrow, huh? Does he mind having me around?"

"Course not. He probably expects you to be there. For the party. He knows, I mean…this isn't a date, is it?" The room was suddenly sweltering. "Lenka, seriously. I think you'd better come—so it's clear. Anyway. He doesn't really have a choice."

Lenka chuckled. "Got you a little flustered, did he?"

"Shut up." Kasia spun on her heels and nearly face-planted over her sister's shoes. "You always leave stuff in the middle of the floor. Clean up once in a while."

"Hey, I'm a guest here."

Kasia chucked a pillow at Lenka. As she walked back to her desk, she mumbled, "Thanks for calling him back for me."

"No problem, dork."

Kasia dragged the chair out a few inches farther to sit.

"Who sent you this letter? Jane Austen?"

Kasia stilled. Had she left Blake's note out?

"Kosh?"

"Somebody slid it under the door. It's from Blake."

"Does he not get that the two of you are over?"

"He's struggling."

"You should go on a real date with somebody. Let Blake see you're moving on. Hey, I know. Kyle." Lenka pointed at her.

"What?"

"Kyle Compton. The guy who just asked you out. Plays guitar, hangs on your every word?"

Kasia drove her knee into the seat cushion. "Lenka, I'm done with dating for now. He's wasting his time."

"Maybe you're not ready to date right now, but seriously. You've got your whole life ahead of you. When you're ready, I think you're gonna want Kyle around. Don't be too quick to blow him off."

Kasia sat and dragged her toe across the carpet. "I am dead serious. I've wasted too much time already. My relationship with Blake was…monopolizing, I guess. I don't want that again." She repeated the words under her breath, her conviction solidifying like setting cement. "I don't want that again."

Lenka's observant gaze bored into her, calculating.

She needed to press on. "Don't worry about me. I'm all about what God has in store for me. I don't want any distractions."

"Huh."

Kasia flicked her gaze in her sister's direction. Lenka tapped the edge of Blake's envelope against her palm. "So explain why you didn't throw this away?"

She stomped over and grabbed the envelope. Her

stomach curled as her eyes traced the lettering. That penmanship—no way it was Blake's.

"Kasia? What's going on?"

Could Lenka quit being so stinking astute for five minutes? "Nothing. Did you want to read the note or not?"

Her sister snatched it back and sat on it. "If you won't trust me, we've got nothing to go on here."

"Blake didn't write it—the outside I mean. You can see his handwriting in the note, but that's not it on the front."

Lenka tugged the envelope out and inspected it, opened the stationery to compare the script. "I don't like it, Kosh."

"I don't even get it. Why would he have somebody else write it for him?"

"Because you'd toss it if you knew who it was from?" She was probably right. "He probably wasn't even the one who delivered it. Does he have a minion?"

"He wrote the inside—only did what he had to so I'd read it."

"It's underhanded though, you know? It's just…it wouldn't be a big deal if he weren't the type of guy who watches your car in the lot, tails you across town, and kidnaps you from a coffee shop. But he is that type."

"That's a little much, don't you think?" Kasia snapped.

"Is it?"

"Kidnap" was ridiculous. Way too criminal for Blake. Still, even as she defended him, phantom fingers seized her elbow and dug in. Half of Kasia tried to come up with something to justify Blake's need to control her every move; the other half wanted to scream in exhaustion. Why couldn't he make it simple and leave her alone? She buried her face in her pillow and let rip a muffled moan.

The bed shifted underneath her. Lenka rested a hand on her shoulder.

Kasia kept the pillow in place until her breathing evened out. Then she tilted her head to the side and peered at her little sister.

Lenka tried to smile, but the effect was depressing. "I'm sorry."

"No, you're right," Kasia admitted.

"I know. That's why I'm sorry."

Now it was her turn to offer an awkward smile. "Lenka, what do I do?"

"I don't know," Lenka whispered. "But I'm here."

Kasia could only nod.

~*~

When Kyle pulled in the next day, Lenka ran out and dove into the back of his car.

Kasia would have to ride shotgun. She climbed in. *This is not a date. This is not a date.*

Kyle shot Lenka a smile in the rearview. "Good afternoon, ladies. What's first on the to-do list?" At least he didn't mind her sister tagging along.

"I need to buy a few travel adapters and batteries for my camera."

"Your parents gave you the go-ahead, huh?" He turned onto the main road.

She leaned into the upholstered seat. "Not yet, but I'm getting ready anyway." If they did forbid it, would she fight for this? Or would she give up?

"You'll be phenomenal."

She crossed her legs and picked at a thread on her sandal. "I'm sure I'll learn more than I teach."

"I think you don't give yourself enough credit."

Kasia shrugged.

Kyle eyed her for a minute but then reached over and turned up the stereo. He must've understood that, sometimes, not talking was better.

~*~

The three of them made their way around the store, found the things on Kasia's list.

Kasia parked the cart next to the register and started unloading. Until she spotted Forearms walking toward her and the batteries fell out of her hands.

Somehow he was more handsome every time they met.

Her stomach turned acrobat, and she spun toward Kyle, tried to keep her face from view. "Who'll be at your party tonight?"

Kyle tilted his head and looked past her. Her ploy must've failed. Forearms had seen her.

"I'm startin' to think there must be a God after all. Seems like Somebody sure wants us to keep running into each other." His baritone voice with that drawl.

She turned slowly, tried to meet his eyes and miss everything else about him.

"Good to see ya, Auburn."

"My name is Kasia, Forearms."

He laughed hard, his voice almost musical. She bit the tip of her tongue, determined not to participate. He ducked his head a little. "Did you just call me Forearms?"

"What? No." *Oh, sweet mother.* She had, hadn't she?

"I sure thought that's what I heard. I don't mind though. At least I know you think of me enough to give me a nickname." He eyed Kyle.

Kyle's stomach pressed against her elbow. *Right. Stake your claim.* She couldn't possibly be an independent person here. Kasia wanted to pound her head against the cash register.

"Anyway, I'm on my way back over to school. Just stopped in for a cola." Forearms held up his stupid bottle. And flexed.

Welcome back to high school. She tossed a travel adapter on the belt.

She shrugged, but a smile kept trying to bypass her defenses.

"Maybe when I move here, we'll get a chance to have that glass of sweet tea at the same table next time. My treat."

"You're moving here?" *Well, crud.*

"Just had lunch with Oconee State's new coach. I'm transferring to play ball."

She put the luggage tags down and faced him. "What kind of ball?" *Please don't say soccer.* Then her whole family would be interested in this guy.

"Baseball." He unscrewed the lid of his cola and took a few long pulls. The cashier was entirely too distracted by him.

"Hm. Not really a fan."

He grinned, pointing at her. "You're kind of merciless, you know that?"

Kyle chuckled behind her.

Forearms narrowed his eyes and screwed the lid back on his drink. "That's cool. Some days I can't stand baseball. See y'all around." He gave her a nod and walked off.

"Who was that?" Lenka's fists were on her hips.

"I can't remember his name. He changed my tire once and thinks I owe him a date."

Her sister frowned. "Can we say 'cocky'?"

Kasia glanced at Kyle.

He stepped back a foot and slipped a casual hand in his pocket. "Want to choose the songs for the playlist on my next indie show?"

"Absolutely."

Forearms who?

11

Radio stations—music—had always held the power to win her over. Truly, Kyle's skill and taste had impressed Kasia. But even after a day crammed with positives, as she drove past Blake's on the way to Kyle's party, her whole body tensed.

She parked, dropped her keys in her bag, and stood to stretch. Her skin absolutely crawled.

Kyle got out of his car and walked over. He spoke, but Kasia heard nothing.

Blake had to be watching her. "I've got to hurry inside—restroom."

Kyle nodded but missed the note of urgency. So did Lenka.

She tried again. "Is anybody up there yet?"

"Yeah." He scanned the area. "I see a few cars…A.J.'s there, it looks like."

"I'm gonna take off, then." She darted across the lot like a four-year-old scrambling up dark basement steps.

Shutting herself in with all the nonchalance she could muster, Kasia found A.J. making a few cheesy birthday posters. She dropped her bag. "Let me color that while you do the next one." A.J. handed over the marker.

A few minutes later, Kyle popped his head around the corner. "I want to have a little worship session with everybody tonight. Would you help me pick the songs?"

A.J. stood. "I'm going to hang these."

Kasia followed Kyle into the main room and joined him on the sofa. They paged through his binder. So full of her favorites—"Yearn" and "Sovereign over Us." And there—"Wholly Yours."

The song he sang at Common Grounds.

"Feeling ready for Peru?"

Kasia rested her head against the back of the couch. "As soon as I can. I need this."

"How long have you wanted to do mission work?" He rested an arm behind her.

She scooched forward. "Mama used to teach ESL classes to other immigrant families through our church. She let me hang around, and—after a year or so—when I turned twelve, she let me lead a group of kids. Just conversation, but I loved it."

"Bet you were pretty amazing even then. Determined, for sure." Kyle touched her shoulder, his fingertips strange against her skin.

Her ears warmed, and she turned to let her gaze wander over the faces of the new arrivals. "I loved the people. I made friends more easily with them than the kids at school, even. But my heart has always been…"

"You're compassionate."

She wished her hair were down so she could hide behind it. Too much attention.

"It's cool."

"Mama and Tatuś always joke that I'm either going to marry someone of a different ethnic background or live abroad. I'm entirely too fascinated by other cultures. Could be the Polish-American thing."

He grinned. "So, live abroad, huh?"

Time to make sure Mama's cookies were out. Actually, Kasia hadn't seen them. "Excuse me, Kyle. I need to check something."

Their cookies weren't on the counter or the table. Lenka must've forgotten them when Kasia dashed out of the parking lot. *Oh*. She'd have to go out to the car for them.

Anxiety nailed her as she approached the door, and her hand stilled on the knob. Maybe someone would go with her. Her eyes scanned the room. Almost everyone was involved in something.

Kyle would take it as interest.

She caught Lenka's eye and pointed outside.

Her sister held up a finger. Evidently an important conversation.

It was broad daylight. Seriously, Kasia could walk down the steps to her car all by herself. She opened the door, peered out. Blake's car was nowhere in sight. It would take…what? Two minutes? She signaled again to Lenka that she was stepping out and, finally, felt brave.

Proud of herself.

She closed the door and walked to the top of the steps, glanced around. Just an older woman carrying some groceries. Kasia jogged down and crossed the lot toward her car, keys in hand. This was the first time she wished Mama and Tatuś had sprung for a new keyless entry fob. When they'd bought the used car for her and the fob was missing, neither thought it mattered. A manual key worked just as well. If she was honest, until now she hadn't thought it mattered either. She picked up her pace toward the car.

When she reached it, she eyed the container on the center of the back seat and stuck the keys in the door.

She ducked inside, grabbed the cookies, and stood up.

Eye to eye with Blake, with only the car door between them.

"Didn't you get my note?"

The sadness in his voice pulled the air out of her lungs. "I did. I wasn't ready to call."

"I thought the bracelet would make you remember."

She always seemed to hurt him and had to hustle to make it better. "What you wrote sounded…like you were asking me to call if I wanted to. I felt like I had a choice." She left the words in the air for a moment. "Didn't I?"

A mirthless laugh tumbled out. "Of course you had a choice. What kind of person do you think I am?"

She'd been tossed on the waves of his temper too many times to answer.

"I guess I'm not used to having to work so hard for your attention."

"If you respected me a little more, I might not mind these chats, but I…don't trust you."

"Wait. You don't trust me? What about how you've made me look to my parents? How do you think I felt when I had to tell my mother *you* were through with *me*?"

"It hasn't been easy for me either." This conversation was going nowhere good. "Blake, I've got to go."

"Just a minute!" He stomped his foot like a five-year-old.

She held up a finger. "One."

"What?" He scowled, eyes on fire. Wounded Blake was no more.

She swallowed but held steady. "You have one

minute. I have somewhere to be, and if I'm not back, people will come looking for me." *Please let that be true.*

"Listen to me for two freaking seconds!"

She cast her gaze around, embarrassed. Her hand clutched the car door, ready to close it.

"We were it for each other. I won't watch you fall for someone else!"

"I'm not! Blake, I don't want to be with anyone. I just want you to leave me alone."

His hands scraped through his hair.

"You're scaring me."

"You act like this is so easy. *Just forget everything and go on like we never existed.* Well, I can't do that. I won't—" His fist careened into the window of her driver's side door. Before she could make sense of it, a splintering pop sounded and her stomach was sprayed with tiny pieces of glass.

She staggered back, dropped the plate of cookies.

Dark red blood painted Blake's knuckles. He bent in pain, held his wrist.

Shattered. Her window was shattered. She absently picked a shard of glass from her T-shirt and saw three angry, sticky stripes of crimson across her wrist.

When she lifted her gaze to Blake's face, for the briefest moment, she caught a hint of regret. But then his eyes met hers and something in them hardened. Everything crawled to a stop. Kasia's mind buzzed in panicked confusion, images disjointed and distorted.

Breathe in. Kasia turned her back on Blake and planted a hand on her sun-warmed trunk.

Breathe out. She stepped out of the parking place—the car door and splintered glass the only barriers between her and Blake.

Breathe in.

Lenka's voice shouted her name from the balcony.

Breathe out. The car door slammed. Metal and glass crunched behind her. Blake was on her heels.

Breathe in. Kasia moved toward her sister's voice. A motorcycle roared into the lot.

Breathe out.

Tires squealed and the stench of hot rubber burned her nostrils. "Kasia! Look out!" She turned. Jayce.

His bike could've crushed her.

Breathe in. Kyle thundered down the stairs and across the pavement.

Breathe out. Kyle. Lenka. A.J. Jayce.

Breathe in. Where is Blake? Her frantic heartbeat drowned out all other sound.

Kasia rotated exactly once, desperate to absorb the scene. A.J. open-mouthed. Kyle with his hand on crying Lenka. Jayce next to his bike right in the middle of the lot.

And Blake beside her car, chest heaving. Fear filled his eyes.

Kyle stepped in front of her then, his body her shield. Her pulse hammered in her skull.

Jayce lunged at Blake, and Blake dodged him, hit the back of her car.

"Yeah, ya better be afraid, you little—" Jayce charged, barreled toward the man she had almost married. Almost spent forever with.

Kyle turned toward her, but Kasia dropped to her knees on the blacktop and watched the threadlike trail of blood trickle down her arm.

Breathe.

~*~

The crunch of gravel under the tires jerked Kasia back to the real world.

She opened her eyes.

Langston Falls.

This was not how she pictured her homecoming. From her own passenger seat, she blinked. The last several hours blurred in her mind.

Lenka drove Kasia's car up their long driveway toward the old stone church and turned hard left toward their house. The side porch light glowed, and the screen door swung wide. Tatuś and Mama came down the steps to meet them followed by an eager, scampering Samson.

Kasia opened her door and heard the hiss of the engine, the crickets.

Mama asked if she was all right, while Samson pranced a few feet away, head cocked.

Tatuś bent down and met her eyes. "*Cześć, córeczko.*" Sweet daughter. He offered a hand. She took it, watched his hand enfold hers. He tugged her out of the car.

He wrapped his arms around her. "It's good to have you home."

She gripped the soft cloth at the back of his button-down, shut her eyes, pushed the evening from her mind, and soaked in her daddy's affection while she could.

He squeezed her shoulder as he let go. Too soon.

"Let's get you inside." His stubble scratched her temple as he kissed her hair. "I'll get the bags, Lenusiu. *Daj mi klucze.*" He held up a hand.

Lenka tossed him the keys and followed Mama inside. Samson pressed his wet nose to the back of

Kasia's knee as she watched Tatuś turn away, keys in hand. She bent to pet her Lhasa Apso. "Samku," she whispered. His doleful eyes were another reminder she'd been missed.

She stood and followed Mama and Lenka up the steps. They left their shoes next to the door, each of them slipping into a pair of house shoes.

Kasia kicked off her flops on the other side of the doorway, next to her dad's soccer ball. She stood barefooted on the cool linoleum, grit under her toes, and breathed in the aroma of home in late spring, freshly picked mint leaves and lemons.

"*Czy chcesz herbatę*?" Mama asked.

"No thank you." Hot tea always meant conversation. "I'd rather…can I just go to bed?"

There it was—the exchange of anxious glances. Kasia couldn't make herself care.

Without waiting for a response, she shuffled down the hall, took off her shorts, and climbed into bed. The bed Tatuś had built for her.

Home.

Her eyes closed. Just being here overwhelmed her.

~*~

Moonlight filtered into Kasia's bedroom window. The bedside clock said 1:13 AM. Cocooned in the soft blanket, she couldn't shake the chill in her core. A tub of ice wouldn't feel much worse. She swung her feet off the mattress and sat up, shivering.

Something stiff and uncomfortable gripped her right arm. A bandage.

"Kosh?" Lenka's voice spoke into the quiet. "You awake?" Why wasn't Lenka across the hall in her own room?

Kasia leaned toward the foot of her bed. Lenka stretched out on her sleeping bag, her face lit by the moonglow. Samson snuffled on the floor beside her.

"I guess I'm awake. Aren't you cold?"

Lenka sat up. "I'm fine. Do you need something?"

"I'll get it." Kasia padded over to her dresser and dug through her bottom drawer, pulled out a heavy flannel she'd stolen from her dad. Not quite as comforting as his worn Chicago hoodie, but it'd do. "Why are you down there, Lenka?"

"I just wanted to stay with you—in case you needed somebody. Didn't know if you'd feel like being alone or—"

Kasia forced out a bitter laugh. "Alone is dangerous." Her gaze fell to her arm, wrapped tightly. Kasia plopped back down on her bed and pulled on the soft red socks Busia had knitted her last Christmas.

She perched at the edge of her mattress, silent for a while before she scooted back. Once her pillow was arranged comfortably behind her, she hugged her knees to her chest and scanned the room. The walls needed painting—something drastic. "I'll be glad to get away."

"I bet."

"Think they'll be fine with Peru?"

"I don't know." The silence was strained for a moment before a snore ripped through it, and Lenka chuckled softly. *Samson.*

"Did you bandage my arm, Lenka? It's probably a stupid question, but—the whole evening's fuzzy."

"A.J. ran upstairs and got Kyle's first-aid kit, because he wouldn't leave you. We might have overdone the bandage a little. It was only a nick, but

Kyle didn't like seeing you bleed."

"Thank you. For that and staying with me for the police report."

"Like I'd miss that. I needed to hear what happened."

"Do you really think I have to get a restraining order?"

"I don't know. Probably."

"They could let me get a plane ticket and get out. Blake won't bother me in Peru."

"Not my call. But I think you need to have one in place when you come back."

"Hmm."

"Kasiu? Don't you think you should try to get some sleep?"

"I guess. I never sleep well anymore." She laid her head down on the pillow, squished and fluffed it until it was just right. "What did Jayce do to Blake?"

Lenka huffed. "Chased him all the way upstairs and stayed outside his door until the police showed. He was pretty sure Blake was crying in there."

Her stomach turned at the thought. But not for the reason she expected. Blake could be so weak. Why in the world had she let him bully her for so long?

Yeah, she was done with that. She wouldn't give him anything—no more reason to assume she would let him push her around.

Life would be on *her* terms.

12

The Lowcountry.

Zan blew out a lazy, contented sigh as he rolled into Charleston. His cell rang, and he grinned, answered with his hands-free. "Hey, Li'l Mama." She'd swat him if he ever called her that in person.

"Alexander Maddox." His mother may fuss, but she loved it.

"Sorry."

"I bet you're sorry. How long will you be?"

The sour stink of the paper mill hit him, but today it smelled like homecoming potpourri. "Twenty minutes, give or take. Please tell me there's some sweet tea ready for me?"

"I'll do you one better. Your father's gettin' out some shrimp and steak to put on the grill right now. We'll be out back waitin' for you, sugar."

His mouth watered. "Hey, Mom? Have you and Dad heard from Bailey?"

"Yep, she calls a couple times a week."

"Are y'all as bothered as I am that she's staying with some strange family and not coming home?"

"Now, Zan, from what we hear, these are good people."

"I'm sure they are. But we're"—he reached up for the roll bar with one arm. "Does she sound happy?"

"Yes. And she sounds strong. You go on and hang up the phone now so you're not talking as you get to traffic. I'll see you in a few minutes."

"Yes, ma'am." He disconnected the call and willed his shoulders to relax. He'd partied with too many "Christians" to trust them. Nothing but fakes.

Two plates full of chargrilled steak, baked beans, and fresh cantaloupe later, Zan stretched out in one of the long, comfortable chairs Li'l Mama had picked out for her swanky bash this year. A sought-after interior designer, she had turned her gift for charm and hospitality into a lucrative complement to Dad's investment firm in the historic district. All around them, iron furniture anchored soft red and beige canvas cushions to the worn brick. Framed by willow trees and Spanish moss, the area could fit thirty people with ease, but his mom's parties never felt crowded.

"I could get used to this chair." He kicked off his leather flops and flexed his feet, tapped his fingertips against the thick padding.

"You said you had some news to share, son." Dad settled back in his seat.

Zan stared up at the sunlight lancing the chinks in the treetops.

"Zan? What is it, sugar?" Mom squinted one eye.

"I've decided to change schools."

Dad set down his bottle of lager, and Zan watched a drop of condensation cut a quick trail. "Now listen. You've got an ideal situation—a scholarship at a great school, great ball club. A hasty decision will only complicate things."

Water darkened the brick under the bottle, and Zan looked up, shrugged. "It's done."

His mom's mouth opened and closed right back.

"I ran into Coach Markman in Huntington the other night, on a fluke. He's just signed at Oconee

State—"

Dad rubbed his chin. "I had heard that was a possibility. But it's against collegiate rules for him to bait you—"

"Well, I guess he got in touch with the university between the hearing and my meeting with Coach, because Coach is the one who mentioned it. Said if I wanted the chance to resuscitate my ball career, I ought to take Oconee State's offer." Zan turned away from their gaze. "Why would he have a problem letting me go? I mean, he gets another open spot on the roster, and it costs him nothing."

"Of course it cost him nothing—you threw your scholarship right back in his face!"

Zan sat up. "You don't have to invest a dime, Dad. Markman found some money for me—"

"Money's never been the issue, son, and you know it. Where's your perseverance? Where's the fortitude? Don't rush at this without thinking." Dad glanced at Mom and reined in his temper. "I'll have a word with the coach and—"

"Dad."

His mom's eyes pleaded with them. She hated the bickering.

Zan made his body relax. Consciously kept his voice level. "It's too late. When I saw Coach Markman before I left school, I signed off on everything. Admissions, financial aid, had a copy of my transcript sent over. As of this morning, I'm an Oconee State Bearcat."

Mom swirled the ice in her cup. "Markman has always taken care of his boys, Phil."

"I suppose he has." An unspoken question hung in the air.

Zan used his right heel to rub his left ankle. He was a fool to bring this up now, but something in him screamed to finish it. "One more thing."

The Great Eyebrow arched. Ever the skeptic.

Zan dug his hands in his hair, tried to massage the stress away. "It's been a while since I played consistently, and this is Markman's first year as a college coach."

"So…" His father leaned forward.

"He's made arrangements for me to spend the summer in the Northeastern Wooden Bat League. Refocus."

Dad picked his bottle up. "The Wooden Bat League's not a bad opportunity."

"No. But I've got to be in Geneva, New York, in a week and a half."

"A week?" Mom swatted away an invisible bug, which she obviously hated.

"I've got to do everything I can, Mom. I've worked too hard to not even get a chance. And with this blemish on my record now…"

"I know, sugar. I was just so lookin' forward to having some time with you again."

"Do you want me to drive you up?" Dad wouldn't expect him to take the offer, but it was there all the same. Family trumps everything.

"No, sir. Thanks though. I'd rather have a car in case I have free time."

Dad stood, and the patio did actually seem crowded. "You'll concentrate and work hard though."

"Yes, sir. Absolutely."

A stiff nod was the only affirmation he got. No surprise there.

If he couldn't have a real relationship with his

father, at least he still had ball.

~*~

"Herbata?"

"Tak, proszę." Kasia slid out one of the oak chairs at the kitchen table. "Hot tea sounds perfect today." Who cared that it was practically summer?

Mama bustled around, obviously choosing every word with caution.

Kasia sat with Samson's furry head on her lap and helped select neutral topics. A little respite before the heartspill. "How's Busia doing?"

"Better this week, I believe. Looking forward to seeing you again. You girls could make some cookies and take them over."

"Do you have the stuff for gingersnaps?" Every Christmas, Kasia and Busia baked a batch of her favorites, the only non-traditional holiday dish Busia ever made.

"Of course." She poured steaming water into each of the mugs. Once the blue-stamped pottery dish filled with everyone's favorite teas was on the table, she sat. Kasia pulled it over, tapped the smooth ceramic. Busia's eyes had landed on it as soon as they entered the shop in Bolesławiec. The last time Busia had visited Poland with them.

Kasia flicked through the packets, searching for chamomile. She needed its soothing effects. *"Czy jest rumiankowa?"*

Mama hopped up and stood on her tiptoes, reached for one of her small tins of dried herbs. She spooned the tiny white and yellow flowers into an infuser and placed it in Kasia's cup. Then she set a mug full of Prince of Wales tea on the table for Tatuś.

Samson curled up on the floor by her feet, his long hair over his eyes.

When Tatuś breezed back into the room, he gently touched Mama's shoulder before joining them. "How many exams do you have left, Kasiu?"

"Just one. Tomorrow afternoon."

"I'll drive you down for it, and we can pick up your things."

"You did well on your other finals?" Mama slid her a plate for the dripping tea infuser.

"Yes. I just stayed in my room." Kasia dumped in a spoonful of sugar and stirred. With her free hand, she traced the white embroidery against the deep indigo tablecloth.

"It was easier that way, hm?" Her mom reached for her hand.

"I guess." Her eyes moved back and forth between them.

Tatuś rubbed his temples, studied her. Under the weight of his sympathy, she cast her gaze downward again.

He circled his hands around his mug and leaned in. "Kasiu?" His gaze didn't let up.

She gave in and met his blue eyes.

"What made you change your mind?"

"God told me to walk away."

He sat back and smacked the table. "Then that's exactly what you do."

Her mom squeezed her hand. "And what's your version of last night?"

"My version?" Were they kidding? Kasia pulled her hands into her lap.

"Lenka told us the officers said Blake will be

charged with destruction of property and second-degree assault."

"What? Assault?" *No, no, no!* They would make things worse.

"He hurt you."

She shook her head. "No. He got angry and accidentally hit the window. He probably had to get stitches! The glass only nicked me." He had yelled—been demanding—but that was all. "Blake isn't a violent person."

"No?" Her dad's cup hit the table, and tea splashed out.

"He just doesn't understand my decision. Can you imagine Mama breaking up with you three months before the wedding?" She'd broken his heart.

"He still needs to act like a gentleman." Mama spoke quietly.

Tatuś pressed his fingertips against the table edge. "Whether he understands or not, he doesn't respect your decision. He needs to deal with it." He frowned. "Blake was never good enough for you."

Kasia bit the inside of her cheek and tasted blood. She wasn't the wonderful girl they believed either.

Tatuś gulped down a swig of tea and sat back. "Well, the D.A. is the one prosecuting. You can decide whether or not you want a civil case—for protection—but the county can charge Blake with assault whether you want them to or not. Sheriff Schilling said—"

"Why did you ask him?" Kasia couldn't believe this. *Deacon* Sheriff Schilling? His pal from church? The rumor mill would crank up by the weekend.

"He's my friend, and I trust him." Tatuś ran a hand through his hair.

"Then can you ask him to see if the D.A. will drop

the charges? I won't even need the restraining order if I go to Peru."

His shoulders tensed.

"Kasiu," Mama said, "maybe we should talk about Peru later."

Tatuś pinched the bridge of his nose. "Last night your safety was our sole concern. So today forgive me if I don't want to ship you off to another continent where I can't protect you."

The phone rang, and Mama excused herself, answering as she left the kitchen. "Hello? Ah, yes…yes, she's home, Roberta."

Kasia lifted her tea and blew across the surface. "Excellent. Miss Roberta will let her Sunday school class know I'm being harassed so I don't have to wear a sign."

"I'm sorry, Curly-Q." Tatuś held out a hand, and she rested her palm against his. He'd called her that forever, and when she was younger, tugged on a springy curl each time he said it.

"Please just handle the gossip for me. Let me go, Tatusiu. Let me do something meaningful."

"Escape solves nothing." His callused thumb ran across the back of her hand.

"I don't think of it as escape as much as a new start. I want to serve somewhere this summer. Get over myself. It's the only way—"

"Whew." Her mom came back around the corner, dusting off her hands. "That woman." Her eyes were filled with compassion. "I think I understand why you've set your sights on another country."

Tatuś stood abruptly, pulling his hand from beneath hers. "I'll be out in my wood shop."

The door slammed shut. Kasia squeezed her eyes

closed.

"Are you well, Kasiu?"

No. Nowhere near it. "I don't know."

"The truth."

Kasia hesitated, but—if she wanted to serve in Peru—she needed to go with a clean slate. And now was as good a time as any. She could wrap her cold heart in the love and concern Mama offered. "I need you to understand something, Mamusiu. The way I broke up with Blake—he had no idea it was coming. And I haven't listened to him. He didn't mean to hurt me. I promise."

"Kasiu, that's still no excuse. It worries me how quickly his temper—"

"Mama. We were having sex."

She caught the note of distress in her mother's eyes before they closed, as if she could wish away the confession.

Her hand slipped into her lap and scraped along the thread at the hem of her shorts. "Blake never had any reason to think I wouldn't marry him."

Kasia's shoulders sagged under the burden of her honesty. "I know when I was younger I promised I'd wait—that my husband would be my first. That's the reason I said yes when he proposed. And it took me a while, but I realized marriage wouldn't make it right. It would only add another mistake to my too-long list."

"Kasiu." Mom's watery eyes blinked, and a stream of tears ran down each cheek. She cleared her throat quickly. "I'm glad you realized marriage wasn't the answer." She pulled a tissue from her pocket and dabbed at her nose. "So glad."

Kasia clenched and relaxed her fists a few times, tried to exorcise the tension that had dug its claws into her all week, but it was fruitless. "I couldn't explain it all to him though. I hurt him. That's why I want the charges dropped. If you could talk to Sheriff Schilling…" She smoothed her shorts.

Kasia's hand felt a squeeze, and she drew from it the strength to continue. "Anyway, the part I struggle with the most is—would God still want to use me?" *And what about my music?*

Mama turned her chair and cupped her hard-working hands around Kasia's cheeks. "Your life is not ruined. Do you understand that? Jesus can use you for beautiful things yet."

Kasia nodded. "Mama? I don't want Tatuś to know. He can't—I couldn't stand it if he saw me differently." She glanced down at his soccer ball, well-worn from countless seasons of backyard practice. The day she'd scored the championship-winning goal, he'd hoisted her up onto his shoulders. That warmth and pride in her dad's eyes—that's what she wanted to maintain more than anything.

But she'd never have a chance at seeing it again if Mama told him the truth.

The sadness in her mother's face matched her own.

But Mama nodded.

~*~

Tatuś read to the three of them in English that night, and Kasia curled up beside his feet. She smiled against his knee as he still read the old neighbor's dialogue with thick Slavic pronunciation. His mellow tone and accent—everything about his voice—she found restful.

Halfway into the story, his fingers tugged on her hair, and a lump of hope formed in her chest. Maybe she could find peace at home after all.

The hope remained as she shuffled down the hall to climb in bed.

But under the covers, sleep evaded her. She twisted and stretched, wrestled with the sheet and blanket. She tensed up muscle groups one at a time and let go, quoted verses she'd memorized as a child, whispered the same verses in English.

Nothing worked.

Kasia bolted upright in the bed as panic seized her. A glance at the clock told her she'd managed to fall asleep after all. It was a few minutes after five in the morning. Her eyes searched the darkness for the nameless fear that had chased her—that hunted her every time she tried to find rest. She would absolutely not be able to go back to sleep; the whatever-it-was was still out there, skulking at the edges of her consciousness.

Why did this not let up? What was she missing?

She couldn't think any further.

She turned on the small lamp on her nightstand to dispel the suffocating blackness and hugged the pillow beneath her head.

The silence hummed in her ears.

13

The rich smell of coffee wooed Kasia from sleep. She lifted her cheek from the kitchen table, worked her jaw to ease the ache. A delectable aroma wafted in her direction, and she sat straight up, blinked away the fog. Homemade cinnamon buns.

Samson snuggled against her legs, her feet tucked in warm beneath his belly. When had he come to keep her company? "Sorry, Samku. I've got to get up." She slid her feet out and stretched.

Tatuś grabbed a potholder and bent to slide the pan of rolls out of the oven. Her favorite mug—the one with the pic of the bluebird of happiness replaced by the chicken of depression—sat next to the coffeepot instead of on the table beside her.

She reached for it.

"Morning, Kasiu," Tatuś said. "Your tea was cold and very, very black when I got in here. You left the bag in a bit long this time."

"Coffee sounds like a better idea anyway. *Czy chcesz?*"

"I've already got a cup, but you can top it off for me." He pointed to his mug.

She poured the coffee, and sweet-smelling steam eddied around her face.

He smiled his thanks. "Did thoughts of Peru wake you so early—or Blake?"

The perfect dose of cream and sugar required her

focus. She stirred her coffee. "Just restless, I think. It's been a while since I really slept soundly." She couldn't even remember when that would've been.

He turned the bacon with a fork. "When I came in, your snoring gave old Sam a run for his money."

"I guess I sleep better at the table than in my room."

"I noticed you used my Bible as a pillow." Her dad took a deep breath. "Listen. Summer is only beginning. Can I remind you of something Paul said?"

"Sure." She closed her eyes, tried to take his words to heart.

"'Forgetting what lies behind, I press on.' Try to drill into what God has in store for you, Kasiu. Don't miss out on His best because you're sifting through the sawdust."

She opened her eyes; his were full of compassion. "*Dobrze*?"

If Tatuś knew everything she'd done, he wouldn't make it sound so easy. Worse, his compassion would probably disappear quicker than cookies at Christmas. "I'm trying."

"Small steps are still steps." He peeked back at her over his shoulder. "And…I believe you're right. A summer in Peru will help." Encouragement deepened his crow's-feet.

Her throat clamped shut at the news, and she set her coffee down to squeeze him tight around the waist. As she pressed her face against the back of his strong shoulder, he patted her hand. "You might want to go check your cell phone, Curly-Q. It's been ringing all morning. We'll talk more today at the garage. And file for your restraining order."

~*~

Friday morning, Zan inhaled deeply, welcomed the smell of the briny summer breeze out on Beresford Creek. He rowed against the tide, needed the burn in his abs and shoulders to prove that effort could get him somewhere. He needed the stress of college politics and the what-ifs of his new opportunity to stay put, stranded on the shoreline behind him.

As he reached the shallows off the shore of the islet, Zan set down the oars and hopped over the side to enjoy the cool water against his sunbaked skin. He gripped the side of the jon boat and beached it.

Satisfied that his boat was secure, he flipped open the storage box and scooped out the tattered baseball, fingered the familiar tooth marks.

This was the hardest moment. He could almost hear Shoeless yipping and barking as he raced around the boat and pounced in the sand, urging Zan to hurl the ball over the rise for him to fetch. He flipped the ball a foot into the air and caught it before slipping it into his pack and pulling out his cross trainers. The overgrown path was no friend to bare feet.

Zan stepped around the scrub and walked right over the tall salt grass, made his way under the trees toward the end of the islet. The mammoth boulder stood in stark contrast to the wild vegetation around it. He set his bag on the rock and hopped up to sit beside it, enjoyed the heat of the stone's surface against his legs.

For a long time, Zan stared out at the beach and the moving water, listened to the call of the gulls.

And he remembered.

Racing Shoeless to the boulder. Sketching with his

charcoals as his dog's head rested on his lap. Chucking the ball into the water and getting showered when Shoeless retrieved it and shook the water from his coat. Enjoying a picnic lunch with Bailey—and the deli-sliced turkey cold cuts she'd brought along for Shoeless.

And the silent, still afternoons last year when his childhood best friend, the white-muzzled golden retriever couldn't join him in the boat for their usual trip. On top of this very rock, Zan had realized putting Shoeless down was the merciful route.

He pressed the heel of his hand against his chest, tried to ease the ache that resurfaced too readily at the stream of images in his mind.

He reached for his pencils and sketchpad.

Within minutes, he captured the solitude of the deserted beach fairly well. Satisfaction settled in as he recorded those details most significant to him—the shadow of the pathway, the glint of the aluminum boat in the sunlight. He penciled in a thick horizon line in the east, smudged the darkness into a slab of gray clouds.

As he shaded the distant water, he left choppy whitecaps. A storm brewing.

He drew the curve of her waist and hips first, a single elbow evident at her side, arms crossed against her chest. With little effort, his pencil outlined her petite frame, standing with her back to him, head turned slightly. Waves and swirls of hair whipped back from her face in an imagined breeze as she gazed out at the rippling surface of the water. He slipped the bronze pencil back into the box and chose a fiery orange for her highlights before it struck him. He meant to draw Bailey, but the girl on the beach was most definitely Kasia Bernolak.

So similar, the two seemed to him—something about Nail-in-the-Tire made him fear for Kasia the way he did for Bailey.

But Kasia was also very different from his sister, and he couldn't quite shake her. She crept up on him at the strangest times, and he wondered where she might be. Whether she was having any luck with peace.

He wished he knew how to find her. Maybe he should try to friend her online. Just to check on her and tell her…what? To be careful?

What would his sister want him to say?

~*~

Kasia pulled a piece of gum from her purse, because mint had to be better than axle grease and new rubber. Friday afternoon, Kasia sat in the hard plastic chair at the back of the body shop. The replacement window should've been in already.

This trip would've been easier if it had been.

Her dad winced as he took a swig of his burnt coffee, and she turned to study the plethora of dingy business cards tacked to the corkboard next to her.

"I'd like to take you down to Huntington today for lunch, if you're up to it."

Lunch with Tatuś. Across the table from her, gentle eyes boring right into her. Right into her mistakes. If he found out, if her choices did anything to risk his ministry, she'd have a hard time forgiving herself.

"Today? I thought I could get some packing done."

His forehead crinkled. She wanted to reach up and

smooth the lines away. To smooth all of this away.

"Mama said you needed a few bigger items for Peru, and I thought we could run by the sporting-goods store and pick them up." He rubbed his chin. "Before we stop by the police station."

Her spine went rigid at the thought of the restraining order. "About that last one. Can I not? It won't do me any good in Peru."

His jaw tensed and relaxed, tensed and relaxed.

"I'll get one as soon as I get home if you want. The day I come back to Huntington." She didn't know if that's how it all worked, but she'd say just about anything at this point. "I don't want all of this to taint my last weeks here. I want to spend every moment with my favorite people. I promise not to go anywhere alone."

Tense and relax. Tense and relax. His jaw jutted forward, angry.

"*Dlaczego nie*?" Why not? It was a fair question.

"It'll make things worse. I'm sure things will blow over before I get back. I just want all this to go away. Please, Tatusiu."

After what felt like years, he cupped her cheek in his rough carpenter's hand and stared into her eyes. "You will not go back to school without taking care of this. We can't trust that it's blown over. And if he so much as texts you before you leave, you tell me. I'll..." He blew out a powerful breath and pressed absently at a callus on his left hand, eyed the clock on the wall. "I won't discuss what I plan to do to him. *Coś złego*." Something bad.

She squeaked out a mousy, "*Dziękuję,* Tatusiu."

"Don't thank me yet." He practically growled his answer. "And don't you dare keep anything from me."

But she was already keeping so much. She shook her head.

No more allowing the worry to call the shots. The only thing that could convince her dad—herself—everything would be fine was forward thinking.

"So…'bigger things,' you said. How do you feel about buying a hard guitar case? I want to take it with me. Start writing and singing again."

"That sounds just about perfect."

14

Oh, how Zan could do without all the silk, starlight, socialites. He hadn't seen Tasha since the frat party, and it'd be pretty fantastic to keep it that way.

Black-aproned kitchen staff hustled all around their home, inside and out, arranged centerpieces and prepared serving trays for his mom's annual summer soirée. Zan stepped to her side and waited until she'd gone over her checklist with the caterer.

"…finish with the mint juleps. I'll swing through to sample the ceviche at quarter till. Everything looks fabulous, Bryan, as always."

"The fact that our client lists overlap has never hurt." He smiled, then turned to shout instructions.

When Zan caught his mother's eye, she slipped her hand around his bicep and escorted him to an out-of-the-way spot. "Thank you for all your help, Zan. Did you decide to have anybody special join you tonight?"

He scratched his head. "No, ma'am."

"Why ever not? There are scads of young ladies who'd be thrilled—"

"Don't want to run into Tasha. I'd rather hit the batting cages. Would you mind terribly if I skipped out?"

"I love your handsome face in the crowd, but if you need to sneak away…"

He bent to kiss her forehead. "You're the best Li'l

Mama in the world."

She smacked his leg with the clipboard. "Don't you forget it."

Backpack loaded, Zan picked up his shades and keys off the mosaic table in the foyer. He slid his sunglasses on and headed out.

It took him ten minutes to navigate his way off the property with all the trucks and staff. As soon as his tires hit I-526, he slipped a hand up on the roll bar. The wind whipped at his hair and the side of his T-shirt, and Zan let himself relax as he drove up and over the Cooper River. Sunshine and sailboats dotted the surface of the rippling water below him. He hadn't gotten a chance to wander down by Waterfront Park or jog on the beach at Sullivan's Island. But with only one night free, he'd rather spend it getting his head back in the game.

Besides, downtown was Tasha's summer stomping ground. And on the off chance she was out clubbing with her friends instead of making an entrance at his house, North Charleston was a safer bet.

By the time he reached the sporting complex, the sky was already a lavender haze.

Duffel at his side, he snaked around the throng of parents watching soccer practice and bought ten bucks' worth of tokens.

He claimed an empty cage near the back, pulled out his old bat, tugged a worn glove onto his right hand, and took a few dry swings. Zan warmed up with the first set of balls, twelve easy grounders, stretching his back and arms. Then game on.

Four dollars in, Zan hit his stride. Nothing but him and the ball. Five dollars. Six. He reached over to drop another couple tokens in the slot.

Auburn flashed into his mind as he swung again, and a genuine smile came out of nowhere.

Zan dropped in his last two tokens. He gripped his bat, took his stance, and connected with a solid ping. The ball hit the back of the net. An easy home run.

This ticket to Oconee State could be just the change he needed. Auburn didn't have to like baseball; he'd take it as a personal challenge to win her over himself.

~*~

Samson bounded out of the house—as excited to meet Kasia's friends as she was to bring them home. When Tatuś had suggested they come up for an impromptu cookout, they all jumped.

Kasia called Samson back and knelt to pat his belly. Her guests could do without wet dog kisses. Tatuś came outside, and Kasia introduced him to everyone. He reached for the cases of soda they'd brought. "*Witajcie.* Please, be at home."

"Nice to meet you, sir." Kyle stuck out his hand.

Tatuś glanced down at it. Smiling, he set down the drinks he'd just picked up and then shook Kyle's hand.

"Why don't I get those for you?"

"That's all right, son," Tatuś said.

Kyle looked as if he could kick himself.

As Jayce reached out to greet her mom, her eyes widened just a touch. "Jayson McEwan, Mrs. B." His voice softened a bit as he leaned in. "Listen, I'm, ah, real glad to be here. I like that ya keep your family tight."

"Glad to have you, Jayson."

He grinned sideways. "If ya like me, call me

Jayce."

Laughter was the soundtrack to the next half-hour as her new friends swapped stories with her parents.

Whenever Kyle spoke, Lenka caught Kasia's eye. What? Was falling for someone new supposed to be easy? Kasia's heart still just felt…unresolved somehow.

"A.J., do you live on campus?" Mama asked.

"No. I live over my Uncle Frankie's garage for now. I do detailing in his body shop."

Mama shaped a ground-beef patty and set it on the plate. "Where's home?"

She met Jayce's eyes for a beat. "Here."

Jayce's brow furrowed. "Her parents live in Manhattan," he added.

"Oh? What brought you down South?"

A.J. scowled at Jayce for half a second before he turned in Kasia's direction. "Actually, Kasia, I plan to move on campus next semester. Need a roommate?"

"I do." Kasia swirled the ice in her glass, wondered why A.J. had dodged the question.

"Cool. We should take care of that before you flee the country."

Jayce reached for a slice of bell pepper and scooped up a full tablespoon of dip with it. "I thought maybe you'd make your slammin' southwest snackers." He pointed half a stick of pepper at Kasia. Smooth subject change.

"Nope. I made dessert though."

A.J. never did come back to life-before-Uncle-Frankie. She artfully maneuvered the conversation away from herself every time, changed the topic with questions and jokes. Her crazy guffaw kept everyone laughing.

But Kasia wouldn't pry.

Girls were entitled to their secrets.

~*~

Kasia stood by the sink, slicing fresh sweet onions for the burgers. Kyle came in from the yard and leaned against the counter. "Your dad's got a decent arm." He wiped his forehead with his bicep.

Kasia smiled. "He likes playing football almost as much as he does soccer." Forearms and his entirely-too-handsome smile flashed into her head. Out of all his favorite teams—all Chicago—Tatuś had grown up watching more baseball games than anything. He used to wash windows for money to see his team play at Wrigley. But there was no way she'd admit that to Forearms. Especially when he *lived* near her.

"It's cool to see you in your natural habitat, with your family and all, I mean. I get why you're so real."

She waited to see if he'd elaborate.

Jayce came in. "Mr. B's got the grill about ready." He grabbed two colas from the cooler. "Either of ya want me to toss over a tonic?"

Kasia shook her head and set the onions aside. She pulled a fresh tomato from the windowsill.

"You can throw me a tonic—the green one, with all the caffeine." Kyle twisted and held up a hand.

"Absolutely. And thanks for not raggin' me about my colloquialisms or anything, Kyle." Jayce passed him the can and headed back out the door.

Kyle wiped the condensation off with his shirt and popped the top. He tipped up the can of soda and drank deeply. She'd never thanked him for watching over her so closely after Blake's display the other night. Should she say something now?

The can clunked on the counter, and she glanced over. Kyle's wavy hair hung in his eyes, dark with post-football sweat.

"I'm making you a playlist." His voice startled her.

"For what?"

"Peru. Your being in a different country shouldn't keep you from new genius. I'll send you more as I get it if you'll give me your email address."

"Yeah. I'd like that." She probably should've at least hesitated.

Kyle reached over and tucked a strand of hair behind her ear. The door swung open and Tatuś strode in. He reached over her to the shelf next to the stove and gathered his burger seasonings. As he turned, he whispered, "You two should come outside with the rest of your friends. Don't be in here alone." He pecked her cheek and left.

Rather than sweetness, his kiss felt full of admonishment. What had her dad thought they were doing in there?

Kasia carried out a tray of burger toppings and condiments. Kyle shouldn't have touched her in such a familiar way. Too soon. Too presumptuous.

She slowed. Jayce held everyone's attention near the grill, faced Tatuś as he spoke. "Ma sobbed in the kitchen every night for weeks. Sayin' the same word over and over, like some messed-up mantra. Then one day nobody woke me for school. She was gone—up and left."

Kasia glanced at A.J. and could tell the story wasn't new to her. It wasn't easy either though. Her bottom lip had blanched under her teeth.

"So," her dad said, "that's the word your mom repeated?" He pointed to Jayce's shoulder where the thick lines curled around his arm above his bicep. Κϱισις. She hadn't seen that one.

"Yeah. I asked my old man about it, and he said it meant justice. I guess—when Ma was the most broken, she slid back into her first language. I've heard of that."

Kasia wondered if she could be hurt so badly she'd revert to Polish. Her heart language.

"My Uncle Colin—runs the tattoo parlor—didn't care that I was only eleven when I showed up askin' for one." Jayce quirked a smile. "It made me feel like Ma was still around somehow—and ah, you know." His voice trailed off, and he had a far-off look in his eyes. Jayce shrugged and said quietly, "I was after justice too. Everybody in Southie's lookin' for justice."

The sizzle of the grill was the only sound Kasia heard for a minute. Her stomach growled, and Lenka's eyes teased her. She spoke up. "Um, I thought you said the other tattoo meant justice."

"Yeah. But a different kind. Southie's full of single moms, but people talk when a man gets left. I honestly don't remember a day my old man wasn't wasted for a few years there. Uncle C barely kept us alive. Then he and my dad threw down one night after some hard words, and whatever he said flipped a switch. Pops did a 180."

As he elaborated, Kasia studied A.J. It almost seemed as though Jayce were trying to be open enough about his past to make up for A.J.'s silence.

A.J. suddenly glanced at Kasia.

Kasia dropped her gaze. She could analyze others all day long—infinitely easier than solving her own riddles. Firmly in the middle of the spectrum, Kasia wanted to be open enough to regain trust, maybe salvage her family relationships. But not so open that people would judge her.

Like even her sister had done when Kasia first shared everything. But Mama hadn't. How was she supposed to know who was safe to tell?

Jayce was still weaving his tale. "The change in my old man had me riveted, but I was an angry little punk with no use for Jesus-freakery. So we worked on restoring Pop's bike. Together—and over hours and hours of wrenches and ratchets—I started to understand who God is."

He chuckled at himself again. "Then it was wicked simple. So"—he shrugged—"the second tat."

The ink was thick and dark down his forearm. Δικαιοσύνη.

"Righteousness," Tatuś said. "I bet the pair of them start interesting conversations." He slapped Jayce on the back and lifted the lid of the grill.

Smoke from the grill wafted over them, and Kyle inhaled next to her. She smiled at him, wished Tatuś would approve of him like he did of Jayce. Then maybe he'd trust her judgment too. Trust her not to embarrass him in his own house.

Had he known about the time she'd been with Blake behind his shop? The only time she'd ever brought Blake home—because of that.

When darkness had swallowed up the daylight and kamikaze mosquitoes began bombardment in earnest, her friends loaded up to return to the valley.

Kyle hung back a minute. "Can you squeeze in a little time with me before you leave?"

"Not for a date though, right? Because I can't…go there right now."

He nodded slowly, entertained. "I get it. I just enjoy your company."

If he meant that, she'd like to hang out. "Can I get back to you?"

"Of course. Maybe. But if I don't hear from you by Saturday, I'm trying again." His boyish smile coaxed out a slight grin.

"Deal."

He climbed into the back of A.J.'s car and rolled down the window.

"Your car is quite a classic, A.J.," Tatuś said.

Jayce laughed and knocked on the hood. "It was a wild piece of junk when her Uncle Frankie got ahold of it. Thing's prob'ly as much Bond-O as steel at this point."

"Truth." A.J. climbed behind the wheel. "It can't be worth much at all. But I feel tough driving from A to B." She cranked the muscle car and made a slow circle in the drive. As it rumbled down the hill, the phone rang inside the house. Kasia shouted goodbye and jogged in to answer it.

"Hello?"

Silence.

No. Someone was breathing.

After her third hello, she slammed the receiver on the counter and stalked back to her room. On the edge of her bed, irrational fear crowded her senses. Her cell phone buzzed and she jumped, slammed her knee into the corner of the nightstand. *Ugh.* Her knee throbbed.

A text from Blake.

Nice. Press charges because I broke your window. I posted bail. See you soon.

Her heart slammed against her ribs. She erased the message.

15

Well, there wasn't sand and beach, but Zan couldn't say he minded the scenery.

The Northeastern Wooden Bat League consisted of small teams across the Finger Lakes region. Deep, thick forests and meandering hills filled the horizon all along the back roads. Plenty of signs for locally owned vineyards. Maybe he'd squeeze in a little wine tasting.

Early afternoon the first Sunday in June, Zan rumbled into the historic district of Geneva, New York. Home of the Geneva Catfish, his summer team. As he sat at the red light, he wrapped his fingers around the bar, pulled up a few times, stretched.

A brick church, a library, and some colorful storefronts dotted Main Street. Quaint little town. But the gas station, laundromat, and handful of municipal buildings weren't going to provide much entertainment. Nothing compared to the heat of the Carolina sun on his back as he spiked a volleyball into the sand, the salty waves only a hundred yards out.

Still, his ball career wasn't over.

He picked up his keys and housing assignment from his new coach, a gruff guy from Tennessee, and found out where to be the next morning. The rest of the day was his.

He found the bungalow without much difficulty and pulled alongside the curb. A car and a pickup that'd seen better days, both with Georgia plates, were parked in the drive. The grass, littered with cans and bottles, waved about knee-high, completely gone to seed. The rest of the welcoming committee was a boarded window, moldy siding, and a broken flowerpot with crisp, used-to-be geranium stems.

He cracked open the door and stepped in. The house was too warm even with all the windows open, and a musty, been-a-long-time-since-this-place-was-inhabited smell hung in the air. Stained, threadbare carpet reminded him of moss in a drought. Would his housemates help him clean the place up? Zan heard some laughter and music upstairs. He shouldered his duffel, headed toward the noise.

He found an empty bedroom, dropped his bag on the dusty parquet floor, and tossed his keys on the dresser. Ideally, the metal bedframe in the corner would be able to support his weight. He could try it out, but he'd rather vacuum it and put his sheets on it first.

Man, he missed his mama somethin' awful.

He turned to go back out to get a box of stuff.

"What's up, man?" A guy with Asian features and close-cropped hair gave him a nod from the doorway. "Todd Chen, catcher."

"Chen's all right," drawled a stocky blond. "We caravanned up here, and he drives like a maniac, but other'n that I like him. I'm Caleb." He stepped into the room.

"Zan," he answered. "Not much to do around here, is there?"

"Nah, but I figure we'll be pretty busy anyway. And I found an old grill out back. Maybe we can clean it up and use it." Caleb tossed a ball near the ceiling and snagged it with a snap of his wrist.

Chen leaned back against the doorframe. "Yeah, my last semester was a killer. When I'm not playing ball, I plan to be chilling. We've got to do some work on this place to make it a little more satisfactory."

Zan smiled. "I like the sound of that."

They made plans to hit the supermarket and pick up a few items from the hardware store.

Caleb stretched. "I'm gonna rest for half an hour or so before we head out." He turned back on his way out of the room. "You go to church, Zan?"

Zan stared at him. He did not get stuck in this house all summer with a Bible thumper. "Uh, no, man."

"No problem," Chen said. "We were just wondering. We're going to try the one in town on Sunday. If you change your mind, let us know."

Zan offered a tight, half-hearted smile in response, and the guys left.

Two Bible thumpers.

Was it too late to switch houses?

~*~

Zan relished the feel of the wood grain in his grip. He'd spent his whole life playing with aluminum, so the bat in his hands at the moment was a big deal. Wooden bats were only for the minors and up. Though the balance was almost identical to the metal bat he was used to, this one was weightier.

He adjusted his grip and stretched his upper body. A scuff mark right on the label caught his eye. He winced. It hadn't been there before the last pitch. He could've broken the bat, letting the ball hit it against the grain like that. Label up, label down. He couldn't forget all these little nuances in the wooden league. He dug in.

The ball came in hard and fast, but Zan nailed it on the sweet spot, sent it down the right-field line. Perfect.

He dropped the bat and took off for first, his stride long and even. He pushed himself, but this time, it wasn't about impressing anybody. Zan passed first base and jogged back, shielding his eyes from the sun as he took in the scene.

This first game of the summer was exhilarating. There were even fans.

"What's up, Geneva!" sang Dannyboy Rollins. The disabled vet was a local hero, and he never missed a practice, much less a game from what Zan had been told. The atmosphere of this local ballpark—no stadium, no diehard alumni, no ever-present boosters—made the politics and stress of collegiate ball seem a world away—exactly what he needed.

A redhead in the stands filled his head with Kasia Bernolak for a second, but he shook it off. *Be here. In this moment.*

Hedge, one of his oldest teammates, hit a shallow line drive, and Zan took off, hustled around second.

The base coach signaled him at third. "Hold up! Hold up!"

He slowed.

The pitcher rolled his neck, and Zan took his walking lead, remained watchful. After three pitches, the batter was up two balls and a strike. And third base wasn't on the pitcher's radar. Zan decided to steal home. Wished Auburn really was out there in the stands, watching him.

A few steps farther.

As the pitcher wound up, the third baseman was a few feet away from the bag. This was it. Zan waited to catch Hedge's eye, shuffled farther down the base line for an extended lead. Hedge turned his head, and Zan touched his helmet; the batter tapped the plate in answer.

Twice more, he stepped toward home, never breaking stride. The moment the pitcher's foot broke contact with the rubber, he made his move. His feet pounded the base line.

"He's going!" someone called out behind him. "He's going!"

The pitcher would have to throw low and away to get the ball out of the strike zone and into the catcher's hands, but Zan knew Hedge was ready for him. As he sprinted toward home, Hedge planted his feet and swung wide. The catcher dove for the ball and stretched his glove toward the plate.

But Zan had the momentum of a locomotive behind him. In one fluid motion, he slid behind the batter, kicked up a cloud of rust-colored dust, and reached around Hedge's feet to tap the plate.

"Safe!"

The crowd went wild. Dannyboy's melodic voice rose above the roar. "What's up, Geneva!"

Zan's confidence soared. Four innings later, the Catfish won.

The first victory of the summer.

As soon as he had a minute, Zan used his smartphone to search for Kasia on a few social networks. Tried to figure out how to spell her name. So unusual.

There. He'd found her. He clicked on her picture. Other than the photo, he could see nothing.

Unless he followed her. Would she even consider it?

He let his gaze wander over her penny-colored hair and wide, gorgeous smile. No wonder he couldn't get her out of his head.

His fingers hovered over the keypad. With guys like Nail-in-the-Tire and the dude she ran into outside of the Warehouse, she didn't need to believe a psycho watched her every move. He understood how a woman who's been threatened and mistreated could hesitate to trust. Look at Bailey.

A direct question was probably his best bet. He typed a message and hit send.

~*~

Kasia's burdens rolled off behind her in the jet wash. She slumped in the constrictive seat and studied the cloud pattern that stretched beside the airplane.

Everything she wanted to run from was miles behind her. Thousands of miles. She leaned her seat back the one oh-so-relaxing inch and tried to rest.

Thirty thousand feet above Venezuela, she jetted toward Peru, toward new purpose, new people, a new country—may as well be a new world.

Sheriff Schilling had called just before they'd left and informed her dad that the D.A. had, in fact, decided to drop the assault charges against Blake. So everything would settle down while she was out of the country, and—when it was time to fly home—none of this would be an issue.

But it wasn't time to think about home.

She was on her way to the Andes.

Kasia selected Kyle's playlist, tucked in her

earbuds, and turned off the overhead light. She settled in, closed her eyes, and saw them: Tatuś filled with an awkward mix of love, tension, and relief as he waved goodbye. Busia, not to be left behind on such an occasion, sandwiched between Mama and Lenka, her eyes shut tightly in that endearing blink—the Polish version of a wink. She'd called out, "*Z Bogiem,* Kasiu!" With God.

Kasia had blinked back and then blown a kiss to Mama.

Just before she walked through security, Lenka had yelled, "Get me a picture from the highest place you can find. Climb if you have to."

Kasia's lips curved at the memory as she drifted off.

Three hours later, her feet touched the floor of Jorge Chávez International Airport, and her soul flooded with excitement. The air was an odd symphony of unfamiliar words, lilting accents that spoke of distant lives, raucous laughter, and shouting.

At the conveyor belt, Kasia kept her distance. She knew better than to step up before she saw the red-and-white striped ribbon on her bags. The pushy swarm reminded her of a Polish deli counter.

But the people! Some of them looked as if they'd just stepped out of a magazine, tall, tanned, and blond. Rich, charming men swaggered around women who commanded their notice. And right in the middle of the glamorous were worn, tired people. Blue collar, or whatever they were in this country. These people—rather than make demands of life—stood still, content to be a part of the background.

It was their ebony eyes that called to her, their stories she wanted to know. If Lenka were here, they'd people-watch together, dream up plots for the oblivious cast of their play.

She wrestled her bag off the conveyor and heaved her pack onto her back, picked up her guitar, and scanned the long line winding away from customs. As she stepped up to the tall desk and lifted her gaze to the border guard, her heart tried to match the rhythm of the loud passport stamping in the room. Was it more anxiety or anticipation?

She'd call it anticipation. That answer felt better.

The disinterested guard stamped her passport with the joy of an undertaker. He handed it back and said with a thick accent, "Have a nice stay in Peru."

"*Gracias,*" she said.

The international concourse exit was the gateway to another world, way more lively than Passport Guy would have her believe. Kasia scanned the crowd, noticed her name on a fluorescent pink placard. If it hadn't been neon bright, she'd have missed both the sign and its bearer, a tall, wispy girl who looked as though she wished she could disappear.

Kasia approached and stuck out a hand.

"You're Kasia?"

"Yep. Is everything all right with Patty? She was supposed to meet me, I thought."

"She's fine. Just getting your apartment ready. I'm Grace, Mark and Patty's daughter."

So did they not need Kasia to be here? "Oh! I hadn't realized—"

"It's no biggie. I travel a lot and had to come through this week anyway. I'll take any excuse to spend a few extra days in Lima."

"So you have a car?"

Grace smiled. "I don't like to play chicken with

third-world busses. You up for one more quick flight?"

"Can I buy a ticket at the counter?"

"Follow me."

When they stepped out onto the tarmac and Kasia saw the teeny plane parked on the runway, propellers spinning, her heart might have stuttered a little.

They boarded and sat near the back, in different rows. After a few incomprehensible comments from the old man beside her, who apparently liked to waggle his eyebrows at young Americans, Kasia gave up trying to understand and stared out the window. Mercifully, Señor Too-Friendly gave up too.

The plane shuddered as it took off, and Kasia prayed it would stay in one piece until they landed in Cajamarca. Crystal-blue sky surrounded them, and she touched her head to the cool Plexiglas of the tiny window, tried to see more. The buzzing vibration of the engine traveled through the window and into her head, and she smiled. Was it wrong to want joy? Jayce's words from Bible study echoed in her head again. *Spend our time on what matters. On Christ. That's it.*

For a passing moment, she wished she could be at small group on Monday night, but she'd be teaching her own class by then. Besides, Lenka would tell her about it.

Kasia leaned toward the window as the plane banked to the left and glanced downward, inhaling sharply. Sunlight had stamped a silhouette of the plane on the cloud below them. A rainbow—a complete circle—surrounded the shadow like an embrace.

Determination welled up in her, and she steeped in it.

The plane bounced as they hit the primitive

runway. Kasia took mental snapshots of the sights around her—the sun-bleached stones lining the rough tarmac, the small crowd milling around outside the simple brick-and-glass airport, the large pineapple-ish plants pleasantly disguising the fence behind them. Tatuś had given her a new journal. She'd capture these memories first.

As she climbed down the stairs, Kasia scanned the waiting faces. The Cleavens' blond hair and peachy complexions shone out of the throng.

Mrs. Cleaven chatted as they left the airport. "The first thing we'll do is take you home for some coca tea, and then you can rest awhile."

Kasia forced a smile. She didn't want to rest. She'd been sitting on planes and in airports for hours and hours. "I'd rather just get busy learning my way around, if you don't mind, Mrs. Cleaven."

With a sympathetic hand on her shoulder, she said, "Please call me Patty. And I'm glad you're ready to get going, but the first seventy-two hours can be a little touchy. The air's thinner up here, and altitude sickness isn't a good way to start."

"It's like the flu, but ten times more awful," Grace volunteered.

"So I have to stay in and rest for three days?" she asked. Three days?

"Well, the tea really helps. It's an old Incan trick. Then we'll go over to your place. As long as you take it easy, you can get settled. Make the apartment feel like home. Mark has your internet connection ready, and Grace has some information about the area that might be useful. Just keep drinking lots of water too."

At least Kasia would have time to get her bearings and touch base with home.

Mark tossed her backpack and guitar into the back of an ancient SUV, then drove them around Cajamarca, pointing out a few places of interest. She tried to form a mental map of the city and found it difficult to gauge the direction. Tall building façades and walls lined the narrow streets, obstructing her vision as if she were in a ravine. She did notice, though, that the center of the city seemed higher than the outer areas.

"Why is the middle elevated?"

"This was an Incan city, and their leader—the Inca—had a spot up there so he could look out at all his territory," Mark said.

"His seat's still there," Grace added. "It faces three directions."

Perfect. She'd head up there and map out her plans as soon as they let her out. And get a picture for Lenka.

Mark whipped the old SUV down a back road and parked next to a mustard-yellow door. "This is where you'll teach English classes. Want to see inside? It's nothing to shout about, but it'll do."

The step beyond the yellow door was nothing like she expected. The façade fronted a small courtyard with a few potted flowers and two benches. Beyond that were two other doors.

"The back room there could maybe be turned into an office—you know, if we decide to spend more time in the city," Mark said. "For now, though, you'll just use this one."

Patty opened the door to a plain, sunlit room—everything but the dingy white walls the color of clay. A long table sat in the middle with lime-green benches on either side.

"We know you'll have three students, but it could

be as many as six—and then they might invite their friends," Mark said.

"And I'll help you dress it up a little more. Curtains, maybe, a tablecloth? Something like I did with the flowers in the open there. We just rented the place last week."

Kasia nodded, imagined the table surrounded by students. "I planned several lessons already—you said just topics for discussion, right? They know the basics?"

"They've all studied at least a year of English, but they need practice. A few might want to get together outside of class for more, if that's all right with you."

"Of course!"

Patty smiled sweetly and nodded to Mark. "Hon, we really need to get her settled. I don't want Kasia to overdo it." She placed a hand on Kasia's back and nudged her toward the yellow door.

Kasia's mind spun with ideas, frustrated by this flu-thing. She just wanted to get started. But she climbed into the vehicle beside Grace.

The city thinned as they drove on, and Kasia's gaze roamed the landscape. "Where are we going now?"

"To home base," Patty said, "about ten kilometers outside the city limits in a little town called Los Baños del Incas. It's a little quieter and right at the foot of the mountains. Makes Mark's travel a bit easier."

Every kilometer seemed to shave off wealth. Not that Cajamarca was a city full of riches and prestige, but out here, the buildings were smaller, more rundown. There were fewer cars and more donkeys—carrying firewood, newspapers, enormous milk cans.

And she began to see more hats. The city people

wore dated clothes, from the eighties and nineties, but these were the Peruvians whose faces graced the pamphlets and travel guides. Every one of them—old, weathered men, plump women with tired eyes, dirty and laughing children—wore a tall straw hat. The hats sat high, especially on the little ones' heads, but the children were so beautiful. "The people don't mind having their pictures taken, do they?"

"Not like some other cultures, but you should ask permission first," Mark said.

"Does everyone out here wear those hats?"

Grace answered. "It's a regional thing. Highlanders—around Cajamarca—wear those. The people in Cuzco wear felt derbies, around Chiclayo they wear fedoras, and—I'll have to show you a picture of the Islanders."

"Islanders?"

"There's an island of reeds in Lake Titicaca. Houses, boats—everything's made of reeds. Their hats are knitted…strange and colorful."

"Have you been out there? To the island?"

Grace snorted. "No, but I do a lot of research about the people of Peru." The corner of the girl's mouth lifted as she turned to gaze out the window.

Kasia did the same.

Minutes later, they parked at the curb beside an immense gate. Iron bars surrounded a landscaped lawn and a sprawling house, a stark contrast to the rest of the neighborhood. Kasia followed the Cleavens inside, feeling a little guilty passing such poverty as she entered this…complex. But it was lovely to have a soft, homey place to stretch out. The brief walk inside already had her head swimming—maybe she could overdo it.

"How far am I staying from here?" she asked.

"Right over there." Mark pointed.

Kasia turned to look out the large picture window and swallowed. Across the street, a crumbling concrete wall framed a bright green door and one tiny barred window with frosted glass.

Away went the guilt.

16

After the game, Zan caught a ride to Hedge's in the back of a too-small coupe.

Hedge's split-level seemed only slightly better maintained than his own housing, but Zan was after a buzz, not a vacation home. He grabbed a couple of beers and stepped out back into the quiet. Somehow, he wasn't up for the party scene tonight.

He called home and chatted with his mom, found out Bailey had filed for divorce. *Good for her.* She needed to sever the connection with Mike as completely as possible.

Was Kasia having luck with that? Cutting ties with Nail-in-the-Tire?

He took a few long pulls of microbrew and stood there, alone, wondered what the year would hold. Markman's team. New classes. And…

Back to Kasia Bernolak. Was she really as put off by him as she seemed at the store? Nah. He'd seen the almost smile. And she'd called him Forearms.

That was it. She just liked him more than she'd meant to. By the time he'd finished both bottles, daylight had dimmed.

This party had nothing to offer, so Zan headed back, took his time. Geneva was no sprawling metropolis.

After a month with Caleb and Chen, it still messed with him that they were so—so normal. At practices and ball games, they gave 110 percent. They cut up with the team and had the guys over to grill all the time. In fact, the only difference he'd noticed—other than their churchgoing and wholesome language—was how they'd just disappear when everybody went over to Hedge's after a game.

The warmth of alcohol flowed through his veins, and the world floated in a mellow haze. With every breath, he tried to absorb the salmon-pink sky, swooping sparrows, and summer breeze. The gravel driveway crunched under his feet as he headed to the back door.

He let himself in and dropped his duffel beside him. Were the guys home? Zan flopped into the ripped-up five-dollar recliner, checked the den for signs of life.

The TV was off, but an open soda can and a half-eaten bowl of popcorn sat on the corner of the coffee table. Next to a Bible. Man, the thing looked like it'd been run over a few times. By a semi. He picked it up and turned it over in his hands, chuckled at the duct tape all over the binding. Somebody didn't do much to take care of it.

"'Sup, Zan?"

He dropped the book.

Caleb grinned. "Had enough for tonight?" He bent down and picked up the Bible, set it on the table.

"Felt like relaxing is all," Zan said. He poked at the Bible. "This yours?"

"Yup."

"Why don't you take care of it?"

Caleb picked at a loose corner of tape. "Rough-lookin', ain't it? I guess I read it a lot."

Zan laughed louder than he meant to. "Is that why

you don't drink with all of us?"

Caleb sat. "Yeah, I don't drink anymore."

"Not allowed?" Got him this time. "One of those 'thou shalt nots'?"

"Actually, the Bible says not to be drunk, but it doesn't say flat-out not to drink. Just warns that it can bring trouble." Caleb looked at him a second longer than was comfortable. "I don't really miss it."

Zan stared back, tried to figure him out. At least he seemed sincere. Zan picked up the book and thumbed through the pages. Stopped. "'O Lord, how long shall I cry for help, and You will not hear? Or cry to You 'Violence!' and You will not save?'"

That sounded about right. "So the Bible might not be *only* crazy stories."

"There's truth in there."

"I'm not into religion."

Caleb slapped the arm of the couch. "Me either, man. Religion is a waste of time."

Zan blinked.

And he almost asked what Caleb meant.

~*~

Kasia followed Mark and Patty across the street and stepped up onto the high curb. Strips of blistered paint peeled off the green door. Mark jangled the keys in the lock. Though a few parts of the outer wall had lost chunks of plaster, the brick underneath was strong. Ugly, but nobody would knock it down and come to get her. Blake couldn't touch her here.

His threat to see her soon never had come to anything. Unless he'd followed her downtown when she'd met Kyle for coffee. Who cared anyway? She wouldn't waste a second more on him. Not in Peru.

Patty hadn't slowed her orientation spiel, so Kasia needed to tune in before she missed something crucial. The door led into an open courtyard. The grass—if you could call it grass, all wiry and coarse—was sparse, but it was still her own little corner of the world. And there was a hot mineral spring right in the middle of it.

Steam rose from the pool, wet the roughhewn steps down into the dark water. "Is this safe to get into?" she asked. If she had to spend the next three days here within the walls, a personal hot mineral spring would be fantastic.

"Oh, sure," Patty said. "The perfect way to end a long day. This area is full of them. This is where the town got its name—the Incan Baths. The landlord put in some pipes and a drain, so you can just let the water out and clean it if it gets murky. Grace'll show you how."

Cool. A reason to spend some time with Grace. She definitely had a busy schedule of her own with all the behind-the-scenes aspects of the Cleavens' work. She designed and maintained their websites in both English and Spanish, wrote their prayer letters and updates, blogged, and handled all their publishing and literature. Kasia planned to read her orientation packet—right after she emailed her family.

Maybe she could bring it out and enjoy the spring awhile.

Her apartment was bigger than she expected but had only the bare bones: beds and well-worn living-room furniture. Mark offered to hook up her laptop while Patty showed her where everything was.

Kasia wandered into the kitchen. An old gas stove sat in the corner next to the sink and one standalone cabinet. A cast-iron candlestick was the only decoration, but she liked it. A small, wobbly-looking table rested against the wall. "You know how to cook with gas?" Patty asked.

Kasia shrugged and offered a smile. "I'm a quick learner." She ducked to do a brief inventory of the cabinet contents.

"I'll drive you into town tomorrow morning for some staples to get you through the next few days. Make a list of the things you think you'll need. You'll have to soak any fresh vegetables in iodine before you eat them."

"I got a typhoid immunization before I left the States."

"That's good, but they could still carry cholera. You can't be too careful. Most volunteers stick to sandwiches, pancakes, simple stuff. So there's some of that already in the fridge."

"Sounds great. I'll explore and experiment on my own first, though, and keep a list of questions. I don't want to bother you every five minutes." Kasia smiled as she took in the ancient contraption that must be the refrigerator, humming with effort. How could she have missed that old clunker?

Mark rejoined them then. "All set. Ready, Pats?" Her hosts headed toward the door. She was almost free to do her own thing—inside.

But Patty turned back suddenly. "Oh! If you want a shower, turn on the water heater and wait about two hours. Gosh, if you'd just hopped in there, I'd have felt awful. Icy, icy. I forgot to tell that to the last volunteer team. Poor guys."

And then they were gone.

She had her email up in a heartbeat.

Wow. Kyle was totally making himself at home with her family while she was away. Lenka was already way too avid a fan, and Kasia did not need extra pressure when she got home. She blew out a breath, sat back in the chair, and loosened her braid—just needed to be in control of something inane for a minute.

She might have re-braided her hair a little more roughly than she needed to.

She opened one from Lenka:

Subj: Seriously. RU there yet?

I check this thing every two seconds, I think. I should know better. Dad looks glum already. He puts on his brave face whenever Mom asks how he thinks you're doing though. Don't you love him? ~Lenka

PS—Mom says she wishes she could be there with you.

PPS—Also, can you BELIEVE you would've been getting married at the end of this month? Thank God, huh?

The last words sucked the breath right out of her. She'd totally blocked that out. All those things—last-minute arrangements, bridal photos, packing for her honeymoon. The thought shook her.

Nope. Not doing this. She shut her notebook, defiant. What she needed right now was a whole lot more Peru. She stood up and knocked her braid back over her shoulder. Where should she start? She could unpack, maybe take a shower and let the warm water wash away the stress…in two hours.

Well, at least she knew the first order of business. She strode into the bathroom, flipped the switch on the side of the enormous tank hanging right over the small toilet, and the whoosh of the igniting flame made her jump. *Dear Jesus, please do not let this thing explode in my face.* Her eyes dropped to the toilet. *Or fall on my head when I least expect it.*

Her laptop caught her eye again. She'd forgotten to let her family know she'd gotten in safely. Two minutes and done.

Now to fill her mind with anything *but* Blake Hamilton. She pulled over her lesson-plan book and jotted down a few new ideas.

17

When the Catfish finally had a Sunday off, most of the guys decided to grill out and invite local girls again, but Zan felt done with that whole scene. He'd hang with the wholesome crew for the day. Not go to church with them and all, but he could occupy himself while they were gone.

Zan knocked on the broken bathroom door. Made a mental note to buy another set of hinges and fix the door while they were at church. "Hey, Caleb. Can I use your tablet for a sec?"

"It's on the kitchen table," Caleb shouted over the spray of water—at least the shower had good water pressure.

Zan pulled up his social-media account. Still nothing from Kasia. Well, he wouldn't bug her. But man, he'd give just about anything to hear back.

A couple hours later, when Caleb and Chen came home from church, he'd just dropped the last tool in the box. The bathroom door now hung properly, and he had a spread of twelve-inch subs on the table. After lunch, they decided to take a road trip to see the baseball hall of fame. The guys jumped into his Jeep, and Zan kicked up gravel as he pulled onto the empty New York road.

The two-and-a-half-hour drive went by quickly, and—as they followed the main route into Cooperstown—a sense of reverence settled over them.

Nobody spoke for a while.

The town itself wasn't a big deal, except that it was the mecca of every true baseball fan. Zan's father would love it. He'd have to find a souvenir and get Caleb to take his picture in front of the museum.

The street was lined with memorabilia shops, and it was all Zan could do to ignore them. He'd enjoyed countless hours with his dad, collecting cards, when he was in Little League, and things were so different now. The slideshow of memories almost made him call home.

But not quite.

The guys wandered through the exhibits, lingered longest in the oak-walled plaque gallery. Light glanced off the bronze faces of the baseball greats, and Zan stood there, reading about their feats. He swore to himself he would do whatever it took to stay in the game. He couldn't blow this opportunity.

In the gallery, they split up for a few minutes, each drawn to their own heroes. The Honus Wagner card sheet had Zan's attention.

"Incredible story, huh, man?" Caleb stood behind him.

What a powerhouse Wagner was. Zan's dad had joked for years that he'd find the card one day. Up in an old attic or somewhere. Never mind that the card was worth over two million because it should never have been printed. "It's pretty incredible to see an entire sheet of them—uncut."

"Pristine. But I'm more impressed with the dude's integrity," Caleb said. "That's what makes it worth so much."

The Pirates shortstop had demanded the American Tobacco Company pull his card from their cigarette packs. "Could've been because he wanted more money." Zan enjoyed playing devil's advocate with Caleb. Their debates had been fun—and intriguing.

"Or it could be what everybody else believes. Wagner didn't smoke, didn't want his baseball card encouraging kids to smoke."

"Yeah, maybe." Zan grinned and knocked Caleb's hat off.

"Or maybe the money. Naw, seriously, man. When I grow up, I want to be like Honus."

The more than thirty-eight thousand pieces of memorabilia crowded Zan's senses after a while. He wanted to remember everything to rehash with his dad so he could enjoy the camaraderie baseball offered, but he was cruising toward overload.

Chen fell asleep in the back on the way home, and Caleb was mercifully silent.

Zan was the first to speak into the quiet. "You and your father get along, Caleb?"

"Yeah. He ain't perfect, but I respect him. And when he messes up, he's quick to try and make it right."

Zan ran his fingers through his unruly hair. "My dad's a financial advisor. Always with clients, investing…you know. I see him at parties, business dinners."

"We've never been rich, but my dad's good at investing his time."

There it was. As far as time went, their relationship was bankrupt. Ironic.

"Money isn't all there is, is it?" Look at Mike Weston. Zan's brother-in-law had a phenomenal career but was an arrogant, violent jerk. Always provided bruises along with the cushy income.

"There's way more to life than money. I don't lack for anything, man."

An unfamiliar restlessness gnawed at Zan. He wanted Caleb's brand of contentment. Wanted to be a man of integrity too. A man who protected the people he loved, knew how to be strong and kind at the same time. Knew how to show them they mattered.

Zan needed to be a different kind of man altogether.

~*~

Kasia leaned in, arms on the table. "When the market closes for the day, what do you all do?"

"I am…I read…about economics and business," Arturo said. Deep brown eyes watched for her approval. He'd been the first to answer every single question she asked. Juan, the older boy with glasses, listened carefully, but he only spoke up if she spoke to him by name.

"Do you study all summer, Arturo?"

He shrugged. "It is difficult to find work in Lima. I must be…do best I can."

"That makes sense. Do any of you have any hobbies? What do you do to relax?"

Arturo squinted.

The girl with the long, wavy hair tilted her head and lifted her hand. "I may answer?"

"Sure, yes! Rosamaria, right?"

"*Si.*" She laughed. "Sorry, yes. If…if I am not have to watch my little brothers, I like to help my mother make cloths. I like the…colors"—she used her finger to trace the design in the tablecloth—"this pattern?"

"Oh! Yes. This has a beautiful pattern. You make

cloths like this?"

"Yes, this one—this my mother's work."

"It's beautiful."

A genuine smile graced the girl's face as she ran a hand across the cloth and dipped her head in thanks. Kasia made a mental note to buy a tablecloth for Mamusia.

"Juan?"

"I play *fútbol*."

"I love that," Kasia said. She spoke slowly but didn't over-enunciate the words. "My family enjoys *fútbol* too. In America, we call it soccer. My father grew up in a small neighborhood where all the families had moved from Europe—from Poland. They played soccer in the streets, many nights until dark."

All the heads nodded. Juan smiled. "We do too. We play in streets."

"*Donde esta* this—Poland?" Inez asked Arturo.

"Polonia."

"Ah." She nodded, quiet again. That was the first time Kasia had heard her say more than her name.

"So, all of you like soccer?" Kasia asked.

Heads bobbed.

"What else do you do to relax, for fun?"

Most everyone shifted, eyed the others, waited.

"Kasia, you want to go places, do fun, with us? After class?" Rosamaria asked.

"I would love to. Maybe some of you could show me around. Take me to your favorite places—important places I should see before I leave. I want to take pictures for my family in America and show them your beautiful city."

Suddenly, everyone was talking—and Kasia knew that the plans her students hatched now would be her favorite times. One-on-one. She could learn from them, listen to their stories, and build real friendships.

~*~

Scruffy grass pressed into Kasia's thighs as she dangled her feet in the steamy spring—her new favorite spot.

Every afternoon siesta, she rested in her courtyard, played her guitar, and poured her thoughts out onto the pages of her journal, more poetry than story. She might not have the songwriting bit back, but she could play. And she could sing songs she already knew.

But she wouldn't complain. After two silent years, music had relented and given an encore. That was something.

Besides, if she wanted rest, naps were pointless.

Kasia set down her journal, pulled her feet from the water, and scooted back against the wall. She reached for her guitar. Her fingers picked along the strings as she sang through Psalm 40. The instrument felt like an old friend, but her fingertips throbbed, and she set it aside.

Wow. Her index finger had actually cracked. No wonder it ached.

Shadows had lengthened and the sun rested on her boundary wall. Siesta would be over soon, and the *kombi* would shuttle people back into town. If she missed the bus, she'd be late for coffee with Rosamaria. She ran inside, set her guitar on the bed, made sure the darkening circles under her eyes were well-disguised. Then, with her backpack and water bottle, she hurried toward the door, kept an eye on her watch.

Time with her students outside class was her

lifeline. In the midst of real conversations—about life, dreams, plans—she could feel.

Kasia caught up with a group of young girls, age ten at the most, who also headed down the street. She hung back a bit, tried to stay under their radar. She etched the picture in her mind: their vivid wool skirts puffy enough to be hiding crinolines, vibrant blouses, cardigans, and high-crowned straw hats. What intrigued Kasia, though, were the striped cloths—the kind Rosamaria and her mother made. Each girl wore one against her back, her burden bound closely to her. One girl, maybe four years old, carried a load of alfalfa, which Kasia had learned would be for the family's sheep. Another older girl toted a load of firewood.

The tallest carried a hefty black-haired toddler with wide ebony eyes. Kasia smiled. His big sister kept passing him bits of bread over her shoulder. Kasia knew the moment he noticed her.

He stared at Kasia openmouthed and called out to his sister. "*¡Naranja!*" The girls turned, all evidently surprised by her fiery curls.

"*¡Hola!*" Kasia waved.

The three girls giggled, but the little boy whispered a greeting back to her.

Kasia stopped under the tree that marked the local bus stop. Since she only headed as far as Cajamarca proper, she'd actually be in a twelve-passenger van. Bigger busses were used from one metropolitan area to another. She'd learned the hard way, though, the *kombi* could hold way more than twelve of the locals. Kasia eyed the waiting crowd. Who knew how many they'd squeeze in today?

The mud-splattered van approached, filled the clean, village air with diesel fumes. It chugged to a standstill, and a lanky man unfolded himself from the front seat and stuck out an open palm. Kasia dropped two *soles* in and climbed into a seat as close to the door as she could manage. It did no good. Within a minute, she was twisted and squeezed so she could barely breathe, and a strange man bent over and perched directly on her right shoulder.

Oh, and she didn't want to breathe. The rank air burned her nostrils and throat.

Mercifully, the ride didn't last long. When Kasia stood upright once again, she gulped in the fresh air like water in the desert. She met Rosamaria at the café, and the two of them wandered the city for hours.

By the time they said good night, it was late enough the shuttle wasn't running. Rosamaria walked Kasia to a taxi stand and gave the driver the address before she told Kasia the fare was a little over one *sol* per kilometer. So…ten or twelve *soles* to Los Baños.

"He might think you don't understand. Don't pay too much. Okay? Tell him you know what is fair."

Kasia nodded and hugged the girl before she climbed in the back of the car.

The night was so dark that Kasia only saw her own tired reflection peppered with red and blue flecks of light from the instrument panel. The driver watched her in the mirror. She wished her Spanish were decent enough to tell him to concentrate on not running his crazy little car off the road, but she must've bored him eventually. Just as she started to relax, he pulled to a stop in front of her place.

"Veinte soles," the driver said, without so much as a glance in her direction.

Twenty? Not a chance. She reached across the front seat and dropped twelve *soles* into his hand.

His head jerked up, offended, and he repeated the price.

No, sir. "*Doce*." Twelve. Not a cent more.

She opened the door to get out, and as she stood, he jumped up as well, irate. He held out his hand in arrogant expectation, and she gave him one icy look before she marched toward her door. She half wished she'd knocked his hand out of her way.

But she fumbled with the lock, and the whole time, his voice rose and rattled her composure. As the green door relented, he shouted a final nasty insult, slammed his door, and peeled out. All she'd understood was *gringa.* Would she have paid twenty if Rosamaria hadn't warned her? She hoped not. She wanted to be strong, the kind of girl who said no and meant it.

She closed the door behind her, locked the deadbolt. What she wouldn't give to have Samson greet her right now—all wet kisses and whimpered hellos.

Kasia leaned an arm against the cool wall and kicked off her shoes. The hot spring beckoned her again. She sat on the edge to roll up her pant legs. As she slipped into the warm bath, the heat melted away her fatigue. Her indignation drained out as well, and Kasia breathed in the solitude. The sounds of deep silence swelled the air, disrupted only by an occasional shuffle out in the street.

This was where she wanted to be. Behind her wall, safe in the warmth of her sanctuary, under the heavens and the ever-watchful eyes of her Savior.

The sky above her held familiar constellations, but out here, miles from the city lights, there were more stars behind Orion the Hunter than she'd ever known. Clusters twinkled in and around the three stars of his belt. Tatuś always looked up at the sky in Langston Falls as he closed his day, and she imagined him beside her now.

I miss him—all that strength and stability. If I can't get back to who I was, at least help me be worthy of his love.

18

Kasia sat still as the night air settled around her. Cold.

She'd emptied her heart and mind of all her thoughts, confessions, and hopes. Her feet, prickly from the heat, had soaked in the steamy mineral spring long enough.

But dread filled her as she considered sleep. She knew it: As soon as she drifted off, the demons would return.

Maybe she could touch base with friends back home.

Once her feet were dry and her comfy pajamas snuggled her warmly, Kasia opened her laptop to see what was new.

A new message from Alexander Maddox. Who?

Oh.

Oh. That haystack hair. She studied his profile pic—he leaned back in the sand while a golden retriever pawed his chest and gave him a big, wet kiss. The day they'd run into each other in the store, she'd seen him laugh like that. His laughter filled her head. Those dimples would probably stick with her for a while.

There was something about a man and his dog. She could imagine their day at the beach without even knowing him.

Forearms.

Alexander. He'd called himself something else before.

She tore her g away from the photo, missed Samson even more, and read the message.

Auburn, first: I'm not a stalker. You've just come to mind once or twice. Second: I thought it'd be nice to know someone on campus when I start school. Friend me, if you want. Or don't. Forearms. (Best. Nickname. Ever.)

A smile pulled at her mouth. She clicked on his profile. Charleston, South Carolina. So maybe not a surfer, but she'd nailed the beach-lover aspect. Great taste in music. Baseball fan. No surprise there.

Sure. She could friend him.

After a shower, she climbed in bed and prayed the nightmares wouldn't come.

But they did.

She traced the creamy threads in the black marble floor next to the Hamilton family's towering Christmas tree and tucked her feet beneath her on the plush rug. Blake knelt in front of her and held out cupped hands, lifted one to reveal a dark velvet box. Kasia sucked in a breath and covered her mouth with trembling fingers. He wasn't supposed to ask her yet.

His straight blond hair fell into his eyes, and his gorgeous smile curved his lips. He set the box on the floor between them and took both her hands in his. "Marry me, Kasia."

He was earnest, his eyes bright and eager. So why was she breaking into a cold sweat? The world seemed to shift, and she closed her eyes, tried to regain her balance. She slid her hands gently out of his, covered her face. She could not let him see her panic.

"Ka-sia…" he sang. "I surprised you, didn't I? You never expected the ring for Christmas." Smug satisfaction laced his voice.

With a deep, calming breath, she peeled her hands away from her face and hoped he'd see the surprise he wanted rather than the shock she felt. "I…I don't know what to say, Blake. I can't believe it."

He laughed. "Then just say yes, Kosh."

She nodded, her bottom lip tight between her teeth. "Yes, Blake." Saying it out loud made it feel better. "Yes. Thank you."

His eyes flashed, and he was on his knees within seconds, his hands tangled in her hair. The kiss was urgent, possessive. She tried not to shrink away, and he didn't seem to notice.

Blake's fingers dug into her skin. The room darkened.

"Ow! Blake, that hurts."

He released her for a moment, but she found no comfort in his eyes.

Everything in his den blurred, a gray haze hiding warped, faceless evils.

With a snarl, he came at her again, bound her tight.

This wasn't Blake anymore.

She fought with her arms and legs, screamed for help. This thing could not pin her down. But the more she writhed, the more tangled she was in its grasp.

Wham! Her head slammed into something solid and unforgiving. She was suddenly flat on her back. The world spun as if she were on a merry-go-round, and she gripped fistfuls of something soft, desperate to ground herself. Her heart beat so loudly in her ears it sounded like someone banging on a door.

Finally, the vertigo eased, and Kasia noticed the faint light slanting through the barred window from the streetlight. In Peru. She was in Peru.

Thud! Thud! Thud! Wood splintered in the courtyard outside.

Wait. Her heart wasn't making that sound. Someone was breaking in. The clock said 3:30 in the morning. Who in the world would be there at this hour?

Fear gripped her. No one good. Someone was after her.

She stood too quickly and wobbled out into the main room, leaned against the walls. Her head pounded, but she had to think. What could she use to fend off an attacker? Her gaze landed on the heavy candlestick, and she grabbed it. She made it the final few feet to the bathroom, slammed the door behind her, locked it. She wiped the sweat from her forehead. Her breaths echoed too loudly in the tiled room. He'd find her.

Had Blake come all the way down here? No way.

The sound of jarring wood reached her ears, followed by footsteps. The door to her apartment slammed into her hallway wall. He was almost here.

She gripped the candlestick and held it like a baseball bat. She would not miss. She couldn't. *God, help! Stop him!*

"Kasia? Kasia? Are you hurt? Where are you? It's Mark. Answer if you're all right."

Why would Mark be there?

"Kasia, honey?" Patty's voice. "Are you here? Are you alone?"

The relief wiped her out, and she sank onto the cool tile floor. She tried to speak. "In here."

"Kasia?" they called.

She banged the inside of the bathroom door, found

her voice, but it was shaky. "I'm in the bathroom." She raised a tremulous hand and unlocked the door.

It swung open, and Patty stuck her head in. "Honey! What in the world? Are you all right?" The woman flipped on the light and knelt beside her. Kasia squinted at the brightness as Patty pushed Kasia's hair back from her face and searched her eyes. She smelled clean and soft, like shampoo and cotton.

Mark stood over them. "There's no one here. She's alone." He squatted. "What happened, Kasia? We heard you scream and call for help."

How humiliating. The whole neighborhood had probably heard her. She looked up at Mark, afraid he'd be angry she'd woken them up for nothing. "It was a nightmare. I'm so sorry to bother you at this hour."

Mark blew out a breath. "Bother us? Scared us out of our wits is more like it. I wouldn't be surprised if somebody called the police."

Kasia's pulse was beginning to even out, and she realized what she'd put them through. "Really, forgive me. I won't let it happen again." She pressed her palm against the back of her head. "Could you—may I have some ice for my head?"

Mark left to get some.

"Kasia," Patty said, her eyes full of compassion, "I don't think this is something you can control. You sounded terrified. Do you want to come and stay with us?"

"Oh, no. No. I'll be fine. You don't have to—"

"I'll stay here with her." Grace. When had she come in?

Kasia's eyes locked on the other girl's. "You…you don't mind?"

Grace shrugged, her eyes full of kindness. "No. I'll

get my things and be right back."

"Do you want me to make you some tea?" Patty offered.

What Kasia wanted was for Mamusia to make her a cup of tea and help her figure out why these nightmares wouldn't quit. Gently, she shook her head. "Thanks though. I'll be fine."

Patty stood and gave Kasia a hand up. They walked out and sat on the sofa, waited. Kasia didn't know what to do. Sleep scared her, but she didn't want to sit and talk about it either. Thankfully, neither Mark nor Patty asked her about the dream.

"I love these Scripture verses you've put up around the room. They're so inspiring," Patty said.

"Thank you. They're the ones I'm memorizing."

"Make you want to rise to the challenge, don't they?" Mark meandered around, reading each of them.

Grace soon arrived and put her things on one of the bunks.

Mark prayed for Kasia before he and Patty left, and Patty gave Kasia's shoulder a motherly squeeze.

"You girls get some rest now," she said.

Both Kasia and Grace nodded, but Kasia knew. Sleep wouldn't be happening tonight.

~*~

Kasia studied Grace in the silence. The older girl wasn't asking the million questions that she had to wonder. Grace sat, long legs folded beneath her in the corner of the sofa. She'd pulled a book from her backpack—it looked like a history of the Quechua people, the highland descendants of the Incas. She had wordlessly placed the ball in Kasia's court. Available but not pushing.

Picking at the crack in her fingertip, Kasia watched Grace bite down on her yellow highlighter, keep the lid in her mouth as she underlined something important. With practiced precision, she stabbed the point back into the lid and went on reading. If her facial expressions were any indication, it was intriguing.

Her eyes flicked up to meet Kasia's. Kasia felt her cheeks flush pink, but she offered a half-smile to Grace. "Thanks. You know, for staying."

Grace nodded and returned to her reading. "A night away is always a welcomed change of pace."

Inspiration struck, but Kasia had no idea how Grace would react. "I, um, could use somebody to shake me awake before I scream the entire neighborhood out of their beds. So, if you want…"

Grace cocked her head. "You don't know me at all—you don't want to take a few days to think about it?"

"Nope." One thing Kasia knew. She didn't want to be alone at night.

Grace met her eyes, intent. "I won't be in your way. I sort of keep to myself." Her eyes fell again as she muttered, "I'm sure you've noticed."

Kasia shrugged and smiled. "A roommate would be nice. Will your parents share you?"

Grace didn't answer, but her mouth turned down.

"How old are you?" Kasia asked. "If you don't mind saying."

Grace smirked. "I'm twenty-five."

"Oh."

"Yeah. I guess my parents assume since I want to be a part of their ministry team—and because they're family—I want to stay there forever. I've mentioned before that I wouldn't mind having my own place, but it's not practical, I guess. Still, I could do my work from almost any city." She pulled her highlighter out again and marked a passage, effectively ending the conversation.

Family dynamics were always complicated.

Kasia decided to write her parents a letter. She wouldn't mention the horrific dream, but there were plenty of other stories to tell.

19

The night smelled like fresh-cut grass, and the temperature was perfect for an evening run. "All right, man," Zan said to Caleb, "it's bugged me for weeks. You're a Bible-thumper, but you can't stand religion. It doesn't add up."

Caleb laughed. "I'm gonna go ahead and take that as a compliment. True Christianity has nothing to do with religion."

"Huh?" Zan checked his watch.

"Let's jog a minute. I don't want to get winded while I'm tellin' you this."

Like that would happen. Caleb's stamina blew Zan's out of the water.

Caleb set the pace.

"There's a million different versions of religion"—Caleb's voice was country twang and solid resolve—"all based on whether or not we're good enough. Christianity is for the man who can admit he's hopeless."

Zan quirked an eyebrow but said nothing.

Caleb looked like he was weighing his options for a second. Then he smiled. "Whatcha think about the Bible?"

"Not into it. Could've been messed with—changed by the people who want you to believe it."

"Have you read it?"

"No. Probably won't."

"All right, well…how 'bout historians. You believe them?"

Zan dipped his head, worked to keep his pace steady as they headed toward the park. "Everybody still brings their own bias to the table, but I'm more comfortable with that."

"True enough. Lots of famous and well-respected historians wrote about Jesus. They agree on three things. One, Jesus Christ was a radical. He turned the world upside down, doin' what everybody least expected.

"Two. He made enemies because of His message."

This was "jogging"? A dog-walker waved at them. Zan nodded back at her.

Caleb said, "Hey, how are ya?" and swung his head back in Zan's direction. "The authorities—Jewish, Roman, all of them—killed Him because He claimed to be God. And His followers swore He came back to life. Now, where—of all places—would it be hardest for those guys to sell their story? That Jesus was alive?"

"Where people saw Him die, I guess. 'Cause everybody would know it had to be a hoax."

Caleb squinted and grinned. "Yep, but that's right where His disciples preached it. In Jerusalem. Mocked by loads of people who thought they were insane for keepin' it up—even threatened by the authorities. But thousands became followers anyway. Crazy, right? Thousands who knew about the crucifixion, heard the rumors of the resurrection and His appearances to crowds, the whole thing."

Zan lifted his shirt and wiped his forehead.

"And three. When the disciples split up to take this message to the world, every one of them was either imprisoned or tortured for it. Actually, all but

John were killed—and in sick, nasty ways. Now, my question is this. If it had all been faked—at some point—wouldn't one of His boys have cracked? Given up the others to save himself?"

"You'd think," Zan said. He stopped for a second, rested his hands on his knees.

"You good, man?"

"Cramp." He reached up and stretched. After a minute, he gave Caleb a nod, and they took off at an easy jog.

"Usually, hoaxes fizzle out after a while. But Christians are still willing to die for their faith."

"I've met a lot of Christians who wouldn't die for it," Zan said.

"All right, true. True. A lot of 'Christians,'" Caleb said with air quotes, "in America, especially, don't really get what following Christ is about. They've never had to figure out if He's worth dying for."

Zan wasn't ready to die for anything but Bailey. "I can't go there yet, you know?" He started again.

"Ask me if you come up with a question, though, all right?"

"Yeah."

They turned back toward the house in silence. Zan's head was too full to speak.

~*~

Several weeks later, Zan walked toward their house in the early quiet and saw lights on in a few of the rooms. So Caleb and Chen were up. He sneaked out for a pre-sunrise jog on his own this time because he wanted time to think, wanted to avoid pounding the streets with Caleb. Zan didn't need heavy conversation today.

As he opened the back door, the difference between the outside air and the warmth of the kitchen surprised him. He pulled off his hoodie and tossed it over into the community laundry pile. It was his turn to handle the laundromat run.

Caleb's tablet sat on the kitchen table next to a box of cereal and the jug of milk. Zan grabbed a bowl and decided to check up on Kasia. Li'l Mama's biscuits, eggs, and sausage gravy sounded like heaven to him too, but that wasn't a possibility for another month.

Kasia continually blew him away. He hadn't assumed she was merely a beautiful face, but he certainly hadn't expected to follow her adventures all summer as she taught English somewhere in the mountains of South America. She never answered him when he asked where she was, so he hadn't pushed. Bailey was careful about guarding her location online too.

This morning, Kasia posted a new photo album, packed with the bright colors of fresh fruits, spices, and small poncho-wearing kids. The animated expressions she captured! A million times just clicking through the pics, he wished he were there with her, wandering through this market. She made him want to pull out his sketchpad.

And grab a cup of seriously strong java from the little outdoor café beside the church with her. What took Kasia down there? Some humanitarian-aid project? An exchange program? To spend her whole summer in the Andes—she was a very different caliber of girl than he'd ever pursued.

It only made him want to know her more.

Kyle Compton commented under a photo. *Don't*

they have any normal-colored yarn?

What a jackleg. Zan typed below it.

Awesome. Bring something cool back for me.

She wouldn't, of course, but he wrote it to annoy Kyle as much as anything.

~*~

Steaming bowl of oatmeal and cinnamon on the table, Kasia opened her laptop and checked her email. One from Lenka:

So much is going on, and I wish I could sit with you up on our rock and chat. A new guy came to church the last two weeks. His family just moved into town. His name's Bryce, and he is SOOO adorable. I sneaked a pic on Sunday so you can see him. We're going to see a movie Friday night.

What was it she'd read that morning? In Psalm 69. "Let not those who hope in You be put to shame through me." She hadn't been a good example for Lenka at all in the dating department. But maybe Lenka would be smarter. Hopefully.

Kyle hasn't missed a Sunday evening service since you left. He's even come up a few times to hang out for the day. Samson's not 100% sold, but he'll come around. Kyle's fun. I guess he's still writing you, yeah?

Those photos you posted are beautiful. You don't even seem amateur. ;) Wish I were there to people-watch with you. Miss you like mad. ~Lenka

She knew Lenka would understand the pictures. She'd gotten several great snapshots at the open-air market. Vendors with steaming grilled meat on skewers, a weathered musician with his pan flute on the street corner, girls piling star fruit and fresh mangoes into back slings for their customers. She'd even taken one picture of a table full of sandals made from old tires. Every scene told a story.

She wondered what Lenka's photo of Bryce said about him and clicked it open. Cute. *Just keep her eyes open, please. Don't let her get attached if he's not as good as he seems.*

Another one from Kyle:

Hey, girl. Bible study was great this week. We've been looking at 2 Peter and how we need to be intentional about "cultivating" our faith. What have you been reading?

BTW, I love hanging out with your family. They make me feel so welcome. (And I'll check out that Bryce kid for you. Make sure he's worth Lena's time.) Take care. Look forward to hearing from you.

Ergh. She'd wanted things to get back to normal at home. But Kyle was seeing "normal" without her.

Which meant he'd notice if conversations turned stilted and awkward when she returned.

No, she had to believe things would be better. Still, Kyle would have a whole summer of experiences with her sister—with Mama and Tatuś—that she'd missed.

She needed to mute the negative and be thankful he kept an eye out for Lenka.

And from Zan:

So, I'm serious, Auburn. You're a natural with the photos. I've tried sketching a few. Maybe I'll frame one for you. We can meet up, have that sweet tea you owe me, and then you can tell me some of your stories.

Kasia knew it, as certain as sunrise in the morning, if that boy asked her for a drink again—and if he tossed her that dimpled grin—there was no way she could say no.

Besides, she wanted to see his drawings.

~*~

"Where did you put the list of ingredients?" Kasia asked Grace, who sat at the cluttered table amid the piles of books, papers, and photographs. They'd been roommates for a month now and had decided to make a 365-day photo prayer guide. Kyle would probably think the bright Latin-American color schemes were hilarious.

"It's next to your keys. I'll have October done by the time you get back."

"*Done* done?" Kasia asked.

"Apart from the final touches, but I want you to look over it tomorrow. You're good with words."

Kasia smiled. "I'd be glad to."

"Rosamaria and Lupé are meeting you at the market?" Grace asked.

"Yep, but they said I have to shop on my own. They'll only help in an emergency. You think I'm allowed to use charades?"

Grace appeared entertained at the thought. "Whatever it takes. Survival Abroad 101."

"I'm on it." Kasia waved and left. Tonight two of her English students were giving Teacher the language lesson and then helping her cook *ají de gallina*. So far, every dish that boasted the spicy *ají amarillo* delighted her taste buds. This one was supposed to use the hot pepper in a chicken sauce over rice and potatoes.

She strolled to the bus stop, thought of Mama's last question when they'd chatted. She'd wanted to know if sleep came any better in Peru than at home. Kasia admitted she never felt quite rested, but she'd held back about the nightmares.

Kasia was convinced she needed to cling to God

this time.

No one else.

Busia's plan had worked. Kasia threw herself mind and body into whatever she saw God doing around her. As long as she could avoid downtime, she felt good. Classes in the mornings; after lunch, she methodically walked the streets of the village, prayed for the people she encountered; every afternoon, she crashed during siesta, played the guitar in the quiet.

Busy mind, outward focus. That was the theme.

"Meh!" A man's voice shouted behind her.

Kasia jumped, startled by the rich baritone. When she turned, her favorite little girls stood there, faces filled with amusement. A sizeable sheep parked beside them, munching on alfalfa straight from the chocolate-eyed toddler's tiny hand. One of the girls pointed at the sheep. As if on command, he swallowed and bleated again. "Meh!"

Kasia chuckled at herself. She'd expected him to baa, like he would in a Mother Goose nursery rhyme, not sound like an eighteen-year-old guy. She pulled out her camera, asked if they'd let her take a picture. After a moment of discussion, the tallest nodded. They stood stone-still, faces uncertain.

Kasia knelt in front of them, scooted forward.

The little boy's hand shot out to stroke her hair.

"Tomás!" his big sister cried.

He pulled his hand back. Kasia reached for it, and his chubby fingers gripped hers tightly. She tickled them with a red curl, and he giggled. Lifting her camera with the other hand, Kasia gestured to Tomás. The smiling sister approved. One, two quick snaps, and she'd captured both the grinning doll and the curious girls.

"Gracias." Kasia waved goodbye to the kids and backed away.

She leaned against a thick tree to watch a game of street ball until the *kombi* arrived. The kids played with a passion and skill that surpassed their youth. Did they each dream of growing into professional athletes, hope it could provide their ticket out?

The ancient van lurched to a stop in front of her, and she squeezed in. Escape must be a universal desire.

20

Lowcountry air—especially out by Daniel Island—always smelled sweet. Like pine straw and magnolias.

Zan turned at the light and slowed, enjoying the pattern of dappled sunlight on the road at the entrance to his neighborhood. He pressed the button and waited for the iron gates to swing inward. As he wound lazily past the mailboxes and the dock, a jogger waved at him. Zan was eager to hit the trails himself.

He hopped down onto his driveway in front of their sprawling stucco villa. Man, he'd missed the Spanish moss, the sticky humidity, the tranquility of the slow-moving brackish water behind their house. Summer in New York had been necessary—good even—but here it was the second week of August. He wanted to get a little time on the water before heading back to the mountains of the Upstate.

Kasia's recent posts had sounded like her activities were wrapping up too. He tried not to think too much about seeing her again. Failed constantly.

At least that brand of failure kept him smiling.

He stepped inside and kicked off his shoes, enjoyed the cool terra-cotta tiles under his feet.

"Anybody home?" The echo of his voice was the only answer.

He walked through the foyer and into the great room. The sun's rays slanted through the skylight. As he set his keys in the bowl on the large mosaic table, a

Bible surprised him. Whose was that? He scanned the room again, looked for signs of company.

He jogged back down the front steps to grab his belongings and high-stepped on the heated asphalt. Before he went back inside, Zan jogged over to their three-car garage and peered into the tinted glass. Bailey's white coupe. Oh! Cool. She must be visiting.

Li'l Mama's ice-cold sweet tea on his mind, he tossed his duffel into his bedroom. In the kitchen, he pulled down a glass and spied a pair of petite, tan legs stretched out on one of the back-porch chaise lounges. He slid the door open and stuck his head out. "Bay?"

"Hey, Zan!" she said, a genuine smile in her voice. "How fast were you driving?" She jumped up and hugged him tightly.

"Fast enough. I didn't want to miss the water all summer. I was just going to fix some tea. You want some?"

"Yeah, I'll come in with you." She stepped in and set her sunglasses on the table. Half her face was purple and yellow.

"What the—"

"It's all right." She rested a hand on his arm.

As if that would erase it.

"It's over now, but that's why I'm here. I was doing fine with the Beistlines. Then I joined a support group for battered wives at church." She shrugged.

With every word she spoke, Zan's short fingernails bit deeper into his palms. He could kill that loser for hurting his sister.

"The counseling has really been beneficial, but um…Mike didn't approve of my support group—wasn't a fan of being labeled abusive."

Zan pounded the counter, and she jumped.

"I'm sorry, Bay. I just—you don't deserve that." He pressed his hands flat against the cool marble. The last thing she needed was somebody else losing it. He reached a hand up, gingerly traced the evidence of his brother-in-law's rage on her face.

"I know." She offered a meek smile. "But it'll make the divorce proceedings easier on me. No one will make me stay with him now. Besides, if I can forgive him and walk away, then I want you to be able to let go of it too. I know it'll be hard, but—for me. Let's put it all behind us."

Forgive Mike? For all he'd done to her?

She stood taller, took his hand in hers. "What he did to me was not all right. Not even a little. I'm smart enough to get away. Forgiving him is for me. I won't carry around all that bitterness forever. Michael needs Jesus."

How long had it taken those Beistline people to snow her like this? She even spoke their language now. He bit down on his mouthful of irritation and wrapped his arms around Bailey's fragile frame. "How long are you staying?"

"I moved back in—indefinitely."

~*~

Zan baked in the sun out on the waterway as the breeze blew across his dad's boat. The waves rocked him gently, and he loved every minute of it. He sat on the back of the boat, allowed his toes to dip in and out of the water as he used his smartphone to see if Kasia was back in the States yet.

Nope. But she'd posted another batch of pictures. He'd enjoyed back-and-forth banter with her all summer—no deep discussions, no unearthing great mysteries—but he could ask her out when they got back to OSU for sure.

One picture had him hooked. The best she'd posted—three young girls with the darkest eyes he'd ever seen and a chubby toddler clearly reaching for Kasia. The kid knew, just like Zan had somehow. He thumbed in a comment.

This little muchacho thinks you're fabuloso. I'm fairly certain he's spot-on.

He stared out at the blank horizon. Bailey needed to meet Kasia. For a moment, he glanced back over his shoulder to where his sister sat reading. Her bruises had faded. A week could cover up a lot. He stood and moved past her.

Her peaceful expression confused him. How was peace like that possible when her whole world collapsed around her? She'd run away from her hellish marriage and moved home with no answers about the future. He ducked into the cabin, tossed his phone onto the couch.

Her gaze flicked up from the book, found Zan's as he sat on the driver's seat and studied her. "Something on your mind?"

"Tryin' to figure you out."

She laughed. "Good luck with that."

"No, seriously. You're so…different from the last time I saw you."

"Well, my whole life has changed. What do you expect?" She got up and joined him, let her toes tickle the surface of the water. "The last time we saw each other, I had just gotten rescued from a marriage like quicksand. It always seemed safer to do nothing than try to escape."

"So this church really helped?"

"It wasn't only the people. Jesus is the One who made the difference for me."

Jesus. Did He just make her feel safe? No, there had to be more to it. Like with Caleb. Her faith—whatever it was—was genuine.

Several questions came to mind, but he ignored them. "I'm gonna swim awhile."

She scooted back a foot or two and gave him a measuring look. "Go on, get in." As soon as he felt her foot on his back, he hollered, but it was too late. Where'd she get that kind of leverage?

The water stung his face before the cool, soothing darkness enveloped him. As he surfaced, her teasing laughter bounced off the surface of the water. He shook out his hair and wiped the water from his eyes with the heels of his hands. His impact had been less than graceful. Probably looked like a dying duck.

She was going to get it now. "Bailey?" he sang.

"Yeah?"

"Hope you feel like getting wet."

~*~

The Andean highlands were simply, powerfully different. Kasia could almost believe she'd stepped back in time.

A week before she was to fly back to the States, Mark and Patty asked if she'd like to travel to one of the highland *campesino* churches for an evening service. She'd wanted to spend some time among the subsistence farmers all along but felt ungrateful asking for more.

She jumped at the chance.

The deep ruts in the dirt road gave Kasia's body a beating. Still, the shock absorbers on the all-terrain vehicle held their own with the three-foot potholes. When they arrived, Kasia snapped photos of anything and everything she could without being rude.

She wondered what Grace and Lenka would think—whether Grace might want to use a few for the prayer calendar. And whether Forearms might actually be willing to sketch a few of them for her to frame. There was something more intimate about a pencil drawing.

That night, she joined the *campesinos* on the dirt floor of the small adobe building, stayed as still as possible. After several of the Peruvians shared testimonies or favorite Scripture passages, Mark asked Kasia to give her testimony.

She stood up and dusted off her pants, cast her gaze around the small, lantern-lit room. Her back ached from the drive, but it was nothing compared to the clamminess that shrouded her then. Every audience she'd ever stood before had been easier than this one. Combined. "Um, I'm a Polish-American. Different nations and cultures have always fascinated me."

Mark translated for her after each sentence.

"My dad is a pastor, and as soon as I started walking, I heard God loved me and created me with a work—a ministry—in mind. All my life, I've been trying to find out what that is."

Except she'd blown it. All she could do was pick up the pieces and survive now. Her well of words dried up, and tears were no more obliging. Pebbles rested in the dirt at her feet, and she kicked at one.

Someone cleared his throat, and she looked up.

Mark's inquiring expression prodded her on.

She swallowed and wet her lips. "One thing I've learned: God works best in me and through me when I put my own hopes and desires aside. When I make my life about serving others, I am truly blessed. Truly happy. And only then."

She heard several thank-yous and compliments as she took her seat once more, but she couldn't meet anyone's eyes. Her eyes burned.

But nothing came. She realized she hadn't cried in—she couldn't even think of the last time. Though there were moments of true joy, something in her heart had atrophied, withered from non-use. She had no idea what it was, but it ached.

The physical pain in her chest crippled her. She hung her head between her knees and breathed deeply.

If she couldn't pinpoint what hurt so deeply, she might dry up too.

No. That wasn't true. She knew how to experience joy. Just keep pouring herself out for others. Keep serving.

Keep busy.

She needed a strategy—every moment purposeful, no distractions. There were people in America she could bless too. Maybe she could take over the homework club. Jen graduated—had she already found someone to keep the club going at Heritage Arms?

Soft guitar music filtered through her thoughts, and she lifted her gaze from the dirt floor. Mark played, accompanying Patty, who sang a lilting melody. The mud building filled with song as everyone raised their voices, praising together.

When three children got up to sing "Amazing

Grace" to an old Quechuan melody, they captivated Kasia. The melody sounded wistful and ancient, and the girls' voices quavered, a guttural sound that reminded Kasia of an Apache ceremonial dance she'd once seen. Otherworldly.

As they closed in a final congregational song, Kasia sang along quietly in Polish, wondered how it would feel to be a part of the multitude at the feet of Jesus.

The crowd remained for fellowship when the service ended before going their separate ways. Kasia seized the opportunity to step outside into the quiet. Myriad stars hovered in profuse clusters, and a few areas were so hazy she wondered if she were looking at a distant galaxy. The cloudy expanse of the Milky Way across the sky was unmistakable.

Out here, the night hung like a curtain over the landscape, but she felt safe.

Truly, unequivocally safe. God was with her.

Footsteps approached, and she turned to see Patty. Just over the woman's shoulder, the moon peeked over the mountain ridge.

"It's beautiful, isn't it? Never gets old." Patty watched the moonrise with her for a moment. "We'll probably pack up and return to Los Baños in about ten minutes."

Patty left silently as Kasia stood and the moon slowly raised its head to peer at her over the silhouetted crest. She half believed that if she hiked to the summit, she could reach out and touch it.

Her heartache subsided. Out here, the darkness held none of her demons.

Only peace.

21

Zan relished the flavor of the spicy shawarma at their favorite local Mediterranean deli and bakery. Was happy to score lunch with Bailey too. Every minute he could spend with her before he moved to Oconee State was worth gold.

She smeared her forkful of fresh spinach through the puddle of house dressing at the bottom of her bowl and lanced a tomato, and glanced back up at him. "I realized how much mercy God had shown me."

"Bay. You're not a bad person."

"But I'm not perfect either."

"Of course not. Nobody is."

She wiped her mouth on the cloth napkin. "Do you believe there's a God?"

"I guess. I mean, I believe there's Someone out there who sort of oversees everything."

"And do you think He's pleased with the way we run things down here?"

"Doubt it. I seriously can't figure out why He doesn't just hit His all-powerful smite button and end it. I mean—to sit up there somewhere, just watch all the suffering and let it go on? You'd think He would intervene."

She nodded. "He did, Zan."

He focused on the last bite of his flatbread. God sure had let Bailey suffer for ages before He got her away from Mike.

"He could 'smite' us all—the whole world—any time He wanted. That's what would really be fair. But He'd rather offer us the relationship He created us for."

Caleb would freaking love that Zan was having this conversation again. "Jesus, right?"

Her eyes lit up, and he almost wanted to believe—just to make her happy.

Bailey's phone rang. She checked the number. "I've got to take this. It's about the administrative position at the financial firm."

"Sure, yeah."

She stood and walked through the archway into the shopping area. Zan finished his last bite of curried pork and washed it down with sweet tea.

She bounced back to the table. "I don't want the conversation to end here, but he can interview me at two. Can we come back to this?"

Zan smiled at her. "Bailey, if you can prove a God who would execute His own Son—for someone like Mike—is loving, you can wake me up in the middle of the night."

"Good. I'm going to call Mom and tell her about the interview."

"Go on out and call her. I'll get this." He reached into his back pocket and pulled out his wallet.

She picked up her purse. "Deal. And thanks." She gave him a quick peck on the top of his head.

She wound her way past the imported olives, grape leaves, curries, and freshly baked breads. She'd been through so much pain. He wished he could undo it.

When he stepped out into the sunlight and glanced around, her car door was open, but he couldn't spot her. He walked toward the corner and peered down East Bay Street. Had she walked to the back of the deli for some reason?

No. Bailey's purse and phone were on the front seat, and the phone was on. Something was wrong. He picked it up. "Hello?"

"Where's Bailey?" His mom's voice was filled with panic.

"I don't know. Her phone is—"

"Zan, go find her. *Now*. Michael was waiting outside for her. The police are on their way, but—"

Zan pitched the phone back onto the seat and raced toward the lot behind the deli. He found the closest alley. Nothing but empty crates, a dumpster, and the stench of rotten vegetables.

But then he heard muttered threats behind the dumpster.

"Michael, don't…"

The pain in his sister's voice ripped through him as he sprinted around the corner.

"Hey!" he shouted.

Mike straightened up and faced him. Blood streamed from the side of Bailey's mouth, and her arm was bent at a strange angle. She whimpered as she tried to stand behind her husband.

Mike spun back to her. "I told you to sit down!" His words slurred; he was a tower of drunken rage.

Before Zan could react, Mike kicked Bailey in the chest. Her body slammed into the corner of the dumpster, limp. And then everything tinted red.

Zan yanked Mike back by his collar and a handful of hair. As soon as the wife-beater was on his feet, Zan pummeled him—face, chest, stomach, face—anywhere his fists could make contact. Mike's nose crunched against Zan's knuckles. Mike swung at Zan a few times, but a bloody lip was the worst he could give. Zan was too fast, and Mike was too wasted.

When Mike collapsed in a heap, it was all Zan could do not to punt him across the alley. "Please. Stop." Garbled words and a broken voice stilled him and pulled his gaze to the tangled mat of hair and blood that framed Bailey's face.

Zan's eyes stung, and she blurred as he knelt beside her, held her face in his trembling hands. She shrank from his touch, and it nearly killed him. "Bailey, tell me you're all right."

She drew in labored breaths, her voice nothing more than a whisper. "Fine…" She gripped his hand, and the lack of strength in her sucked his hope like a vacuum. "Mom?" she tried.

"She said the police were—"

Feet pounded the pavement behind him as two officers approached. One of them surveyed the scene and swore right before he radioed for an ambulance.

Zan kissed his sister's temple and slumped beside her, hung his head. Why had he let her go outside without him? One mistake—one simple mistake—might cost him more than he could afford.

~*~

Adrenaline shot through Kasia until it was hard to breathe.

As the flight from Miami to Charlotte began its final descent, people repacked their carry-ons, women touched up makeup, flight attendants collected trash.

Kasia's heart hammered. The door opened, and she tasted the metallic tang of gate-side air pouring in. She raced up the Jetway, thanked the Lord once more that she'd gone through customs back in Miami.

Her family would be at the baggage claim, waiting. She almost ran.

And there they were.

Kasia slipped into Tatuś's embrace, smiled at Mama and Lenka over his shoulder. He grunted a laugh. "Squeezing the life out of me, Curly-Q." She pulled back and looked into his eyes.

"I missed you, Tatusiu."

He squinted as he studied her face. "It's good to have you back." He cupped the back of her head and planted a firm kiss on her temple.

"All right now. Let her mother get to her." Mama's eyes were all misty, and she sniffled her greeting into Kasia's ear while they hugged. "*Kocham cię,* girl. I hope it was what you needed."

Progress at least. "I love you too."

Lenka hugged her without a word. There was too much to tell, none of it airport conversation. Lenka's tear-filled eyes said enough.

Coming home felt better than she'd dared to hope.

Things could only get better from here.

Kasia sat in the back seat of Tatuś's four-door truck. She relished every bite of a grilled-chicken sandwich slathered with honey mustard and tried to field the barrage of questions coming at her rapid-fire but failed.

First-World America overwhelmed her more than she'd expected.

Lenka gestured to the shopping centers plastered with back-to-school-sale signs. "Maybe we should wait until you've taken all of this in."

How different from the humble simplicity of the Andes. "I can't wait to give you the gifts I brought,"

Kasia said. They passed a burger joint, the lot flooded with cars. "Monday night kids eat free," the sign read.

Monday. Small group.

Her parents spoke with hushed voices in the front.

"Um, would it be awful if I wanted to swing by Kyle's for small group?"

"He would *love* to see you!" Kasia almost couldn't handle Lenka's giddiness.

"You're not exhausted?" Mama asked.

"I am, but…it'll be next *week* before everyone's together again."

"Do you want to drop in or stay?" Tatuś asked.

"I don't know. I want to get home, but it's been so long, you know?"

"Well, I'd love to see what all the hype is about, so I'm up for staying. We'll leave it up to you, Curly-Q."

She chose to go, directed them to Finley Lake Apartments.

They parked, and Tatuś helped her down from the truck. Mama and Lenka walked to the sidewalk and waited for them.

Kasia scanned the area, relieved that Blake's car was missing. She noticed her movements mirrored her father's. He took her hand as they walked across the lot and up the steps.

Kasia heard the guitars and djembe from outside Kyle's apartment. The African drum was her favorite percussion instrument. Ever.

Her family stood back, motioned for her to open the door. As soon as she could see inside, Jayce spotted her.

"No way! Hold up, everybody!" His crazy laughter filled the room as he jumped up and met her. "Kasia Bernolak!" He pulled her into a one-armed hug, more like a headlock, and pointed at her. "Who knew 'bout this? Who knew she was comin' tonight?" Jayce's sideways grin looked about to slide off his face. "You, Kyle? Keepin' it quiet?"

"It was a last-minute decision," Kasia said. "I missed you guys."

Kyle stood, set his guitar down. "Come on in."

People moved legs and Bibles out of the way for her to get across the floor, and A.J. hopped up to give her a huge hug. She smelled like mangoes. Kasia's mind immediately flew to the half-dressed children playing beside Cajamarcan fruit stands.

"Where can two senior citizens sit and be out of the way?" Tatuś asked.

Almost as soon as they all got settled, Kyle squeezed her shoulder and winked a quiet welcome. "Why don't you share something? Anything."

"Oh, I could do that so much better next week, you know? Besides, tonight's not about me." She tugged a curl from the nape of her neck and twirled it around her finger.

"One thing. Sum it up so we can look forward to next week."

She chewed at her lip, weighed her options. "God showed me He can use anyone. And I realized I need to be less about myself, more about others."

Kyle nodded. "I think we all do." He fingered the edge of his guitar, his gaze distant.

Thunk. Jayce popped the body of his guitar with the heel of his hand. "Tune in next week for the real story."

People chuckled.

And then the room filled with music. She almost felt like grabbing a guitar herself. Kasia reveled in it.

For months, she'd missed these songs, these friends. But she wouldn't trade the experience of worshipping with Peruvians on a packed-dirt floor up in the mountains.

She opted out of the discussion, listened as the Bible study went on around her.

Closing her eyes for a moment, she lost herself in prayer.

Her eyes opened.

People stood around her, chatted and gathered their things to leave. She'd slept through the end of the meeting. Unbelievable.

"Somebody's exhausted." Kyle offered her a hand up.

He looked as if he had a lot to say, but Kasia lacked the energy for conversation. She smiled at him and quickly searched out her dad's face. When she met his gaze, his eyes crinkled in the loving smile that was all Tatuś. He held out an arm for her to find shelter under.

"You tired, Curly-Q?" His voice buzzed against her ear.

She yawned.

"We look forward to seeing you, A.J.," Tatuś said. "All of you."

Kasia nodded. In two weeks, she'd live down here again. Close to all of them.

She followed Tatuś out the door and glanced in the direction of Blake's window. The blinds moved. Kasia blinked.

The fatigue must be playing tricks on her.

22

Hollow.

Zan's heart was an empty fifty-five-gallon drum. He'd sat by Bailey's bedside for hours every day, willed her to give him any indication she'd be all right. Other than the slight rise and fall of her chest, she was still as stone. She could hear him in there, couldn't she?

They'd shaved the left side of her head for the emergency surgery to stop the bleeding in her brain, and the bandage around her head looked tight and miserable. Probably light-years better than the injured spine and broken jaw though. Part of him was thankful they'd decided on a medically induced coma. At least she wouldn't hurt herself trying to move around.

But he needed to hear her voice before he left Charleston. Zan spilled his fear and regret into her hospital room, but he found no peace. If he'd just been a few moments sooner…if he'd walked outside with her…

The blood-pressure cuff broke the silence with its occasional beep and whirr. He took her frail hand in his own and wished for a miracle.

His mom startled him as she rested her cool hand on his neck. "What time does check-in start?" She kneaded the taut muscles gently. It didn't help much.

"Three."

"Zan, it's already noon, and you've got at least a three-and-a-half hour drive up there. You need to get on the road."

"I know. I'm loaded up and all, but..." He studied the pattern in the floor tiles. "Doesn't feel right leaving. How long will she be like this?" he asked, his voice hoarse.

"Maybe another week. I think she's as comfortable as we can hope. But you've got a second chance at this new school, and Bailey wouldn't want you to throw it away on her account."

He nodded. "It's just hard to drive away—not saying goodbye."

"I'm sure she hears you." Li'l Mama's eyes filled with compassion. "She's stable, and the doctors said they'll start weaning her from the meds at the end of the week. I'll call you if anything changes."

He dipped his head, resigned. Bailey couldn't be in better hands. Michael was locked up for aggravated assault and battery, and for ignoring the restraining order.

Zan hoped he'd rot in prison. The attorney said although Mike could press charges against Zan for beating him senseless, it'd be foolish. One look at photos of her swollen, misshapen face would convince anyone Zan's defense was reasonable.

His eyes burned.

He stood and wrapped Li'l Mama in a hug. "She'll be fine. You get some rest too, all right?"

"I'll do my best."

He gave her a definitive nod and a smile as he turned to go. When the door closed behind him, he let the strong façade drop. Walking away from Bailey like this was the hardest thing he'd ever had to do.

~*~

Kasia woke with the sun. For the bulk of Wednesday morning, she recorded her homecoming thoughts and reread her journal. *Oj,* was she naïve when she got there.

The only things left to do were to order a bound copy of the photo calendar she and Grace had finished and drop off her signed housing contract.

As she burned her file to a disk, Mama knocked and peeked in. "Hey, I wondered if I could interest you in a break and some Lady Grey. Give us a chance to talk while Lenka and Dad aren't around."

"Sure." She slid her work into her backpack and hopped off the bed, followed her mom into the kitchen. The teacups were already on the table. Steam swirled up from the rims. Kasia pulled out a chair.

Mama poured some loose tea leaves into infusers and set them gently into the cups. "I really only have two questions. What was your favorite part? And what was the hardest part?"

Kasia chuckled. "Can I start with the hardest?" She tilted her head, sifted through her experiences.

"I guess—the biggest thing was…" She thought of the language barriers, of the effort it took to build trust with her students so the real ministry could happen outside of class, of the lying taxi drivers who treated her like a stupid *gringa* tourist.

But one thing stood out from all that.

Kasia set her gaze on Mama's face. "I'm still not sleeping."

"Still? Oh, Kasiu. You must be exhausted."

"I don't even want to try to sleep, because I always have nightmares."

Her mom's mouth quirked in compassion. "To do

with Blake?"

She nodded. "Sometimes. And other times, I feel like I'm being watched, hunted. It's like there's something lurking out there. Mama, what else can I do? It's not like I haven't asked God to take these from me. I've begged."

"I don't know, Kasiu. Is there something you're holding on to?"

"Like what?" It was hard to keep the irritation out of her voice. "I've asked God to forgive me. What else do I have to do?"

"It's not what you need to do, as much as…I don't know, love. But I'll pray the Lord shows you. And I'll listen any time you need me."

Her mom paused. "There's the matter of getting a protective order…"

Ah, the unwelcome reminder. "Mamusiu, how do we know if I need it? And they might not even let me. Blake hasn't done anything to me for months." In her mind, getting the order equaled letting Blake win.

"Your dad has already spoken to Sheriff Schilling about it. Since Blake was charged with assault—even if the charges were dropped—a temporary restraining order would most likely be granted immediately. Until the hearing can be scheduled."

"Can we wait and see if he's a bother? If he's not, I just want to drop it, you know?"

Her mom covered Kasia's hand with her own. "Your dad and I aren't convinced—"

Kasia sighed. "I know. But have you guys seen him? Talked to any of the Hamiltons? He's probably moved on—maybe even dating someone by now. I'd like to start the year in good faith. See what happens."

"I'll talk with your dad again, but no promises."

"Thank you." She sure wouldn't expect a miracle.

"Tell me about your favorite part."

"The stars. Definitely the stars. The further we got from civilization, the brighter they were. Matchless."

~*~

Zan sped north, one hand on the roll bar, one on the wheel. The mellow tunes of Jack Johnson weren't working their usual magic. All he could think was Bailey. Thankfully, there wasn't a whole lot of traffic, and he made good time. It only seemed like the hours dragged.

There hadn't been much opportunity for sleep in the last few days, what with bedside vigils, police reports, and legal pow-wows with the family attorney. He needed to get his brain in gear. In ten minutes, he had an impression to make, and he needed it to be stellar.

He smiled as he passed the store where he had his surprise run-in with Auburn. Would she be friendly this time around?

Back and forth on the serpentine road out of downtown Huntington and onto campus, he began to focus. He checked his map and found the lot closest to the field. Only ten minutes late—better than he'd expected. He parked the CJ and hopped out, tossed his duffel over his shoulder. Were they going to throw awhile or just get room assignments and practice later?

A few guys stood over by the dugout, so Zan made his way over. Nobody was dressed for practice. Markman lifted his clipboard in greeting. "Good to see you, Zan. How was your summer up north?"

"Beneficial, I think."

The other guys gave him nods of welcome and took off.

"I heard about Bailey, and I'm sorry. How is she?"

He gave a quick rundown.

"You ready to be here?"

"I can't lie. I'm pretty distracted, but I know I need to be all in—I want to."

"Give me what you can. We don't start until Monday morning at nine. It'll be all day every day until the semester starts though."

"Yes, sir. Thanks again for the opportunity. "

Coach picked up his duffel and stuck the clipboard under his arm. "Come on."

Neither spoke until they got to the lot.

"Zan."

He lifted his head.

"If you need me, I spend a lot of time at Bleacher Bums. You know the sports bar downtown?"

"Yeah, I've seen it."

"Come by if you need to talk."

Zan dipped his head and climbed into the driver's seat. "Thanks."

He drove toward the dorms and found a parking spot. Nobody much was back on campus yet. Maybe his roommate was still at home for the summer. At least he'd have time to sort out his junk without a whole lot of get-to-know-you.

He found the door to his dorm, hoisted his load of bags and packs, and hit the stairs. His footsteps echoed in the stairwell. No obvious signs of life here, just the stink of fresh paint in a confined space. By the time he made it to the end of the hallway, a headache whizzed toward him like a line drive. Priority number one: open the window.

He turned the key and shoved the door open.

Well, either his roommate didn't believe in packing up for breaks, or he'd been here for the summer session. Zan pulled in his stuff from the hallway, tossed his bag onto the empty bed, and let his gaze wander over his new home away from home. Not exactly spacious, but this guy had managed to make his side look decent. His bed was elevated, his desk underneath, and the wall dotted with photos. A guitar and some other instrument in its case sat in the corner underneath a picture of some old jazz trio and a poster of Fenway Park. One of the dressers had a coffeemaker and an iPod docking station—with a killer set of speakers mounted near the ceiling.

So, a musician. Probably all studious and reserved if his neatness was any indication. Zan could stand a little working music himself. The silence made his head ring, and Bailey's face was always there. He wished they'd dived right into baseball. Thirty-six hours to kill on his own.

He flipped open his phone and checked in with his mom—pretty much the same.

Fifteen minutes later, window open, Zan blared his music and started unpacking. Had he heard the door? He glanced over his shoulder as he tucked some shirts in a drawer.

And smiled. He'd been dead wrong about studious and reserved.

His roommate tossed a pair of drumsticks onto his desk and extended a hand. "Jayce McEwan, man. You here for ball?"

Zan gripped his hand and tried to place the accent. Probably Boston if he was a Sox fan. "Alexander Maddox, but Zan works. Practice starts first thing

Monday morning."

"Good deal. Ya got meetings and stuff tonight, or ya want the grand tour?" Jayce didn't look the invasive-questions type.

"Just campus, or were you thinking downtown—you don't have anything else going on?"

"Nah, whatever you want. My girl's workin', and I'm wide open."

The busier, the better. "Yeah, man. I'll take you up on that." The last thing he needed was to lie in bed and stare at the ceiling—and see only his sister's bruised and bandaged face.

The place Jayce took him smelled like one of those greasy dives that completely satisfied. Zan slid into the vinyl booth across from his roommate, hoped his stomach would begin to feel full again. The whole weight of Bailey's suffering bore down on him, and he studied the laminated menu. Didn't matter that he had no appetite.

Jayce drummed a distracting rhythm on the tabletop.

Zan tossed him a half-hearted smile. "I saw that Fenway poster in the room. You a fan?"

Jayce laughed and popped the edge of the table with decision. "Am I a fan? You ever meet anybody from Southie before?"

"Nope."

"Welp, back in the day, my old man used to take me and a few o' the boys up to every game we could afford. We shoveled walks all winter, washed cars all summer. Woulda cut grass if anybody in Southie had a yard. If we got the seats up on top of the Green Monster, we could go about once a month. It was rowdy, but watching Manny Ramirez hit a home run at me before he got run outta town was the sweetest part of my childhood. 'Zat answer your question?"

Zan grinned. "I guess it does. Did your dad ever get to see Roger Clemens play?"

"Yeah. He loves Clemens. Who're your boys?"

"Chicago."

"Fly the W, yeah? You a long-time fan or just proud of 'em for finally winning the World Series?"

Zan grinned. "Generations. My middle name's Banks. After Ernie."

"Respect." Jayce nodded.

Jayce made conversation easy. By the end of the night, Zan looked forward to the semester. It'd be good to have somebody around that he didn't have to spend every day and every road trip with. And there was some sort of unspoken agreement to stay out of touchy territory.

When they got back to the room, Jayce hopped in the shower. Zan took the opportunity to call and check in with his mom one more time. No change. He hadn't expected any different, but it still deflated him somehow. He slumped onto the bed, kicked off his shoes, pulled his shirt over his head. The day felt too long again.

He was almost under the covers when Jayce stepped out and set a folded pile of clothes on his chair.

"Goin' somewhere?"

"Church. 9:30 tomorrow mornin'." He plopped a worn-out Bible beside the clothes and grabbed a helmet from underneath his desk.

Was there some cosmic force putting Christians around Zan everywhere he went? Bailey. Caleb and Chen. Now Jayce. The fact that Jayce was into all this surprised him though.

Jayce lifted his chin. "Wanna go with?"

Zan narrowed his eyes at Jayce, studied him for a minute. "Well, I won't ride on the back of your bike with my arms around your waist."

Jayce smirked and set the helmet back under the desk. "No problem. You can drive."

Wait. Had he just agreed to go to church? At 9:30 in the morning? For a minute, he thought about telling Jayce he was just mouthing off. And then he saw Bailey's face the last time it looked whole and perfect—telling him how much she loved Jesus.

Jayce didn't stand there waiting for an answer. He did a few other things and then stood by the door, hand on the light switch. "You all right if I hit this now?"

"Yeah, man."

Jayce turned off the light, and Zan could hear him climbing into his bed.

In the darkness, with no eyes on him, Zan spoke up once more. "9:30."

Jayce shifted and the bed creaked. "Yup. And you don't have to dress up."

Zan turned over. Thank God.

23

When the soft light streamed through the blinds, Zan's bleary gaze wandered the room. It took a minute to think where he was.

And then he remembered he was going to church today for the first time in his life.

So. How was he supposed to do this? Not dress up, Jayce said. Shorts? Jeans? He stretched, swung his feet out of bed, actually curious. Sort of.

Maybe.

He climbed into the shower, let the water hit him straight in the face.

He wanted answers to those questions he'd asked Bailey. Wanted to know how forgiving a wife-beater could possibly be right. His heart welled up with emotion, and Zan didn't try to contain it.

He let his words fall with the stream of thudding water. "Hey, God? Why didn't You handle Bailey better? I was right there. You could've made her stay with me or something."

Zan pressed the heels of his hands into his eyes. He wanted to shout but couldn't stand the possibility of Jayce hearing him. "There's so much I don't get. I don't know if I can trust You, but—if You'll take care of Bay—I'll give You a shot. It's all I've got for now, but I'll give You that."

Jayce wasn't kidding about clothes. He sported a black U2 T-shirt with jeans, his wallet attached with a chain.

Zan chose a plaid shirt with khakis, rolled up the sleeves. "Do I need to take anything?"

"Nope."

If Jayce had any idea this was Zan's first time going to church, he didn't act surprised.

They swung into Java the Hutt for breakfast and coffee to go, and Zan choked down his bagel and cream cheese just as he climbed back behind the wheel.

When they pulled into the church lot, Zan's chest was tight. "Listen, Jayce. I've never…I don't really know why I'm here. I'm not a church guy, and I don't know what I believe about God. This is my first time."

Jayce cracked a wide grin. "I thought maybe. First time at any church?"

"Yeah."

"Good. Then you don't have anything to compare it to. Do you want a heads-up about how we do it here, or just want to ask if you've got a question?"

Zan's shoulders sagged with relief. "Just let me hang back and check it out. I'll ask if I need to."

"You got it." Jayce gave the bar a quick drumroll and ended with a thump. Then he jumped out.

They walked toward the doors, and Zan's heart raced so fast he thought maybe Jayce was using his drumsticks on his back. *Bailey, this is for you. I owe you this.* He knew somehow, as he crossed the threshold, there was no return. He couldn't stop until he had the answers he needed.

Jayce's face lit up. "Zan, this is my girl, A.J." Earthy. Artsy.

"Zan, huh? Interesting name." She shook his hand. Good grip.

"My first name's Alexander."

"Gotcha. I'm Aurelia Jane."

Zan grinned. An Aurelia she was *not*. She suited Jayce McEwan to a tee though. They all went in and found a spot near the back of the auditorium. Jayce excused himself for a sec to say hey to some people he claimed he hadn't seen in a while.

Zan studied the program he'd picked up, checked out all the activities. This church was busy.

"Jayce said you're from Charleston." A.J.'s blue eyes watched him closely.

"Yeah."

"Have you lived there long? I mean, your family."

"All my life. Why?"

"I just…know a guy who moved down there about five years ago."

"What's his name?"

"Felker. Stefan Felker." She studied him as she said the name.

"I mean, I may have heard of him, but I definitely haven't ever met him." Was she relieved?

"Only curious." Her eyes softened. "I've got to work this afternoon, but Jayce and I usually grab lunch together after church. You joining us?"

"I won't be in the way?"

"Course not. As long as you'll drop me off at the body shop after."

Zan's eyebrows shot up in surprise. "What kind of shop did you say?"

She probably knew exactly where his head was. "My Uncle Frankie owns a body shop. I used to just handle the office stuff, but I'm the airbrush girl now too."

He was impressed. He'd pegged her for artistic, but—with her confidence—he could believe she was serious. Besides, biker-looking guys obviously didn't faze her.

"Yeah, no problem. Lunch sounds good."

Jayce slid into the seat next to A.J. and put his arm around her, whispered in her ear. She glowed.

And Zan wondered when he'd run into Auburn.

~*~

"Zander, you wanna slide the pie my way? What'd you think of the service?" Jayce asked.

Zan took a bite of his thin-crust pizza and thought about it. He pushed the pizza toward the other end of the table, took a second to swallow. "Um, I hate to admit this, but I didn't really listen a whole lot. I sort of watched people, wondered about everybody's life. It was cool that they let me keep the Bible I used though. I've never heard of that."

Jayce laughed. "Yeah, some people don't bother gettin' one of their own—glad ya grabbed it."

"I've got a lot of questions, so I think it'll help."

A.J. used a fork and knife on her pizza like a debutante. Must be the Aurelia Jane in her. She speared a bite and turned his way. "So, what'd you think of the people you watched, then?"

"Pretty laid-back. I like that the preacher has a sense of humor. I guess I expected him to point out everything wrong with my life and make me feel like crud."

A.J. said, "Nah. I'm pretty sure most people at our church would admit they're not perfect. Everybody hurts somehow."

Now was a good time to have a mouthful of pizza. He wasn't ready to talk about pain.

A.J. eyed her watch. "I've got to clock in soon, guys."

"Want me to get a to-go box?" Zan asked.

"Sounds good."

Zan stood up and stretched, pulled out his wallet as he walked up to the counter. Lunch was on him. They'd been patient with his questions.

He followed A.J.'s directions into a part of Huntington he sure wouldn't want his girl living in. A.J.'s Uncle Frankie had better be scary. With big dogs.

He turned into a drive packed with old cars and cycles. A few were impressive, obviously done and ready to be picked up. But most looked junky. And the nearby businesses and clientele all seemed pretty sketchy from where Zan sat.

Jayce walked A.J. inside. While they were gone, Zan thought back to one thing he'd actually caught during church. By both His words and His actions, Jesus Christ claimed to be God. If someone went around today claiming they were God, they'd be locked up. Or killed by extremists.

Caleb had hit on the very same thing though. The guys who'd been closest to Jesus—saw Him executed and swore they saw Him alive again later—those men believed Him with absolute certainty. And two thousand years later, with only a book of stories to go on, Bailey did too.

Jayce jumped in beside him just as two burly bikers pulled into the small lot. "You mind drivin' back to the church so I can bring her car back out here? I know it's a lot of back and forth, but—I don't want her out here without a vehicle. Frankie's around now, but he won't be later tonight."

"Not a problem." Zan could respect a guy who

kept all his bases covered.

~*~

Kasia breathed in the scent of mountain laurel and a hint of late-summer wildflowers from the meadow. She propped herself up, the blanket softer than the hard ground. Worship in English and Tatuś's sermon that morning had warmed her heart, but when he prayed the benediction, the church members and all their questions about her trip flew at her like arrows.

On her way out of the building, she spotted Jim Schilling, the chairman of the deacons, at her dad's office door. The question was whether he played the role of deacon or county sheriff at the moment. Everybody needed to drop the subject of Blake Hamilton and let her move on once and for all.

After lunch, she'd craved space and taken off. A large white oak beckoned her to enjoy its shade near the trail. No sooner than she'd pulled out Tatuś's old blanket and stretched out on it, sleep had taken her.

The nap had been relatively peaceful for once. She reached over and checked her phone. Jen had replied.

Oh. She'd already gotten two underclassmen to commit to running the Heritage Arms club. Well, Kasia wouldn't give up that easily. There were other neighborhoods. She grabbed her notebook, jotted down a few complexes where she might be able to start an after-school club. She'd have to call around tomorrow to gauge interest.

A twig snapped behind her. She sat up and spun around in one move.

"I didn't mean to scare you," Tatuś said.

Her shoulders sagged. "Just surprised me, that's

all." She patted the blanket beside her. "Come sit by me and enjoy the view for a minute."

He breathed a creaking sigh as he squatted next to her and eased himself down. "I thought you'd worn holes in this old rag long ago." His fingertip traced one of the lines on the plaid blanket. "I'm sure it had a few in it when I gave it to you, in fact."

"Even if it looked like a net, I'd still love it."

His head bobbed in a silent chuckle.

"Were you just out for a walk?"

"No, I thought you and I could chat."

Her heart stuttered. "'Bout what?"

He picked up her list of Huntington neighborhoods close to school. "What's this?"

"Some possible places for me to start up a neighborhood ministry. I need to make a difference, even back in the U.S."

"What kind of ministry?"

"I thought maybe an after-school club. Help the kids with homework, give them something constructive to do."

He held the list up, reading over it. "That'd fit you tongue in groove, but some of these neighborhoods are…"

"Neighborhoods that need something like this the most."

He nodded and rested his arms on his knees. "I understand. But you don't have to climb into a woodstove to prove you can handle fire. I'd like you to cross these two off the list." He set it down, tapped the paper. "Do you plan to do this alone?"

"No, sir. I'll ask for help."

"I want you to have a partner with you all the time. If you can't find somebody to commit to it all week, maybe your friends would take turns."

What was she, a project? "I can do it, Dad."

"I believe you. If you didn't have Blake to worry about on top of this, I could—"

"I can't let him win. I won't hide like last year. I'm happier when I do something for others."

"And I won't squelch that for a minute, Kasiu, but we don't need to be foolish either. Sheriff Schilling said to come by and fill out the paperwork for the protective order tomorrow morning."

Her fist pounded the blanket—on the side away from him. "I hate that he knows everything. How am I supposed to 'press on' if church people are keeping tabs on me?"

"That's not fair, and you know it. Jim and I are working together for your protection."

She set her hand on top of her dad's strong one. "It's been three months since anything happened, and he didn't even mean to hurt me when he hit the window. I saw his eyes, Tatusiu. He looked shocked and sorry." She wouldn't add how briefly those emotions had registered. "Would you let me go back to school and truly put all this behind me? Blake's over me. He must be. *Na pewno.*"

"There's nothing 'for sure' about that boy." He flipped his hand over and held her hand in his, stroked the back of it with his thumb.

"What about me? Do you trust me?" She wished the question back a thousand times before he answered. A no would break her; a yes would remind her of how far she'd fallen.

His thumb stilled.

She peeked in his direction. His jaw knotted so hard she could see it in his temple. Why did she have to put him through so much?

"Kasiu, can you be honest with an old man?"

"Yes." Maybe.

"It is my job—my heart—to keep you safe. It's what dads do. You know that's all I'm after, right?"

She dipped her head.

"Do you think Blake is dangerous?"

"No, sir. I think he was hurting—and I caused it. Can you imagine being dumped for no good reason?"

He snapped his head in her direction. "How is following God not a good reason?"

"You know what I mean. To him it wasn't."

"That communicates volumes." He let go of her hand.

"Tatusiu? I'm positive this has all gone away. It has for me. I don't love him. I don't miss him. I'm focused on other things. He probably is too."

Her dad looked as if he were in physical pain. "It's not a wise move."

"For me, Tatusiu. Let me have the chance to show you I can walk away from him and be fine. Let me show you."

He stood and fisted his hands.

Kasia didn't know whether to stand or not. "Besides, we shouldn't make trouble. If Blake has moved on, a restraining order all of a sudden would only stoke the fire again."

His jaw knotted, and she wished she weren't the source of such stress.

"God, don't let me live to regret this one." He looked down at her. "I will tell Sheriff Schilling we'll wait and see. But if Blake—"

"I refuse to live in fear. I can't let him win, plain and simple. I'll be fine. Promise."

He shook his head. "I hope it's plain and simple." He left her sitting there.

24

Kasia pulled into Frankie's at three o'clock and found a space between a classic Mustang and an El Camino.The El Camino was in better shape. Pricey cars filled the lot today, but bars on the windows and razor wire on top of the security gate sang a different song. Kasia offered up a quick prayer of thanksgiving that A.J. had decided to move onto campus this semester.

Her cell phone rang. Kasia locked the doors and stayed in the car to answer it. *Kyle Compton.* "Hey, Kyle."

"You readjusting to life back in the States?"

"Getting there. America in the throes of New School Year is certainly different."

"I bet. When do you think we might be able to hang out? I'd love to see you and hear more about Peru."

But not a date, right? "How is it I've been in the country for one week, and my schedule has already gotten totally slammed?"

"Are you too busy?"

"A.J. and I move into our apartment tomorrow, and I plan to start a new after-school club over at the Mill. I have a meeting with Mrs. Anderson, the director, today, and then I'll do all the prep between now and next week. I want to start in mid-September."

"Before or after homecoming?"

"Whatever Mrs. Anderson wants. The sooner the

better for me. Why?"

"You need volunteers? I've got most afternoons free, but until homecoming, I've got all the legwork for the concert. Trying to nail down a few more local bands for the lineup. You'll be there, right?"

She hadn't thought that far ahead. "No idea, but it sounds cool. I'm trying to focus on one thing at a time. What did you say about volunteers?" Tatuś would *not* want her to pass up this offer. Besides, the center director had asked that there be at least two adults present at all times. "It's every weekday afternoon. All semester."

"I can't do Tuesdays, but sign me up for the rest. We can catch up while we hang with the kids."

"Excellent. How about we catch up before the kids get there and after they leave?"

She could hear the laughter in his voice. "You don't play around, do you? I promise I'll do whatever you say."

"I'll hold you to that."

"So, what time's the appointment with the director?" he asked.

Kyle was not easy to deter this afternoon. "Six."

"I'd love to join you, see the center and stuff. Would you mind?"

She tried not to sigh. "It would probably be wise for you to meet Mrs. Anderson too."

"You want to swing by my place on your way?"

Did she want to voluntarily drive into Blake Hamilton's apartment complex and sit in the lot? "Meet me at OSU. I'll be over there with A.J., signing the housing contract. I could meet you at the bagel shop—around quarter till?"

"Sounds perfect. I'll see you then."

~*~

A.J. met Kasia at the door. "Welcome to my lair."

"Rough neighborhood."

"No kidding, but nobody's fool enough to mess with my uncle."

A gruff laugh sounded behind her. Kasia tried to see into the darkness.

"Come on inside. Your eyes'll adjust. Here's Frankie himself."

Kasia followed A.J. over toward an antique pickup truck painted with flames. A muscle-bound guy with a salt-and-pepper ponytail inspected the work. "Nice job, A.J. Looks like you've been doing this for years."

"Wait," Kasia said. "You painted this?"

A.J. grinned. "Gotta earn my keep."

Frankie wiped his hands on a cloth. "So you're the infamous Kasia Bernolak."

She shook his hand. "I try to lay low."

"A.J.'s spreading her wings, leaving this joint. Can't say it bothers me to see her get out of here though. You two move in when?"

"Tomorrow, I think."

"You need some of my boys, A.J.? To help you get everything in?"

She shook her head. "Jayce signed his new roommate up for the heavy lifting."

Frankie laughed. "All right. Don't forget the contract. Kasia, make sure she behaves."

"Gotcha."

A.J. turned Kasia around and pointed toward steps in the back. "I need to run up to my room and grab my stuff."

At the top of the steps, they paused on a small landing with two doors, and A.J. pulled out her keys. She unlocked the door on the left and Kasia followed her into a tiny studio apartment. One wall was yellow, one orange, and one gray. The front wall—the only one with a window—must have been A.J.'s easel. Every inch of it was covered with designs, some small and detailed, some painted over. Caricatures of Jayce and Frankie floated in the middle of the artistic mayhem, along with a few faces Kasia had never seen. One, a young girl, drew Kasia's attention. Painstakingly detailed, she stared off toward the gray wall, arms crossed in apparent displeasure.

"That's my sister."

"Oh?"

"Don't ask. Hey, what furniture do you want to take with? We can use any of this we want. It's all mine."

"How about all of it? I have bedroom stuff and a bookcase. I'm sure I can get a few other things if we need them, but I love your style."

"I had to make it be my home."

Kasia waited a beat to see if A.J. would unpack her statement, but she busied herself, tossed a few last-minute items in a box on the bed.

"What's Frankie's story? How'd he get into body work and all?"

A.J. grabbed her bag and stopped by the fridge to get two waters, tossed one over. "My father and Frankie used to be a lot alike."

"Who's older?" Kasia followed A.J. down the steps.

"Uncle Frankie. He was the heir, the favored son. All that."

"The heir?"

"Hang on a sec till we're outside." She jogged over to the counter and slipped a manila envelope into her bag.

Once they were in the car, A.J. continued. "My grandparents were loaded. But Uncle François became the world's biggest letdown and got into racing."

"François, huh? Does he still race?" Kasia drove toward campus.

"Nope. Quit a long time ago. He lost everything in a bet. That's how he got into body work. Started working in a place that fronted for an illegal chop shop and made his way up through the ranks."

"As in, he helped run it?"

"Eventually. People knew not to mess with him either. He was one bad dude."

"I can see vestiges of the scary," Kasia said.

A.J. nodded with a smile. "But then Aunt Dahlia got his attention."

"You've never mentioned her."

"She passed away the year before I moved down here, but her last request was that Frankie quit anything that could be interpreted as crime. So he did."

"Wow."

"I'm real proud of him." A.J. offered Kasia a piece of gum. "He could make loads more money in a better part of town, but he didn't want to walk away from all his connections. He's strictly legal now, but those rich thugs pay him well when they want something legit."

"Do you think he misses his old life?"

"I don't know."

"When did you move in with him?" Kasia glanced over in time to see A.J.'s shoulders tense up. She'd crossed into forbidden territory.

"The summer after eleventh grade. Tell me more about Peru."

~*~

Conversation buzzed around Zan, bounced off the walls of the locker room as if it had nowhere better to go. Zan ignored it and instead checked his phone. He *needed* some news about Bailey.

He towel dried his hair and tugged on his clean shirt. Practice hadn't provided enough distraction today.

Markman caught his eye as he hiked his foot onto the bench and tied his shoes.

The man waved him into his office. "You're as unfocused as I've ever seen you, Zan."

"I'm sorry." Zan closed the door behind him. "Bailey's still in a coma, and Mom's radio silent—or there's nothing worth hearing. I've got a court date soon—to testify against Mike."

"When?"

"Two weeks from now. Just for a couple days. My testimony's at the end of the trial. Do I need to have it recorded or something?"

"Sit down a minute."

Zan sat, immediately as uncomfortable as he'd been in his former coach's office.

"Let me level with you, Zan. I understand a lot's weighing on you here, but you need to find an outlet for it. Or let baseball be your outlet. When you step between the lines, you've got to be one-hundred percent, or the guys who do give it everything will play right over you. Competition is high, and I need to field the best team I can. I pulled quite a few strings to get you here, and both our reputations are on the line. Can you give me one-hundred percent on the field?"

"Yes, sir. Everything I've got left."

Coach nodded. "Since it's fall and we alternate days on the field with days in the gym, I can let you go for three days—but no more. If you think they'll need you longer, you'll need to make arrangements for your testimony. And when you're here, I want you completely here. Understand?"

"Yes, sir. And…thanks."

"Any time. And my offer still stands. Or you can call me on my cell." He scrawled a number on an index card and handed it to Zan.

Zan stepped out into the rowdy locker room and shouldered his duffel. He needed to take his time back to the dorm. Clear his head for real.

He pulled out his phone as he left.

A new post from Kasia. *Back home and missing Peru already.*

Home. Awesome.

~*~

A.J. said goodbye to Kasia as she entered the art building. She needed some studio time to finish a project, and then she had plans with Jayce. Kasia had about twenty minutes to occupy until Kyle showed up. The campus seemed deserted but peaceful. Next week, it would be a different world.

Kasia wandered toward the lake, took in the sights and sounds. Everything was so alive. Birds dive-bombed the lake for food. A woodpecker drilled for insects somewhere nearby.

She paused to breathe in some fresh perspective,

closed her eyes. *Thank You, Lord, for this moment of solit—*

"Peru treated you well." The familiar voice was a claw against slate. Blake.

She refused to look in his direction.

"Listen," he murmured. "The last couple months have been good for me too. I had a lot of time to think—away from you. You were right. We needed that."

She eyed her watch and started walking, headed in the direction of Westing Hall, where the public-safety department was located, just in case.

He reached for her. "Wait!" He grasped her elbow. "Please?" he added softly. "I…I need to say I'm sorry. I never meant to scare you before. I was hurt. I just didn't understand."

So she'd been right. She turned to face him. "But you understand now, right? I'm not—"

His nostrils flared, and she bit her tongue. But instead of losing it, Blake drew in a measured breath, and so she wavered. Maybe she should hear him out.

"I do understand, now. It overwhelmed you, didn't it?"

She nodded.

"If we slowed down, if we spent time together, really got to know each other again. I mean, I know you've changed. I have too—"

"No."

He blinked, his face an expressionless mask.

"While I agree I was overwhelmed, I'm not interested in starting over. I'm in a different place now. Very different."

A scowl marred his face. "What is that supposed to mean? You're better than me?"

She wiped his spit off her cheek. "That's not what I'm saying—"

He swore, and she spun away. His fingers, like talons in her elbow, held her in place.

"I'm sick of your mouth," he hissed. "Sick of you putting me off. You're so full of yourself!" He jerked her to face him, but she would not give him the satisfaction.

She turned her head away.

And saw Forearms walking past Addison Science Complex.

He might not even recognize her—but he was her only option. "Zan! There you are!"

His brow creased in confusion, and he stopped.

Blake pressed his face against her ear and filled it with vulgarity and humiliation. The fight left her, and she hung her head. He shoved her away.

"I'm glad you caught me." Zan's words were gentle, but his voice sounded tense to her. He closed the distance between them, draped an arm around her shoulders, pulled her into a strong hug.

Blake stalked off.

The arms around her were all warmth and safety. She remained there, her cheek against Zan's firm shoulder, and the tension ebbed from her body.

25

Zan stood, rooted to the ground, Kasia pressed against him. When her hands fisted in the fabric of his T-shirt, he sucked in a breath. She smelled like fresh apples, and dark copper curls hung over his hands. He resisted the urge to see how soft they were. Instead, he prayed for wisdom.

God, if You're seriously there, now would be a good time to help.

It had only taken a second for the desperation in her eyes to hit home before he'd rushed over, but in the time it took to get to her side, the loser had whispered something that had made her face crumple in pain. Zan's heart swelled with rage.

When the guy had the audacity to shove her away like so much trash, Zan almost spun him around and knocked his teeth out. No one should be treated like that.

And this wasn't just anyone. This was Kasia.

She was the important one right now. His arms tightened protectively, and she trembled. He ached to find a way to make her smile again. This was not how he saw their first reunion going down.

She cleared her throat softly, released her grip on his shirt. He let her go. As she stepped back, she tucked a long wavy strand of hair behind her ear.

Zan didn't think it'd be wise to speak first. He was angry, and he wanted to tread carefully, to be what she needed in that moment.

She wet her lips. "Thanks," she finally said. She avoided his eyes.

That wouldn't do at all. He bent his knees and ducked his head to eye level.

Her gaze lifted to meet his, so he spoke. "You all right?"

She checked her watch. "I need to head toward the bagel place."

"Perfect. I'll walk you." He didn't want to push her too much, but he had to know she was all right. He matched her pace, and they strolled back toward the center of campus. "Are you honestly all right?"

She shrugged.

"Was that the guy who hammered a nail in your tire?"

She blew out a sigh. This was clearly not a favorite topic. "He's so unpredictable, you know?"

Zan scratched his chin. He could certainly guess.

"We dated—were engaged, actually."

Whoa. Not what he expected to hear. It explained a lot though. The guy knew her well enough to wound her where it hurt the most.

"With Blake, I was…a different person. Somebody I didn't like. So, I broke it off last spring. Right after you and I met." She shoved her hands in her pockets. "I don't trust him. But I don't think he's really dangerous."

Debatable. "I don't trust him either."

She huffed a laugh, endeared herself to him even further. "I get that a lot."

He jogged a few steps ahead and opened the door to the bagel place. She stepped in.

"So, I've got to ask. Are you a coffee drinker? I

hope you're just not a fan of sweet tea. It's too humbling to think you might be stonewalling me."

She smiled and walked toward a table. "I don't need anything."

"Water, maybe?"

"Do they have hot tea in the summer?"

"Serious?"

Her expression said "utterly."

"I'll ask."

~*~

Kasia took off her messenger bag, hung it over the back of her chair, and sat down. *Deep breath.* She needed to get off the emotional roller coaster.

Joy. Her day had been going perfectly. And then…

Frustration.

Fear.

Embarrassment.

Relief.

Swoon. What?

A little. Not really.

She would not be fooled by a sweet accent and a charming smile. She'd been down that road before. Besides, if she could pick the one person she least wanted to have to rely on, it would be Alexander Maddox. He was entirely too full of himself.

She flicked a crumb off the table. And that other crumb.

Today was supposed to be so uneventful.

Blake always interfered. And she was furious with her gullibility—again. Had she really thought he was capable of sincerely apologizing, changing? Really almost considered his hoard of lies?

She turned toward the counter and inspected Zan a little more closely. A backpack slung over one shoulder, he leaned on the arm closest to her, placing his order. At least five sinewy muscles ran the length of his arm. She spun her head and focused on whatever was outside the window. A bush.

Very green.

"Hot tea in August. And they didn't even ask for credentials."

She forced her gaze to his face and was met with a smile like sunshine.

"They had fresh-baked muffins today too, so I got one of those. If you don't want it, I'll—"

"What kind?"

"Apple cinnamon."

She plucked the bag from his hand and opened it, inhaled the sweet aroma, and pulled a muffin out. "They're still hot."

"Taken out of the oven about five minutes ago."

"Yum." She broke a little of the crusty top off and popped it into her mouth. It melted into sweetness. "Thank you."

"My pleasure." He took another out of the bag and peeled off the paper cup, wiped the stray crumbs off the table, and dropped them in the bag.

Mamusia would appreciate that. "Listen, if you need to be somewhere, I'm fine here."

"Nah, I just finished ball practice, so I'm done for the night. I can stay awhile." He stuck his fingers in his hair, made it all disheveled. "Are you meeting someone?"

"Yes. We've got an appointment with the director of a multi-housing complex. I'm starting an after-school club over at the Mill. Had to do something to get my mind off myself, you know?"

"I understand needing distractions." Something about him had changed. He'd never seemed this easy to talk to.

The door opened, and Kyle strode in. His smile faded as soon as he saw she wasn't alone.

Forearms stood up and extended a hand. "I'm Zan."

"Kyle." He grabbed a chair from another table and scraped it across the tile so it faced Zan. Right beside her.

Kyle stretched his arm across the back of her chair, not around her, but close enough. "Baseball player, right? We saw you at the store last spring. Did you have a good summer?"

"It was all right." Zan sat back down.

Kasia scooted her seat a few inches away from Kyle, toward the window, turned it slightly so she could see both guys—and not be claimed by either.

Kyle reached into his pocket and set his keys on the table. He leaned toward her. "Are you about ready to leave?" he asked softly. "I thought maybe we could have dinner afterwards."

Before she could answer, Zan stood. "I'll see y'all later." He picked up his backpack and slung it over his shoulder. "Have a good meeting."

Kasia bit the inside of her cheek. This wasn't how she saw the conversation ending. Yes, they had to leave, but she hadn't needed Kyle to waltz in and wrap up for her.

"It was nice to talk to you, Kasia. I'll see you around."

"You too. I'm sorry—"

He smiled kindly and turned to go.

She stood and reached for her messenger bag. *Oh, Kyle is holding it out. How chivalrous.* She took it from him and slipped it across her shoulder. Every single thing Kyle had just done irked her.

She felt like the rope in a tug-of-war match.

Except Zan wasn't pulling.

And that disappointed her more than she cared to admit.

~*~

Zan tossed his pack onto his bed.

"Hey, man." Jayce spun on his stool. "Tough practice?"

"You could say that."

"Your ma called."

Zan's heart raced. "She say anything?"

"Just to give her a call when you get in."

Zan pulled a water from the mini-fridge and picked up his cell. Should he go outside? He didn't want to have this conversation with an audience. Jayce must've read his mind, because as Zan turned around, his roommate stood at the door, helmet in hand.

"I'm out, all right? The road's callin'."

"Yeah, cool. See you later."

"A.J. and I are gonna go see a movie with some friends around nine. You game?"

"Maybe. Ask me at eight."

Jayce gave him a nod and shut the door on his way out. Zan speed-dialed his mom.

She answered, breathless. "Zan?"

"Mom? Is she awake?"

"Yeah, sugar. And she asked for you."

Tears brimmed as Zan slumped onto the bed. "She

can talk?"

"Well..." His mom sniffled. "She uses a lot of body language to get it across. Her jaw is wired closed for a few more weeks, but she's real good at notes."

Zan chuckled through his tears. "Tell her I love her."

"Zan loves you, baby," his mom said away from the phone. He heard some shuffling. "She says she knows. She saw you fight for her."

Zan's heart swelled about halfway, until his conscience reminded him that if he'd stayed with her, he wouldn't have had to protect her. "Mom? Can you hold the phone to her ear for a second?"

"Sure. One sec." More shuffling. "Zan, sugar?" she called. "She's there."

"Bay?"

It was quiet. Then she cleared her throat.

"Listen, I just—I want to tell you I'm sorry. I shouldn't have let you go outside alone. I should've—"

"M-mn." Was that a no? More emphatic now, she said, "Hm-*nn*." Three hundred miles away, jaw wired shut, his sister was telling him to shut up. Part of him wanted to laugh. The other part still cried.

His mom called out that Bailey was writing. Then she said, close to the phone, "She says thank you for saving her life, and all you're allowed to say back is 'You're welcome.'"

It took him a minute, but he made himself say it. For her. "Hey, I went to church on Sunday."

A high-pitched squeal of either disbelief or delight sounded through the phone.

"I won't say I believed it all, but I went. And I'm asking some of my questions up here, since you won't be able to chat for a while. I hope that's cool."

"M-hm."

Once he was off the phone, he left a note on Jayce's desk with his cell number. For the first time in a while, Zan had a raging appetite. He grabbed his sketchpad and pencils and threw them in his pack. He'd go to the greasy joint Jayce took him to the first night. He could sit there for hours, and no one would bother him.

Which was what he needed. Food, anonymity, and a blank canvas.

~*~

As the side door opened, Kasia inhaled the spicy aroma of *bigos*—a Polish favorite made with mostly *kiełbasa* and cabbage. Her stomach growled as she watched her mom set a loaf of fresh-baked bread on the table.

"Perfect timing. It's still warm," Mama said.

What were the odds of fresh-from-the-oven treats twice in one day? Kasia smiled, at least as much at the memory of the warm muffin as at her mom. She kissed Mama on the cheek and made her way down the hall to set down her bag. Her mind swelled with unbidden images of Zan coming to her rescue—he'd searched her eyes, delivered her hot tea, asked questions—all sincerity.

Those eyes. Like the blue of Peruvian dusk. She felt like if she hung around for a while, she might get to see the stars again.

She wanted to.

Voices converged in the kitchen. She needed to get back in there. Kasia jogged down the long hallway and joined her family for dinner.

"And how was your day?" Mama set fresh butter

on the table.

"Busy, busy. But good. Signed the contract. We can move in after ten. Met A.J.'s Uncle Frankie, had my appointment with Mrs. Anderson at the Mill, toured the center. Kyle went with me."

Lenka snapped to. Sweet. She would avoid discussing Zan.

"Nice of him," Tatuś said as he poured water.

"He's actually volunteered to help out four afternoons a week."

"My goodness." Mama offered Kasia the bread plate.

They prayed, and then Lenka tossed her a napkin. "You'll love working with Kyle."

"I'm sure. He met a few of the kids this afternoon and played a little pickup basketball before we left. They were killing him, but he took it well."

Her dad laughed quietly as he chewed.

"I can't imagine little kids beating him that badly," Lenka said.

Kasia shrugged and reached for the butter. "It may have been a bit exaggerated, but from what I saw, he was awful." She smiled at the mental image.

"He just let them win."

Kasia smiled. "Maybe." She was thankful no one asked if she'd seen Blake on her first day out alone.

26

Zan sat in the back-corner booth, sketched Bailey as he wanted to remember her. Her sun-warmed smile on the back of the boat, peaceful, content. He drew until his meal came and then put his pad and pencils away. If he got grease on the drawing, he'd kick himself.

He wolfed down the burger and wiped his hands. His head was packed—not just with thoughts of Bailey.

This idea of a "loving God" wasn't easy to reconcile with what he'd seen happen to his sister. He snagged another napkin, began to write. His thoughts rambled and his hand cramped, but by the time his cell rang, he'd filled three napkins front and back.

"It's eight. Feel like a movie, or no?" Jayce asked.

"Sure. Meet me at the room in a few?"

"Yup. I'm here. I'll wait for ya."

Zan paid and packed the napkins in his bag. They'd make interesting reading later. He felt like he was actually getting somewhere.

Ten minutes later, he jogged up the stairs. Jayce had the music cranked up, so Zan could hear it in the hall. When Zan opened the door, Jayce stood beside his loft, white drumsticks in hand, drumming out the beat on his mattress...and the ladder, and the wall. The corner of the room had become his drum set.

Zan let the door close with a thud. Jayce turned and grinned. He tossed his drumsticks on the bed and turned down the music. "Glad you're gonna go with us."

Zan's cell buzzed in his pocket, and he pulled it out. *Tasha.* Why was she calling? He silenced his phone and set it on the dresser. "Girl I used to date."

"So ya don't answer."

"We knew each other in Charleston—different high schools but same social circles. After graduation, we ran into each other at a party, and I couldn't say no. We had one real intense summer, both left for school, and it was over. That fast."

"You miss her?"

"Not. At. All. I might've last year, but—I don't know." He gazed up at the ceiling. "Sometimes I'm surprised at myself when I think about who I was. I'm just—different somehow. Not sure why."

"Interesting."

"What?" McEwan shouldn't just analyze his life.

"Listen, ah, I'm not about makin' you uncomfortable," Jayce said. "Just sounds like you've had some heavy things goin' on this year. That'll change somebody."

How did he know?

Jayce answered the unvoiced question. "You seemed a little keyed up when your ma called." Jayce knocked on the side of his mattress. "Know I'm prayin' for ya about it. Whatever it is."

Oddly, that opened the floodgates. Friends who were honestly interested in him—more than his errors in the last game, more than splitting a case of brews—were new to him.

"My sister, Bailey, woke up from a medically induced coma this afternoon. Her ex-husband put her there, because I got to her too late."

Jayce's eyes burned with intensity. He wiped his mouth with a fist. "What happened? He beat her?"

"Yeah."

Jayce sniffed and Zan eyed his hand—clenched and unclenched. Repeat. It obviously cost Jayce some effort to speak calmly. "How'd it go down?"

"She stepped out of a café while I paid, and he was waiting for her. Pulled her into an alley and let loose."

Jayce turned his back on Zan and thrust his fists at his desk. Zan stood quietly, wondered what was up. Finally, Jayce spoke. "Sorry. Let's just say I can relate." He faced Zan again, arms crossed over his chest. "What'd you do?"

"I went after her. Ran up and saw him punching and kicking the life out of her, and I lost it. Snapped. Pulverized him. Couldn't even see straight, man. I don't know what I might've done to him if Bay's voice hadn't broken through."

"She stopped you?" Jayce asked, eyebrow quirked.

"This weak little voice..." Zan's eyes stung. "She said, 'Please. Stop.' What could I do? I left him in a heap and held on to Bailey until the cops got there. I was afraid she wouldn't make it."

Jayce's gaze dropped. He spoke softly. "She's fine though?"

"Alive. Awake. But who knows if she'll ever get out of her wheelchair? I testify against the scum in two weeks."

Jayce nodded. Glanced at the ink on his arm. "Justice. He'll get what's coming to him. One way or another." His phone rang.

While Jayce talked, Zan wondered about that statement.

Jayce set the phone down and said, "A.J.'s raggin'

on me. Says I make everybody late. How 'bout that movie?"

Zan laughed humorlessly and grabbed his jacket. "Let's go."

~*~

"Are you cool with A.J. driving out to Frankie's alone this late?" Zan asked. They'd gotten out of the movie around midnight.

Jayce sat on the chair by the door to take his boots off. He looked up. "No, but it's the last night."

"You worry about her out there?"

"I try not to, but it's hard. I mean, I know she's careful and whatnot, but I don't trust all the shady characters. Gotta trust her though. And I gotta trust God with her."

Zan grabbed the baseball off his dresser and tossed it into the air, caught it as he talked. "That's not a sure thing, man. God lets good people get hurt."

"He allows it, yeah. But He can use it too. God can bring wholeness to anyone. Your sister, Zan. God can bring her back even stronger."

"Why does He allow people to suffer at all though?"

Jayce propped his arms on his knees. "I think you got the wrong question, Zander."

"What do you mean?" Toss, catch, toss, catch.

"The way God made everything in the beginning—it was perfect. People did the one thing He asked 'em not to, though, and sin hit the world like a wrecking ball. Now everybody hurts everybody else. People are all messed up, lookin' out for number one, oblivious to the pain right next to 'em. Think about it.

The right question is why doesn't God just let us all go to hell where we belong? Why did He do what He did to make a way out?"

Zan held the ball and sat on his bed.

"I mean, seriously. He's perfect. Holy. Won't tolerate sin in His presence, and every one of us deserves hell. But He sent Jesus—the part of Himself who could walk among us, suffer like us—to earth. Jesus shook things up and laid His own life on the line—willingly. Why do that?"

Zan pointed around the ball. "That right there. Why would God kill His own Son?"

"There was no other way, man. It's who He is. He's all love, completely just, and crazy merciful. Those parts of His character are all intertwined. Ya don't get one without the others. So, His justice was satisfied with Christ's death, and His heart of love is satisfied when people take Him up on His offer. The mercy part is what blows me away—that it's for somebody like me. But I'm not gonna turn my back on it, ya know?"

"Even if He allows you or the people you love to suffer." Zan tossed Jayce the ball.

Jayce caught it, and his eyes never wavered. "Even then."

Zan sat there for a while, and Jayce let him. He actually got what Jayce was saying. If there were some other way to save the world and God had just sent His Son to die, then Zan couldn't stomach it. But if there wasn't…

Still. "All right, let's say I decide to trust Him myself. I'll have to be willing to risk whatever He allows me to suffer. But what about Bailey? How can I be good with Him letting her get hurt? Or this other girl I know. Kasia."

"Somethin' happen to Kasia?"

"Kasia Bernolak. You know her?"

"Yeah. What happened?"

"I ran into her today after practice. What's up with this Blake guy?"

Jayce squinted. "She told you about him, or he was there?"

"He was with her when I came out, but he took off."

"Pshhh. Guy's an absolute wuss. He's all threatnin' and whatnot when she's alone, but try to have a little man-to-man, and he's outta there faster than a Yankees fan in the middle o' Southie. Jerk's never hung around long enough to look me in the eye. Was, ah, was Kasia good?"

"After a while. We talked a little."

"She's a cool character." Jayce spun the chair around and sat down, used its back as an armrest. "What'd ya talk about? 'f ya don't mind my asking."

"Not much. Just got her some hot tea while we waited for her boyfriend to show up."

Jayce's head jerked back almost a foot. "Boyfriend?"

"Kyle, right? He met her to go somewhere, and they seemed…I just assumed."

Jayce laughed. Hard. "Well, I guess it depends who ya ask. Kyle would flippin' love to hear ya say that, but Kasia's never seemed to be real interested."

"Oh." Zan chewed the inside of his cheek to keep his smile under wraps. Because it wouldn't be as complicated to keep an eye out for her now.

Jayce's eyebrow was cocked in a silent "I saw that."

Zan dropped back on his bed and stared at the squares in the ceiling. "Seriously, man. I'm one thing, but Kasia and Bailey? Someone won't always be there to step in and rescue them, you know?"

"There's no trustin' God halfway, Zander. If ya trust Him, ya gotta trust Him with all of it. Either He's God or He's not, right?"

"Maybe."

"My sister was real scared before she died." Jayce set the baseball on the floor.

Zan turned so he could see Jayce. "How old were you?"

"Ten. I don't remember everything, but I remember that. She'd been looking over her shoulder for weeks. I asked her what was chasin' her. She never told me. Then she was gone."

"How did she die?"

"Murdered. They found her in an alley. Called it overdose, but we all knew better."

"So nobody ever got arrested for it?"

"Nah. Me and my old man wrestled with that for years—each in our own way. What finally got me to come around was knowin' one way or another, whoever hurt Nora will get their justice. Either here on earth, or—if they never cry mercy—then in hell. For a while, I loved thinking about 'em in hell, but…I don't want that for anybody anymore. If I can experience God's mercy, anybody can."

Zan had to let that sink in for a minute. "Wait. What about earlier? You looked like you were ready to start taking names and cracking skulls. And now you're good with your sister's murderer in heaven one day?"

Jayce laughed. "Well, I'm not gonna lie to ya. I'm

willin' to throw my hands when I need to. There's some things you gotta fight for. But that doesn't mean I want the guy to go to hell. Don't forget—I deserve hell too."

"You're a better man than me."

"Does Bailey trust God?" Jayce asked.

Zan studied his hands. "Yeah."

"She angry at Him?"

"No. And somehow—at least before—she was able to forgive Michael for all his abuse." He kicked off his shoes and tossed them in the corner of his closet. "I bet she'll forgive him for this too."

After a minute Jayce spoke. "She's strong."

"She is." Zan took a deep breath. "And smart. But I've never gotten why she stayed. Why she always believed him when he said he was sorry. One side of me wishes she'd killed him a long time ago, and the other knows how wrong that is, right as the words come out of my mouth. It's different for her now though," he said. "She doesn't turn a blind eye to it like she used to, but she's freer—in her heart anyway."

Zan went quiet as he thought about his sister.

Bailey sure was restricted physically—couldn't even open her mouth at the moment. But nobody who talked to her could miss her joy and peace.

"I wish I could feel freedom like her." Zan scraped at a hangnail.

"What's holding ya back?"

He should've expected McEwan to call him on that.

27

"Tatusiu, I'm about to pour a glass of ice water. Want some?" Kasia leaned against the doorframe of her new bedroom.

In her new apartment. So much better than the dorm.

He slid his pencil behind his ear and set down the level. *"Nie. Dzięki."* He tugged a screw from his pocket. "How are we on time?" Strong muscles moved in his arm as he turned the screwdriver, made a hole for one of the anchors. Her corner shelf rested on the floor a few feet away.

"A.J. said eleven. They should be here any minute."

She and Tatuś had already brought in all her boxes and moved the university-issued furniture in her bedroom around so she'd have room for her freestanding bookcase. The one he'd built her for her tenth birthday.

Her favorite piece of home.

The scent of spiced pear from her three-wick candle permeated the air of the apartment. Her clothes were put away, her bed made, and a few photos strategically placed. Maybe decorating with A.J. would lead to honest conversation.

Kasia padded into the kitchen and pulled down her *Far Side* mug from the cabinet. Her ice popped and cracked as she added cold water from the faucet.

The front door opened. "Move-in day!"

A.J. bounced over and greeted Kasia with a hug. She glanced around. "Is your dad here? That's his truck outside, right?"

Tatuś stuck his head into the hallway. "Hey, A.J. I'm hanging a shelf, but I'd love to get Jayce's help with that bookcase I left in the truck bed."

"Jayce's roommate is down there too, so I'll just have them bring it up."

"Sounds great." He pointed at Kasia. "Curly-Q, help me hang the corner shelf, *dobrze*?"

She joined him, avoided the desk in the middle of the floor. Raised her end of the piece over her head, supported it as he guided it into the corner.

"Keep it level. We're aiming for an inch above the anchors."

With a steady hand, her dad touched the shelf to the back wall. They eased it to her left—

"Hey, Auburn," Zan said. "Where do you want this monster?"

Clunk. The mounting bracket bonked her head. "*Oj,* sorry, Tatusiu." *How in the world is Zan here?*

"Are you all right?" Tatuś peeked beneath the walnut plank.

She cleared her throat and pointed toward the window. "You can set it against the wall by the window, please."

Zan backed into her room and Jayce came around the corner.

She turned back to her dad.

His eyes were such an all-seeing blue. "Let's get this mounted so I can meet your friend."

Right. Of course. Lifting her end, she noticed the bracket had scraped the wall a little. Neither of them mentioned it. As soon as they had the shelf firmly mounted, Tatuś strode over to the guys.

"What's good, Mr. B.?" Jayce said. "Zan, this is Kasia's dad, Pastor Bernolak."

Zan wiped his hand on his shorts and reached out. "Nice to meet you, sir."

Kasia's stomach clenched. If he mentioned Blake, Zan could ruin everything.

~*~

Whoa. Kasia's dad had a grip and a half.

"Have you known Kasia long?"

Zan glanced over at Kasia. She tensed at the question.

Zan squeezed back. "I met her last year, and we keep running into each other."

Kasia's shoulders relaxed. What was she nervous about?

Zan met Mr. Bernolak's eyes. A pastor. Zan stood there with no doubt that he wasn't worthy of her father's stamp of approval. For multiple reasons. But he was better than the last loser, and he ached to make a good impression.

Kasia's dad released his gaze and turned to move Kasia's desk into the corner underneath the shelf, so Zan picked up the other end.

"Thanks. Listen, gentlemen, I appreciate your willingness to do the heavy lifting. Let me help unload A.J.'s things before I head home."

Jayce clapped his hands together. "Not gonna turn down extra manpower. Let's make short work of this and get somethin' to eat."

Pastor Bernolak slipped into a pair of shoes at the

door. Zan couldn't remember the last time he'd seen his father in jeans, much less barefooted.

"What's Kyle doing today?" her dad asked. "I thought we'd get to see him."

Kyle.

Jayce jogged down the steps in front of everybody. "He's got a shift at the station."

"Tell him he was missed." So Kyle was Pastor B.'s pick. This wouldn't be an easy win.

Jayce and Pastor Bernolak caught up like long-lost friends.

Probably because Jayce and A.J. were so serious. No threat from Jayce's end. Zan couldn't fault the man for being protective—even skeptical—of new guys. Zan would be the last guy to jeopardize Kasia's safety, to hurt her. He was on the same page as her dad there. Besides, he was still sort of reeling from the whole Kasia-was-almost-married thing. As much as he thought of her—wanted to be around her—there was a whole lot he didn't know.

Still, she attracted him more than he knew how to handle.

Kasia was a mystery he wanted to solve.

He stretched his shoulders and back, took in the overall impression of the girls' place. A funky piece of A.J.'s artwork here and there, candles and books all over. Kasia stuck colored cards to cabinet doors, windows, the fridge. Eyeing a purple one in her hand, she walked back to her bedroom.

While she was gone, he stepped over to examine the last card. A piece of moss-green card stock framed a cool recycled-looking one. *When I am afraid, I put my trust in You. In God, whose word I praise, in God I trust. Psalm 56:3–4.*

Zan scanned the apartment, and he spotted several others, each with its own artsy script. All Bible verses?

"Here." She came up beside him and his world suddenly smelled like fresh apples. She held out a tightly woven leather strap.

"What's this?" As he reached for it, his fingers grazed her hand. Adrenaline flooded his bloodstream, and his heart kicked it up a notch.

Kasia sucked in a breath, stepped back. Her eyes brightened. She'd felt something too, he was sure of it.

The leather was smooth and cool, seasoned like a well-worn glove, but he wished he could replay the last minute and brush her hand with his fingertips again.

She crossed her arms. "You asked me to bring something back from Peru for you. It's just a bookmark or whatever." Around her slight wrist, a similar leather strap was tied. It looked earthy and unusual—a reminder of where she'd been and all she'd seen.

He rubbed the gift between his fingers. "Thank you. I didn't really expect anything."

She waved his compliment off. "It's not that great. I hardly know you."

He smiled, mentally promising himself to change that fact. "You wear yours on your wrist."

She looked down and blushed.

"It's not the same thing. I got them from the same kid, I guess, but…they were cheap. I liked the intricate pattern."

"Hey!" Jayce shouted from A.J.'s room. "I just called for Chinese. You two want to go pick it up?"

Zan tilted his head as she gazed up at him. "I'm in. Do you mind?" Zan asked.

"Let me grab my bag."

When she returned, they walked out to his vehicle.

"You said a kid made these?" Zan asked. "How old?"

"Twelve or so. It might've been the only income his family gets too. You wouldn't believe some of the things I saw."

Zan flipped his keys in the air and caught them. "Tell me."

Her nose scrunched up. She wasn't buying his interest.

"I want to know about it. Seriously. All summer, reading your updates was my favorite pastime." He hadn't commented on most of them, because he didn't want to push. But she had to know he was genuine.

"The people are so content with the little they have. They don't worry about what I would've considered suffering or sacrificing. There's an acceptance and a peace—it's hard to explain. But I appreciated it." She traced the pattern in her bracelet. "Felt a little jealous of it, actually."

It was still warm in the evenings, so he hadn't put the canvas shell on his CJ yet. Still, he followed Kasia around in case she needed help climbing in. Kept his hands near her back.

A minute later, he started the engine. "So seeing their suffering changed you?"

She closed her eyes, probably remembering the faces she saw in those village streets. When they opened, her answer was quiet. "I saw things in those mountains that put my whole life into perspective. Who am I anyway? No one important. But if God wants to use me, I'm His. He does things—allows things—I don't understand, but I belong to Him. I know He's good. I can be content with that."

She was definitely important.

Kasia stared outside, still and silent.

Zan couldn't comment. It wasn't that he was at a loss for words. He had too much to say, but it didn't feel like the right time to correct her on the "important" thing, no matter how wrong she was. He bit the inside of his cheek, tried to find a place to launch. "You remind me of my sister."

"Oh? In what way?"

Yeah, he definitely wasn't going to say everything on that subject. "The way you love God."

That got her to smile.

They made it to the Chinese take-out place and back in fifteen minutes, and Zan parked at the back of her lot. "Smells great, doesn't it? I'm famished."

She didn't answer. Pale as the moon, she hugged herself and stared out the window.

"What's wrong?"

"The black sports car in the corner, right beside the sidewalk. It's Blake."

"D'you want me to make him leave?"

Her voice was a weak whisper. "I don't know."

"Are you all right walking past him?"

"What if he says something?"

"Kasia?" Zan whispered. He touched her arm and wondered if that was all right. "I'll be right there. Between you and Blake. If he does anything or says anything, I'll handle it."

She turned to face him and searched his eyes. Whatever she was looking for, she found. With a blank expression, she picked up the bag of take-out and nodded, climbing out.

Zan walked around to meet her, moved to her side. "Let's go."

They walked toward the apartments. Toward Blake. About ten yards from Blake's car, the driver's door opened, and Blake stood, rested his hands on the roof. Zan swallowed. He'd expected Blake to stay in the car.

Kasia hooked her hand around Zan's bicep and stared straight at the sidewalk.

"Behind me," Zan whispered. "Stay there."

Kasia slowed a step, but her hand stayed locked on his muscle.

"Problem?" Zan asked, his voice steady but full of warning. He didn't need Blake angry. He locked eyes with Blake, tightened his jaw and fist at the same time. Narrowed his gaze and stared the guy down. All he wanted Blake to see was that he would intercept anything he threw at Kasia.

And Blake would pay for it.

One yard out, Blake lost the staring contest.

That's what I thought. Zan allowed himself a smirk at the loser's expense, pulled Kasia to his side. "Walk in front of me now." She did, and Zan kept his hand at her back.

One yard past, Kasia let out her breath with a shudder.

"How are you doing?" Zan asked softly. He could still feel Blake's gaze on them.

"Fine."

Yesterday that answer hadn't satisfied him either.

They walked slowly—deliberately—to the building, up the steps, into the apartment.

As soon as the door closed, Kasia grabbed him around the waist with such desperation she all but knocked him into the wall. Cautiously, he closed the embrace, held her until her breathing evened out and her grip relaxed. He leaned against the wall, waited for her to speak first.

But she didn't. Even once the tension had drained, she held on to him.

"I know you don't know me well yet, but I'm here—however, whenever you need me. All right?"

She nodded against his chest and whispered. "I like this spot. I don't know why, but I feel safe here."

"You can stand here any time you like." God help him. He didn't trust himself at the moment. He needed to step away.

"Oh no."

"What?" he whispered.

"I think I broke the chicken." The bag of Chinese food was on the floor, and an orangey-red sauce pooled out of a corner of the bag.

He reached down and picked it up. "Let's check the damage. But I vote for making A.J. and Jayce go out if we need a replacement."

She nodded. "Me too."

28

Friday afternoon, drumsticks played a tattoo on their front door.

Jayce. Maybe Zan too.

Kasia leaned her guitar against the bookcase, content, hopeful. *Coraz lepiej.* Fingerpicking—playing at all—was getting better, easier, all the time. Alone, she worshipped through song, her fingers and voice in full cooperation. Finally. Even if she could only play familiar songs, any progress satisfied.

She'd compose again.

One day.

She opened the door.

"All right, ladies! Zander and I have decided we must participate in the homecoming festivities. Bare minimum, the bonfire tonight." Jayce, the king of laid-back, had a bounce in his step.

Good. Kasia wanted to hear the music. Kyle had promised a great show.

"I thought we'd decided to avoid the crowd and watch a movie," A.J. strode out of her room.

Zan closed the door behind Jayce and raised a plastic grocery bag over his head. "This wasn't part of the equation until now."

"What's in the bag?"

"S'mores stuff." Jayce counted off, drumsticks in the air. He played a drum solo on every piece of furniture within his reach.

"Are we going early enough for the concert?" Kasia asked. "Kyle said he's got a killer lineup before the bonfire. Nick Flora, Green River Ordinance..."

Zan stuck a hand in his hair and messed it all up. She loved that for some reason. When he caught her looking, he grinned. "Unless y'all want to go to the Warehouse for dinner first," he said. "I haven't been there in a while, and I'm craving some excellent java and a meatball sandwich."

"Mm, but I do want to get back in time to see some of the show if we can. The Beggars' Guild plays first. They don't play together much anymore."

"I'll call in our order so we can pick it up and have dinner in my CJ. Best seats in the house."

Could the night get better than that?

Kasia packed Tatuś's hoodie and blanket in her backpack while A.J. grabbed a jacket. Mountain autumn had come to stay.

The four of them ate dinner in the stadium lot, serenaded by Nick Flora. The brisk night air was full of change. Kasia's stomach knotted into a ball of solid anticipation, and she found it hard not to shiver. Especially when Zan looked at her. With eyes like the Andean sky.

Maybe it was time to get up and walk around. "Let's go over by the fire."

Clusters of students milled around near the parking lot.

Their group stuck together as they wound their way through the crowd, but the throng of people near the stage was pretty impenetrable.

Kasia's neck prickled. She searched the sea of faces for Blake's but couldn't spot him. She moved a step closer to Zan.

He leaned down. "You all right?"

"I think Blake's out here somewhere."

"He won't bother you if you're with me."

His confidence was a warm blanket. "Thanks."

She noticed Kyle under a tent at the big soundboard and waved.

~*~

Zan blew out a breath. *Kyle.*

All four of them were headed straight toward him, but Kyle's eyes were all for Kasia. By the time they made it over to him, he still hadn't taken his eyes off her.

"Hey, Kyle," Zan interrupted. "How's it going?"

"Decent." He finally tore his eyes away. "You?"

"Same."

The conversation remained stilted and awkward for way too long. When music came up, though, everyone loosened up. Kasia knew The Gray Havens, Waterdeep, Christopher Williams, Andrew Greer—a lot of the bands Kyle mentioned—and a lot about the local concert venues.

Zan knew nothing. Except that he loved Kasia's passion when she talked music or Peru. Her eyes came alive, and her smile lit up.

"If we don't get in there and claim a spot, I'm gonna have to make these s'mores Southie style. With a burn barrel and coat hanger."

A.J. smacked Jayce's arm.

"What? Bonfires are frowned upon—would be if anyone had a yard anyways."

"I'll go to see if one of the other guys will give me thirty minutes to hang with you," Kyle said. "Nicholas and a few others from small group are around too."

"I'll text them and tell them where we are," A.J. said.

They made their way fireside and pulled out the bag. Their Bible study friends found them, and they claimed a good slice of ground. Zan didn't let Kasia get too far from him, but there was the Kyle factor. Neither of them had any right to claim the spot at her side as their own, but they both wanted it. That much was obvious.

Rather than compete, Zan hung back as the small group connected, and he occupied his time getting to know Nicholas and a few other guys—always keeping an eye out for Blake.

Just in case.

Every so often, he caught Kasia straightening up and scanning the mob. Kyle noticed and stepped closer. But Kasia went into stealth mode each time, moving away from Kyle and closer to Zan.

Zan stood a little taller in those moments. Not that he would be a punk about it.

Kasia nudged him. "Feel like roasting some marshmallows with me?"

"Absolutely."

"You hold the hanger. I'll skewer the little suckers." And skewer she did. In record time. She licked the sticky off her fingers and shrugged. "Sorry. I know that's gross."

Zan squatted down and opened up the chocolate bar, breaking it in pieces. When the first marshmallows came out of the fire, Kasia held the hanger down, and he used the grahams and chocolate to slide them off. "You try first."

She bit into hers, and her eyes fluttered shut.

He looked away for a second.

"Are you going to try yours, Zan?" she asked. "*Przepyszny.*"

He hoped it was as good as she made it look, because all he could think about was the dot of chocolate right beside her lip. And he did not need to be going there. "What's that mean?" He bit into the graham crackers.

"Better than delicious. I can never get enough melty chocolate." Her smile was sweeter than the chocolate though. "Oh, you've got"—she reached up and, with the tip of a finger, wiped his cheek, and Zan felt it inside. Like a shockwave—"some chocolate."

She tugged a tissue out of her pocket and wiped her finger on it.

"Thanks."

She held out the hanger again. Time to skewer some more.

"Hey, Kasia. Have you checked out the new Josh Garrels studio project?" Kyle asked.

Zan had almost forgotten he was there.

"It's incredible. He's *such* a poet—and I love that he does so much with humanitarian projects." She pulled her hair back, tied it in some kind of adorable knot.

"Do you have a favorite album?" Kyle asked.

"Can't pick." She positioned their marshmallow-kabob over the outermost flames.

"He's going to be at Escape to the Lake this year—you know about that?"

"Yeah? I'd love to get there some year. Love everything Under the Radar does."

Zan had no idea what they were talking about, so he decided he'd find Jayce and reload their graham-cracker-and-chocolate cache. Kyle had finally gotten her attention. He deserved to enjoy it.

~*~

Whew, it was warm. Kasia pulled the marshmallows back and tapped them. Not done yet.

"Kyle!" Nicholas called. "Come let me introduce you to somebody."

He turned to her. "You good with me going a minute?"

She nodded. Kyle ducked back into the crowd, and Kasia pulled out her marshmallows, leaning back to see if she could spot Zan. They needed to make their s'mores before the mallows got cold.

Ow! She sucked in a breath and her hand flew to her neck as her eyes locked onto the flames, stunned. Had a spark hit her? She pulled her hand back and saw blood. Her eyes skimmed the faces around the edge of the fire.

That's when she saw him. A satisfied smile twisted his mouth as he stepped backward into the throng, blended in. Disappeared.

Her insides turned to ice, and everything went black.

29

Ugh. Kasia's head swam and throbbed, swam and throbbed.

"Kasia? Can you hear me?" That was A.J.'s voice, right? "Open your eyes."

She tried for a split second, but her head ached, the pain constant and awful. "Too bright."

Footsteps, then Jayce's voice. "Kyle, get on the mic. Find a doctor."

More voices, and then a thud beside her. "Kasia. It's Zan. Can you look at me?"

"It's too bright," A.J. said for her.

"Here," he said. "Try now." His voice had moved in front of her.

Her head still pounded, but maybe whatever Zan had done worked. Scrunching up her face, she cracked one eye a slit. It was better. She opened her eyes and found A.J. kneeling right beside her head, holding her hand.

"What happened?" Zan asked. Kasia tried to make out the dark mass in front of her. It sounded like Zan, but what in the world was he doing?

"Do you think you can sit up?" A.J. asked.

"Probably, but that doesn't mean I want to." Seriously.

"We shouldn't move her until somebody checks her out anyway," Zan said. He turned and shouted into the crowd, "Where are we on finding a doctor?"

That's when she figured out why Zan's voice was shrouded in darkness, why it blocked out the too-bright flames. He knelt, spread his sweatshirt out behind his head, giving her a shadow to hide in. Good thing they were next to the fire. He'd freeze in just that T-shirt.

"I'm a paramedic," somebody said. He rushed over.

"Good." Kyle's voice was right behind the blur of the paramedic.

The guy immediately started hounding her with a penlight. She couldn't tell if he preferred the interrogating or the poking and prodding more. He never asked the right question though.

"Blake."

"What?" Zan snapped.

A.J. leaned down. "You saw him? Here?"

Her head swam for a second. She breathed deep. Equilibrium slowly returned.

"Something hit my neck, and I…I don't know why I fell." Unless it was possible to collapse from sheer shock and disbelief. She'd never expected Blake to actually hurt her. He'd always made empty threats. But this…

"Let's have a look, all right?"

Soft, cold fingers gently turned her head. Penlight whistled. And Zan swore. The fire suddenly brightened. Zan was still there, but he wasn't holding his shirt up.

"Kosh." A.J.'s voice was too whispery.

Kyle and Jayce mumbled something to each other, and Kasia didn't like their tone. Her vision was still blurry.

The shadow came back, clearing its throat.

"I'm…I'm sorry I cussed. You said you saw Blake. Did he do this?" He sounded furious. She didn't answer right away.

Penlight was being as gentle as possible, but her neck was so sore. He prodded a particularly sensitive spot and she inhaled through her teeth. "Do you think you can sit?"

He slowly helped Kasia sit up. She closed her eyes for a moment, found her balance.

When she opened them, Jayce squatted beside A.J. "Kosh, where'd ya see him?"

"Over there." She pointed. Twenty feet away, two o'clock. "Right before I fell."

"On it." Jayce was gone before she could take a deep breath.

"Me too." Kyle started off in the other direction but stopped suddenly. "Kasia?"

She looked up at Kyle, sucked in air at the pain.

"You should call your dad. He'll want to be all over this."

The words stung as much as whatever Penlight was dabbing on her neck. For all kinds of reasons. Kasia had broken her promise to Tatuś and gotten herself hurt. She had to admit she was in way over her head. And there'd be no way to avoid the protective order after this.

As much as she wanted to, she couldn't pretend this wasn't crazy serious. And terrifying.

Blake wasn't playing.

~*~

Zan knelt beside her, his heart ripped in two directions. Leave Kasia to help find the jackleg who hurt her and beat him within an inch of his life, or stay and make sure she was all right.

Kasia won.

Zan's shoulders burned from holding his sweatshirt up for so long. He'd brought it down for a bit, and then raised it again. His shoulders were strong, but it'd been, what, ten minutes? He'd never tested their stamina before. "You good with the light now? Or do you want me to keep holding this?"

"Um, I'm a little chilly. Can I wear it?" she asked.

"Of course." He offered it, and she frowned.

"Never mind. I—can you get the hoodie out of my backpack for me?"

"I'll get it," A.J. said. She mouthed, "And call her parents."

"Just one more moment," the paramedic said. "Bandaging *this,* and then I need to peek at the back of your head. I think you just jarred it from the fall itself."

"What about my neck?" She sounded so lost.

"You've got an abrasion there, but it's going to bruise deeply. I'd like you to change the bandages twice a day. Do you have antibiotic ointment?"

She nodded, winced.

"Use that. I saw a few pieces of black debris, and pulled them out easily. It appeared to be asphalt."

Was he kidding? The loser pulled up a chunk of pavement and hit her with it? Zan couldn't keep his questions to himself anymore. "Is there any danger of whiplash or concussion? Anything like that?"

"It's possible. She should be watched closely tonight, woken every half-hour or so. Will you…" He appeared to be searching for A.J. Where was she?

Still on the phone. "I'll be there," Zan said, as if that'd been the plan all along. "At least long enough to deliver a message to her parents." His announcement seemed to surprise Kasia, but he wouldn't let her out of his sight until he handed her over to her father.

"Good." The paramedic continued his instructions and then got up to leave.

Kasia tried a thank-you smile but didn't quite get there. It squeezed on Zan's heart.

As soon as campus security got her statement and left, Zan knelt in front of her. "Hey, Auburn. You good?"

She shrugged. A painful expression still marred her face.

"If I promise to stick to yes or no questions, will you stop shrugging and hurting yourself even more?"

A half-smile crept up her cheek. "Yes."

"Are you ready to go?"

"Yes." He didn't quite believe her. Something about the way she tightened her lips right after she answered.

"Wish you didn't have to?"

"Yes."

"I was having a lot of fun making s'mores with you. We'll have to try again sometime."

He got a real smile, dialed back just a notch with carefulness.

He eased her to her feet and held her steady for a moment.

A.J. walked up and joined them. "You go on and get her out of here. You're taking her home for the night?"

He nodded.

"Why don't Jayce and I drive up with you so you can sit in the back with her?"

"Sounds like a plan."

"We'll meet you at the parking lot."

Zan kept a hand near Kasia's back as she took her first few steps. She wobbled every now and then, and her hand shot out to grab his. He held it tightly and hoped she wouldn't take it back.

She stopped suddenly. "I don't think I can…can I sit right here and let you drive over and pick me up in a minute?"

He looked around. They were still in the middle of the crowd. "D'you mind if I lift you?"

"What?"

"I'll carry you."

She was dazed. Of course, that might have had nothing to do with his offer.

She turned to him and held out an arm, willing to let him do what he'd wanted to from the second he'd spotted her on the ground. He scooped her up and held her small frame close to his chest.

She said nothing, but settled into his arms as if she belonged there.

He maneuvered her gently through the crowd, stepping carefully around the curious onlookers. "How're you holdin' up?"

"Huh?"

"You going to make it?"

"He hurt me." The words cut him, her voice tired and childlike. "Blake actually hurt me."

His heart stuttered at the hopelessness in her voice. He stopped and tilted his head so he could see her face. She looked shocked—as if she'd been betrayed by her best friend.

"This isn't the first time he's hurt you." She had to see that.

Her forehead wrinkled in confusion.

As they rounded the corner, Kasia sighed, exhaling utter exhaustion, and nestled into the spot where his shoulder and neck met. He sucked in a breath and inhaled the scent of apples and wood smoke. Keeping his heart out of the equation wouldn't be easy.

~*~

Kasia drifted in and out of consciousness for a while. When she was lucid, she appreciated the cool, smooth lining of someone's coat. She was in the back seat of an old car. A.J. was driving. Zan sat beside her. He hadn't left her side. She breathed in the scent of leather and woods from her makeshift pillow, finding enough comfort to fade back into her own dark shadowlands.

She wished it weren't so easy to be lulled back to that place. It was desolate, and sometimes, the shadow-lurkers would peer out at her. She could see the same bitter sneer that distorted Blake's face.

She wanted to leave but didn't know how. She'd gotten herself lost here anyway. Tatuś had warned her, and she'd let her guard down.

The sky lit up, flickering, and she saw herself standing, clueless, at the edge of the bonfire. Like an old film reel crackling to life, the whole scene began to play out before her. The rock whizzed at her from across the edge of the fire, hitting its target. She saw herself touch the wound and search the crowd, watching her expression shift the instant she recognized Blake.

She should've screamed at Blake. Should've charged straight at him, pointing and shouting his name loud enough for people downtown to hear. Asked him where he got off throwing a hunk of rock at her head. What was he trying to accomplish anyway?

But she hadn't. She'd seen the blood on her fingers, seen the malice written all over his face, and she'd given up. Bit it. Dropped to the ground like a worthless rag doll.

And she hated herself for it.

Why? Why couldn't she fight him when it counted?

Why couldn't she stem the tide somehow?

She drifted back into the darkness. Made herself get up. *Stop him. Don't let him take any more from you than he already has.* She scanned the perimeter. For the first time, she noticed a heap of stones and bricks. Maybe that's what they were supposed to be used for.

Working in a circle, she began building a wall. Every brick was well-placed, because the wall had to be strong enough to stop all this. She lifted, climbed, spread the mortar, stacked some more. The wall grew higher.

It became a tower. Safe inside, she could see upward, the only direction that mattered to her. She could connect with God, could feel His love. His love mattered.

"Kasiu!" Lenka called. *Thump, thump, thump.* She heard the voices of her family and knew she had to let them in too. She could trust them, but they were the last ones. The higher the tower, the safer she would be.

"Kasia, your dad's here." Zan's voice tugged at her. "I'll unlock your door."

Home. She opened her eyes and saw Tatuś's face through the back-seat window. She sat up, winced, and pulled the coat onto her lap. Tatuś opened the door and inspected her, his gaze on her face, her neck. He reached for her, and—even though his eyes were on fire—his hands were gentle. *He's so strong.*

He cradled her, carried her into the house, left A.J. to introduce Zan to Mama and Lenka. Into the kitchen her dad carried her, the door swinging shut behind them, down the hall to the family room. He set her down gently.

In his chair.

He knelt beside her, his blue eyes searing, and she waited. She knew she deserved every ounce of his rebuke. His jaw clenched and unclenched. His eyes were so full of words. Why weren't any of them flying at her?

He stood suddenly, and she flinched.

He made a choking noise, and she turned her head back to him, met his gaze. It was infinitely different now. A tear slipped from the corner of his eye, and he tilted his head. His eyes remained fixed on her. Cautiously, he reached out to her and brushed a curl out of her face.

She waited, expected him to tell her how she'd let him down.

But he didn't. He left.

~*~

Zan stepped into the Bernolaks' kitchen and was immediately struck by the sense of home. A cinnamon candle glowed in the middle of the table, empty coffee mugs and tissues nearby.

"Where's Dad?" her sister asked. "Did he take Kasia to her room?"

Mrs. Bernolak offered a warm shrug. "Why don't

we stay in here for a bit and let Kasia get settled. Zan, can I pour you a cup of coffee? A.J.?"

They each fixed a hot drink the way they liked it, and Mrs. Bernolak directed them to the table. "I think I need to hear what happened tonight again—slowly this time."

Just as they began, Pastor Bernolak joined them, quiet but intense. "Marta, Kasia needs you in the den. Right away."

She hurried out of the room.

Zan stood, a knot in his throat. Was something wrong?

Mr. B. turned and inspected him again. "I didn't thank you properly…I don't remember your name."

"Zan." He grasped Kasia's dad's hand. "Alexander Maddox."

"I appreciate you seeing Kasia home safely. Please. Sit." His accent stood out a little more than before.

Mr. B. poured himself a cup of black coffee. He drank it straight. "Talk to me."

A.J. gestured to Zan.

He spoke. "The paramedic said the neck injury wasn't major in and of itself. The fall is what jarred her head, but she was in the grass. They don't think it's a concussion. Still, you're supposed to wake her every half-hour, keep an eye on her. She got a little weak on the way to the car."

"I'm fine," Kasia rasped, standing in the doorway.

Mr. B. shot out of his chair and slid it over, right beside her. "Sit down."

"Let me make you some tea." Her mom shuffled in behind her. Mrs. Bernolak walked that fine line Li'l Mama knew so well—between keeping up appearances and letting the worry win.

Kasia tapped the counter. "No. I don't want anything."

"Then you need to go rest," Pastor Bernolak said.

She nodded, gingerly. "Thanks, Zan. For everything. G'night, A.J."

He nodded, missing the vivacity that belonged in her eyes. Her little sister—he remembered her from the store—studied him, clearly wary. Zan reached down to pet the frumpy brown dog that sat by his feet, also watching him.

Everyone wanted to know if he was trustworthy.

30

With a deep sigh, Kasia rolled to her side. The pain that stabbed through her neck caused her eyes to widen in instant alarm. With a whimper, she rolled onto her side again and stared at the sky-painted ceiling of her old bedroom.

But what she saw was Blake's face at the edge of the fire, familiar headlights in her rearview mirror, shattered glass.

The scenes that followed were hazy, confusing—they conjured demons she didn't recognize. An indefinable menace groped at her, pulled her farther into the depths until drowning in the fear seemed a better option than fighting.

Her survival instinct kicked in. She had to get out from under all this—this pressure, this defeat. This fear. Her heart pounded so loudly she could feel it in her head. *Oh, God. Help me.*

"Kasia?" She turned toward the soft voice and found A.J. watching her from the air mattress by the wall. "You good?"

"I'll be fine—just need to get up and going, I guess." Kasia listened to bumps and the rush of water in the plumbing.

"Let me get dressed, and I can help if you want."

"You stayed."

A.J. smiled sadly. "Yeah. Jayce and Zan will come back and get us this afternoon if you're ready to go back. Or you can stay. Whatever."

Kasia sat up slowly. It only took a few excruciating mistakes for her to remember to use more careful, measured movements. One more deep breath, and she headed to the kitchen.

Her mom met her at the table with a pain reliever and a cup of coffee. "You all right this morning?"

She nodded.

"Good. Then as soon as you've finished your breakfast, we'll go take care of our to-do list, all right?"

The protective order. Of course.

~*~

Zan followed the same winding road A.J. had driven ten hours before.

Jayce adjusted his seatbelt. "You and Kosh seem to hit it off pretty well. She relaxes around ya." Jayce was matter-of-fact.

"I hope so. She's definitely different. She's good for me, I think. "

"And you? Are you good for her?"

Was he kidding? "I'm watching out for her."

"You don't ever consider the possibility of more than that? I can tell she gets to you."

"She's nothing like other girls I've known, so yeah. She's got my attention, but—"

"You might not understand this, man, but following God isn't just something she says she does. It's another kind of life altogether. Kasia and you—you're after different things. The last thing she needs is to get confused by another guy."

"We're friends. I'm not going to hurt her." *Leave it alone.*

"That's great, but, ah, I gotta ask you not to distract her either."

Zan rolled his neck. Tried to shrug it off. Jayce had Kasia's back. They were on the same page. "Right."

"Nah, Zan. I'm sayin'. If ya get to the point where ya start thinking of yourself, and ya hurt her—even a little—I'm gonna knock a knot on your head the size of Fenway."

Zan cast an irritated glance in Jayce's direction. "All right, I get it—"

"As long as we understand each other."

~*~

A temporary restraining order was granted immediately, based on her statement and the earlier incident with her car window. She'd have a hearing in a few weeks.

In the meantime, Kasia was sure Blake would be irate. She'd just kicked a hornets' nest.

Zan was parked next to the carport. The thought of seeing his smile buoyed her spirits. He made everything better. Safer. More fun.

"Send Jayce and his roommate out to get the pizza and drinks. You don't need to do any lifting."

"I feel fine, Mamusiu. It's not like pizzas—"

"Boys. Pizza and drinks. If you want to do something, go and tell your dad it's time for lunch. I'm sure he's hungry." Mama leveled her gaze at Kasia, and she took it right between the eyes. "You two could use a minute to chat anyway, hm?"

"Yes, ma'am." Kasia closed her car door and walked toward the church building. Even if her head had felt perfect, the walk would've been a long one.

She opened the side door and took her time in the dark hallway. Knocked on the door.

Tatuś cleared his throat and shuffled some things around. "Come in."

She opened the door partially, kept it between them in case he was still upset. Her gaze wandered the photos on the walls instead of meeting his. "Mama says to tell you lunch is ready. We bought pizza."

He was quiet for a moment. She looked at the floor beside his desk, then his desk…his shoulder…the top of his head.

"Won't you look at me?"

"I am." They made eye contact for a millisecond—then she studied the worn carpet under her feet.

He stood and walked over, wrapped her hand in his. He led her farther into his study. "Last night, Kasiu, did you think I was angry with you?"

"I promised I'd be safe."

He tugged on her index finger. "I don't remember that. I remember you said you'd be careful, and you wouldn't be alone. And you kept your word. This Blake is the only one who made me angry."

She risked meeting his eyes. They were only filled with love today.

"But you left."

"Kasiu, I had to get out of that room. Seeing you like that—my anger frightened you, and I knew it."

"I'm sorry, Tatusiu. But I can't make him stop. I thought it would go away. What if he follows me again and I don't notice?" *Ugh*. She hadn't meant to say any of this. His hugs always did that to her—made her pour out her feelings. She clamped down on her bottom lip and said nothing else.

"Sheriff Schilling said if Blake does anything

else—anything—you report it. Until then, Jayce will be there, and this Zan. You don't think they'd mind escorting you to classes, do you?" His chin moved on top of her head.

"Zan already does."

"*Na prawda*?"

She picked at the button on his chest pocket. "Really."

"Look at me again."

She turned up her face.

"*Zrób to dla mnie.*"

Her heart stuttered. What would he ask her to do?

"I need you to remember that no matter where you are, no matter what happens, no matter what mistakes you make, I love you. *Zawsze*." Always.

"Yes, sir."

She knew Tatuś honestly thought he meant it.

But if he knew everything, that would change.

31

Time dragged.

The week that had passed since the bonfire felt like a month. Kyle had come by to check on her twice—bearing flowers and sheet music. She'd played guitar awhile, even pulled out her Peru journal. Her notes about Psalm 40 tugged at her heart. She'd written that getting away from Blake felt like getting out of the slimy pit. Peru had been new, firm ground. A solid place to stand.

And oh, for a new song. Even now, she toyed with an idea—that whole transition.

About how, without Christ, she'd been too weak to climb out on her own.

But here she was, out and scrambling for shelter. What good did it do to get out of the muck and mire only to keep hiding?

At least her fingers had developed calluses from playing guitar in her sanctuary.

Kasia plopped into A.J.'s overstuffed chair. "Think Zan's in Charleston already?" He'd dropped her off after class, made sure she had what she needed, and turned her over to Jayce.

"I'd think so, by now." A.J. had almost finished her book. They'd agreed to enjoy a quiet evening of reading.

Kasia rubbed the pads of her left fingertips. Should it bother her that even *they* were beginning to numb? "You know why he had to go home? All he told me was that he had a court date." He'd seemed way too burdened for a speeding ticket though.

"Jayce said it had something to do with his sister."

She hoped it wasn't something tragic. Every time he talked about Bailey, worry creased his face and hunched his shoulders. Maybe one day he'd open up about her. Let Kasia pray for him.

She stared at the wall inches from her face, let her vision blur and focus and blur again. It didn't help the intensifying headache.

But she needed to feel something.

She'd gone numb.

"A.J.? Why don't you ever talk about what happened before you moved down here?"

A.J. set her book aside. "You're blunt tonight."

"Sorry. Guess the rock Blake threw knocked off my verbal filter."

"Yeah, maybe." A.J.'s voice held compassion.

Kasia didn't know what to do with it. She decided to keep frustrating her eyes.

"You remember I mentioned my dad's loaded, right? So picture those Manhattan social circles. That show *Revenge* was my life—prep school, ritzy parties, the high life. Church wasn't on the radar."

Kasia glanced over.

"I'd had a thing for my brother's best friend, Stefan, for years, but he never paid me any attention. The summer I turned sixteen, my parents let me go to Paris. I spent the summer with some family friends, and…I guess I grew up a little. In the ways that Stefan noticed anyway."

Kasia shifted and faced A.J.

"My parents threw a welcome-home bash before

school started, and everyone was there. Finally, Stefan danced with me and ignored the rest of the crowd. He actually apologized for never noticing how beautiful I was before." She blew her bangs out of her face. "It was a load of crap."

"Been there," Kasia muttered.

"Sorry."

Kasia could tell she meant it.

"Luke, my brother, was nervous that I was in over my head with Stefan. I totally ripped into him and told him to mind his own business." She mocked her sixteen-year-old self. "'Honestly, Lucian, do I tell you what to do with the girls you go out with?'" She smiled sadly. "He stopped bugging me about it."

"Do you wish he'd stayed on you about it? Now?" Sometimes Kasia wished a friend would've grabbed her by the shoulders and asked what she was thinking. But no one ever did. She'd never had those kinds of friends.

"Luke kept an eye out for me. And yeah, I'm glad. Stefan was charming around our classmates—but alone? Different story. Sure, we messed around. Did all kinds of stuff that I really liked at the time, but I always drew the line before sex. I guess he thought he could convince me. I was so enamored, I made excuses for him every time he pushed me about it. Sometimes…I even liked how he pushed."

Kasia chewed her lip. *Sometimes the wrong thing feels good.*

"So this one afternoon, I went over to his house to study, and he'd gotten this porn flick. He literally made me sit and watch it. Told me to take good notes." She wore an expression of disgust, but her eyes were sad.

"I went home and—of course—didn't talk to anyone about it."

Kasia swallowed.

"I just showered for an hour or two and told myself I wouldn't mind doing some of that stuff someday…as long as Stefan loved me."

Kasia's stomach turned. Before Blake, she'd believed sex was supposed to be beautiful. But the real thing always felt like she was in some sick movie.

"I had planned to go to a football game with Luke that night, but I didn't feel up to it. He went without me and came home an hour later with a broken nose. Apparently, Stefan had been rolling around under the bleachers with some skank from the other school. Luke beat the snot out of him—tried to protect my honor.

"I was grateful…till he demanded I break up with Stefan. I should've, totally. I know. But I was jealous that Stefan had wanted somebody else. I thought I could change his mind. Be whatever he wanted, you know?"

Kasia smoothed a long curl between her fingers. She knew.

"I was so blind. Psychotic, the things we do when we're messed up in the head, isn't it?"

A.J. looked right into her. Kasia massaged her temples.

"Does your head hurt again?"

"No, I'm fine."

"I can tell. Give me two minutes to finish, and I'll get you some medicine. Yeah?"

Kasia nodded. She half regretted asking about it all. A little too close to home.

"That weekend, there was this big party. My parents forbade it, so I lied. Said I was going over to my friend Charlotte's. I don't remember much, except I found Stefan at the party and acted like an idiot. He went to get us drinks, and…I woke up in the hospital several hours later."

How awful. Kasia thrummed her finger across the nubby upholstery.

"Apparently, Luke—the meddler—had called Charlotte's and found out I wasn't there. He raced to the party and searched every room until he found me." A.J. drew in a shaky breath and dropped her gaze. "I was out cold on somebody's bed…with my shirt torn and my pants cut off. And there were bruises on my neck and shoulder too."

Kasia gasped. "I can't even imagine."

"People probably still talk about my brother going ballistic that night, much to my parents' dismay. Seriously, more than half the people ditched the joint before he even got up the stairs. So I heard. Stefan had put some Rohypnol in my drink and done whatever he wanted with me. By the time Luke got there, Stefan was gone, but…he left no doubt about his identity."

A.J. uncurled herself from the couch and brought Kasia two pain relievers and some water. "Needless to say, we pressed charges, and he spent a night in jail before his daddy bailed him out. His high-society parents kept it as quiet as possible. At least they made him plead guilty though. He was charged with first- and second-degree rape, three counts of aggravated assault, assault on a minor, and first- and second-degree sex offense, and sentenced to ten years in a state penitentiary with possible parole after three years. Which I heard he got."

She rattled off that list of charges as if they'd been old friends for years.

"For a long time I was a shell. In denial about all of it. My parents put me in therapy, and I got to deal with it a little. Basically, I decided not to let him hurt me anymore. I had a life to live, and I was going to live it. I didn't make it a secret though. I talked about it—sort of became the school spokesperson for date-rape awareness."

"I bet your parents were proud after all that."

A.J. closed her mouth and eyed her watch. "Sheesh! I didn't realize we'd talked so late. We'd better hit the hay, yeah?" She stretched and grabbed her book.

Kasia reeled at the abrupt ending.

A minute later, A.J. stood beside her door, switched off the lamp. "Night, Kosh."

But Kasia felt as if she needed to know, and the darkness made it easier to ask. "A.J.? What happened with your parents?"

The silence was loud for a heartbeat. "My socialite parents didn't want to be known as the family of Date-Rape Girl. They told me to quit talking about it or they'd ship me off to school."

Silence. A.J. drummed her fingers on the doorframe.

"After everything I'd already been through, all the progress I'd made, they were ashamed of me anyway. Someone drugged me and raped me, and I was a blemish on their reputation."

How awful. "And they wouldn't listen when you talked to them about it?"

"Didn't try. I left. Tracked down the black sheep of the family and took off to join him."

A.J. walked into her room and shut the door.

Kasia sat still in the blackness, with only the

streetlights slicing through the blinds.

She couldn't believe what A.J. had been through. The world was so sick and broken.

As she let her gaze trace the stripes of light, she felt it again. Something was out there, at the edges of her memory. Why couldn't she just remember it and have it *done*?

32

Kasia was a guitar string wound ten steps too sharp.

She got up and shuffled through the dark hall to the bathroom, slid her palm the length of the cool wall. She filled a glass with water and took more pain reliever before climbing back into bed. But her head throbbed, shoulders aching all the way down her spine.

This couldn't still be from the rock. Blake hadn't even given her a concussion.

She readjusted her pillow and tried to distract her mind—homework club would begin next week; a short story was due on Friday for her creative-writing class. She could write about Peru.

Snippets of A.J.'s story crept into her mind like vines. Twisted, stretched, tugged. They hunted something. Other recent conversations joined them.

This isn't the first time he's hurt you.

I always made excuses for him.

An infuriating disquiet lurked at the edge of her consciousness—constant. Always worse in the darkness. She'd love to face the foreboding once and for all. Name it, stare it down. Maybe it would slink back to wherever it came from.

God, I need to be done with this. I need rest.

She tossed and turned for almost an hour, unable to figure out why she couldn't shake the sense of dread.

Finally, mercifully, she dozed off.

She gasped suddenly and sat up. Her breaths echoed in the stillness around her.

Her memory was even louder, and she could not—for anything—quiet it.

She remembered a landscaped garden, remembered the rolling hills behind Blake's house in Georgia, the weekend of that three-day concert. His parents had been so welcoming and friendly. Until they'd hosted a loud, crowded dinner party and Kasia had declined the wine.

"Kasia, don't be ridiculous," his mother said. "It is a glass. One glass. Hardly a crime."

She'd never even tasted alcohol before, and she knew her parents would disapprove. But she'd be drinking it with Mr. and Mrs. Hamilton, after all.

Before dessert was even over, her senses hummed.

Blake led her up to his suite after dinner, away from the crowd, and she was relieved. And impressed. A fire crackled in the corner. He opened a set of French doors and led her out onto the balcony. He stood behind her, snaked his arms around her waist, and rested his chin on her shoulder. "That wasn't so bad, was it?" he whispered.

She felt the heat of his breath on her neck and shivered with pleasure. "No, your parents are nice. I like them. But I like it better up here with *just* you."

"I'm glad. I locked the world out, so no one will bother us." He pressed his lips to the hollow beneath her ear.

"That feels nice." She laced her fingers with his arms across her stomach.

His hands squeezed hers, and he pulled one hand

away, piled her hair on top of her head. His lips ran all over her neck, and he pulled her back against his body. When he spun her around to face him, she was surprised by the darkness in his eyes. They were so filled with…lust. He ran his fingers along her collarbone, pulled the thick strap of her dress aside, covered her shoulder with strong, firm kisses. "Do you have any idea how much I need you, Kasia? I physically ache."

No one had ever spoken like that to her before, and her stomach curled at the words. She wanted him to say something more, something that made her feel right about this. That he loved her. Wanted to marry her. She wondered if the wine might be affecting her too much. "I need to sit, Blake. Would you mind if we sat inside, on the couch?"

His eyes smoldered. "Perfect." He led her in toward the sofa. "I'll be right back."

She sat, her mind fuzzy—her body very, very awake. When he came back, he had their wine glasses refilled. She'd already had too much.

But he scowled when she edged away. "I want to propose a toast."

She hadn't realized it was important to him. She took the glass.

"To Kasia, my oak. You're so strong, and I admire that. But I love the effect I have on you. The way I make you smile, the way you shiver when I touch you, and the way you let me know what you want without words. Here's to much, much more of that. More of us."

He clinked his glass to hers, and they sipped a mouthful of the warm liquid. "Now," he said. "You toast me."

She had no idea what to say and felt ridiculous even trying. "To Blake. I hope I make you as happy as you make me." Another swallow. Her throat burned. She set her glass down.

Blake finished off his wine and wiped his mouth with the back of his hand.

And then it was overwhelming. It was a mess of desperate hands, hungry lips, shallow breaths. It was fear and confusion. Her stomach was in knots.

She didn't want this. The room was hot, dark, spinning. She tried to pull his hands back to her face, to kiss them and turn it back into a romantic moment, but he was overpowering. She let him do more than she wanted, hoped at some point he'd be satisfied and just hold her.

But it wasn't enough.

"Blake, I can't—I don't want to have sex. Not before we're married. We haven't even—"

"Shut up. You're doing this tonight."

She tried to shove him away, but he was too heavy against her.

Eyes full of tears, she whispered, "Please, Blake. Don't. Don't do this to me."

But he shoved her head to the side, held it there so he didn't have to see her face. She stared into the flickering orange of the fire as a tear ran down her cheek and into her mouth.

Kasia reached out and placed her palm against the cool of her new bedroom wall, grounding herself in the present.

That had been the last time she'd cried.

She lay there in a cold sweat. Her stomach clenched. She jumped out of bed and ran to the bathroom to vomit. When she was empty, she curled up in a ball beside the toilet. How had she not remembered that?

Oh, God, I think I liked it better when I was oblivious. Feeling guilty was better than feeling victimized.

The whole time A.J. talked about her rape, Kasia had pushed away the memory. If she could keep it beneath the surface, she could pretend it wasn't there. But tonight she'd asked for help. For strength to face her demon.

So there it was.

The bathroom door opened, and a sliver of light hit her. And then light flooded the room. She shielded her eyes with her arm.

A.J. padded across the floor and touched her calf. "Kasia? Are you all right?"

She couldn't answer.

"Are you sick?" A.J. pressed her hand to Kasia's forehead.

"No. I—I had no idea."

"No idea? About what?"

Kasia pressed her hand against the tile. "Blake. He…" She couldn't gather her thoughts, couldn't form a sentence.

"Did he call? What did he do now?"

"No. I remembered."

A.J. knelt beside her.

"The first time…we…he…I was—" *Oh, God, please no.* She pushed herself up off the floor and dry-heaved.

A.J. pulled Kasia's hair out of her face and held it back. Nothing left but bile. When Kasia sat back on the cold tiles, she unloaded every gut-wrenching, sickening detail.

And she wished she'd never remembered.

33

Zan appreciated one thing about the legal system: Victims of violent crime—in imminent danger—were given priority on the docket.

Seemed like they understood the need for immediate justice for Bailey. If not a preemptive strike, at least a quick reaction.

God, however, had taken His sweet time.

Wednesday morning, back in Charleston, Zan woke around five to fix Bailey breakfast before they were due at the courthouse. If he could've been in town last week too, for Bailey's entire trial, he would've. But the three days Coach Markman allowed him to testify would have to be enough.

Tomorrow the jury would announce their verdict, and Michael would receive his sentence. No way he'd get off.

The only downside, as far as Zan was concerned, was that capital punishment wasn't on the table.

He grabbed the banana he'd stuck in the freezer the night before, broke it, and dropped it into the blender with the milk and ice. A few squirts of chocolate syrup, and it was almost done. Before serving Bailey, Zan topped her glass with a fuchsia-and-yellow drink umbrella. She may be on a liquid diet, but her drinks didn't have to be boring.

"Voilà," he said. "Chocolate Bliss a l'Alexander." Zan bent to place the drink in her hands and gave her a gentle peck on the forehead. Bailey's eyes filled with affection.

He pulled up a wicker chair and sat across from her, angled so he could look out at Beresford Creek too. A boat purred past slowly, headed toward the Cooper River. "Are you lookin' forward to Mike's jail time as much as I am?"

Her lip quirked into a misshapen frown.

That wasn't the effect he'd aimed for. "You're not sorry for him, are you?"

She picked up her marker and wrote on the whiteboard. *No, he deserves it, but—I wish none of this had ever happened.* She sat, pensive, for a moment and then wrote again. *I will feel safer knowing he can't get to me.* Her mouth formed a tight line.

"But..." Zan prompted.

She scribbled more and spun the board toward him. *I'm not afraid of him anymore. I am more than just my body.*

Zan sat back and blew out a breath. "You're something else."

An eyebrow lifted before she remembered that hurt.

He winced with her. "But you're right."

"Zan." It pained her to say his name. His gaze locked on hers, and she pointed at the board. She wrote each letter with strength. *I trust God with everything.*

"Listen, I'm...I'm real thankful you've got that kind of faith."

She searched his eyes.

"I'm working on it too," he mumbled.

She bloomed.

"We can talk about that later though."

She pointed to a previously written list at the top

of the whiteboard. *~~School~~. ~~Baseball~~. Roommate.*

"You'd like him. He looks really rough—the type of guy you don't want as an enemy. But he's a good guy. He's the one who answers most of my questions—he invited me to church."

Name?

"Jayce."

Tell him I'm praying for him.

"Ha, ha. Yeah, I'll do that."

She wrote something else. Spun the board back to him. *That bracelet you're wearing. Where's it from?*

He tipped his head back and smiled. "Kasia. She brought it to me from Peru."

Bailey's face filled with questions, and she wiggled her marker over the board, almost like she didn't know where to start.

"How 'bout I just tell you everything? I could use a little insight anyway."

~*~

Watching Bailey have to sit there in her wheelchair with her jaw wired shut was pure torture. Mike's smug face behind the defense table on top of it was too much. It had taken every ounce of self-control Zan could muster not to lay him out right there in front of the judge and everybody. It was just like that day in the alley, when every fiber of his being had thrummed with the need to kill Michael Weston.

Which was why Zan headed out to his island. To think things through. His lats burned as he rowed against the current. His head was so full he'd taken off as soon as they'd come back from court this afternoon.

The skiff rocked in the surf. Zan hopped out,

hissed in shock as the water hit his pant legs. He hadn't rolled them high enough, and the October wind would freeze him now. He dragged the boat up onto the sand and checked his watch. Three hours before high tide.

He hefted his backpack and followed the overgrown trail. Five minutes later, he set down the pack and rested a hand on the smooth boulder, chilly against his palm. He'd use it as a backrest today rather than a seat.

Staying indoors to look through his notes made more sense, but he hadn't considered it for a moment.

He tugged on his sweatshirt hood and buttoned his jacket collar.

He unfolded the ragged blanket he'd grabbed from the garage, flung it over his legs, and pulled out the handful of scribbled-on napkins and his notebook. Reading over all the thoughts he'd scrawled out would take some time.

Bailey. It wasn't easy to trust God with her, with the trial and all, but he'd never been in control of any of it anyway.

What was it she'd written on her whiteboard that morning?

I trust God completely.

Zan leaned his head back against the boulder, mulled over her unbelievable confidence. Maybe God did take care of His own. Just not in the ways they expected all the time.

He tapped his thumb on the page in his notebook that rattled him the most. Yesterday, at Mike's trial, he'd written:

This waiting kills me. I hope the jury sees. I told Bay I'm worried Mike will get off too easy. She said God already knows the outcome of the trial.

Que sera, sera.

I know worry won't change a thing. But sometimes I want to bring back lynching.

At least I'd feel better.

Scrawled beneath that were the words that had shaken Zan to his core last night.

I'm as guilty as Michael. Not because the creep doesn't deserve to die.

Because of how many ways I've thought of killing him. Torturing him. Like…planned it out. Dreamed of making him suffer.

Back at school, Jayce had shown Zan a verse that said it didn't matter. To hate is to kill. One and the same. In his heart—Zan had destroyed Mike over and over again, mercilessly. Inflicted as much pain as he could.

And what about all the other junk Zan had done for his whole life, when he was just being a regular, self-absorbed guy? He was a mess.

Zan thumbed through the pages of his journal again. Somewhere along the line, as he'd been thinking through this spiritual dilemma, he'd pretty much decided his course of direction.

Every time he looked in the mirror, it was clearer: Guilty.

Zan couldn't stand before God as he was. God wouldn't let sin go unpunished. Any sin. And like Jayce said, that might help him rest a little easier where Mike was concerned, but it scared the life out of Zan. He didn't want what he deserved.

The only reasonable choice was to take Jesus up on that offer of mercy.

Ask God to consider the debt paid.

~*~

In the late afternoon, he tied the boat off and strolled up the pier toward the house. Inhaled the Charleston air and let it fill him. What God had done to him, in him—whatever—felt different. His step was lighter. Every burden that had weighed him down was gone.

Zan stepped onto the patio. His concerns weren't gone. Bailey was still inside, hurting. Baseball waited for him and his two-hundred percent. Blake hadn't left Kasia alone yet.

But nothing nagged at him like it had. Some stuff was his to handle, and some wasn't.

And he wasn't alone.

Zan closed the patio door behind him and stepped into the sunroom. Bailey looked up from her Bible. Figured. She was probably praying for him.

"Hey, Bay. If I decided I wanted to believe in Jesus and all…you know, follow Him? How would I go about that?"

Her eyes filled with such hope he almost confessed his decision on the spot. Jayce had gone over the basics a few times, and Zan had no doubt that he'd surrendered his life and everything in it to God. But the question was still serious.

She flipped toward the back of her Bible and pointed to a verse. He read along with her, and then she picked up her board. Wrote quickly.

He stretched out in his chair, pretended nonchalance, gazed out through the glass into the sunset. "I think we're good then. I did all that."

The board smacked against the tile floor. He cut his gaze in Bailey's direction. Instant tears. When her lip quivered, Zan was undone. He knelt in front of her and gingerly took her hand in his.

"I need to say thanks. It was the peace you've had this whole time. Your argument was pretty hard to ignore."

She sputtered out a crazy mixture of laughter and sobs and squeezed his fingers. "I love you."

Zan kept his teeth clamped tightly shut as he returned the sentiment. "I love you too."

~*~

The next morning, Mike was sentenced to five years. Piles of evidence, previous police records, 9-1-1 calls, testimonies of Bailey's friends—it had all been enough to establish a prior pattern. Plus, Mike had no alibi. Jerk didn't even have any friends. Bailey's written statement and the paramedics' testimony probably would've been enough to convict him even without Zan.

Two officers pulled a stunned Michael Weston to his feet and cuffed him.

Bailey brushed a genuine tear from her eyes.

Zan clenched his teeth and sat, silent. No satisfaction.

This wasn't how he was supposed to feel. Or maybe it was.

Maybe this was right.

34

"Zan called," A.J. said. "He'll meet you outside at quarter till."

"'Kay." Kasia pulled her hair up, put on Tatuś's hoodie, and hid the shadows under her eyes with concealer. She looked like she hadn't slept since he'd taken off for Charleston.

She sipped her tea and picked at some dry toast.

Loud footsteps sounded outside, and Kasia peeked through the blinds. Zan was almost to the door. Pulling her boots on, she yelled bye to A.J., hefted her backpack, and left.

"Good morning," Zan said. "That's the best sweatshirt I've ever seen."

He must be a Chicago fan. "You're chipper. So your sister's all right?"

"Bailey's…great. Still not a hundred percent, but on her way."

"What happened again? Have you already told me?"

He tugged off his skullcap and scratched his head. "We haven't talked about it all, no. I went down to testify in a trial against her husband. Assault and…a lot. But they put him away. You'd like her. She's got rock-solid faith. Sort of mind-blowing to me with all she's been through."

"I'm glad." He'd never talked with her about faith before—his or anyone else's. "Zan, forgive me for never asking, but…are you a believer?"

He jerked his chin back. "Huh. I've never heard it that way. Uh, yeah. I am. Only recently though. It's taken me a while to come around."

That news truly did brighten her day, even with…everything else. "How recently?"

"Yesterday." They stood outside the door of her lecture hall.

A smile broke through. "That's really great news. I needed to hear that."

He touched her arm. "It's good to see you smile. Don't walk back without me, all right? I'll be here just after. Even if I have to leave my class early."

"I'll wait." She nodded. He left once she was inside.

She chose a seat near the far wall. Creative Writing. Not how she wanted to spend her morning.

The professor cleared her throat. "We'll begin with poetry today. When we let our emotions, the aesthetic beauty of nature, or any universal theme lead us, the words tend to flow more easily. I think you'll be surprised…"

The silver-haired professor droned on. Symbolism, Truth, Love, Beauty.

Kasia doodled in the corner of her notebook. Trees of every season—some with leaves, some in the process of changing colors, a few skeletal silhouettes. *If I'm supposed to let emotion and beauty lead today, go ahead and give me the F.*

Another memory of Blake rushed into her head.

And finally, a poem came after all, and she scribbled as the professor's voice competed with the radiator at the back of the room.

I lived in the summer…

Inhaled the warm air
Soaked in the sunshine
Danced through meadows
Savored the scents of wildflowers
Reveled in lazy-afternoon freedom
Gazed at crisp, sun-bright colors
Steeped in strength, until
He brought the autumn…
To chill me with the breeze
To steal my daylight little by little
To sap the life out of me
To wither me with decay
To blind me in a haze
To paralyze me slowly
To draw out of me all that was my own
To make me brittle
And now it's winter…
And I am frozen
I stand in the gloaming
Overcome by grey
Brittle and broken
Glazed with ice
Breathing in emptiness
Numbed by barrenness
Quieted by the stillness
And spring might never come.

~*~

Zan's class let out early, and he jogged over to meet Kasia, scoured the handful of faces he passed. He didn't want any more surprises from Blake.

The door opened, and students filed out—a trio or couple here and there, a lone student on a cell phone…no Kasia. Zan peered into the lecture hall.

Kasia sat in a desk against the wall, her head in her hands. He walked over and slid into the seat next to her, nodded at the professor as she left, unconcerned.

"Hey."

Kasia's head shot up, her gaze so empty, he almost hugged her on the spot. But he was the one who wanted that.

Today clearly needed to be about her. "Want to walk around, enjoy the leaves?"

She stood.

He held the outside door open and followed her into the autumn chill, snugged his skullcap down on his head.

Hey, God. How about a little wisdom here?

He tried to read what she needed. He was so new to this praying deal. Sometimes he'd walk beside her, and other times she pounded forward. He let her go, stayed in her shadow.

She stopped suddenly. "You mind a real hike?"

"I'm up for whatever."

"I want to climb the ridge. To my thinking place. There's this tree up there."

"Go. I'm right behind you."

She took off with such determination he backpedaled. "Are you sure you want me up there with you?"

She spun toward him, her mouth open. "Yes. Please—I don't want to be by myself right now."

He nodded.

She veered off the pavement and strode straight into the woods. A trail was marked, but definitely not well traveled.

Twenty minutes later, they reached the ridge, and

she marched up to a towering tree, leaned against it, and gazed out at the valley below. Zan hung back, slightly out of breath. She breathed deeply and closed her eyes. Her arms hung limp.

He found a spot at her side against the giant oak and leaned against the trunk. His arm bumped hers.

"You said the rock wasn't the first time he'd hurt me."

"I remember." A cold blast of air whipped around them.

"I didn't understand, but I do now."

"Why? What made the difference?" He moved to face her, stood so his body would shelter her from the cold.

"I remembered something last night. You were right. He hurt me a long time ago."

She studied the dead grass at their feet like there'd be a quiz on it, twirled a strand of hair around her finger.

"I wish I'd been wrong." He watched her go to work on her lip. "If you ever need to talk, you know I'll listen, right?"

She finally looked into his eyes, then nodded. "I know. But if I tell you, you won't stay."

"I'm willing to prove you wrong any time you feel like unloading."

Her finger twisted and twirled—wrapped her bronze curl tight and then pulled it straight down. She set it free, then started the process all over again. A few times.

Finally, she inhaled as if she were about to jump into a lake, and her expression went blank. Like she'd switched off her emotions.

"Blake raped me."

Zan felt the words like a kick in the gut. Fury pumped so hard through his veins he could hear it. He fisted his hands in his pockets, willed himself to breathe. Took air in through his nose and slowly released it. Breathed again.

Meanwhile, Kasia went on as if she were reporting the weather. "I remembered my first visit to his house. His parents served a little wine, and I'd never had any before…I guess I don't have much tolerance."

She offered a wry smile, and Zan wished it would go away. That kind of smile didn't belong on her. The finger that had played with her hair stilled, turned a bright purple-red.

Zan reached up and unwound the lock of hair from it. He kept her hand in his, rubbed her finger to get the circulation going. At least, that was the plan at first. But as she talked, eyes wide open, expression blank, he just couldn't let go.

"I told him I wasn't ready, and he got angry. Said we'd been together long enough that I needed to show him I loved him."

Zan clamped his back teeth down. Of all the manipulative clichés.

"When I realized he was determined to…finish, I begged him to stop."

Zan's eyes burned at the word *begged*. She still stared at the ground.

He swallowed the acid in his throat and looked away. Barely bit back the rage. He needed to scream, track Blake down, make him beg for mercy. He pictured Kasia begging, terrified and unable to stop Blake. Bailey's battered face flashed into his mind too.

Please don't tell me there was any more. To watch her stand there and relive it—especially when she was numb to the sick tragedy of it all—was too much. He sniffed and rubbed her hand.

A single hot tear broke free from Zan's eye. For her.

"And now you think I'm a weak, disgusting whore. So, I get it if you want to take off."

"I'm staying." As if he could walk away.

She finally allowed her gaze to turn his direction, and the bitterness he saw pressed on his heart. She honestly did expect him to leave, and she was steeling herself to cope alone. He couldn't have stopped the tears now if he wanted to.

"Wait. What are you doing? Stop that."

He dried an eye with the back of his sleeve.

"Why are you crying?" she asked.

"Because you're not."

Kasia blinked, swallowed. "I wish I hadn't remembered."

He rested his forehead on hers. "But now that you have, you can deal with it. My sister said God showed her, in chunks that she could handle, so she could give them to Him. One at a time."

Kasia met his gaze.

"He beat her until she was unrecognizable. Bailey said the only way to let go was to face it head-on. Ignoring the pain doesn't make it stop."

"'Chunks that she could handle'? I can't handle this one. What if I…what if I remember more? What if I've buried other things that hurt?"

"You might have."

"I don't even want to deal with this."

He chewed the inside of his cheek, refused to offer some useless platitude.

"Maybe it was lonely and numb, maybe even fake,

but it was comfortable."

God, make her see. "Kasia. Have you ever broken a bone?"

Her face wrinkled in confusion.

Yeah, it was abrupt. But stick with me.

"Yeah?" She waited.

"Before you got a cast, the doctor reset the bone, right?"

"Sure."

"Well, imagine you broke your leg and there was no one around to reset it. Desert island. What would happen?"

"I guess the bone would heal itself."

"In the wrong position though."

"So…bent up, then. Ugly."

"You might even get comfortable with it eventually. You could still do what you'd always done. Only with a limp."

"Which would probably make climbing difficult."

He nodded, let a half-smile win for a heartbeat. "And dancing."

She shrugged, but he caught a faraway look in her eyes before she dropped her gaze to the ground again.

"I think your heart works the same way. You can shut out the memories and keep going, but you'll have to live with a heart that's healed wrong."

"I don't know. I'm sort of a fan of numb at the moment."

"Kasia, you'd be able to dance again."

For a moment, hope filled her eyes and then flickered out just as quickly. "What if I'm too afraid of the pain?"

He needed her to see how serious he was. He cupped her face in his hands, ducked enough to gaze evenly into her eyes. "You deserve to dance—and climb. And if you'll let me, I'll help you."

Jayce might kill him, but he meant it.

Besides, they weren't going in such different directions anymore.

He tucked a curl behind her ear. "I'm not going anywhere. If you wake up and need to unload at three in the morning, I'll listen. If you get angry, I'll take whatever punches you need to throw. When you're finally ready to cry, I'll hold you if you'll let me. And when you're ready to dance, I'll be there."

~*~

Kasia stared into those dusky blue eyes that held the same fire as her daddy's. He meant every word.

She wanted to hug him and cling to him, believe for all she was worth.

She wanted to run. He might expect something in return. Sure, he'd been wonderful so far, but he was a guy.

God, clear my head. Help me to watch for the things I missed…with Blake. To walk every step with my eyes wide open.

"I don't have any expectations," he blurted out.

"What?"

"Well, I don't expect you to tell me everything. You don't have to tell me anything. And I don't expect to be the only person in your life that matters. I mean, I know you've got A.J., Jayce, your family. Just whatever. If you need me, say the word."

"All I know for sure right now is I have no idea how any of this will work. I don't know how to be your friend. To be anybody's. I hardly know how to be myself."

"I get that this feels like your whole world right now, but it's not. Please remember you're more than this, and"—he stared off over the valley—"God can bring you through this. Stronger."

She could only pray that was true.

~*~

Zan was the last person who should offer free consultation on what God would do. Yeah, he trusted God, but his faith was wrapped in the acknowledgement that God can—probably does—disagree with people on what's best.

A sobering thought.

They followed the trail back down in weighty silence.

At the edge of a large boulder, Zan climbed down backward, the roots and stones beside it his footing and handholds. He offered Kasia a hand, and she took it, used the same footholds as a precarious staircase.

Back on a level trail, he caught her eye. "After you."

She paused and her mouth quirked into a sad smile. Her fingers tugged at his hand, kept him at her side.

She didn't let go. Her hand felt slight—not weak, but small and soft—against his. Like it belonged there. The hardest part of all this was—again—trusting God for someone he cared about. While he watched her hurt.

Or shut down and choose not to hurt.

But God came through for Bailey. He would come through for Kasia too. Somehow.

That much Zan knew.

Never in his life would he be able to forget this day. The smell of decaying leaves, the thud of their feet on the packed-dirt trail beneath them, the rich hues of the treetops nearby and at a distance in the valley below—Gamecock garnet, Vanderbilt gold, a hint of Clemson orange.

The day Auburn described being raped.

35

Fresh honey-wheat bread, deli ham, crisp lettuce and bacon. Kasia's stomach was intensely grateful for the club sandwich Zan bought her. Her stomach had been rumbling louder than his old Jeep. She could have eaten two.

She sat, crossed legs pulled up on the seat, and bit deep into the messy sandwich again.

They were on their way to the Mill so he could help her set up the activity center for the first day of homework club.

She craved it. Craved the purpose and the chance to get her mind off herself.

Her gaze fell on his wrist as he shifted gears. He had on the bracelet she'd brought him from Peru. Something unfamiliar pinched her heart.

"I meant to ask before if you could use some company up here. I'm free two afternoons a week."

"You don't have practice?"

"Tuesdays and Thursdays we take a quick batting practice and work out. As long as I sign in and do my gym time before it closes at eleven, it's flexible."

"I could definitely use you on Tuesdays. Kyle's got the rest of the week covered."

"Tuesdays for sure, then."

Ugh. Why did she mention Kyle? She wished Zan had told her he didn't care whether Kyle had it covered or not. "Thanks."

"Kasia Bernolak, that's not you, is it?" A woman in purple scrubs called from the end of the sidewalk.

Shea! Thank You, God. Kasia jogged down the walk and hugged her, looked around for Ki-ki.

"'S been too long, girl. Your grandpa and grandma still running the old neighborhood?"

"No, Dziadzia passed away almost a year and a half ago. Busia's in a home now, but she's well. How about you?"

"I got my nursing degree. I'm doin' all right." She didn't sound sure. "We're doin' all right." Shea eyed Zan over Kasia's shoulder. "Got yourself some fine company."

"Oh no. He's just a friend." But he did look entirely too handsome for her own good.

"If he treats you well, you might want to see if you can change that." She winked. "I heard you gonna be up here tutoring the kids. Ki-ki's 'bout to bust wide open. She can't wait to see ya."

"I bet she's changed so much."

"Nine and a little miss priss. Listen, I know you probably want to meet with Mrs. Anderson, but come by and see us sometime, hear?"

Kasia smiled. "I will." She hugged Shea again and the woman left.

In the activity center, Kasia scoped out the workspace, and Zan helped her move tables around. The busyness helped, but her thoughts drifted back to Shea. Her strength. Her husband never could hold her back, trouble that he was.

~*~

As Zan drove back through Huntington, he kept

an eye on the rearview mirror. A sporty black car had pulled out behind them as they'd left the neighborhood, but he wouldn't mention that to Kasia. It hung about two blocks behind for a while, and he managed to lose it with the traffic lights.

It may not have even been Blake.

Zan shouldn't be paranoid. Somebody needed a clear head, and that fell to him. He turned up the heat and made sure one of the vents was pointed at Kasia. The hard top didn't keep the inside warm enough. He should start keeping a blanket in the back for her.

Kasia's phone rang, and she checked the caller ID before she answered. "Hey, Tatusiu…no, I'm fine. Yes, sir. I'm with Zan now…"

She told him about reconnecting with Shea, about class, her new apartment, her plans for homework club. But she neglected to mention Blake. The rape obviously wasn't a phone conversation, but Zan had expected his name to come up.

He cast his eyes to the rearview mirror again. No little black sports car.

When Kasia hung up, Zan peeked at her sideways. "Did you tell your dad about Blake waiting for you in the lot last week?"

"No." She crossed her arms.

Zan stopped at a light, and a black sports car like Blake's pulled up next to him, its roof about level with his knee. He could only see down into an empty passenger seat. He decided to let Kasia keep staring out her window.

But he did punch the gas and beat the car off the line the second he saw green.

The car stayed on his six, and Zan prepared himself for another face-off in the lot. He made a mental note of the tag number so he could report Blake to campus security. But the car turned left into the Finley Lake apartment complex across from campus.

Exactly where Jayce said Blake lived.

That clinched it.

Kasia was oblivious though, and for once, Zan was glad for it. He parked and then turned off the ignition. He jumped out and stretched before he walked around to help Kasia down.

When he got to her, she pointed to the middle of the lot. She made no move to get out.

"What is it?" he asked.

"My car." He could hardly hear her.

"Which one's yours again?"

"The one with my name on it." She bit out the words.

He turned and scanned the lot, stopped cold. An old gray sedan faced them the next aisle over. Thick, spray-painted letters sliced across the entire hood.

SLUT.

~*~

Zan lifted Kasia down and wrapped her in a hug. "That is not your name. It's not you."

She held onto his jacket pockets and spoke into his collar. "Who's already seen that? How many people know what I've done with Blake? I can't—my ministry, Zan. How can I serve God if that's what people think of me?"

"Kasia," he said, "you are not—you never were—*that*. I can't even say your name in the same sentence as that word. That name is a lie, and anyone who knows you will see it for the slander it is, all right?"

"All right." Barely a whisper.

"Let's get you inside. I'll call Jayce and we'll take care of this." He dialed immediately. "Hey. I need you to meet me at the girls' place." He hung up and told her, "Jayce is on his way." Her face smiled, but the rest of her didn't know it. She looked absolutely lost. When he offered a hand, she took it.

The walk was silent, but a few times, she squeezed his hand and he squeezed back.

I'm here.

Jayce sprinted toward the steps of her building as they approached. He slowed, caught his breath. "What's up?"

Zan guided Kasia to the steps and let go of her hand, followed as she started up. "Kasia's car was vandalized. I thought we could get her settled here and go handle it together."

Jayce nodded once. "You got it. Hey, Kosh." She looked back.

"This is gonna end soon. One way or the other, Blake'll stop. If I have to pound him. We'll finish this."

She thanked him, tight-lipped, and climbed the steps.

A.J. jumped up from the kitchen table. "What happened?"

Zan reached for Kasia's hand. "I'll come back when we're finished, just to check in, but I'll probably need your registration to file the security report. Is it in the car?"

Kasia pulled her keys out of her pack. "Glove box."

He took them, pulled her into one last hug. "It's not true," he whispered once more.

She hugged him back this time, but her expression

said she still wasn't convinced. And that wrenched his heart.

"Hey, ah, lemme pray real quick 'fore we head." Jayce waited a moment, until he had their full attention. "God, You know the truth about Kosh, 'cause she's Yours. Blake is a liar, and it'd be nice if You'd shut him up. Mostly, though, I'm askin' You to speak the truth into Kasia's heart. Tell her how beautiful she is. How much You love her. That You and us—none of us are goin' anywhere. Tell her heart, since her ears are skeptical. Thanks. Amen."

The guys were out the door and both on the phone within seconds. Jayce with campus security, Zan with Huntington Metro PD. The police arrived in minutes.

"Security said they'd pull the video footage and see what they had," Jayce informed Zan.

"She's got a protective order against this guy," Zan said to one of the Metro officers. "He's getting progressively worse. What do we need to do?"

"Where is she now? We need a statement."

Zan gave the apartment number, and the officers left. He snapped some pictures with his phone, for insurance.

Jayce ambled over as campus security left. "What a mess, huh?"

"This guy. Every time I think of him, I want to hurt him more," Zan said. "Do you have Pastor Bernolak's number in your phone?"

Jayce cocked an eyebrow. "You callin'?"

"He needs to know."

"Oh, I'm with ya on that. Just…"

"He needs to know. If Kasia and I both end up telling him, he'll hear it twice, but I'm not a hundred percent sure she'll call. If she doesn't like that I did it,

I'll deal with it."

Jayce nodded and passed his phone to Zan.

Kasia's dad answered on the second ring. "Jayce, what can I do for you?"

"Mr. Bernolak, it's Zan, not Jayce. Kasia's fine, but something happened. I thought you should know." He ran down the list of offenses. "Jayce and I filed reports tonight, and we'll try to clean up the car after we check in on the girls."

Mr. Bernolak asked a few questions before the conversation wrapped up.

Zan answered them all as honestly as he could, tried not to betray Kasia's trust but to still take care of her.

"Zan, does Kasia know you called me?"

"No, sir. But I'm sure she'll call you herself soon. She needed to get a handle on things first, I think."

A measured breath. "Thanks for keeping me in the loop. I may see you tomorrow."

"Yes, sir." Zan returned Jayce's cell and knocked on the hood of Kasia's sedan. "What do you think?"

Jayce scraped at the spray paint. "She needs a new paint job."

"Well, let's get her one then."

"Yeah. I know a guy." He smirked and dialed his cell. "Hey, Frankie. Jayce here. How busy are ya tomorrow?"

~*~

Kasia was clean—on the outside anyway. She pulled on her pink-and-green flannel pajama bottoms and her dad's sweatshirt. Her fuzzy black slippers completed the bedtime ensemble, and she didn't care what it all looked like together. She needed hot tea.

She padded out into the main room and saw Zan and Jayce with A.J.

She went into the kitchen and found her favorite mug. The tea kettle whistled before she'd even picked out the tea she wanted. A.J. must've put it on the stove for her.

"Kasia." A.J. appeared at the bar that separated the kitchen from the den. "Jayce and I want to run your car out to Frankie's tonight for a couple of hours. It's 7:00, so…maybe we'll be back by 10:00, 10:30. Is that all right?"

She wanted company. Distraction. "Um, sure. Do you think I should go?"

"No, we got it."

"I'll stay with you," Zan offered.

"Oh. *Dobrze.*" Her heart picked up tempo. He affected her more than she needed him to.

He tossed her keys to Jayce, and they left. "Are you hungry?" he asked.

"Not really."

"If I ordered a pizza, would you eat some?"

She shrugged and pulled her teabag out of her mug.

He sat on the couch and brought her up to speed.

"Thank you. I couldn't have stood out there and done all that," she said.

"The police came by here though?"

"Yeah, just for a few questions. I was in a better frame of mind by then, so…"

"Did you call your parents?"

She played with the faux fur of her slipper. "I don't want to worry them."

She glanced over at Zan. His furrowed brow

confused her. "You don't plan to tell them at all?"

"I wasn't." His gaze felt heavy. She didn't like the pressure. "You disapprove."

He picked up one of A.J.'s batik throw pillows, gave it a squeeze, and set it back down. Then he adjusted it. Twice.

"You think I have to?" Kasia asked. Of course he did.

"Well, I…sort of already called."

What? "You didn't think that was my decision?"

He leaned forward, elbows on his knees. "I guess I expected you to make a different one. I figured I'd let your parents know Jayce and I took care of the police report and campus security. Things they'd probably have wanted to come down and handle."

What's up, presumptuous? Why did people think they knew what was best for her? The word on the car. "Who'd you talk to?" *Do not say Tatuś.*

"Your dad."

She shut her eyes. "Did you tell him what the graffiti said?"

"Yes." His head dropped.

"Was he disappointed in me?"

It snapped back up. "What? Disappointed in *you*?"

He didn't get any of this.

"Your dad is furious with Blake—just like the rest of us. And concerned for your safety. I think he'll check on you. Said he might run into me tomorrow."

If Tatuś was driving down, she had to call and be upfront about it all. Keep the peace. "Excuse me." She snatched up the phone and walked into her bedroom, shut her door.

~*~

Way to go, Zan. Her irritation didn't surprise him. What dumbfounded him was the fact that she could honestly be afraid that her dad—that anybody—would think less of her because of this. She didn't see anything clearly. He blew out a long breath and called for pizza.

Zan straightened up the den while she was in her room. Then he read all of the verses on the walls and studied her pictures. One had to have been taken on that ridge they'd climbed that morning. She sat on an old plaid blanket, her shoulders and legs sun-browned, a braid hanging over her shoulder.

Her smile. He'd never seen her with that level of joy, but he missed it.

On the kitchen table, Zan spotted a notebook and pen. He was about to turn away when he noticed the trees in the margin. That was the page she'd doodled on in class earlier. Against his better judgment, he sat down and read what she'd written.

A poem. About Blake sucking the life out of her.

She'd hit the nail on the head, except for two things. One, she still had life in her—buried underneath the snow. And two, God hadn't given up on her spring.

Zan scrawled a note at the bottom of the page. How many lines could he cross tonight? But things needed to be said whether Kasia wanted to hear them or not.

~*~

Jayce and A.J. came back at nine. The tension had never fully dissipated.

Zan picked up his keys. "I've got to get to the gym, Kasia. See you tomorrow."

He got a half-hearted wave back.

Zan jogged to the lot and grabbed his duffel.

In the sports complex, he yanked his sweatshirt over his head, tossed it, and found an empty bench. He threw free weights on the bar and did a set of ten reps.

More weights, more reps.

He slid on more, his reps getting fewer.

More weights. "Rogers," he breathed. The trainer came over. "Spot me, man."

He could only do three reps before his arms felt like they would explode.

Rogers took the bar. "Zan, that's 325! You never do that much."

"Tonight's different."

"I hear ya." Rogers got out of his way. "Don't kill yourself though."

He did the same thing on the leg press. He finished out with pull-ups and squats, three sets to failure. As hard as he could until he broke.

And then he ran. His mind was clouded in fury as his feet pounded the treadmill. He'd rather have messed Blake up, but that was wrong. The rhythm of his stride matched the beat of the soundtrack in his head.

Blake. Liar. Slanderer. Manipulator. Misogynist. User. Rapist. Stalker. Vandalizer.

As Zan wore down, the rhythm altered. The soundtrack changed. It was Kasia. Vulnerable. Hurt. Confused. Broken. And then he ran toward her.

Beauty.

Compassion.

Heart.

All that.

More.

He ran until he was spent, and then he slumped onto a bench and closed his eyes.

36

The morning wasn't as awful as she'd expected. So far anyway.

Zan had written her a note about the beauty he saw in her winter. His apology, maybe. Whatever he meant, the words buoyed her. There was still frozen muck and mire to wade through, but today she could trudge ahead.

And—perhaps—forgive him for calling Tatuś. But the jury was still out on that one. She palmed the curl-softener into her hair, inspected her face in the mirror.

"Kasia, phone! It's your dad," A.J. said through the bathroom door.

Kasia reached out and grabbed it.

"I want to make something clear before I see you," he said.

She held her breath. Here it comes.

"I'm on your side, and we will push this hearing request as far as it will go today."

"Yes, sir."

"*Dobrze*. I'll let you get ready. I'm almost there."

Kasia ran to the kitchen to pop a bagel in the toaster and pull on her boots. The phone rang again. "Hello?"

"Hey," Zan said, "if you need a witness for the hearing, let me know." She heard a muffled "What?" And then, "Jayce says count him in."

"Thanks."

Ten minutes later, Kasia was on the way to the courthouse. Her stomach was one solid ball of lead. "So, what is this supposed to be like?"

Tatuś looked at her sideways and offered his encouraging half-smile. "It's only a meeting. Just sit and speak with the judge about everything, answer questions. Sheriff Schilling says because of the temporary protective order, you have the right to ask for an emergency hearing within three to five days."

"*Dobrze*."

"I'm glad you called last night."

Her heart thudded. He must have known she hadn't planned to. Way to cut to the heart.

"I know you'd love to pretend this isn't happening. We're all tempted to do that, but we need to face this. It will not get better otherwise. I want to help."

She nodded and stared out the window as he pulled up in front of the building. She climbed out of his truck, and Tatuś met her on the sidewalk. He held out an envelope. "This is a copy of every report that's been filed—school and police. The car window, the bonfire, the incident Zan told me about in the parking lot, the graffiti, and the time he followed you."

"Followed me? When was that?"

"Zan didn't tell you?"

"No." She also didn't know he'd told Tatuś about Blake waiting for her in the parking lot.

"Yesterday, on your way back to campus. Zan gave the tag number to the police, and they confirmed it was Blake."

She reached for the envelope and walked up the steps to the courthouse.

~*~

Tatuś drove her toward the Mill that afternoon. "There's a warrant out for Blake's arrest—they have video footage of him vandalizing your car. And by tonight, the Hamiltons will know that Blake's hearing is on Tuesday. We don't need an attorney for it, so that's good news. Your friends can testify. Over all, it should be relatively simple for us. Blake's built a solid case against himself."

Easy wasn't the word she'd use to describe facing Blake in front of Tatuś and all her friends. Or to describe being honest.

"There's no way Blake will come in there without an attorney. Will that be bad for me?" Today—with the judge alone—had been nerve-wracking enough. But they couldn't afford a lawyer.

"Let's remember the Holy Spirit is your Advocate. And you've got a lot of documentation. You'll be fine, Kasiu."

But she wasn't so sure. She trusted God still. She *did*. She just believed that He allowed bad things to happen. Even to His own.

Tatuś parked, and Kyle strolled over to her window. She rolled it down.

"Hey, what's up, Mr. B.? Helping out with homework club?"

"No, Kasia's got a protective order against Blake now, so you keep an eye out, all right? We want this boy stopped."

"Yes, sir. On it."

Kasia leaned over and kissed her dad's cheek. "I'll be fine. I've got a whole posse to watch my back."

"You call me if anything happens, Kasiu."

"I will." *Or if I don't, Zan will.*

The middle-school bus rolled in as soon as Kasia and Kyle had everything set up. Kids herded in, stayed close to their buddies. Mrs. Anderson stepped out of her office to remind the kids she expected them to behave like shining stars.

The kids were gone before she knew it.

Time for the little guys. While Kasia explained the reward chart to Kyle, the elementary students arrived.

Mrs. Anderson gave her spiel, and Kasia explained the chart. The more days they came, the more stickers they'd get, and stickers equaled prizes. Cheers erupted. Kyle passed out name tags and carrot sticks, and everyone got to work. He ended up at a table full of little girls.

Kasia stepped over and knelt down. "Mr. Kyle, who are these lovely ladies?"

"This"—he turned to a sweet blonde girl with the biggest green eyes Kasia had ever seen—"is Mallory…and this is Maria." The small Latina girl with doe eyes and curly black hair tugged on Mr. Kyle's sleeve.

Kasia smiled and got them on task. Mallory pulled out a worksheet right away. Maria, reticent to let go of Kyle, finally relented when he promised to help her personally. She showed him her backpack. "It's got *wheels*."

"That's pretty awesome," Kyle said.

A finger poked Kasia's back as she turned. A young girl gazed up at her, doing the twist, nervous. Her eyes…this couldn't be Zakiyah Freeman.

"You recognize me, Kasia?"

"You know, I think I do, but I'm sure those sweet eyes belonged to a much smaller girl."

Ki-ki laughed. The beads in her hair clicked as she shook her head. "Mama says I'm 'bout too big."

Kasia knelt and met the girl's charcoal eyes. "Has it been too long for me to ask for a hug, Ki-ki?"

"Nuh-uh. I was real nervous comin' today, but Mama made me. I need some help with math." She wrapped her caramel arms around Kasia's neck and squeezed. "But now it's you. I miss you…and those cookies we made at Busia's."

"Mmm. Those *were* yummy." She'd lost track of Ki-ki the year before Dziadzia died. Ki-Ki and her mom had moved into another neighborhood, closer to the school where she took night classes. But Kasia could've tracked them down. Should've. Another ball she'd dropped. Well, she'd make up for it. "How about I bring the ingredients and come over sometime? We'll have a cookie fest with your mom. Sound good?"

"You know it!"

"Good deal, sweet girl. Write down your phone number for me and then get out your math. I'll call your mom to work it out."

"M-kay." Ki-ki was all determination and cuteness.

~*~

Sweet conversations peppered the hour and a half, and before they knew it, it was time to go. Hugs, high-fives, and fist bumps almost knocked Kasia and Kyle over as the kids rushed out the door.

"You were great in there." Kasia buckled her seatbelt.

"I honestly enjoyed it. Who knew kids could be so fun?" He turned down the radio. "Hey, I thought maybe you'd like to start playing with the worship crew for small group. Get yourself back into the swing."

He made it sound so easy. "I'll think about it."

"Yeah, definitely. And maybe get back on a stage too. If that's what you want. Even if you just sing with Jayce and me."

She'd love to be ready for that but wasn't there yet. "Maybe small group. Oh, almost forgot. I was supposed to meet A.J. by the library at five. Can you drop me there?"

"Yep. I need to swing through and drop you off though. I've got a five-o'clock meeting myself."

"Cool. No problem."

"Hey, Kasia, listen." He reached for her hand, traced the length of a finger.

She pulled it back.

"I want to take you out to this new place Saturday night. Audrey Assad will be in town, so we could do the concert too—after dinner. What do you think?"

"Kyle…no." *Jejku*, she hoped this didn't ruin their working arrangement. But she thought she'd been clear.

"Sure, no problem. You're not into Audrey Assad?"

"I am. For sure. But…I'm just not…that feels too much like a date."

"Gotcha. No dinner first? Bring Lenka?"

"Kyle."

"I won't push it." He smiled, but his gaze locked on the road. She wanted to roll the window down to let the tension out.

Two minutes from school, Kasia's gaze landed on her side mirror. If that black car was closer than it appeared, Blake would be breathing down her neck. Kyle didn't notice her skyrocketing stress level. She swallowed, willed herself to calm down.

Kyle parked near the library, and Blake disappeared.

Half an hour to kill before A.J. showed. She had no clue where Blake'd gone, which made it worse. Tatuś would go ballistic if she stayed alone. Or walked to her apartment.

She didn't get out. "Give me just a minute? I shouldn't stay here alone."

"Oh, yeah." Kyle waited but kept an eye on the clock, bounced his leg to mark the passing seconds.

"Listen, I know you've got to go. I'll get in touch with somebody else." Zan.

"Aw, that'd be awesome. I really don't want to make Pastor Sean wait too long. We're talking music for an upcoming conference."

"Sure, I understand."

Her cell buzzed. She opened the message. *ETA two minutes. Coming from science complex.*

"Zan's on his way. Can you wait until he gets here?"

"Zan?"

"Zan. The baseball player."

"Oh." Confusion marred his face.

Silence filled the car. She searched the darkening landscape for Zan. Because he was doing what he promised he would.

Kyle checked his watch and watched for Zan with her. He fidgeted in his seat. Drummed on the wheel.

"Kyle? Thanks. You didn't have to stay, and I…"

"Honestly, I'd rather hang out with *you* all night than go to this meeting. Maybe later…"

He followed her gaze out the window.

Zan sprinted toward them as if the fate of the world depended on a five-second arrival deadline.

She tried to hide her smile, unsuccessfully.

"So…forget what I was saying."

"Kyle, I'm sorry. I—"

"Zan's—is he even a Christian?"

Whoa. Settle. "Why does that matter?"

"Be careful."

What was he implying exactly? "I'm not seeing him, Kyle. He and Jayce just—"

"Look out for you. I know."

She opened the door. "Thanks for waiting a few minutes with me."

Kyle shrugged. "Any time."

She shut the door and stepped up onto the sidewalk.

Zan jogged to a stop beside her. "Thanks for the text. I wasn't sure you believed I meant *any time.* And after last night…"

"You're a man of your word." That meant more than she could say.

~*~

Back in the girls' apartment, Zan sat at the kitchen table to finish his lab report. He'd completed the experiment just before he got Kasia's text but hadn't recorded a blessed detail. Thankfully, his professor had responded with only an alarmed nod when Zan shouted that he had an emergency. He'd thrown his stuff in his pack and taken off. He'd have to pay the prof a visit later to explain.

He erased the smooth endoplasmic reticulum and

redrew it. Too much the perfectionist.

Kasia studied on the couch behind him. Right? He hadn't heard anything in a while. He pushed his chair back and stood, leaned over to get a look at her. Curled on her side, she slept with her book tucked under her arms. Auburn hair spread out like flames.

Zan went into her room and pulled an old blanket off the foot of her bed. He draped it over her. So peaceful. She needed more of that. He walked back to the table and finished recording his final observation. She would have to eat when she woke. Bailey's chili recipe sounded perfect to him, and Kasia had picked up all the ingredients at the store with him last night. He decided to use them and restock her fridge later.

An hour later, when Jayce and A.J. arrived, a big pot simmered on the stove.

A.J. waved and headed right to her room. "Smells delicious."

Jayce sauntered over and sniffed the chili. "You been holdin' out on me."

"I never said I couldn't cook."

Jayce rubbed his hands together. "I'm thinking some grilled cheese would set me up."

"The girls don't have any cheese though."

"I'll go pick some up," Jayce said.

Kasia yawned like a cat. "Can you get some Edam? That makes the best grilled cheese."

Zan smiled at her.

"On it." Jayce drummed on the counter. "Be right back." He picked up his keys and tossed them in the air. "A.J., you comin' with?"

Kasia stood, kept the old blanket cocooned around her. "What smells so good?"

Zan shrugged. "My sister's chili recipe."

She shuffled into the kitchen and leaned against the counter. "Tell me more about her."

A.J. pulled on her down jacket and followed Jayce out the door.

~*~

Zan's blue eyes filled with mirth as he talked about his sister, and Kasia wanted to keep the stories coming. "How much older is she?"

"Eight years."

"Wow, that's a big difference."

He nodded. "She wasn't the bossy, aggravating type though. She watched out for me."

"Does she live far away, or do you get to see her sometimes?"

"She lives with my parents. Had to move in with them…" His laugh lines disappeared, and he stirred the chili.

"Because of her husband?"

"Yeah. Ex, almost."

Kasia fiddled with the edge of the blanket, tugged at the fray.

"It was actually her faith that drew me to God. I couldn't understand why He turned His back and let all that happen to her, but she trusted Him anyway. She said Jesus didn't promise to make everything easy."

"Once upon a time, I didn't want to run when God asked me to go through hard things. Of course, they weren't anywhere near this bad."

"So," he asked. "You still trust Him like that?"

She looked him in the face. "I want to."

~*~

Kasia pulled the sandwich from her lips, and a string of melty Edam stretched until she pinched it off with her fingers. The night had turned out better than she'd thought possible.

Her heart had thawed a little while she talked with Zan about Bailey. His sister's story was terrible, but her determination filled Kasia with hope.

Jayce took a swig of cola. "So, Kosh. What happened this AM?"

"The hearing is scheduled for Tuesday."

"Want us to come?" A.J. asked.

"Yeah, I think I'll need it. Blake'll probably have a lawyer."

Zan almost choked on his cheese. "You don't have an attorney?"

"No." She swallowed, alarmed by his reaction. "Is that a big deal?"

"Sorry if I scared you. I don't know. Bailey had one though."

"We don't really have the money."

"I'm sure you'll be fine," Jayce said. "We'll all back ya up and whatnot. It's not like this was a one-time deal with no witnesses."

"That's true," Zan said. "But I'll call Bailey. She can at least let you know what you're in for."

Kasia nodded. "That'd be great. I'd like to talk to her anyway."

The grin that spread across his face warmed her. "She'd love that."

"So," Jayce said. "Other than plotting Blake's legal demise, what are the plans this weekend?"

37

Saturday afternoon, everybody gathered around the Bernolaks' kitchen table, and Zan watched their crazily intense game of Spoons. The only game his family had ever enjoyed together was baseball.

Kasia had a great laugh. His favorite part was her high-pitched squeal when someone grabbed a spoon. Then everybody clued in and chaos broke loose.

Jayce got the credit for taking her up to her parents' for the night. Anyone could see Kasia would go stir-crazy trapped inside. She wasn't the veg-in-front-of-the-television type, and with no classes or club for the next two days, her options were few.

Zan's phone buzzed in his pocket. *Bailey.* He stepped outside. "Thanks for calling back."

"Absolutely. Mind if I actually talk to Kasia?"

"Uh, no. That's cool. Let me get her." He hated to interrupt her when her smile was on a roll. "Kasia, it's Bailey. About the hearing. Do you want me to—"

All seriousness, Kasia stood up, took his phone, and walked down the hall with it.

~*~

Kasia shut her bedroom door behind her. "Hello?"

"Hi, Kasia. I hope you don't feel weird about my call, but Zan said you could use a heads-up about Tuesday."

"Oh, I appreciate it. More than you know."

"How about I tell you how it went for me, and you can ask questions. Sound good?"

"Sure." Kasia pulled a pen and notepad out of her nightstand and sat on her bed.

"First off, you need to know that a hearing isn't like a trial. There's no jury. You'll present your side, and the guy…"

"Blake." Kasia hated saying his name.

"Blake—or his attorney—will get a chance to cross-examine you. Ask questions. And then Blake will get to tell his side. The judge decides."

Blake could be the one to ask questions? "Can Zan and everybody help?"

"Yep. That's part of your side of the story. But you'll go first."

"How was it for you?"

"Easy enough to talk about. By the time of my hearing, I wasn't numb anymore—I had a lot to say. The biggest challenge was laying blame squarely on Michael while he glared at me the whole time."

"Were you afraid?"

"Um…intimidated. But not afraid. I was angry—I liked angry better than numb. And I needed to do it. Speaking up—saying out loud that you were abused—is a terrifying thing by itself, but silence doesn't help anybody. Michael was wrong, and it was time to fight back…but I did it in a way that I felt honored God. I probably could've killed him in his sleep or something, but that—"

"Would've been frowned upon," Kasia said. It felt good to joke. The gravity of it all overpowered her most of the time.

"So what questions do you have?"

"What's most important for me to say? Just tell the story from beginning to end?"

"Start at the breakup—unless he was abusive while you were together. Was he?"

He was jealous and pushy. Overly sensitive. And he'd raped her that weekend, but after that…their relationship was almost all about sex. It was safer to keep him happy, so she did. He'd always anticipate and tease her about the next time; she'd constantly dread it.

But several times, she had initiated it. Blake could be gentle when he was satisfied. He'd laugh, treat her well. Make her feel like a treasure. Whenever she resisted, he'd scared her.

She had to take responsibility for her part.

Didn't she?

"Kasia? Are you there?"

"Oh, yeah. Sorry. Um, it's probably just better to start with the breakup." She didn't want Tatuś to know all that. Or for the church rumor mill to have any details.

"Mention any threats or acts of violence. Emphasize the fact that you feel afraid for your safety. And it would be good to have witnesses mention those too."

"Um, what kind of questions did Michael and his attorney ask you? For the cross-examination."

Bailey blew out a breath. "It was awful. They belittled me, tried to make me look completely incompetent. But, Kasia, listen. You can do it. You've got to. Look 'em dead in the eye and tell the truth. Blake is the one who is wrong."

"I guess," she said. Conviction settled in her gut. "No, you're right. I'm done making excuses for him.

This has to stop."

"Exactly. Stand up to him. Zan and I have been praying for you."

"Really?" She'd been covered in prayer this whole time? By someone she didn't know?

"Yeah. He's really impressed with your love for others—the people of Peru, he's mentioned a few times."

Kasia pictured little Tomás reaching out to touch her hair. "I'd love to go back. I learned so much."

"Sometimes God pulls us away from normal just long enough to begin something great in us. So, how can I pray for you? To you, what's the biggest thing?"

"The not-having-an-attorney makes me nervous. And that I'd…deal with what's happened. Get back to normal."

"Better than normal. Stronger."

"Right." Stronger. Yes.

~*~

A few hours later, Zan sat beside Kasia on the sofa in her parents' house, with a giant mug of coffee and rubbing Samson behind the ears. She liked Zan there. On her couch. With her dog.

With her.

Samson always sandwiched himself *between* her and Kyle.

But he rested his scruffy head on Zan's knee—on the far side.

Zan pulled out his phone and bumped her arm, passed her a text. His fingers brushed hers as he let go.

Kasia read the text from Bailey. *Thought my attorney could be helpful. She'll call tonite @ six for a consult. Let me know if time's not OK. My gift 2 U.*

Whoa. "Did you know about this?"

"Not until now, but it doesn't surprise me. Bailey deals with the real possibility of never walking again, and she's thinking about others." He stared at the floor.

She reached for his hand, squeezed.

He squeezed back.

Silence reigned for a measure or two.

"So," he said, "do you have someone to act as your advocate at the plaintiff's table?"

She blinked. "Hadn't thought about it."

"You should ask your dad. That'd seem right to me—the way he protects you. Maybe her lawyer can talk to him too."

"Good idea." She'd better do it right then.

She left Zan with Samson and found Tatuś sanding planks in his shop. The air smelled of sawdust and pine.

"Kasiu?" He wiped his hands on a rag and had some coffee, waited for her to speak.

Her palms felt clammy. "I know you come out here when things weigh on you. Is this a good time?"

He nodded, silent.

"Um, thank you for helping with all this. For wanting to protect me."

"Of course."

"During the hearing, would you…will you sit at the table with me, do the question-asking?"

His eyes crinkled, softened. "I planned to. Jim gave me a list of questions. It might be hard not to just give the boy an earful, but I'm already praying about it. Several people from church are praying with us."

Again, so many people knew. She hoped no one

would show up on Tuesday. If they would just pray from home, she could be more upfront about everything. "Zan's sister's attorney is going to call at six, to go over things with me. You can talk to her."

An eyebrow lifted.

"She was in an abusive marriage—did this whole hearing thing last spring."

"Hm. I'll talk with the attorney at six, then." His brow furrowed slightly. "I didn't expect to pay for an attorney."

"It's on the house." She showed him the text.

Both eyebrows this time. "That's quite a gift from someone you've never met."

"She's been praying for me for a month. That's an even better one, I think."

Tatuś nodded. "It is. *Na pewno.*"

For sure.

~*~

Zan and Jayce cleared the table, kept an ear out while Pastor Bernolak consulted with Bailey's attorney.

Mrs. Bernolak rolled up her sleeves. "If you boys'll put all the leftovers in the fridge, I'll wash the dishes. Aryk will be done soon, and he'll want to sit with all of you. Here, Jayce." She tossed him a wet rag. "*Dziękuję.*"

She ran hot water in the sink. "Zan, call the girls inside for me, please."

Zan opened the side door, spotted them in the driveway with Kyle, who'd apparently just arrived. And today had been going so well.

"Kasia, Lena, I think your dad's ready for everybody."

He waited until they started toward him and

headed in.

Pastor Bernolak sat at the table with a legal pad full of notes, still on the call. "No, no, I'm not sure who his attorney is. Kasiu? Do you know?"

She shook her head and closed the door behind her. "His father is the CEO of some big marketing firm, so they have a whole team to choose from."

Kyle touched her arm before he sat next to Lena. Kasia smiled at him.

Zan rolled his neck.

Mr. B. set down the phone. "All right. Let's get started."

He welcomed everyone and had Kasia go through her story. While she talked, she made eye contact with everybody but her dad. Over and over, she traced the design on their tablecloth. It must kill her to talk about all this stuff in front of an audience. Better to get used to it now though. Bailey'd been uneasy before her hearing too.

Blake had pulled a lot of junk before Zan had come around. It was good she'd had everyone else. Even Kyle.

"The letter under your door too," Lena added. She whispered something to Kyle and eyed Zan thoughtfully.

Kasia told her dad about Blake's letter.

"And that's all?" he asked.

Kasia shrugged. "I think so."

Nope. "Don't forget the nail," Zan said.

Kasia turned his way, genuinely perplexed. "I haven't thought of that since it happened, but you're right."

"What nail?" Her dad leaned in, arms on the table.

"The first time Kasia and I met, I helped her

change her tire on the side of the road. There was a nail in the sidewall."

He narrowed his eyes, studied Zan. "I owe you my gratitude again."

This time, Zan bore up under his measuring eyes. "My pleasure."

"Tatusiu?"

Her dad swung his head in Kasia's direction.

"That was before we broke up. Is it relevant?"

He jerked back in disbelief. "Relevant? It could've caused a lot more than a flat, Kasiu." He fisted his hand. "You don't see Blake clearly."

Right. And a lot she still wasn't telling. But this wasn't Zan's show.

"Did he contact you in Peru?" her father asked.

Kasia shook her head. "He'd already done enough damage here, I guess. I had nightmares most of the time—haven't slept well in a year. But he definitely wants to make up for lost time."

The fight was on its way back. More evidence of the thaw.

"And when you got back? He waited for you in the parking lot—that was the first thing?"

Her gaze dropped to the floor. "No, sir."

Zan chewed the inside of his cheek. She recounted the day she'd called out to him for help. The day she'd clung to him like a lifeline. She didn't mention what Blake had said into her ear that hurt her so deeply.

Pastor B.'s jaw pulsed. "There's a good bit you kept quiet."

"I know. I'm sorry. As much as I wanted it to, pretending didn't make it go away."

Her dad reached for her hand. "No more secrets, *dobrze*?"

She nodded.

So would she tell him about the rape? With everyone here?

No. She was done.

Pastor B. asked all of them what they'd seen. Kasia sat, listened, fingered the bruise on her neck, lost color by the minute.

As soon as they were done, she took off like Shoeless after a ball.

~*~

Kasia ran to her room, pulled on her coat, and strode through the house. Her palm hit the glass and shoved the door open. Outside, she sucked in the cold, cleansing air. All that mattered was escape.

At the edge of the woods, though, fear hit. The taste of adrenaline soured her mouth. Anybody could be in the woods.

She shuddered and turned around, headed for her dad's wood shop.

The door creaked as she opened it, and the scent of sawdust and turpentine hit her. She flicked on the light and wandered through the room, paused to inspect each of Tatuś's creations. The smooth edges of another bookshelf, the curved back of a bentwood rocker, the skeleton of a small boat. A roughhewn cross stood in the shadows at the back of the shop.

She stepped toward it, mesmerized by the jagged, unfinished wood. And she prayed.

You went through so much worse.

She spoke aloud. "They're all inside, rehashing the garbage, but they don't know half of it. I probably don't know half of it. The one thing I know—the worst of them all—I can't say."

"Why can't you say?"

Lenka. Superstealth. She turned and faced her little sister. "I don't want to."

"Not even to me?" Point-blank as usual.

She tried point-blank back. "Blake raped me."

Lenka ran to her. "Kasia! When? Where did it—"

"Two years ago. While we were dating—our first time."

"I hate him."

Kasia didn't have anything to say to that.

"But then you *weren't* just sleeping with him." Lenka's eyes were full of hope. As if this one tragic fact magically made the hundred other times okay.

"He only held me down the first time."

"I'm sorry." Lenka wiped her hands on her pants. "So, will you…tell Mom?"

"I don't want to talk about it at all. Honestly, I just want to think of it as the thing that made me realize I needed to stand up to him. Maybe, *maybe* I'll tell her after all this is over. Besides, after Blake broke the window, Tatuś admitted he wanted to hurt Blake. This would—I've got to protect his ministry. Do you mind if I just pray right now?"

"I'll get out of your way." Lenka almost turned to go but spun back and hugged Kasia with some fierce love. "I love you, Kasiu."

Kasia managed a small smile. "I love you too." She listened as Lenka's boots clunked across the cement floor and the door creaked shut.

Then she knelt at the foot of the cross. She should've left Blake immediately after the rape. Called the police. But she'd stayed with him and mired herself down even further. Whatever part—if any—was her responsibility, she wanted to make right.

Dear One, you do not need forgiveness for things done to you.

"But God, I'm sorry I kept offering myself to him—not to You."

It is finished. Your choices from here on are your own. Will you follow Me?

"I will. I don't want to live like a victim anymore. Help me keep my eyes locked on You."

38

Late that night, after everyone had gone to their rooms, Zan and Jayce stepped out onto the back porch. They were still in the mood to cut up, and the house was quiet.

"That dog sure loves you," Jayce said.

"What, he doesn't like you?"

"Stares at me. Sits, cocks his little dog head, and glazes over. Like I'm an alien or whatnot."

"Maybe he thinks you're ugly." Zan chuckled and propped his elbows on the rail, watched the gray cloud slide in front of the moon. "I'll tell you what—I'm not Lena's hero."

"No? Things seem good now."

"She's in Kyle's corner all the way."

"Yeah, she's a big fan. The way ya said that intrigues me though."

Zan raised his eyebrows in question.

"You said, 'Kyle's corner.' Like, ah, like you decided to get in the ring."

Zan smiled. Caught red-handed. "I didn't decide anything. But I couldn't quit thinking of Kasia the whole time I was in Charleston. And the not-following-God rule is off the table."

Jayce studied him, and Zan held his gaze.

"Look, no matter what I want—I know all she needs from me right now is friendship. I can't turn off what I feel, but I won't hurt her."

"Your call, man. But I'm tellin' you the same thing I said to Kyle. She needs guys to look out for her—not hit on her."

The door slid open behind them. "Gentlemen?"

They both straightened up as if their drill sergeant had shown up. "Yes, sir?" Zan asked.

"I'm going to bed, and I'd suggest you two come in as well. Your voices carry farther than you think." He cocked an eyebrow at Zan.

~*~

Kasia and Zan ate *gołąbki* and potatoes with her family before they left.

As they said goodbye, Lenka's eyes were full of strength. "I'm praying hard. You don't want me to give Mom even a heads-up?"

Kasia shook her head. "No, please let me decide how to do this." As if it were possible to give a "heads-up" that someone raped her daughter.

"Hm." Lenka squeezed her once more and whispered. "Zan's growing on me, by the way—not as arrogant as I thought."

He came around and opened the door for Kasia. When he'd shut it behind her, she smiled at Lenka through the window.

On the way to Huntington, Kasia answered at least a hundred questions about Peru. They talked about everything—the people, the angry cab driver, her class, the night she gave her testimony and couldn't cry. As she remembered, shared things so important to her—she felt warm. Like her heart was awakening.

Why didn't she talk about Peru more often?

She tapped his bracelet. "I'm surprised you still wear this."

"Well, there's no clasp. I had to tie it on. All or nothing."

"You chose 'all.'"

His cheek slid back into those too-handsome creases. "I did."

A slow burn began right in the center of her, spread its warmth all the way to her fingertips. She gripped the seat beneath her.

When he drove into the parking lot, she spotted A.J. and Jayce. Jayce straddled his bike, and A.J. sat on the hood of a shiny, maroon sedan. A.J. dangled Kasia's keychain in the air.

That was hers? Kasia's mouth wouldn't stay shut. She jumped out and walked a complete circle around the car, traced the metallic paint with her fingertips. New rims, detailing. She loved the color. On the driver's side, at the rear, a black stripe faded into a few music notes.

"It suits you better," A.J. said.

Jayce whipped out a pair of fuzzy dice. "Interested in these?"

She laughed. "I'll take 'em. If I had dashboard carpet and a bobble-headed dog, I could totally be a Peruvian taxi driver."

"We can hook you up," Zan said.

"You guys are too much. Thank you." They all walked up to the apartment together. Kasia tossed her backpack on the couch and noticed the corner of her cell between the cushions.

"I knew this must've fallen out of my bag." The screen showed a missed call. She dialed voicemail.

"You are unbelievable, Kasia." Blake's sister

hissed through the receiver at her. "Such a gold-digging skank. I told Blake to quit slumming and move on, but I didn't realize how manipulative you could be. You are so completely beneath us. A restraining order? Vandalism? Are you serious? What do you think this is? Some stalker movie?"

Amber's voice dripped with hate. "You don't have a clue who you're dealing with here. Our family will not just sit back and let you smear the Hamilton name. You're just a poor, stupid Polack. Back off now, or this really gets ugly. Worthless wench."

"To save message, press—"

Kasia sat down hard, dropped the phone back onto the couch.

She'd only met Amber once, but she'd been civil at least. Kasia sat there, dumbfounded. Zan knelt in front of her after a moment. "What is it?"

She dialed again, entered the PIN, and handed him the phone. "Blake's sister."

He listened and actually growled. "Write down your voicemail number and PIN for me. This needs to go to security now."

He stalked over to the window. "At least it'll help your case."

"How?"

"She threatened you. His sister pulls the same kind of crap he does. Makes me wonder what his parents are like."

Kasia nodded, tried to shake off the sting of those insults. She scribbled down the information, and Zan pocketed it and left.

~*~

Kasia spent the afternoon in her bedroom with her journal. Her heart was drawn back to the poem she'd started earlier about getting free of the pit. Another poem was due in her creative-writing class, so she might as well explore that idea further. Any distraction was welcome.

The door opened and shut. Her heart quickened. She hopped up and stuck her head out of the room.

"Jayce left to get dinner," A.J. said. "Want some tea or coffee?"

"Hot tea. Lemon, if there's any left." Kasia flopped back onto her bed. "Thank you, A.J. You're the best roommate ever."

Zan probably wouldn't come back tonight. He had to study too. She needed to keep reminding herself of that.

She opened her Bible to Psalm 40 again. *God show me something.* She pulled out that other poem she'd written. About the seasons. The phrases she'd used—she remembered that emptiness. Sapped, withered, blinded, paralyzed, brittle. And this line: *To draw out of me all that was my own.*

That was the crucial difference, wasn't it? Blake drew her out of herself. God drew her out of the muck. He helped her stand. She did a quick search for other Psalms about the pit.

Psalm 103:4. *"Praise the LORD, O my soul, and forget not all his benefits—who forgives all your sins and heals all your diseases, who redeems your life from the pit and crowns you with love and compassion, who satisfies your desires with good things so that your youth is renewed like the eagle's."*

Redeemed. Crowned. Satisfied. Renewed.

With her heart full, she grabbed a pen.

~*~

Three poems down. One about Peru, one about Zan.

One about freedom.

And a melody began to thread through her mind.

Kasia slid around and hung her head off the side of the bed. All afternoon, she'd run her nails along her scalp as she searched for inspiration. Her curls were a wild mess. Still upside-down, she corralled her hair and slipped the elastic band off her wrist, made a sloppy ponytail.

A familiar pair of Chucks stepped into her doorway. "Knock, knock."

She shot up, and blood rushed from her head. She shut her eyes and leaned against the wall.

Zan chuckled. "What were you doing upside-down?"

"Hair."

"It looks like fire tonight."

She exhaled a laugh. "You came back."

"Yeah. I look for every possible excuse to do that."

"Because we have a kitchen."

"And there's you."

Her ears turned hot. Why was her hair piled on top of her head where she couldn't use it to hide? She jumped off the bed and pulled Tatuś's hoodie over her T-shirt, taking cover.

Maybe a beat too long.

He cleared his throat. "Will you be staying in there for a while? I mean, it's awesome and all…"

She peeked out through the top. "Are you a Chicago fan?"

"Since birth."

"This is my dad's." She pushed her head all the way out.

"I respect him even more now."

"But seriously. I didn't expect you back tonight."

He lifted a bag from behind his back. "Thought you might want fresh-baked muffins again—pumpkin this time."

She rubbed her hands together. "I wish I could make hot cocoa as good as theirs. Sometimes chocolate's better than tea."

"I brought one of those too. It's on the kitchen table."

She wanted to hug him, but he stepped out of the way so she could get down the hall.

A.J. must've gone to her room.

When Kasia turned and faced Zan again, his eyes melted her a little. She pulled out a muffin and slid the bag across the table.

"Can we talk?" he asked.

"Ah, an ulterior motive. I knew it."

He smiled, and his eyes were Peru sky again. "I need to make sure of a few things."

She swallowed. "Like…"

"I got to listen to that unfortunate message several more times today, while the security guards and I transcribed it and had it notarized. I need to know you don't believe a word of it."

She sat. "I don't." She didn't want to think about it. Her good mood might disappear.

"You're probably the best person I know, and I don't care what Amber or Blake or anyone else says about you."

She blinked.

"Even though you've got a quirky side. I like it." His effort at humor eased her anxiety.

"Very quirky."

"But everything else she said. It's a lie. You know that."

Kasia nodded very slowly.

Zan reached for her hand and pulled it into both of his. Her heart stuttered.

"I talked to Bailey today. Asked her about healing. What the process is like. You know, because ideally, after Tuesday, you'll be free to work on it without Blake's interference."

"Ideally." She pulled her hand away to pinch a bite of muffin and pop it into her mouth. "What did she say?" *Tell me, "Not so bad."*

"It's pretty intense."

Kasia flicked a crumb into the bag. "Bailey pulls no punches. She told me the same thing about the trial."

"First of all, she said there's *always* more healing ahead—but that's part of just following Jesus, right? She made me promise to say that everything she remembered at first threw her for a loop. But then she started to feel, get mad, work through it. She said the key is to tear down lies you believe about yourself—maybe things like Amber said—and replace them with the truth."

"Sounds all right." If she knew how to go about it.

He pulled a piece of paper out of his pocket and unfolded it, spread it on the table. His gaze locked on hers, held her attention. "Amber said you were a gold-digger and being with you was slumming."

She tried to look away but couldn't.

He leaned in. "Being with you makes me want to

be a better person. And"—he looked down at his notes—"Zephaniah says God rejoices over you with singing."

She squirmed.

"She said you're manipulative, but she and her brother are the ones who have manipulated and hurt *you.* You're the one telling the truth, and the truth will set you free."

Kasia swallowed. He could not do this with the entire phone call.

He looked back at the paper. "She said you're poor, a stupid Polack. But you're wealthy in the ways that count, and your family has a rich, beautiful heritage. God designed you with a purpose, and"—notes—"God's King of the universe, right? So...you're a princess."

Kasia's eyes stung with absentee tears. He was speaking simple truth, but this was Zan. These truths—forgotten when she needed them most—were brand-new to him. His effort alone affected her.

"Blake called you a slut." He turned away for a second, and his jaw knotted. "Sorry. I swore I'd do this with zero anger. Just truth."

She cleared her throat.

"And this chapter I found in Romans was...I didn't understand it all. Romans 8. But there's something you need to hear."

He read, "'Who will bring any charge against those whom God has chosen? It is God who justifies. Who then is the one who condemns? No one. Christ Jesus who died—more than that, who was raised to life—is at the right hand of God and is also interceding for us. Who shall separate us from the love of Christ? Shall trouble or hardship or persecution or famine or nakedness or danger or sword?'" He looked up at her, his eyes burning with blue fire. "It says no. No! You're more than a conqueror."

Her chest filled with confidence—not in herself, but in Christ.

Nothing can separate me from the love of Christ. Not a pit. Not a wall. Not my sin. Not my shame.

He cleared his throat, folded the paper, creased it with more precision than necessary. Was he embarrassed?

He started to put the paper away, and she pressed his hand back to the table.

His gaze lifted. "It was too—"

"Can I keep it?"

"This?" He eyed his work.

"Yes, that. Thank you for taking the time to write all that."

His eyes were moist. "I don't really know what I'm doing. I just looked some things up."

"Zan. Quit it. It was perfect." She leaned over and pecked his cheek.

"Kasia, I—" He stood.

Oh. She'd made him uncomfortable. "I shouldn't have done that. Sorry." She tugged on her ponytail.

"You don't have to be careful with me." He pulled her up, wrapped his arms around her. "I just want you to know the truth." His chin rested on the top of her head. "I want you to know how you should see yourself."

Her hands grasped each other tightly against his back.

"Amber said one thing right on the phone," he whispered.

She looked up at him, curious.

"You're unbelievable." When his lips touched her forehead, her heart went ballistic.

"I should go. I'll see you before class tomorrow, all right?"

She nodded. This time, her silence wasn't because of emptiness.

39

Today Zan looked like he was born for the autumn.

And every time she peeked over at him as he drove toward the Mill, Kasia remembered his lips against her head. She heard his words. The truths she needed to believe.

She felt like she could handle anything today.

"You said class went well," he said. "How has your writing been going?"

"Better, I think. I wrote something yesterday I'm excited about. I might even have a melody for it."

He smiled over at her. Did he have any idea what a big deal that was to her?

"So this lady you're having lunch with—is she the one you talked to outside last week? The nurse?"

"Yep. Shea. She's Ki-ki's mom. Used to live in my grandmother's neighborhood."

"You'll be at her place the whole time?"

She nodded, mildly amused. "And Kyle's supposed to get to the Mill around 2:30."

"Are you sure you don't want me to stay? I have some reading I can do. Practice doesn't start until three."

"Zan. I won't ask you to sit out in the parking lot."

"There's the activity center," he offered.

"No. Go and get some work done. Shea said she'd walk me to the center. All the way to the door."

"All right," he said. "I trust you to be careful."

His words boosted her confidence even further, and she smiled. She'd be fine.

~*~

"We've got to do this again, girl, and soon." Shea wrapped her sweater tight around her body and tied the belt.

Kasia buttoned her coat and picked up her backpack. "Definitely. And that cookie fest with Ki-ki."

"Ooh, Ki-ki can't wait."

"She's not the only one excited, and you know it."

Shea laughed, stepping outside. Kasia followed, closed her friend's apartment door.

"So, the hearing's tomorrow, huh?" Shea asked.

"Yep. One way or another, it'll be over tomorrow afternoon."

They strolled toward the center.

"Well, let me tell you, you got to hold your own—even in his face. Nothing worse than a man who thinks you owe him."

"Look at you though," Kasia said. "You're taking such great care of Ki-ki. And you've got your degree."

Shea grabbed Kasia's hand. "Look at *you.* You don't let that boy take no more, y'hear?"

"I won't." Kasia reached for the door.

"You better not leave without giving me a hug, girl."

Kasia chuckled. "No, I know better."

Shea stepped away from the hug, walked backward toward home, and talked while she went. "Thanks for doin' lunch with me. It's been a long time since I did something for myself."

"Thanks for the invitation. And the walk up here." Shea waved and turned around. Kasia went inside.

"Hey, Kasia," Mrs. Anderson said. "Ready for a full week this time?"

"Yes, ma'am. It was hard to wait."

"Listen, I've got to run over to 10B for a minute. Got a complaint from one of the tenants. You'll be all right till the kids arrive?"

"Yes, ma'am." Kasia took off her coat and hung it on the back of one of the chairs, set her pack beside it.

"All right, then." Mrs. Anderson shoved the door open with her back and stepped outside. "I'll be a few minutes." As the door closed, she hollered, "Your friend's already in the kitchen."

The door thudded shut.

Kyle was already here? She hadn't seen his car. He probably just parked around back.

Her body tensed. What if it wasn't Kyle? She shouldn't have let Zan leave.

Blake's car wasn't out there either, but she wouldn't be unprepared this time. She stepped into Mrs. Anderson's office and picked up a few things off the desk, tested their weight. The industrial stapler would work. She held it behind her back, eased toward the door.

As soon as she stepped back into the foyer, Blake appeared from her left. "Mrs. Anderson seemed impressed with me. Said she's always glad to have young men around to help out. Very trusting."

Kasia breathed slowly. "I wasn't expecting you."

"But then, you never are." He glanced over Kasia's shoulder into the empty office. "Did I hear her say she'd be gone awhile?"

"She'll be right back. And another friend is on his

way."

"You certainly have a crowd of keepers these days."

She glanced at the exit, wondered if she could make it.

He rushed at her.

With every bit of her strength, she hurled the stapler at his face and lunged for the door.

Fresh air came at her like salvation, but he was on her heels. And he was wroth.

She sprinted out into the middle of the lot, prayed someone would see or hear. "Don't come near me! Stay back!"

He laughed, and her skin crawled. When she turned around, her stomach dropped into her shoes. The stapler had cut a deep gash below his eye. Blood streamed down his face as he came toward her.

"Stop that girl! Look at what she did to my face!" His voice sounded pained.

But no one heard anyway.

She wanted to run, but turning her back on him was crazy. She backed in the direction of Shea's. A dark blue sedan pulled into the lot and veered toward them. She shouted, waved her hands in the air. "Stop! Help!"

The car did. A tall man stepped out and stood up, pushed his sunglasses up on top of his head. "What's going on?"

Blake ignored him, faced her alone. "Kasia, I just want to talk. I don't want to hurt you. Why are you pushing me away so hard?"

She flicked her gaze back and forth between the stranger and Blake. Was it dangerous for her to ask for help again? Blake was only a foot away. Kasia glanced back at the man. He approached in silence, furtive. Watchful.

She wished Coward-Blake would make an appearance. Had he finally snapped? "Don't come any closer. Stand right there and say whatever you have to say. But nothing will change. We're done."

His eyes blackened, and he dove at her, grabbed a fistful of her hair. "You don't get to say when we're done!" He twisted his fist into her head, and a screaming pain tore at her scalp.

"That's enough, sir!" the stranger shouted. "Let go of the young lady and back away."

"Ow! Blake. Do what he's asking." She pulled in a deep breath and stomped the heel of her boot on his toes.

"Augh!" Blake wrenched her hair, seething. "I will do what I want."

"Take your hands off the lady." The man was now a single step behind Blake.

Without a word, Blake yanked Kasia backward and shoved her to the side. Her knee slammed into the pavement, and she felt the impact in her teeth. The heel of her hand burned. She needed to get out of there. A parked car was only a few feet away. She crawled behind it and watched.

Blake spun and shoved the stranger back.

The man stumbled for a millisecond but regained his balance quickly. "You do not want to do that, young man."

"You shouldn't have gotten out of your car." Blake swung, but the man reacted in a blur of motion. Before Kasia could make sense of it, Blake was flat on his face, one arm pinned behind his back.

"I'm Deputy Brad Osbourne." He flipped his

badge open and showed both of them.

Kasia sat up, stared dumbly at the scene playing out before her.

The man read Blake his Miranda rights and pulled out a pair of cuffs. "You're under arrest for assault."

"There was a warrant for his arrest out already—for vandalizing my car."

"I'm the one pressing charges!" Blake cried out. "Did you see my face? I was only defending myself. She's crazy!"

"You just assaulted an officer of the law, and I watched you attack her, so shut it." The officer leveled his eyes at Kasia. "I'll need you to stay around for a statement."

She nodded. She was a pro at giving statements by now.

Mrs. Anderson hustled down the sidewalk from 10B. "Kasia? David? What happened? Brad, what's going on?"

"This young lady's lucky I forgot my coffee." Officer Osbourne explained what he'd seen, but Kasia tuned it all out.

The officer was Brad… "Who's David?"

"That young man. Your friend from school." She pointed at Blake as if it were obvious.

Kasia shook her head and stood up cautiously. *Enough.* "This is Blake Hamilton. I have a temporary restraining order against him. He's not supposed to be anywhere near me, and he knows it."

"You have a protective order, and you didn't tell me, Kasia?" Mrs. Anderson's hands landed on her hips. "How are people s'posed to help you, if you don't let 'em?"

The plain-clothed officer stood Blake up and put

him in the back of the car. "It wouldn't have done you any good. He gave you false information."

"Lied to me to get in my clubhouse, is what you're sayin'."

Blake whined. "I didn't know if you knew about the stupid restraining order!"

Keep talking, idiot. Kasia brushed herself off. "I'll be inside. I'll make a statement whenever you're ready, Officer." She flipped her phone open and called A.J.

Somebody needed to come help Kyle with the kids.

~*~

Kasia answered the officer's questions but kept an eye on the kids the whole time. The room bustled with rambunctious middle-schoolers, and Kyle quickly gave A.J. and Jayce directions. Of course, all the boys vied for A.J.'s attention.

"Mr. Hamilton could press charges against you for throwing the stapler," he stated.

Kasia turned back to him. "I know."

"I don't think they'd stick, but you should be aware."

"Thanks, um…for everything. I'm glad you showed up when you did."

"I guess the Big Guy upstairs had an eye out for you."

The Big Guy, indeed. She smiled.

Kasia made it back into the meeting room just before the middle-schoolers wrapped up. The kids bounced out the door, already making plans. In the brief interlude when the clubhouse was empty, Jayce gave her a hug that poured strength into her.

"You good, Kosh?"

"Well enough to focus on the kids, and that's all I can ask right now."

She stepped back and noticed for the first time that he was semi-dressed-up. Nice khakis and a button-down with the sleeves rolled up. His tat showed. "Did you raid Zan's closet?"

"Ha, ha. You're so funny. You forget, as a music major, I gotta perform sometimes. Every once in a while, a venue may not approve of my tees and chains."

A.J. and Kyle finished the snacks and came over to join them.

Kasia smiled at Kyle. "Way to run the show. You were awesome today."

He shrugged. "Glad you're back for the small ones. They can get a little moist for me."

"That's gross," A.J. said.

"They'll be here in five minutes," Kasia reminded them. "Let's get in the right frame of mind. A.J., Jayce, this group is super sweet, but really distractible."

"So I gotta use my charm, is what you're telling me."

The group stampeded through the door, left it standing somehow, and found their seats. Everyone was busy from the start, each with their own table full.

Ki-ki bustled in a few minutes late, winded, and ran up to hug Kasia.

"Hey, little lady."

"I did good on my quiz, Kasia."

"I had no doubt you would. Show me." Kasia squatted beside Ki-ki's chair, when she felt eyes on her again. Kind eyes though. She scanned the room and caught Jayce's crooked smile. He gave her a Southie nod and turned to the next table.

"Good afternoon, ladies. I have a granola bar for each of you. How else may I be of service?" Two girls snickered. Mallory actually blushed and hid her little face.

All around, there were smiles and bright conversations. During break time, Jayce and Kasia both noticed a little black-haired boy giving A.J. eyes. Jayce smirked at Kasia, until the kid actually walked over, leaned in, and put his arm on the back of A.J.'s chair.

"Hey," he said with confidence. "My name's Taylor, but you can call me T-Dawg."

"How old are you, T-Dawg?" A.J. asked. "Nine?"

"Ten. I haven't seen you around here before."

"That's probably because I'm usually very busy studying and hanging out with this guy—at college." She pointed to Jayce, who stepped up and offered his hand to Taylor. "Excuse me for a second." A.J. scooted over to the table of girls.

Jayce sat for a little man-to-man. "You must have a pretty smooth-talking older brother, T-Dawg." The boy's chest puffed out. "Lemme give ya a little hint about the older ladies—'specially this one."

When Jayce stood up a minute later, the little man and the big man eyed each other with respect and bumped fists. Taylor asked Kasia if he could put a sticker on the chart as he left.

"Sure thing."

He walked away, dignity intact. *Nice, Jayce.*

They cleaned up after the kids cleared out, and Kyle pulled Kasia aside.

"I'm sorry I wasn't here."

She shrugged. "Don't worry about it. You were here on time. He skulked in early. And I appreciate you letting me have the time with the officer."

"Do you want to grab somethin' to eat, maybe? Chill a little while?"

She had to give him points for persistence. "Sorry. I just want to get back to school."

Jayce walked up. "Maybe we can all hang tonight after small group, yeah? A big group's more Kasia's speed."

Kyle nodded. "That'd be cool."

"We brought my car, Kasia," A.J. said, "so you can ride back with us."

Kasia picked up her belongings and followed them out.

The ride back was quiet. A.J. turned on the radio, and Jayce texted somebody.

When they drove onto the campus fifteen minutes later, Zan hopped down off his hood and watched them park.

40

What Zan wanted to do was hold her, make sure she was all right.

But he didn't know what she would need after her run-in with that creep. Zan didn't even know exactly what had gone down.

And what mattered was how she was doing.

So he leaned back against the grille and crossed his arms. Waited.

She wore the same blue sweater and black pants she'd been in when he dropped her off at noon—no surprise there—but the pants were ripped at the knee, a small piece of material flapping. Her wrist was wrapped in gauze, and her left boot was scuffed up. Left knee, left wrist, left boot. That piece of trash had shoved her on the ground.

God, I can't do this. I can't see how she's been hurt and not want to go rip Hamilton apart. I need a real shift in focus here.

She's here, Blake's in jail, and a heart full of rage accomplishes nothing.

She shouldered her backpack and ambled toward him. He stepped up and met her, took the bag. Then he reached for her left hand and inspected it.

"I'm fine," she said.

Zan nodded to Jayce, who waved and pointed toward the music building. He'd been working on a song for A.J. Must've finished it.

Zan traced Kasia's thumb with his fingertip, searched her eyes. "Quite a day."

"It was definitely something," she said. "I don't know what to say about it."

"Jayce only told me Blake was waiting for you, and he chased you outside. I didn't know he hurt you."

Her mouth tipped up. "Not as bad as I hurt him. I threw a stapler at his face. I'm pretty sure that's the only reason I made it out the door—other than divine intervention."

"What do you mean?"

"I mean—even when none of you guys were around—God had my back. Seriously. As Blake came after me, an unmarked car pulled in right behind him. The officer had left his coffee at home."

Humbled and thankful, Zan tugged at a fraying thread of gauze and traced a line in her wrist. She shivered.

"Hey, you know what?" She took his hand and led him toward his passenger door.

"What?"

"I'm famished. Why don't we go to Pete's for a greasy burger?"

He unlocked the door and opened it. That was easy. He would've followed her anywhere.

His regular corner booth was empty, and he slid in across from her.

The waitress immediately brought two mugs and two waters over. She looked at Kasia. "I know he's havin' coffee. You too, doll?"

"Please. And I know what I want. A bacon cheeseburger with home fries, and a side of honey mustard."

The waitress nodded, filled their coffee.

"I'll have the same. No honey mustard."

Kasia reached for the bowl of creamer and emptied four of the tiny cups into her mug. She noticed his perusal. "What? I'm a fan of lattes."

Real conversation didn't come easily though. Kasia's smile was in place, but she spent most of the next ten minutes sipping at her coffee and rearranging her silverware.

"If you need to talk about anything…" he tried.

"Thanks, but I'd rather have some distraction." She used the condensation from her ice water to draw a picture on the tabletop and said nothing more.

God? A little help?

~*~

Kasia was hungry, but a knot formed in the pit of her stomach that had nothing to do with food. It wasn't nerves; it was…a ball of pure tension. She felt like a nocked arrow, unsure of her target.

Once food was on the table, she ate it, grateful for the warmth, but she hardly tasted it. And it did nothing for the stress.

"Jayce said you're a natural with the kids. Tell me about some of 'em."

Kasia recapped T-Dawg's attempt to woo A.J.

He laughed. "I'll ask Jayce what he said later."

"Perfect. Then there are two precious little girls, Mallory and Maria. They have a huge crush on Kyle…and it didn't take Jayce long to win them over either. I'm really just getting to know everyone though. Except Ki-ki. She's my favorite."

He pointed a home fry at her. "You're not supposed to have favorites."

"You're probably right, but she's Shea's. We've got a history." She rehashed all Shea had been through when her husband got locked up for possession.

The knot in her gut grew. Tension. "Can we leave? I don't feel like sitting still."

"Sure." He slid out of the booth, laid some bills on the table, and they left.

As soon as they got outside, Kasia had to speak. Thinking about all Shea had been through stoked the frustration inside her. "Shea spread herself so thin—studied online, worked crazy hours to provide for the girls. And he got out, waltzed back into her life, and expected her to give him everything. It's not right."

Zan stood next to his vehicle. "No, it's not."

Kasia kicked his tire. Hard. She felt it through her spine, and the sensation threw fuel on her spark of irritation. "Where does he get off?" A few patrons rubbernecked as they passed. Kasia wanted to ask them what their problem was. So she was making a scene. Big deal. "Who does that? You know? He felt entitled to do whatever he wanted, whenever, however. Never *once* stopped to consider how it might affect her. She walked with her head held high until he robbed her, sucked her bone-dry. I mean—Just. Leave. Me. Alone."

Zan's face was etched with concern, and Kasia knew why.

She wasn't talking about Shea anymore.

The knot in her stomach balled into a fist, punched her from the inside out. And she finally figured out what it was made of. Pure wrath. She clenched her fists until her knuckles were white, and her shoulders were so tight she shuddered.

"I loathe him," she hissed. Anger locked her jaw.

"I want to hurt him. I want to take back everything he took from me. I want to—"

Blake's black coupe drove into the lot, made a U-turn, and signaled right.

Everything else faded to black. This was her chance.

Kasia hurled herself at the car, barely missed as his tires spun out of the lot.

Undeterred, she sprinted after him, out of Pete's lot and down the road toward campus. All she heard was the sound of her breath, harsh, strained. When she caught him, she'd damage anything she could.

His taillights shrank in the distance, and she pushed herself harder. Her lungs burned as she sucked in the night air, desperate to catch him. And then her feet were off the ground, someone's arms locked around her waist.

"Get *off* me! You can't stop me!"

The mass of strength behind her carried her, fighting and kicking, several yards off the side of the road into a stand of trees and set her back on the ground. She stood there, crouched in defense, ready to launch herself at anyone who tried to stop her.

And then he walked around and stood in front of her, his face barely lit in the moonlight.

Zan.

"What are you doing?" she screamed.

"Kasia."

"I want to hurt him! I hate everything he did to me! How he made me—what he took from me!"

"I know." His voice was soft.

"No, you don't," she accused. "You *stopped* me. You had no right!"

"You can't just chase him down and attack him."

"Don't you *dare* tell me what I can't do!" She spun away from him, out of words, fury pumping hard in her chest.

She didn't have to listen to this.

41

"Kasia?" Zan spoke quietly, as gently as possible.

She was like an injured animal, baring her teeth at anyone who came close enough to help. "Will you listen for a minute?"

She stared at him, so he took that as a yes. "Blake was arrested today. He probably wasn't even in that car. Could've been a family member picking it up or something. The huge thing, though, is that you've just been granted a protective order. If you went after *him…*"

"Then what do I do?" she yelled. "I want to hit something! I want to kick him. I want to make him writhe in pain. *What do I do with that?"*

Zan's heart broke for her. "You can hit me, Kasia."

"What?"

"Hit. *Me.*" He was dead serious. If she needed to get it out, he would be her punching bag.

Her face contorted into a mask of utter disbelief. She must think he was insane.

"Let it out," he said. "You're right to be angry. What he did was wrong, and this has been a long time coming." Too long.

"You can't fix me, Zan. You want me to be all whole and happy like your sister, but I'm not—"

"No, I just want you to—"

"Shut *up*!" She shoved him, slammed into his shoulder with the brunt of her anger. He staggered backward and then spread his feet, steeled himself. Her eyes said there was more to come. And boy, did she let him have it.

He wanted to cheer for her. Wanted to cry.

Her small fists struck his chest and his stomach, over and over. She never came near his face—wouldn't look at him, in fact. Did she imagine Blake's face as she pounded him with every ounce of strength she had?

She roared. "You showed up in my life and acted like you cared. Said you were drawn to me. Pretended I was special. 'Different,' you said."

Zan stood there and took it. He didn't know what hurt more—the sharp jabs of her fists or the pain on her face.

She spat the words out like they were poison. "And you stole everything from me that mattered. You used me. Manipulated me. Just because I chose to be with you didn't mean I owed you! You think you have some *right* to me. Get over yourself, Blake! I. Wish. You. Were. Dead."

Every word was punctuated with a punch or slap to his shoulders.

She turned her back on him, ran toward a tree, and kicked the trunk.

God, help me to know when to step in. Give me wisdom. Zan caught some muttered words.

"Way to go, Kasia...this—for trusting him." She spoke to herself with such revulsion that Zan couldn't stay back anymore.

She slammed her hands into the rough bark of the tree, punched it. It suddenly made sense—she was trying to punish herself.

He reached around her and gently took hold of her wrists, pulled her back from the tree. He whispered the truth in her ear. "It's not your fault, Kasia."

"I should've seen it!" She sobbed.

"But it's not your fault." *Like yesterday. Replace the lies with truth.*

"How could I be so blind?" Her whimpers nearly broke him.

"It was all an act, Kasia. He was a liar, and it's Not. Your. Fault." He enveloped her tightly now, held her arms against her stomach. He rested his chin on her shoulder.

"He…took everything…so horrible…I was a fool."

She hung her head and quit struggling.

"He was the fool. To not see you." He felt a hot tear drip onto his hand. *Thank You.* His own eyes burned in solidarity.

"I'm worthless now." Her body shook uncontrollably with those soft-spoken words, the dregs of an empty heart.

He turned her around and enfolded her as sobs wracked her body. He whispered to her. "Your worth has nothing to do with this. Don't you know how much you matter? To God?" Softly enough that she wouldn't hear, he added, "To me?"

She cried until she was empty. He held her in silence.

Minutes passed, and he considered everything she said—everything she believed.

She stepped back suddenly. "Oh, your shirt, Zan. It's soaked." She wiped her eyes with her fingers.

"It's all right." He offered a smile and tried to lighten the mood. "Feels good against all the bruises you gave me."

"Oh, *jejku*." Her face drained. "I'm sorry. I just sort of lost it."

"No 'sort of' about it." He grinned down at her. "You've actually got a pretty mean right hook, but I'm all right." He laughed darkly for a moment. "I'm almost sorry you didn't get to do it to Blake, but…it's better this way."

"Yeah." She kicked at the dead grass. "I guess so."

He wiped a tear track dry with his thumb. "You cried tonight, Kasia Bernolak."

Her head lifted, and she sniffed, eyes wide in surprise. "I did, didn't I?"

"You did."

"You know what started all this today, I think?"

"What?" He lifted a wet curl from her cheek and tucked it behind her ear.

"Blake came to the club. I felt something new today, in the pit of my stomach. When I saw him walk around that corner, all smug. How dare he, you know? I mean, it's one thing to mess with me personally. But to bring those kids into the line of fire—"

"It's hard to watch innocent people suffer." How well he knew that.

"Yes! And to come *there.* That's not my personal life. It's my ministry. This is about others, part of my life without him. I…I'm not doing a very good job explaining this, am I?"

"No, I get it. It was another violation. Another way to step in and ruin something of yours that doesn't belong to him."

"Right," she said. "It made me want to fight. I guess I exploded—sorry it was on you."

He chuckled. "I volunteered to be your punching bag. I don't think I expected it so soon, but I asked for it."

He lifted her hand to study it in the moonlight.

Her knuckles were scraped and bloodied, and the gauze from Blake's assault was half torn off. "We need to take care of these when we get back, all right?"

She nodded, and he kept her hand safely ensconced in his as he led her back to the car.

~*~

Kasia's heart felt lighter all the way to her apartment door. She fished the keys out of her backpack and opened it. A.J. wasn't back.

"Thanks," she said. "I actually do feel better—and clear headed. It's been a long time."

"Then it was worth it." Zan followed her inside and flipped on the kitchen light. "First-aid kit?"

She pulled it from the cabinet under the kitchen sink, handed it over.

"Can you hop up on the counter? Your hands'll be higher."

She planted her hands on the counter and jumped but hissed at the pain.

"Sorry," Zan said. "I should've thought of that—lifted you or something."

Oh, he needed to not say things like that, because she already wanted him to hold her again. When he'd hugged her after she'd cried, he smelled like woods and a baseball glove.

She situated herself on the edge. He took her left hand, unwound the old, loose gauze, and used an antiseptic wipe to clean the heel of her hand.

She concentrated on how the bracelet fit snug against his wrist. How it suited him. "It's not a problem to wear that for baseball?"

He tweezed a few splinters from her knuckles too,

with painstaking precision. "Don't care. If there's ever an emergency, they can cut it off me."

After doing the same with her other hand, he dabbed cream on each scrape and bandaged them.

"Did Bailey ever beat you up when she was all emotional?"

He lifted his gaze to hers and smiled. "She tells me she lost it for a while, but I wasn't there for it, no."

"Oh, I thought maybe that's why you were so perfect out there. Practiced."

Zan was suddenly consumed with cleaning the countertop. As he turned to throw a handful of bandage scraps in the trash, he muttered, "…far from perfect."

"I wonder how you know what to say sometimes."

He washed his hands in the sink and grabbed the dishtowel from the oven door, kept his back to her. "I think I get help with the words—or God tells my heart to shut up—because I sure ask Him to. I feel a little lost here. Just praying I won't do more harm than good."

He rehung the towel. Her eyes blurred.

He turned to face her and chuckled. "You must be absolutely spent."

As she met his gaze, a chill ran through her.

"Cold?"

She slid off the countertop. "Yeah."

"Is it all right if I grab a blanket from your room?"

She nodded, meandered over to the couch. A minute later, he was back with Tatuś's old college blanket and her fuzzy slippers. She sat down at one end of the sofa, and before she could react, he had her boots off.

He slid her slippers onto her feet. "It's not just anybody that can pull these babies off, but you make 'em look good—poodle fur and all."

Heat flooded her cheeks, and she pulled her rubber band out of her hair so she could hide behind her curls. She took the blanket from him and wrapped it around herself like a shawl.

"You want to lie down?" he asked.

"Will you leave?" She wanted him right beside her.

He shook his head. "Wherever you need me."

"Thanks." She ducked a little. "Would it be too much…? Am I allowed to ask for you to sit there with a pillow on your lap?" She whispered, "For my head?"

As soon as the words were out, she regretted it.

"I told you, you can ask for anything." He sat down on the far end and chose the softest of A.J.'s throw cushions, settled it against his leg.

Her stomach fluttered at the sight, and she knew this probably crossed some imaginary line in the sand, but she so wanted to curl up next to him.

Her head on the pillow, she pulled the worn blanket tight around her and turned on her side, pulled her knees up close. Zan stretched his arm out on the back of the couch and settled in.

He felt as safe as home.

~*~

Zan swallowed hard when her bandaged hands curled up next to his leg. She was so beautiful, so peaceful. He closed his eyes and prayed for her, for patience. For discipline. There was a time, not too long ago, when a girl might've snuggled up, and he'd have thought about getting her to take it a step farther.

But not anymore. And not with Kasia.

He couldn't let his thoughts head that direction. At all. He shook it off, pulled out his cell, and texted Jayce to let him know what was up.

As soon as her breathing changed, Zan eased himself out of the danger zone. His fingers wanted to run through her auburn hair, and he needed to find something constructive for them to do. He checked the pantry and made a decision.

An hour later, when A.J. and Jayce got there, a pan of warm brownies—Li'l Mama's recipe—sat on the counter, candles glowed, and a Sara Groves album played in the background. Jayce cocked an eyebrow, but Zan smiled and shook his head. "Believe me, she needed it…and I needed some ambient noise so my baking didn't wake her."

"Sure, man, sure. Brownies are always a good idea," Jayce said.

A.J. laughed.

"What? My mom's recipe is easy."

A sharp nod said Jayce was satisfied. "How's she doing?"

"She's getting somewhere."

42

Tuesday morning—courthouse morning—felt heavy. The sky was gray and overcast, and the air smelled like winter. Kasia scanned the municipal building's lot as Zan found a place to park. Jayce and A.J. were quiet in the back.

Her corduroy skirt wasn't meant for climbing, so she stood on the running board and Zan lifted her down. She hugged him on impulse, and he pulled in a breath, slid his arms around her. She lifted her gaze to his, and his eyes made her feel as if anything was possible.

And of course, it was.

Truth.

Tatuś strode down the steps to meet her. "We were in the lobby. Lenka kept an eye out."

They all entered the large marble lobby together. In small groups, they shared quiet conversations—even the tiniest sounds echoed off the cold stone.

The click of high heels sounded in the hall, like a string of small firecrackers. An austere woman in a charcoal-gray business suit, hair pulled back into a bun at the nape of her neck, strode toward them. "I assume you're the Bernolaks? Good morning, Zan."

His head whipped to attention. "Mrs. Johansen. I didn't expect you."

Tatuś stepped up immediately, offered his hand. "Aryk Bernolak. You are?"

"Lydia Johansen. We spoke on the phone. Zan's sister and I felt that Kasia needed the presence of an attorney today. There'll be no charge, but I'd like to act as her advocate, if that's acceptable."

Kasia glanced at Zan, who seemed genuinely surprised. The confident smile and nod he offered calmed Kasia a tad, but—this was so last minute. She'd psyched herself up for something totally different.

Her dad cleared his throat. "Is there somewhere we can discuss this privately?"

"Certainly. Follow me." She clacked back down the hall. Tatuś reached for Kasia's hand as the two of them followed her.

They entered a small room, spartanly furnished, probably designed for conversations like these. The bare walls, straight-legged table, and stiff office chairs offered no comfort, but Tatuś sat beside her.

"I'm sure you have questions," the attorney said.

"I do, Mrs. Johansen. Thank you for your help on the phone. Your suggestions were excellent, and I'll be the first to admit I don't have the experience you do."

"It was no problem at all. Call me Lydia."

"What prompted you to drive three hours up here after our discussion?"

"The Hamiltons' legal team. They're intimidators. They speak first, apologize later. If you'll allow me, I'll act as Kasia's advocate, not her official attorney, but I wouldn't advise her being without professional legal representation."

Kasia watched her dad's jaw as he considered it. He would take care of her. He inhaled deeply through his nose, nodded. "Thank you, then. What do we need to do differently?"

Kasia willed herself to relax. If he trusted Lydia,

she could too.

"Not much," Lydia said. "Kasia, they'll try to poke holes in your testimony everywhere they can. But that's all they can do. They can't make you anything less than you are, and they can't hide the truth. Look them in the eye, and tell your story. You've already got the temporary order. All we have to do today is show that Blake's behavior is problematic enough to deserve an official protective order. Those last a full year."

"Don't I have to prove all these things 'beyond reasonable doubt'?"

"When you press charges in the criminal case, yes. But this is a civil hearing. The judge decides what evidence is acceptable, and after hearing both sides, he'll decide whether or not you need the order."

She explained courtroom protocol, discussed the order of the witnesses, and said they'd have to wait in the lobby until they were called. Mama and Tatuś could come in right away.

"What about Lenka? I want her in there with me for the whole thing."

"She's one of your witnesses," Lydia stated.

"Does she have to be? I mean, if everyone will tell the same stories?"

"If you have three or four other witnesses at each of the events, I suppose her testimony isn't necessary."

Kasia's dad studied her face. "To you, Kasiu. Which is more important? Lenka as a witness or support?"

"I want her in there."

"Then I'm confident the others can handle the testimony," he said.

Kasia squeezed his hand.

Lydia marked Lenka off her list.

~*~

"Alexander."

Zan snapped to attention. Why was his father at the courthouse?

"Mrs. Johansen made it, I hear."

"Yes, sir. You didn't come up here just for the hearing."

"No, I'm in Greenville for business this weekend, but Bailey seemed to think Lydia's services were required. Tell me about this young woman, son. How serious are you about her?"

What? Kyle and Jayce were within earshot, and he didn't want his dad vocalizing any assumptions. He knew how Zan used to be. "Can we go outside and talk?"

They stepped into the biting chill. "What are you asking, Dad?"

"Why did Bailey ask me to take care of this?"

"I didn't realize you were paying for the representation. Thank you." He leaned back on a pillar. "Kasia and I aren't together, but she's—I've never felt like this about anyone."

"You like her as much as you did Tasha?"

Zan shoved a hand into his hair. "She's different—my priorities have changed."

There was the Great Eyebrow again. "Bailey said as much. You're not getting mixed up in all this religion, are you? Bailey—I understand. But you're practical, son. I need to ask: Is Kasia a Christian too?"

Zan's heart was a war zone. "She is. But she's not the reason I am. This wasn't a quick decision for me. I wrestled with it and weighed the facts. I—"

"The *facts*? Please." The disdain stung.

His father's condescension trampled him.

Help me.

A street sweeper rolled past.

Zan lifted his head and met his father's eyes. "I know you're disappointed, Dad. I get that."

"You're an incredible ball player, son. You've got a future ahead of you. Don't risk everything—"

"I need you to hold off on the judgment. I'm not walking away from a single worthwhile part of my life."

Dad's mouth formed a grim line, and Zan could hear him breathing through his nose as he turned to look out at the street. "You were fine without all the confusion."

"I'm not confused, Dad. I feel more sure of this than anything—ever. You've got to trust me enough to let me find my own way."

"I hope things go well for your friend in there." The disappointment in his voice was a bucket of icy water on Zan's fire. His dad turned and walked down the steps.

~*~

No one said much as they waited, the air charged with unease.

Kasia stayed close to Tatuś, looped her arm through his. Zan stood over by Jayce and A.J., and his shoulders seemed slumped with burden, but every time his eyes connected with hers, he filled her with encouragement. She could do this.

Lydia checked her watch and suggested the family find seats in the courtroom. The Bernolaks followed her into the large hall and sat down. Kasia studied the room intently—every chair, every alcove, every plant, each light fixture—memorized their placement and characteristics as if her life depended on it.

Tatuś tapped a silent *I. Love. You.* on her knee, and she tried to smile at him.

Her mouth tasted sour.

The court officer stood and called out, began the session for the day. Then she heard her name. "Miss Kasia Bernolak." Lydia stood, briefcase in hand, and nodded to Kasia. The two of them—without Tatuś—stepped up and took seats at the plaintiff's table. On the other side of the room, the defendant's table was empty.

Then the side door opened, and Blake—head high—strode in between two officers. A well-dressed man followed him in and sat beside him at the table. Blake cast a fleeting glance at Kasia, his eyes full of derision. She felt sick.

"All rise for the Honorable Daniel Wilson," the bailiff called.

A sixty-ish gentleman in a judicial robe entered the courtroom and walked to the bench. Though he had a grandfatherly face, the expression was absolute authority. Kasia swallowed. *Please let there be some grandpa in there somewhere.*

"You may be seated," the judge stated. "We need to be clear on a few things today. Although this civil hearing is, by definition, more informal than a criminal trial, I will tolerate no insolence from anyone. If you can't behave respectfully, you'll be asked to leave the courtroom. Do I make myself clear?"

Kasia nodded.

"Plaintiff? You may begin."

Lydia stood and called Kasia to the stand. The bailiff swore her in.

She sat in the hard chair and stared out at the faces in the room. Every one of them incited a different emotion. Confidence. Love. Anger. Shame. Worthlessness. Nope. She'd look at the faces on the left side, thank you.

Sheriff Schilling, Tatuś's friend, was in the back. No one else from church. She breathed easier. Just a touch easier.

Lydia offered Kasia a slight smile. "Miss Bernolak, what has caused you to feel as if a protective order is necessary?"

She started with the breakup in the spring and listed every detail she'd told Tatuś, hoping it would be enough. Things had changed between them, but there was no doubt of his love. "No matter what," he'd said. And he'd proven it.

"And then," she said, "Blake pretended to be someone else—after he'd been informed of the protective order—so he could come to the after-school club I run. That's where he chased me out into the parking lot, grabbed me by the hair, and shoved me onto the ground. I don't know what he'd have done if Officer Osbourne hadn't arrived and helped."

"Objection!" Blake's lawyer shouted. "That's speculation."

"Sustained. Miss Bernolak, stick to what did happen," the judge advised.

"Yes, sir. I'm sorry. Since I came back from Peru, your honor, Blake's shown up everywhere. It's gotten to the point that I never feel safe. Anywhere."

"Have you asked him to stop following you? Told him to leave you alone?" Lydia asked.

She nodded. "Yes. He gets really angry when I do that. Demands that I listen to him. Tells me he won't just walk away. I don't think he's ever heard me, really. He's too busy telling me what to do. Even his sister called and threatened me."

"Oh?"

Blake's attorney and his father exchanged confused glances.

"Tell us about his sister's call," the judge said.

Kasia explained the details.

"I know that some of these have been reported to the campus security and municipal police. Do you have any further documentation?" Judge Wilson asked.

She handed him an envelope with a dated description of every confrontation, the notarized transcription of Amber Hamilton's voicemail message, photos of the vandalism, and everything else she, her friends, and her family had gathered.

"Is there anything else you'd like to add?" Lydia asked.

"I…I guess not." Nothing she could ever prove.

"Does the defense have any questions for the plaintiff?"

Blake started to speak, but his attorney shushed him and whispered something.

"Isn't it true, Miss Bernolak," the man began, "that Blake has also made several *kind* appeals to you? Told you he missed you, wished you would let him apologize. Brought you flowers."

Kasia looked into the attorney's eyes. "If he starts that way, the kindness never lasts long. By the end of the conversation, he yells, threatens me." Blake's eyes narrowed.

"Do you ever let him finish? Or do your friends interrupt his apologies and conversation?" the attorney asked.

"They step in to protect me and get me out of there."

"The night of the bonfire, did any of these friends see you get hurt?"

Kasia hesitated, and Lydia spoke up. "Objection. My client doesn't know what others may or may not have seen that night. She only knows what she's been told, and that's hearsay."

"Sustained," replied Judge Wilson.

"I'll rephrase the question. Miss Bernolak, did any of your other friends tell you that they had seen Mr. Hamilton at the bonfire?"

"No."

"Do you mean no one saw him throw the rock at you or no one saw him at all?" he pressed.

"I saw him!"

Lydia shouted in frustration. "Objection! He's badgering Miss Bernolak regarding hearsay again."

Kasia balled her hands into fists.

"Sustained."

She met Lydia's eyes. *Thank you.*

Blake's lawyer went on. "I'm sorry. Miss Bernolak, can you tell the court which of your friends were with you the night of the bonfire?"

"Alexander Maddox, Jayson McEwan, A.J. Montreuil, and Kyle Compton."

Blake tapped his attorney's arm, and they had a brief exchange. The attorney stood up straight. "Miss Bernolak, you were engaged to marry Mr. Hamilton, were you not?"

"Yes."

"And you broke it off without warning. You didn't give Blake a chance to ask questions. You didn't even have a reason for breaking off the engagement. Is that correct?"

All that was true, but…

"Is that correct, Miss Bernolak?" His tone was patronizing. Frustrating.

"I didn't have a reason that satisfied Blake."

"And the two of you were sexually intimate. Correct?"

Kasia's eyes flew to her father's. *No! Don't do this! I—*

"Objection, your honor," Lydia said. "That's irrelevant."

"Sustained."

Someone else may have spoken, but Kasia only saw Tatuś's pained expression. His blue eyes cried, *Tell me no. Tell me that's not right, Curly-Q.*

She wanted Tatusiu's eyes to whisper love again. *Don't be so disappointed that you can't love me anymore.*

Blake's lawyer said something, but Kasia heard only garbled words.

She had no idea what he wanted her to say, but if nothing else happened all day, Tatuś had to hear that her innocence had been stolen from her—not given. That was all that mattered right now. "He raped me. The first time we had sex, Blake raped me."

Boom. Everything at once. Kasia wished a million times in the next minute that she could take it back.

Tatuś stood, on fire. "What?"

Sheriff Schilling stepped away from the back wall.

Blake jumped out of his seat and threw an accusing finger at her. "You lying whore!"

The gavel slammed down.

Her dad knocked his chair backward and rocketed toward the front of the courtroom, Sheriff Schilling after him. He reached across the table with both hands and pulled Blake up by his collar. "That's my daughter you're calling a whore! Don't you dare—"

The gavel slammed down. "Order!"

Blake's attorney shouted, "Your honor, this is outrageous. We'd like to press charges for third-degree assault." He pushed Blake back into his seat.

And Tatuś hung his head. "Your honor, I'm sorry. I—" The apology came too late.

"Mr. Bernolak, you are being placed under arrest."

"Yes, sir, your honor. Forgive me."

No!

Deputy Schilling put him in handcuffs and led him out the side door of the courtroom.

Before the door shut, Tatuś turned to Kasia and mouthed, *I'm sorry.*

The Honorable Daniel Wilson spoke firmly. "Mr. Hamilton, I'm holding you in contempt of court for that remark. And if I were you, I'd choose words from here on out that demonstrate your ability to show respect, rather than help Miss Bernolak solidify her case. Am I understood?"

Blake scowled, and his lawyer stepped on his foot.

Like a child, Blake spouted, "Yes, your honor. Sorry."

How had she not seen him like this?

The judge turned to her. "Miss Bernolak, have you pressed criminal charges against Mr. Hamilton for the rape you've accused him of committing?"

"No, sir, your honor. It's way too late for that. I…I just wanted to go on record as saying that I didn't have sex willingly—at least not at first." She glanced at

Mama. Tears poured down her ashen face. Lenka's head bowed.

The judge cleared his throat and asked if the defense had any further questions. Finally, he said, "Miss Bernolak, you may step down."

Kasia rejoined Lydia at the table. Lydia simply whispered, "You did well."

The judge called the first witness, and Tatuś was in a jail cell somewhere.

43

The hallway is a torture chamber.

Zan stared at the marble floor in the lobby, praying for Kasia. It'd seemed like with all the evidence they'd piled up, this hearing was a sure win.

He was just out here, talking music with Jayce, and then chaos broke loose inside. What had happened in there?

After the ruckus settled, the double doors opened. "Jayson McEwan." Jayce stood and nodded to the rest of them. The doors closed behind him.

"Aurelia Jane Montreuil."

"Kyle Compton." Zan breathed a little easier. It had been awkward in the hall with only Kyle and a bunch of strangers.

"Ken Winston." The man who'd taken care of Kasia at the bonfire gave Zan a weak smile.

"Patrice Anderson." The tall woman strode through those doors on a mission.

Only Zan and Officer Osbourne were left. Zan glanced over at the man who'd come to Kasia's rescue yesterday. "I'm glad you went back for your coffee. Good timing, huh?"

"The weirdest. But yeah, I can agree with good timing."

"Thanks. For saving her."

Officer Osbourne dipped his head. "It's what I do. She's your girlfriend?"

Zan chuckled. "No, she's not." *You got an hour? I could try to explain how I feel.*

"I understand."

At least someone did.

The doors swung back open. "Alexander Maddox." Zan straightened his tie and walked into the courtroom, nerves on edge.

~*~

Kasia took a deep breath. After about two hours of witness after witness, Officer Osbourne stepped down and took a seat. The room was silent.

Kasia wondered where Tatuś was. What they'd do to him. How all this would affect his reputation.

"I believe that's all from the plaintiff. Am I right?" the judge asked.

Lydia said, "That's all, your honor."

Then the judge said, "Defense? It's your turn, Mr. Hamilton, to take the stand and speak for yourself."

Blake's lawyer spoke quickly to him as he rose to his feet. Blake walked to the stand, swore to tell the truth, and sat down, looked blankly at the judge.

"Well, young man?"

He scanned the faces of the crowd and gulped.

Jayce muttered, "What a wuss."

Blake glanced at his parents and then back at the judge. "Kasia and I were real happy for a long time," he said softly. "I don't know why she walked away. I loved her—still love her. She couldn't even explain why she didn't want to marry me." With every word, Blake sat taller on the witness stand. Apparently, he was getting used to the limelight.

He pointed at her and looked at the judge. "But

that rape thing is a total lie. She's just afraid to tell her stupid parents we were doing it. Whole family of right-wing fundamentalists."

Her face flushed.

Blake's attorney stood, thanked Blake for his testimony—tried to cut him off.

"Maybe I'm just guilty of giving her a way out of that mess, a shot at a better life. I just wanted answers, you know? If that cop hadn't shown up yesterday, I would've gotten some out of her too."

Blake's father stood then, a tower of authority, eyes blazing. "Not another word, Blake."

Blake slammed his hand down on the podium. "That didn't come out right. That's not what I meant!"

"I agree with your father," said the judge. "We don't need to hear anymore. We'll recess for ten minutes, and I'll come back with my decision."

The tension in the room was palpable.

Kasia felt a slight hand on her shoulder. She turned and saw Mamusia's face.

"Kasiu. I believe you."

"I only remembered last week. And—Tatuś. I'm so sorry."

Mama's eyes filled with tears as she knelt. "I feel like *I* need to apologize for not seeing. I had no idea what you were dealing with."

"Maybe you would've if Blake and I had ever been around. I didn't—"

Mama sighed. "We could apologize all day. It's enough that we can work through it now, but that doesn't take it away. I wish it did. I'm proud of you, *wiesz*? You're brave. *Silna.*" Strong.

Kasia pulled her lips between her teeth. "Thank you."

"All rise," the bailiff called. Mama went back to her seat.

Judge Wilson took his seat. "Based on the preponderance of evidence, I find there is a credible threat to the plaintiff's safety. I believe we've seen and heard evidence here today of both stalking and abuse, according to South Carolina state law. Therefore, I do authorize a protective order…" Judge Wilson explained the limitations.

He stopped reading the wordy decision for a moment and leveled his stare at Blake. "Mr. Hamilton, let us be sure *you* know what this means. There will be no contact—direct or indirect. No letters or flowers, no phone calls, no calls from your sister, no emails or texts. No. Contact."

Kasia felt jittery with relief—finally. She would be safe. Safe enough, maybe, to find healing.

"In addition," the judge said, "the court recommends professional counseling so that you can learn some less aggressive methods of communication."

Blake and his attorney balked at that.

The judge leaned forward over the bench. "It's either that or batterer intervention, son. Which would you prefer to have on your record?"

The attorney pressed Blake's arm to the table. "Professional counseling is fine."

Blake crossed his arms and turned away from the judge. *Petulant child.*

"Well, then," the judge replied. "The clerk will be in touch with the legal teams to schedule the criminal trial, and you can expect it to begin within two weeks. Are there any other questions?"

"No, your honor," the attorneys answered.

"Then this hearing is adjourned."

"All rise!"

As soon as Judge Wilson was gone, Kasia fell back into her seat, buried her face in her hands, and let the tears fall.

With relief. She could walk around without looking over her shoulder.

With pride. Head-on, unshrinking, she'd exposed him for a sick coward.

She'd finally fought when it mattered.

But she also cried with remorse. For too long, she'd accepted Blake's manipulation and lies. He should've been put away for rape, and she'd been too blind to recognize that's what had happened.

And this mess was how Tatuś heard it all. If only she'd risked honesty earlier. Would her delay cost him his ministry?

Her chest throbbed.

A chair scraped against the tile floor nearby, and a hand rested on her knee. That wedding band.

Tatuś? Her hands fell into her lap, and he grasped them tightly. His callused thumbs moved against her knuckles, and she risked a look into his eyes. She saw two things: compassion and tenderness. Her daddy's eyes were half-moons, the creases in his face familiar and warm. She sniffed as he wiped her tears away.

"How—"

"Jim had another officer book me right away, and then he personally posted my bail. I've been in the lobby for a couple of minutes. Kasiu." He waited until she met his gaze. "I asked you to remember something. Do you?"

She swallowed.

He spoke again. "Nothing will change my love for

you. Not your choices, not things that happen to you. Not ever."

"Will you lose your job?"

"I don't believe I will, but listen to me. There's nothing I wouldn't give up for you. For either of my girls."

He hugged her and kissed the top of her head. "I love you, Curly-Q. No matter what."

44

Zan hung back, leaned against the cool wall in the hallway, while everyone else chatted about the hearing and the relief Kasia must be feeling. He couldn't imagine.

Lydia passed Mrs. B. her card. "If you have need of me during the criminal trial, please let me know as soon as possible. I'll take the case pro bono."

Zan walked toward the water fountain to give them some privacy.

"Zan?" Lydia's shoes clacked toward him. "A moment?"

Surprised, he turned. "Sure."

She picked up her briefcase and an envelope, walked toward the exit. "Bailey asked me to pass this on. It's for Kasia, but she wanted you to deliver it, not me."

He reached for the envelope. "When should I—?"

"She said you'd know. It's meant to be encouraging. Give it to Kasia whenever you feel she needs that."

"I will. Thank you, by the way."

"Take care." She walked out the door.

He slid the envelope into his inner jacket pocket and joined the others. Lena sure stuck close to Kyle. Zan wondered if she was still cheering for him or—nope, that smile said she might be interested in snagging Kyle's attention for herself.

Cool. Zan could handle that.

"We were all saying how hungry a hearin' makes ya," Jayce said.

Zan smiled. "All y'all, huh?"

"Prob'ly mostly me, but everybody could eat."

Zan checked his watch and followed everyone toward the lot.

As he got to the exit, a strong hand on his shoulder stopped him. "I think it would be best to get back to normal as quickly as possible," Pastor Bernolak said.

"Yes, sir." Zan glanced over.

"Why don't you invite Kasia to ride with you to Mahoney's?" Mr. B. smiled.

"I thought she'd want to be with you."

"Maybe, but you've been a trustworthy friend, and she…well. Just give her the option."

Zan smiled back. "Yes, sir."

~*~

Kasia's ambivalence was about to drive her crazy. Exhausted but wired. Wanting home, wanting friends.

"Kasia." Zan jogged up beside her. "That went well. How do you feel?"

She shrugged.

"You probably made them nervous. You're stronger than they thought."

She cocked her head.

"What are your plans after lunch? Going home awhile, or jumping back in?"

That was the question of the day. And phrased that way, it was easy to decide. "I won't run. I'll be at the homework club."

"Well, this is the day I'm free to join you. Mind if I

tag along? I'd love to meet Ki-ki." He ran a hand through his well-tamed hair and messed it all up. "Check out T-Dawg."

Kasia felt her whole face smile. "Sure."

"Listen, you want to ride with me still? I understand if you want to go with your parents, but I just…"

"Let me tell Tatuś."

Tatuś was a few yards behind her, with his arm around Mama's waist. She stood, waited for them to reach her. They chatted quietly, whispered in turn. In the middle of the crowd, there were only the two of them.

Maybe one day she would love someone like that.

"Kasiu," Mama said, "would you like to come home for a night?"

"No thanks. I don't want to take any time off. I'm riding with Zan, *dobrze*?"

Her mom looked surprised.

Tatuś didn't though. "See you at Mahoney's, Curly-Q."

~*~

Lunch flew by, and Kasia found it easier to breathe. So much of the weight she'd been under was gone. And homework club was a new experience. Not only were Zan and Kyle there, but A.J. and Jayce too.

Kyle found a moment between groups. "I'm sorry you've had to go through all this. I had no idea it was so bad."

"That's on me. You tried. I didn't open up."

"We missed you at small group last night. Jayce said you needed to decompress."

"Yeah." Talk about an understatement.

"Hey, listen. I know I gave you a hard time about Zan, but—he's a good guy. You should invite him to small group."

"I'll let him know you suggested it. And…I think I'm ready to play for worship with you guys."

"Serious? Kasia, that's—I'm—that's good to hear. Come a little early next week, and we'll practice. And"—he toed a pinecone, shoved his hands in his pockets—"do you think—how would you feel if I called Lena? Took her to a few concerts."

"I'm fairly certain she'd love it."

The bus hissed to a stop outside. As the elementary schoolers crowded in, Ki-ki sidled up to her. "You doin' good?"

"What?" Kasia asked with a wink. "I thought it was my job to ask *you* how you are." She tugged on a tiny braid.

"Mom said we s'posed to pray for you today. I didn't know if you was going to come."

Kasia knelt down. "I'm here, and better than I have been in a long time. Because of those prayers."

Ki-ki hugged Kasia around her neck. "Who's this new guy?" Ki-ki eyed Zan as she turned toward a table full of her friends.

"A friend of mine. Everybody calls him Zan."

"He must be the one Mom was talking 'bout last week."

"Why do you think that?" Kasia asked.

Ki-ki flashed her nine-year-old smirk. "'Cause he's *fine*."

Kasia chuckled. "He's a little old for you though."

"That's cool. Mom says he only looks at you." Without another thought, Ki-ki pulled her homework out of her bag and got to business.

Kasia stood there, speechless.

"Miss Kasia, can I get some help with this?" Dominic called. Kasia rushed to his side to fill her mind with something else.

Anything else.

It worked for about five minutes, until she noticed Zan on the floor beside Leland, a quiet little boy who refused to join a table group.

Leland worked in silence, his lower lip a mile out. Zan got up, walked away. In a flash, he returned with his own backpack. He pulled out a sketchpad and pencil, leaned back against the wall next to the boy. He said nothing but drew quietly.

Kasia smiled as Leland cut his gaze over toward Zan's pad, watched.

She helped Mallory with simple predicates and peeked back. Leland was on his knees beside Zan, pointing at a detail on the paper.

Zan's smile was incredible, with those deep dimples. He said something to Leland, and they chuckled. A minute later, Leland had his notebook back in hand. Zan had earned the right to help.

During break time, Leland told T-Dawg about the drawing, and T-Dawg filled in everybody else. A bunch of boys snatched the sketchpad and piled on the floor to flip through it.

"Aw, *cool*! Check this out." They oohed and aahed about cartoons, caricatures, several sketches of a dog.

Leland shuffled over to where Zan stood at the edge of the little mob and tugged on his sleeve. "What kind of dog is that?"

"It's my old retriever. Shoeless."

"Oh."

"This is just *writing,*" T-Dawg said. "*Bo*-ring. Turn the page."

"Whatcha write about, Zan?" Leland asked.

"Oh, nothing big. Someone who inspires me."

Jayce stepped close to Zan. "That's not the one you have the picture—"

"You know what? Let me see that, y'all." Zan reached out for the pad, but T-Dawg would have none of it.

"Oh, man!" T-Dawg blew a silent whistle. "That looks just like Miss Kasia."

Kasia watched, wondered. Was Zan blushing?

"Nah. Can I get—?" Zan stepped into the center of the crowd. "All right. Takin' it back." He tugged the sketchbook from T-Dawg's clutches and bagged it. "Glad y'all liked it."

"Make sure you throw away your trash and push your chairs in, guys!" she called. Kids got up and cleaned their places, packed to leave. Zan left with Leland, while Jayce helped Kasia wipe the tables.

"You know anything about that sketchpad?" Kasia asked him.

"Sure I do. But I know a guy who could tell ya better."

~*~

When Kasia stepped out of the clubhouse, Zan tossed Leland the ball one last time. "You're good, little man," Zan said. "How 'bout I bring my glove Thursday, and we throw some more?"

"Cool."

Zan walked backward toward the lot, kept one eye on Kasia. "See you, Leland." Who cared if Kyle had every day but Tuesday covered? Zan wanted to be there.

Kasia walked toward him, her eyes full of questions.

"So, I know you're not technically in danger anymore," he said, "but how about I still walk you to class?"

"Do you mind?"

How could his heart beat so loud and Kasia not hear it? "Of course I don't mind." They walked side by side, and Zan fingered an old gum wrapper in his pocket. "So I'm not fired?"

"What?" Her face was half curiosity, half laughter.

"Jayce and I as bodyguards. You're not going to lay us off now, blame it on cutbacks?"

She smiled. "I'll keep you on retainer. I like you around." She reached for the crook of his arm and rested her hand on his forearm. Even with the coat as a barrier, her touch made him shiver.

"That's good. 'Cause I don't want to disappear," he said.

"I'd love to see some of those drawings."

He laughed. *Embrace it, man.* "Yeah, I know what you want to look at."

She shrugged, grinned. "So?"

"I'll show you the picture, but not what I wrote. Not yet."

"Hm. All right. I can respect that."

The air smelled like snow, and the sky was a pale gray. Zan breathed it in deeply, wondered where they'd go from here.

He rubbed his hands together and pulled his skullcap out of his pocket. "Let's get some hot chocolate and muffins."

45

Kasia couldn't wait any longer. This was how she wanted to end the night. She tugged Zan's hand and led him to the chair in the den. A.J. and Jayce were on the couch. Their movie had just ended.

"What's up?" Jayce pointed the remote and turned off the TV.

"I want to play something for you guys."

Zan's face lit up. Why in the world she was playing her first song in front of that smile that made her giddy, she didn't know. But she sure was.

She wanted him to hear it. Whether or not he knew how momentous this was to her.

A.J. straightened up. "Coffeehouse style. We've already got all these candles lit. It's perfect."

It was. Semi-darkness was good for ambience and hiding.

But knowing who was in the darkness with her meant the most.

Kasia sat on the floor, wearing her fuzzy slippers and Tatuś's hoodie. Every little bit of comfort helped.

Her fingers picked the intro, finally at home on the guitar. Jayce's thumb drew her attention, tapping to the beat as she played.

But her stomach trembled a little. What would they all think?

No time to wonder anymore. *God, this is for You anyway.* She wet her lips, and she sang, soft and attentive.

Here I am again, even smaller than before
Bent beneath the weight of all my shame
I am brittle. I am broken, numb to the core
These thorns won't go away,
I am only weak, let me hide and wait.
I can't take another storm.

Jayce's hand had stilled. A.J.'s mouth quirked in a sad smile. Kasia couldn't look at Zan just yet.

I try to find the words as I grieve for all that's lost
Heartache robs my breath, a stabbing pain
I am empty, I am spent, now I feel the cost
Strains of silence are all that remain

So long she'd felt this. Keeping the truth pent up had nearly broken her for good. Fear of honesty, of speaking the truth out loud had caused its own damage. But God hadn't left her to suffer it.

She peeked up at Zan and caught him glancing over at Jayce. Jayce shook his head. When he turned back, their eyes met, and she almost couldn't handle his compassion. Gaze back down, she kept an eye on the chords. This was the moment everything transitioned anyway.

But in my weak and frightened state,
Your strong love lifts me up

She picked up the tempo. When God lifted her, the melody of her whole life had changed.

Out of the pit into the open where I can stand again
My feet on a rock,
My eyes locked on Yours
You pull me from where I've been
You redeem my life, I cling to You
And I let go of my shame
Fill my heart to reflect your beauty.
I am yours, You are Life, so I breathe in.

Kasia's fingers moved quickly as she changed key. She closed her eyes, felt the truth of the words. She basked in the certainty of them and hoped Zan would too. The third verse was her favorite, her redemption song.

Face to face with You, I finally speak the truth
You lavish me with grace, and I am free
You are steadfast, You are peace, You offer me release
Infused with Your strength, I am renewed

Her voice broke as genuine gratefulness overwhelmed her, and she bent her head. Humbled. So humbled. A tear slipped down her cheek, and she played a few extra measures while she tried to rein in the emotion.

When she was steady enough to sing, she did—but softly. Not hesitant, just meek.

Joy restored and rooted deep, I stand tall
I bloom and thrive in You

The words filled her with strength, just not her own. The way she preferred to sing. To live. To do anything anymore. In the strength of her Savior.

Out of the pit into the open where I can stand again
My feet on a rock, My eyes locked on yours
You pull me from where I've been
You redeem my life, I cling to You
And I let go of my shame

Fill my heart to reflect your beauty.
I am yours, You are Life, so I breathe in.

Deep breath. Her redemption song needed to end well. Because it was honestly a new beginning.

Fill my lungs to sing a new melody
I am Yours, you are Love, so I breathe in.
Fill my life to overflowing
I am new, you are Lord, so I begin

~*~

Kasia's voice had cut right through Zan. He wasn't sure what was more right—her hands on that guitar, her voice, her words. Ah, but his chest ached from her pain. He pressed the heel of his hand hard against his heart.

And then he realized he wanted to feel it with her, hurt with her, find whatever peace she was finding—with her.

Jayce got up and pulled Kasia to her feet. He hugged her, and A.J. joined them. Zan sat there in the silence. He wished the impromptu concert would last hours more. And yet that song, that transformation had been enough for the whole night.

And it was late.

He got up and put on his jacket, quiet.

Kasia came to stand beside him. He stood and wrapped his arms tight around her. When she rested her head in the dip of his shoulder, he wanted to keep her there.

He sat his chin on the top of her head. "Your song was…so beautiful. The beginning was hard, but I get it."

"The end kind of makes the beginning easier to sing," she said.

Just kind of. "Oh, hey. I um…I have something for you." He reached into the inner pocket of his coat and pulled out his sister's letter.

"What's this?"

"It's from Bailey. I have no idea what I'm handing you except encouragement."

"I could use some of that."

"Perfect." He squeezed her tighter and stepped back. "I'm going to go, Kasia. I've…um…got a lot to think about. Your song just—"

She looked into his eyes, and his heart constricted. Her eyes plumbed his, and he didn't know what he was searching for, but he hoped she'd find it.

"I need to just sit with Jesus for a while anyway. See you tomorrow?"

"No doubt."

~*~

Kasia felt full, whole, and hopeful as she walked down the hall. She closed her bedroom door with her foot and opened Bailey's letter.

I realize you don't know me, but I've been somewhere similar.

Kasia sat on her bed.

I can tell you, when you look into the darkness and start turning over rocks, you'll uncover some things that you might want to keep hidden. You might want to flip those rocks back over and run. But don't. Expose those painful and dirty things to Christ. It's worth it.

No matter how long and arduous the journey, follow it through.

And the Lord will guide you continually and satisfy your desire in scorched places and make your bones strong; and you shall be like a watered garden, like a spring of water, whose waters do not fail. —Isaiah 58:11

Praying for you,

Bailey

Kasia flopped back on her pillow and switched off her lamp. She covered herself with Tatuś's college blanket and thought about all that lay ahead. She wanted to sit with Busia for a while. She glanced at the clock. 9:17. *Late.* But Busia had always, *always* told her to call whenever she needed to talk. Tonight of all nights, Busia would understand. She dialed Busia.

"*Słucham*. Hello."

"Busia? It's Kasia."

"*Cześć*, Kasiu. *Nie śpisz*?"

"Not sleeping yet. Did I wake you?"

"It's nothing, you know that. How are you after your long day?"

"All right, I guess. I think I've decided to see a counselor at my church."

"Ah. Wise choice, *kochanie*."

"I'm nervous about it though. The whole thing will be really tough."

"What was it you told us about the stars in Peru, Kasiu?"

"There were so many more than I thought."

"*Gdzie*? Right in the city?"

"No, ma'am. The further up we drove into the mountains, the more I saw."

"Your next few months will be like that, I think."

"What do you mean?"

"Driving out into the wilderness, yes? Away from what is familiar and comfortable to you. But you remember this, girl. The deeper your darkness, the brighter the stars."

"*Kocham cię,* Busiu. God must've made me call you."

Busia chuckled. "I love you too, dear. I'm glad you listened to Him."

"Good night."

"*Dobranoc, kochanie*. Come see me soon."

"For sure." Kasia turned off her phone and rolled over. If it meant brighter stars, she would follow God into the darkness.

46

Zan took a swig of his strong, sugary coffee and glanced at Kasia again. They were tucked into their regular booth in the back corner of Pete's.

He loved that they shared a routine.

Tonight his heart and mind were full of questions. About Bailey, about his father. About the future.

He checked his watch, wondered if he had time for a coffee refill, and her gaze met his for the twentieth time. What was she thinking? He searched her eyes for any clue to the mystery. She didn't look away this time, just chewed the edge of her lip and smiled.

Her genuine smile was so different from the smiles of others he'd enjoyed over the years—the ones that were coy, flirtatious, entirely too overt. For all God had done to get his attention, he was deeply thankful.

But a tinge of regret nagged at him.

All those kisses he'd wasted on girls who meant nothing to him. Too many.

But Kasia.

To kiss her would be to anchor himself to something solid, to know something real. That kiss might never happen, but he'd never settle for less again.

Her phone buzzed on the table. "Hey, Tatusiu."

Zan studied her face as she spoke to Pastor Bernolak. Sheer adoration.

There was a father who knew how to make his

kids feel championed.

"Yes! Zan's right here. I'll tell him. I love you too."

She grinned and nodded. *"Dobranoc."*

That had become one of his favorite words. She'd started whispering that into their nightly hug a few weeks before. *Good night.*

"Blake pled guilty at the criminal trial. There was no point in fighting it, I guess. Mrs. Johansen submitted a pile of evidence."

"Let's not forget his own idiotic comments on the official hearing report."

She beamed. "Case closed."

He knew that didn't mean dealing with it all was over. She had a long way to go yet—sort of infinite, Bailey said. But she'd keep on, he was sure of it.

The waitress sashayed over and set down the bill. "You two need anything before I get out of here for the night?"

Zan shot a glance at Kasia, and she shook her head. "No thanks," he said. "I think we're all set."

"All right. Don't stay too long though. It's really comin' down out there."

"Rain again?" Zan could hear his own disappointment.

"No, sweetie. It's snowing to beat the band."

Kasia pushed the door open as Zan left a tip on the table, and a blast of wind hit her, blew her auburn hair back into the restaurant like flames. He heard a squeal and hustled to catch up. The flat black parking lot was gone, replaced by iced cars, trees, and buildings.

Kasia shivered and smiled, stretched out her arms and twirled into the falling snow.

"You shouldn't dance in the snow without a partner," he said. "It's some kind of rule."

She turned and looked at him, snowflakes caught on her eyelashes. "It's a rule you just made up."

"So?" He took her hand, asked for permission with his eyes.

She dared a few tentative footsteps, turned in a slow circle toward him. His arm curved around her, then he unwound her steps. She glanced back, and a slow smile spread across her face. She spun toward him on the slick pavement, and her feet shot straight out from underneath her.

He caught her and held her tight, her face dangerously close. Her warm breath washed over him just before her eyes closed.

Why had she closed her eyes—to ask for a kiss or to shut him out? Zan forced himself to take measured breaths as he studied each feature. The graceful curve of her jaw, her eyelashes against her flushed cheeks. Her lips.

He couldn't risk being wrong. His heart depended on it. Hers too.

He chose to kiss her warm cheek. "I told you when you were ready to dance, I'd be here," he whispered.

Her fingernails grazed his neck as she slipped her hand around him and pulled herself upright.

His stomach trembled at the touch. But he had to do the right thing.

~*~

In front of Zan, Kasia lifted her face to his. Those expressive eyes held all the depth and mystery of the Peruvian skies. But there was a vulnerability in them tonight. "Zan, you know I'm here too, right? To pray with you about Bailey, your dad—everything."

He dipped his head, silent.

She pressed her hand to his face, offered comfort. Grounded herself in this moment. In him.

Even his cheek felt strong. Soft stubble brushed her palm as a dimple appeared under her hand.

He ducked slightly, as though suddenly shy. "May I kiss you?"

His hesitation, the sweetness in that question trapped her breath in her throat. She studied his eyes once more and then nodded.

The corner of his mouth tipped up, and he cupped her face in his hands. She shivered at the touch of his fingertips on her skin, so warm as the snow swirled around them.

His mouth met hers, gentle and sweet—all sugar and coffee and Zan.

This was how a kiss was supposed to feel. She smiled into it.

His lips brushed hers once more as he pulled back, his forehead against hers. His left hand gripped her waist firmly. "Thank you, Auburn." His gravelly voice surprised her.

"For what?" she whispered.

"For being so worth the wait."

She pulled his face to hers again.

He wrapped her up in his warmth, and she felt safe. No, more than safe. Alive.

More than breath, more than the whoosh of blood through her veins, her heartbeat was the song of a heart revived.

Thank you…

for purchasing this Harbourlight title. For other inspirational stories, please visit our online bookstore at www.pelicanbookgroup.com.

For questions or more information, contact us at customer@pelicanbookgroup.com.

Harbourlight Books
The Beacon in Christian Fiction™
an imprint of Pelican Book Group
www.pelicanbookgroup.com

Connect with Us
www.facebook.com/Pelicanbookgroup
www.twitter.com/pelicanbookgrp

To receive news and specials, subscribe to our bulletin
http://pelink.us/bulletin

May God's glory shine through
this inspirational work of fiction.

AMDG

You Can Help!

At Pelican Book Group it is our mission to entertain readers with fiction that uplifts the Gospel. It is our privilege to spend time with you awhile as you read our stories.

We believe you can help us to bring Christ into the lives of people across the globe. And you don't have to open your wallet or even leave your house!

Here are 3 simple things you can do to help us bring illuminating fiction™ to people everywhere.

1) If you enjoyed this book, write a positive review. Post it at online retailers and websites where readers gather. And share your review with us at reviews@pelicanbookgroup.com (this does give us permission to reprint your review in whole or in part.)

2) If you enjoyed this book, recommend it to a friend in person, at a book club or on social media.

3) If you have suggestions on how we can improve or expand our selection, let us know. We value your opinion. Use the contact form on our web site or e-mail us at

customer@pelicanbookgroup.com

God Can Help!

Are you in need? The Almighty can do great things for you. Holy is His Name! He has mercy in every generation. He can lift up the lowly and accomplish all things. Reach out today.

Do not fear: I am with you; do not be anxious: I am your God. I will strengthen you, I will help you, I will uphold you with my victorious right hand.

~Isaiah 41:10 (NAB)

We pray daily, and we especially pray for everyone connected to Pelican Book Group—that includes you! If you have a specific need, we welcome the opportunity to pray for you. Share your needs or praise reports at http://pelink.us/pray4us

Free Book Offer

We're looking for booklovers like you to partner with us! Join our team of influencers today and periodically receive free eBooks!

For more information
Visit http://pelicanbookgroup.com/booklovers